GROWIN' UP WHITE

Revised Edition

DWIGHT RITTER

PUBLISHED BY IRON PRESS
A publishing cooperative
New York City
ironpress101@gmail.com

ISBN-9780990967200
ISBN-13:978-0-9909672-2-4

Grateful acknowledgment is made to the following for permission to reprint previously published material:

Cover photograph. Rose Murray 2008: Used by permission, Will Murray Attorney for Mrs. Rose Murray, 2014.

Permission for use of parts of music lyrics is pending, though conforming to partial use restrictions:

1. Ice, The Penguins, 1954, by Gaynel Hodge, Jesse Belvin and Curtis Williams, Mercury Records

2. Hey Senorita, why don't you call me on the line? The Penguins, 1954 by Gaynel Hodge, Jesse Belvin and Curtis Williams, Mercury Records

3. Earth Angel, The Penguins, 1954 by Gaynel Hodge, Jesse Belvin and Curtis Williams, Mercury Records

4. Sh-Boom, The Chords, 1954, by James Keyes, Claude Feaster, Carl Feaster, Floyd McRae, and James Edwards, Cat Records

5. Maybellene, 1955, by Chuck Berry, Producer: Leonard Chess, Phil Chess

6. It's My Desire, Horace Clarence Boyer and the year of Jubilee, 2001, by Svein-Martin Holt

7. Precious Lord, Take My Hand, 1956, by Thomas A. Dorsey, Columbia

8. Good King Wenceslas 1853, public domain

9. Amazing Grace, John Newton (1725-1807), public domain.

GROWIN' UP WHITE

A NOVEL

DWIGHT RITTER

Iron Press
New York City

"... *Now Sarah watched the son that Hagar the slave woman has born to Abraham, playing with her son Isaac.*

'Drive away that slave girl and her son,' she said to Abraham;

This greatly distressed Abraham because of his son, but God said to him,

'Do not distress yourself on account of the boy and your slave girl. Grant Sarah

all she asks of you, for it is through Isaac that your name will be carried on.

'But the slave girl's son I will also make into a nation, for he is your child too.' "

—Genesis 21:9-13

One

A 1948, faded blue Plymouth coupe drives slowly past the Fox Burlesque Theater, an elegant, old, art deco lyceum located in one of the "gray" zones of Indianapolis—neither colored nor white. The Fox stands alone with an alley on each side, where trashcans roll on slippery bricks and wet spit never seems to dry. Inside, men sit on crusty mohair seats, smoking Camels and nursing a fantasy.

Outside, 11-year-old Ricky Stoner stares out the backseat window of his father's car as it creeps by, hoping to get a good glimpse of the posted black and white photos of half-naked women who dance there. His father drives this route often when making house calls, visiting patients at the nearby city hospital, or taking their housekeeper Georgey home in the evening.

"Slow down now, Doctah. Let's see who's dancin' these days," Georgey says, cranking down the window and staring. The music can be heard streaming through the open doors.

"Boy oh boy, Harvey can certainly play that song better than anyone," the doctor says.

"How you know that?" Georgey teases.

"He's been in that orchestra pit since high school."

"Memories like that never fade, huh?"

Stoner puts a finger to his lips, indicating they had talked enough.

"Who are you talking about?" Ricky asks from the back seat.

"Never mind."

Inside, the orchestra pit is sparse—a snare drum on a rusty tripod with a bent hi-hat cymbal, a worn stand-up piano with few ivories to tickle, and Harvey Johnson's saxophone, yellowed reed and all.

1

Harvey's trio sure could crank out "The Stripper" with all its flourishes, rolls, and umpas. The music drove men's libidos crazy, made them feel like kings again. It also excited the "girls," as Harvey called them. They got dirty about the third bar, removing their stage gowns with one flourish of the armpit-to-floor zipper and stepping out in sheer G-strings and pasties, pulled off with their teeth as they squeezed their bare breasts with painted fingernails. That was the cue for the drummer to lay harder on the beats and accompany the girls' rhythmic steps and grinding humps. Saxophone in mouth, Harvey directed each orchestral move with nods—often winks—to the girls for more. Then the main dancer would step closer to the footlights—just above Harvey's head—and pull her G-string tight into her folds.

Ricky and his brother Andy had heard stories of strippers "doing it" to men backstage for money or in nearby boarding houses, where fat madams lounged in stained nightgowns. Most of their friends believed the two boys' stories because their dad had been the doctor at the Fox since returning from the war. The owner, an old high school friend of Dr. Stoner named Jerry, required most of the women to have medical checkups "to make sure they were healthy." Jerry didn't want any smoldering diseases floating around backstage, and Dr. Stoner didn't want any smoldering-looking strippers dressed in high heels, pink boas, and fishnet nylons prancing through his office waiting room. So he would go to the theater, medical bag in hand, and park in the alley next to the row of beat-up garbage cans and scurrying rodents.

From Ricky's point of view, the Fox was the beginning of it all. It would ring the start of his education into racial hypocrisy in Indianapolis, even though the town had been a hotbed of bigotry for years.

Two

Late one night the phone in our house rang and awoke us with a harsh nudge. My older brother Andy and I slept in the same room and we could always hear it clearly through the radiator pipes, which went directly to Mom and Dad's room. Brief muffled words followed. Dad was talking to the hospital, then Mom and Dad talked. We focused on their sounds.

"Damn! What a stupid idea! I knew this wasn't gonna work," Dad mumbled, still half asleep.

"What wasn't going to work?" Mom asked. The bed creaked.

"Jerry hired a colored stripper."

"A colored girl was stripping at the Fox?"

"Yeah. The Queen of the Congo, she calls herself. She came from a club in Harlem, New York City. I told Jerry this town wasn't ready for that." He grunted as he rose from the bed, pulling on his pants. We heard the metallic sounds of his belt buckle and zipper.

"What happened?"

"Seems she was gang raped in the alley."

"Gang raped? Oh my God, that's horrible!"

"Five white guys tied her over a trash barrel and stuffed a rag in her mouth."

"Wayne, this is terrible! Did they catch the men?"

"No. She said most of them wore white sheets over their heads—masks, like Klan hoods. This could be real bad if it gets out."

3

"If it gets out? Wayne Stoner, this is bad, period. Worse than bad, horrible!"

By then Andy and I were sitting at the foot of the stairs, out of sight but able to better hear the discussion.

I whispered to Andy, "What's gang raped?"

"It's when a bunch of guys do sexual intercourse to a girl."

"You mean they put it in?"

"All of 'em do."

"At once?" I gasped.

"No, stupid. Some of the guys hold the girl down while another guy does it to her."

"Does she like it?"

"Of course not! It's one of the worst things you could do to a girl. Really nasty. Shh."

We refocused our attention on Mom and Dad. He was brushing his teeth, saying something indecipherable with the toothbrush in his mouth.

Mom asked, "Is this something you have to get involved in, Wayne? Can't an intern at the hospital handle this?"

"No. The police are there. So is Jerry. I have to check her injuries and sign her out of the hospital or have her admitted." He gathered his medical bag, clumped down the hallway, and spotted us crouching in the shadows.

"What are you guys doing here?"

"We were, um, just wondering what . . ."

"Go back to bed," he said, as he closed the door behind himself. We heard him start up the Plymouth and drive down the driveway.

"Andy?" I called, after we went back to bed.

"What?"

"Does the girl have babies from every guy that did it to her?"

"God, are you dumb. Of course not. Only one."

"Oh." I wondered which one, but I was smart enough not to ask.

* * *

The gang rape at the Fox Burlesque never saw a headline. As far as the patrons were concerned, the Queen of the Congo had to return home because of a severe cold that was contagious. Her name was taken off the marquee and her glossy photos removed before sunrise. Dad asked—no, *told*—all of us not to discuss the matter with anyone. Later I learned that Dad's anger over the entire event was partially calmed when he learned that the Queen of the Congo was carrying an enormous case of gonorrhea.

"Rife with a venomous case," he told us.

"What's that?" Andy asked.

Dad was very serious. "Gonorrhea is a venereal disease, son."

"What's that?" Andy asked again.

"Wayne," Mom interjected, "don't you think they're a little young?"

Dad agreed. "We'll talk about it later. You guys go in the other room."

We stepped into the hallway with our ears to the wall.

"What's gonorrhea?" Mom asked.

"Lillian," Dad exclaimed in disbelief. "It's a sexually transmitted disease. If it's unchecked, the bacterium can spread through the bloodstream and infect other parts of your body, including your joints. Fever, rash, skin sores, joint pain, swelling, and stiffness are the minor results. You can also die from it."

"That's terrible!"

"It is, but there is some good that will come of this case."

"Oh?" Mom inquired.

"Since it's only transmitted through sexual intercourse, those five men—then their wives, then their marriages—will no doubt suffer. I'm certain we'll hear about it."

So Dad stitched up the nasty gash on the Queen's face—from her ear to the corner of her mouth—and loaded her up on penicillin. Jerry paid her for the entire weekend on the condition that she'd keep her mouth shut and put her on the next bus to New York City. Not one representative of the NAACP was ever called. One policeman, one nurse, Dad, and Jerry were the only ones who knew about it, besides us. They knew it would eventually leak out, but by then it would only be a rumor. "Fakelore," Dad called it.

Several weeks later, rumors indeed swirled within the Negro community. Our colored housekeeper Georgey asked Dad if he knew anything about "that colored girl who took her clothes off at the Fox. Neighbors say she was murdered by the Klan."

"That is absolutely untrue," Dad replied. "She's alive and well in New York City. She was quite sick. I examined her before she left town."

Three

Mom and Dad hired Georgey shortly after we had moved to the big house on the west side of Indianapolis. Totally unexpected, her arrival was an ominous event for Andy and me.

She first appeared on a sunny spring day. Andy was setting a model airplane on fire across the street at the golf course, and I had just finished decapitating a dead chipmunk and tacking its head on a board like those African hunters did. I thought it would look great over the fireplace and I could just see my Dad's proud face, standing beneath the mounted beast and declaring, "My son Ricky shot this chipmunk."

Mom pulled into the driveway in our new 1951 Ford station wagon with the side panel where I had carved my initials. Spike, my younger brother by five years, was with her. A fat colored lady emerged from the car. She wore a light blue maid's uniform and walked unsteadily, supporting herself with a heavy cane. Lantern-jawed and bow-legged, with happy old eyes that squeezed into slits when she smiled, her teeth sparkled in the sunlight.

As a wise 10-year-old hunter, I was suspicious. After all, she was colored.

"Honey," my mother began, "this is Georgey. She's going to be helping around the house."

And oh, my God, that big woman was on me like a lion on a gazelle. She wrapped her arms around me, and my head got lost in her monstrous bosom.

"I is gonna take care a you like you was one a my very own," she said.

"What about Mom?" I asked, worried that this woman was going to adopt us and move us to Africa.

From the start Andy and I were skeptical. What was a Negro lady supposed to do with us? Spike was young and bought her act completely, following her around like a lamb with its mother. But Georgey wasn't like the other maids and sitters we had scared away. For one, she smelled different—kind of sweaty and the odor of Dad's slippery old leather belt. Her skin was moist and shiny, not dry from modern body soaps like Mom's. And she had pronounced nicotine stains on two fingers of her right hand. Yet in a short period of time she quickly became part of our home, shuffling around the house with a feather duster in one hand and her cane in the other, struggling with the vacuum cleaner, banging pots and cookie sheets in the kitchen, and "singin' the Lord's word so all can hear it."

We saw that her relationship with Dad was strange, and we learned that she used to work for Dad's family when he and his brother Gordon were in their teens. She wasn't like a maid or housekeeper really, more like a relative—Dad's sister, perhaps. Somehow privileged. It was very confusing.

* * *

After Georgey had been working at our home for a few months, Andy broke a window in the golf shop across the street and stole some firecrackers. He entwined the wicks of three cherry bombs and blew up empty coffee cans in our backyard, shooting them twenty feet into the air—concussive, beautiful, KA-WHOMP! Our first in a series of rockets to the moon, I stared in awe. Buck Rogers, here we come.

Georgey asked Andy where he got the firecrackers. He lied. She knew it and, holding him firmly by the back of his neck, she squeezed. He writhed, pulled against her, tried kicking her, and finally submitted, telling her the truth.

"All right, I swiped 'em," he cried. "They got millions. They won't miss these."

"That ain't the issue. You stole and you ain't s'posed to steal. Then you lied and you ain't s'posed to lie. It says in the Bible thou shalt not steal and thou shalt not lie. You gotta learn to obey God's rules." Picking up her dog-eared Bible from the kitchen counter, she handed it to Andy.

"Open it to Exodus 20," she said.

"I'll never read this stupid ole book," he said, shoving it back to her. "This is for poor, colored people."

Georgey glared at him, clinched her jaw tightly, and walked out the door.

"Where's she going?" I asked.

"I hope she's goes home," Andy said. "She's not our Mom. She can't tell us what to do. She darn near broke my neck."

Very shortly, Georgey returned. She carried a two-foot-long tree branch—a willow switch, we learned—and had finished cutting the twigs off. Grabbing Andy by the back of the neck, she demanded, "Take yur pants down."

"What?" Andy shrieked.

She squeezed his neck. "That stupid book—the Bible—also says, 'Those who spare the rod hate their children, but those who love them are diligent to discipline them.' Take yur pants down, child, and lean over that chair."

Andy started crying. "No, please, Georgey. I'm sorry."

"Underpants, too." She squeezed harder, jerking down his underwear. "This hurts me as much as it hurts you, Andy boy." She pushed him over the chair, never letting go of his neck. "Hold still. Take your punishment like a man."

"Georgey, don't! Please!" Andy cried.

I reached out to grab her arm. "Georgey, don't," I pleaded.

She looked at me, tears running down her face. "Don't you be next."

I answered, "Yes, ma'am. Sorry, ma'am." I lowered my eyes and focused on the frayed ends of the rug and the toes of my sneakers.

And then she whaled on his bare bottom, striking it unmercifully. The sound of branch meeting injured flesh cried out so loudly that I put my fingers in my ears. Andy screamed "NOOOO, OWWW" as she whupped his skinny pink hind end hard. "PLEASE NOOOO, OHHHH, OWW"—the stick flailed through the air several times, bruising his skin and raising welts.

It was so gruesome that I covered my eyes, grimacing until my cheeks hurt. Spike ran to his bedroom. How could this happen? A devil is loose in our house!

"Now you go to yur room until yur momma comes home. Take my Bible with you and read Exodus 20. Ricky, find Spike and go outside and play."

* * *

I never knew what Georgey said to Mom; they went for a drive as soon as she got home. Mom was not interested in seeing Andy's "bloody butt," nor was she interested in hearing Andy's side of the story. That was not like Mom.

At dinner Georgey said to Dad, "I switched Andy good and hard today, Doctah. Hurt me much more than him."

Dad nodded his head, glancing from Mom to Andy and then Georgey. "What did you do to deserve that, son?"

Andy welled up and whimpered, "I don't know. I guess I stole some firecrackers from the golf pro shop."

"You stole them?"

"I did."

"Anything else?"

"Well, I lied, too."

"Anything else?"

He thought. "No."

Georgey said, "And you referred to the Holy Bible as a stupid ole book only for colored people."

"Really?" Dad asked, rolling his eyes back.

"Yeah. Guess I did."

Dad spoke somberly, "Sounds as if you deserved a switching." It was the first time we had heard and seen Dad act this way—no eye roll, no dancing eyebrows, no glint of fun in his eyes. He was all seriousness.

Georgey said, "I give him my Bible to read the Ten Commandments."

"Did you read them, son?" Dad asked.

"No, Dad. Ohh . . ." He started in with some tearless crying and moaning. "Dad, she really hurt me. Ohhh, she's so cruel and wicked."

"After getting your butt beaten viciously, you still didn't do what you were told?"

"Dad, please. My butt's bleeding like crazy."

"Your butt hurts too much to read, huh?"

"Yeah. Real bad. A bloody mess. Might need stitches."

"Uh-huh." Dad nodded, looking at each of us. "Stand up."

Andy stood.

"Turn around."

Andy turned slowly.

"Take your pants down."

"Da-ad," Andy whined.

"Do it," Dad repeated.

Andy pulled his pants down.

"Turn around."

All eyes focused on his Fruit of the Looms—no blood, no skin hanging in folds beneath his undies, clean as that morning when he put them on. Dad pulled down Andy's underpants—no blood, no open wounds, a few red welts. Dad shook his head, accompanied by an eye roll.

"Andy, I want you to go back to your room and memorize those Ten Commandments. You'll have to stand up since you don't want to lose any more blood. No dinner for you, son. No dessert." We had never seen this side of Dad. "Then I want you to teach them to Ricky. And Saturday, I want you both to recite them to me. Spikey, we'll teach them to you later."

"Dad!" Andy pleaded.

"Let's keep that switch handy, Georgey."

"Yes, Doctah."

Before Dad took Georgey home, she came upstairs and knocked on our bedroom door. Andy was laying on his bed reading Exodus 20. I was laying on my bed scared.

"Boys," Georgey began, sitting on Andy's bed, "I is so sorry this had to happen." Tears filled her eyes and overflowed down her cheeks. "I had to discipline you. You must learn the difference 'tween good and bad. And you can't be bad. I had to discipline you because I loves you, loves you more than anything, more than I loves my own self. You are my children. I don't 'spect you to understand this right now, but you will. That day will come."

Andy didn't look at her; he kept his eyes focused on the Bible.

She nodded quietly. "The pain in your hind end will go away, Andy child, but the love in our hearts will stay forever. Now let's hug one another." Her arms unfurled like angel's wings, and she held us.

Our world changed that day.

After Dad drove Georgey home and returned that night, he came upstairs and woke us up, Spike too. With cigarette and ashtray in hand, he said we needed to have a talk about Georgey. No doubt this was serious.

"Even though you don't remember it," he began, "Andy, you and Ricky have met Georgey before. Actually twice, once before Spike was born and once after. Even when you were six or seven you were a handful, and your mother and I weren't getting anywhere with you. Since we both work, there weren't enough hours in the day to follow you around correcting your behavior. You were horrible." He paused. "Well, you still are."

Andy and I shared a fleeting glance, one of pride.

"The first time you met Georgey, we sat outside at our old house, Georgey, Lillian—that's your mother—and me. You two boys," he pointed to Andy and me, "were playing in the woods. Andy threw a handful of stones at us, lobbed them like grenades." Dad rolled his eyes in disgust. "Your mother looked around and saw you, Andy, with a smirk on your face, chin jutting out, hands on your hips.

"I remember clearly your mother's words: 'You boys be good,' she said. And I remember clearly your words, son, to your mother. You said, 'Don't wanna be,' and Ricky, you made some smart remark, too. Georgey was disturbed, and you know the look on her face when she is angry."

"We call it the I-ain't-foolin' look," Andy said.

"That fits," Dad nodded and continued. "Georgey asked me how old you were, Andy. I told her six or seven and she said, right in front of your mother, without hesitation, 'Acts jes like you used to. Needs a good smackin' for that kinda sass.' You should have seen the look on Lillian's face. Eyes bugged, teeth clinched. That's not the way she believed children should be raised."

"I don't get it," I said. "How did Mom think we should be raised?"

"Oh, a 'free from punishment' kind of thing."

Andy and I nodded at each other as if Mom were right.

"I know what you're thinking," Dad said. "If my—excuse my French—my ass was beaten, I'd probably feel your mother was right, too. But she wasn't. She had never been raised in a family of boys. I had."

"You mean Georgey switched you?" Andy said.

"Not exactly. Remember, I was fifteen when Georgey came to work for us. But once she rapped me on the back of my head with her knuckles for purposely throwing a baseball through our garage window. It was as if I had been hit with a wrecking ball. I saw stars and carried a knot on the back of my head for a week. And I also remember she had a ferocious grip with her right hand on the back of my neck and on your Uncle Gordon's."

"She still does," Andy said, rubbing his neck.

"Anyway, your mother felt that physical punishment was wrong."

"I agree with Mom," I said quickly. "Definitely wrong."

"So," Andy interjected, "are you going to fire her?"

"Not in a million years, son. Lillian and I are 100 percent behind Georgey."

Andy and I shared a glance of fear.

"You boys think that if someone hurts you they can't possibly love you, even though you've hurt Mom many times, even shot paper clips at her."

"I apologized," Andy said.

"Or teased her to tears, or put sand in her brassiere. I could keep on going." Dad nodded and looked at us briefly, continuing, "Lillian and I thought you guys would grow out of it. So came the baby sitters. You were out of control. The crowning blow was when Mom asked Ricky to get Spike a glass of water, and you mixed in some toilet bowl cleaner. You could have killed him."

I flinched. "I was real young, Dad."

"No excuse. Well, your mother didn't know what to do, so she called me at the office and raced to the hospital, where they pumped Spike's stomach."

"I don't remember that," Spike said.

"The next day, your mother and I made some serious decisions. We put Andy and Rick on the bus to school, dropped off Spike with neighbors and went to Georgey's house."

Mom had come upstairs by now and stood in the doorway. "I'll never forget my only rule to Georgey," she said.

"What was that?" I asked.

She sat on the edge of my bed. "I asked her to promise me she wouldn't hurt my boys."

"Hurt me!" Andy shrieked. "Look at me. I could've lost a lot of blood!"

15

"You're fine, Andy. Don't forget, I'm a doctor."

Mom wanted to finish her thought. "Well, Georgey said clearly that if you were bad, she would punish you, and if you were real bad, she'd have to switch you good and hard. That would definitely hurt. I certainly didn't like that."

"Neither do I," Andy said.

"Definitely bad," I added.

"Yeah," Spike finally said.

"Plain and simple," Dad explained, "those were Georgey's rules. Take it or leave it. But it wasn't all about punishment, guys. Georgey's a deeply religious woman. She has a set of rules I learned long ago. It's this: God first, love second, and a strong conviction to goodness, gentleness and fairness. Punishment isn't in there. It's a fallback if the good stuff isn't working."

"And the good stuff—as your father put it—hasn't been working," Mom said. "Lying, stealing."

". . . and calling the Bible a stupid old book for poor, colored people." Dad shook his head. "I don't know what got into you, Andrew Stoner. I consider you lucky."

Andy didn't say a word.

"The irony of your punishment is that the Bible has many references to the religious value of physical punishment." Dad looked up toward the ceiling and pondered. "Like, 'those who love their children are diligent to discipline them.' And boys," he continued, "the most important thing in the world to your mother and me is that all three of you grow up learning what is right and what is wrong. Georgey was my inspiration, still is. She's perfect for our family. She's bringing something that wasn't here before—a spiritual meaning for all of us."

"And your father and I totally support her," Mom added, her first adamant opinion about something other than music.

Through the radiator pipes that night we heard Mom curtly warn Dad, "Against my better judgment, we are doing this your way, Wayne. I hope you're right."

"I know I'm right, dear. I'm also very tired. I hope the phone doesn't ring."

Four

You know," Mom said to Georgey, "I was born and raised in Massachusetts and never spoke to a colored person until I moved here."

"What you people back east do to 'em?" Georgey asked.

"Nothing, I guess. I remember seeing a few in Boston during college, but we never had anything to do with them."

Georgey rolled her eyes. "I 'spose, then, you never wore sheets over yur head or seen a burnin' cross in yur front yard?"

"Oh goodness, no. Absolutely not!"

* * *

Mom was a concert pianist, very different from other moms—never wore an apron, burned SpaghettiOs, hated (oh, how she hated) washing dishes, and often forgot to shave her legs. Her entire being was music. She played it and taught it and it was lodged up front in her personality. Music, definitely; motherhood, not so much.

Mom also taught music at a private girls' school where every girl looked the same—navy blue, pleated skirt, white blouse, black pumps, and red-tipped pimples on her legs—at least the ones that I saw.

Though Mom was not like other mothers, she didn't totally ignore us. She loved us as much as her two Steinway grand pianos residing in our living room. From time to time she would try the motherhood thing because parenting—the concept—still existed in some part of her brain.

Often when she gave a local solo recital, one of us would accompany her to turn the pages of her sheet music. The host or hostess of the affair always introduced Mom, rattling off her credentials. We had them pretty well memorized.

"Ladies and gentlemen," the hostess began. "Our special guest today is Lillian Stoner. How lucky we are to have such a gifted pianist in our town. At nine years of age, she walked onto the stage at Boston Symphony Hall and gave a piano recital, a feat few mature professionals have been asked to do." A few gasps and raised eyebrows from the audience. "The Boston newspapers and classical enthusiasts dubbed her a child prodigy." Random clapping echoing as rain on a tent and low whispers of child prodigy. "She went on to graduate from Radcliffe College, the women's part of Harvard, where she studied with Walter Piston, famed author/composer and professor of music. She has also been under the tutelage of Swiss pianist and composer Rudolph Ganz as well as Arthur Rubinstein, perhaps the finest pianist ever to grace a concert stage." A substantial applause followed.

Mom always appeared gracious and humble during these introductions, but also fidgety, anxious to perform, and distracted. When she took the stage, she briefly introduced her accompaniment (usually just one of us)—that's the part we liked the best. "My son Ricky will be assisting me this afternoon." I gave a full low bow, one arm across my stomach, the other across my lower back. Mom said the "histrionics" were unnecessary (I wondered what that meant). We stood next to the piano while she played, and when she nodded her head, we turned the page of her sheet music. It looked as if we knew what we were doing, like we could read music. Andy never missed a cue—standing at attention and, in military fashion at her command, he turned the page. I was not as dutiful, often distracted by something or someone in the audience and then missing Mom's cue. I sometimes misunderstood and smiled to the audience. Abruptly Mom snatched the page and turned it herself. "Pay attention," she hissed. Strangely, by the time he was five, Spike could follow the music—had his hand on the page before Mom nodded. Turned it at the exact moment. Mom noticed. Spike was different—born with a tuning fork in his brain.

The key words we took away about Mom were child prodigy, Boston Symphony Hall, Harvard, Walter Piston, tutelage, Rudolph Ganz, and Arthur Rubinstein. We heard them over and over again and soon we would be able to introduce her ourselves. We wouldn't need some overweight emcee with fat ankles and a wiggly neck wattle.

Once Andy asked Dad what a prodigy was.

"A prodigy is . . . ," he stopped and thought. "Well, it's a natural-born musical genius."

"Mom is a genius?" Andy asked.

"Well, in a way she was."

"But not anymore?" I asked, relieved.

"Oh no. She still is. Once you're a prodigy, you're always a prodigy."

"You think I'm a prodigy?" I asked.

"Don't appear to be so, son."

"Um," Andy said. "Sorry."

"She's all right, then. Not retarded or anything," I added.

"She's just fine," Dad said.

With a slight edge to her voice, as if she didn't really mean it, Mom once told us that her mother was a "fine pianist."

"We didn't have any money. Father [as she called her dad] worked in a textile mill and sang in the church choir and other choral groups. You could always pick his voice out of a choir. It was the loudest voice, the one that was slightly off-key. But you could never tell him."

From this, a Stoner family expression evolved: "slightly off-key but never in doubt." We used it a lot to describe certain people—boisterous politicians who always spoke loudly about things they didn't understand or that confident guy at the gas station who couldn't find the dipstick.

Mom had a Saturday afternoon radio show with an unlikeable woman named Louise Waring. We called her "Aunt Weeze," even though she wasn't our aunt at all. She was quick tempered and edgy. Divorced from some guy named Bill when she lived in New York City, I heard her tell Mom that Bill was rude, conniving, and had a girlfriend. Aunt Weeze seemed to be intolerant of most people who were poor, uneducated, and colored. When she was younger she moved to New York to be a dancer, but ended up playing piano at the bar in the Gramercy Park Hotel until she got her break providing musical arrangements for the Rockettes—or so she said.

Aunt Weeze loved classical music, but to Andy and me it seemed she loved rich people more than anything. Through the radiator pipes we heard pieces of stories involving wealthy men in town—wealthy married men. Recently she had taken up with Sidney Goldstein, the town's biggest jeweler. He was considerably older than Aunt Weeze and had a massive, shiny, comb-over swirl—like a Dairy Queen chocolate two-scoop. I often wondered what he looked like when he got out of bed, standing there in his drawstring pajamas with hair draping down one side of his body, probably to the floor. A sign on the front door of Goldstein's Jewelers said "NEGROES NEED NOT ENTER." He told Dad that Negroes always stole jewelry and smelled so bad the odor stayed in the store long after they left. Dad rolled his eyes.

Five

Thou shalt not have no Gods except God," Andy began, tail between his legs, reciting the Ten Commandments at dinner shortly after "The Beating."

"Thou can't carve any images or bow down to anyone except God," I followed.

"Close enough," Dad said. "Number three."

"Thou shalt not utter God's name in vain—what's vain mean?"

"No swearing," Dad answered.

"Number four. Thou shalt not work on Sundays," I said. Blank stares were passed around the table.

"Unless you're a doctor," Dad added. "Next. Andy."

"Honor you and Mom," Andy said.

"Make that Mom, me and Georgey, the three of us."

Andy and I shared an audible breath.

"Thou shalt not kill," I announced.

"That excludes chipmunks and mice," Dad added.

"Thou shalt not commit adultery. What's adultery?" Andy asked.

"We'll talk about that at another time," Dad said, motioning me to move on.

"Thou shalt not steal," I said.

"Thou shalt not bear false witness against your neighbor," Andy said.

"That means lying about seeing something you didn't see. Lying, in general," Dad explained. "No lying."

"Thou shalt not covet your neighbor's house, his wife, his servants, his you-know-what."

"His you-know-what?" Dad asked.

"The Bible says 'ass,' " Andy answered. "What's that mean?"

"Well, in the Bible an ass is a donkey," Dad replied.

"A donkey? How do you covet a donkey?"

"Suppose God means cover a donkey? We're not supposed to cover donkeys? Why not?" I asked.

"I think that's enough biblical knowledge for today," Dad said.

"I'll be ready real soon," Georgey called from the kitchen.

Mom got up and went into the kitchen. "I'll clean up the rest."

* * *

Exodus 20 was just the beginning. Bible lessons became frequent with Georgey.

"Before you run off and play, I want you to remember the word of God," she said.

"OK," Andy said, on his way out the door. "I will."

"And I'm gonna tell you what He says now. Right this minute." She pointed sternly at both of us. We had learned to recognize when she meant what she said.

"Oh, come on, Georgey. Not now," Andy begged.

"Right now. Sit right here. This is important. As long as I is here and breathin' you is gonna hear about the Bible. And you is gonna act like God-fearin' young men. I is here to guide you and to love you." She didn't need to say "I ain't foolin.'". . . We knew.

Then, "Genesis. You know Genesis?" she asked.

"First book of the Bible," I mumbled, having recently memorized the names of five books: Generous, then Exodus, Licorice, Numbers, and Deutoronomus.

"Y'all know about Adam and Eve and the Garden of Temptations?"

Eye roll, eye roll, eye roll.

"Yeah, Eve was naked," Andy said.

"No, she wasn't," I insisted.

"Was too. Shows how stupid you are. So was Adam. I've seen pictures. Eventually, they covered their wieners with a leaf."

"I'm gonna tell mom you said wiener," Spike piped in.

"You gonna listen to me, or you gonna write yur own Bible?" Georgey asked.

"Well, they did," Andy said.

"How'd you know that?" I asked.

"Normy Winslow's got a picture book of religious pictures. I seen it."

"You seen her wiener?" I asked.

"No. But I seen her other things."

"What other things?"

"Will you two hush up with that kinda talk? This is the word a God. With the word a God we think about the miracle. We don't think about wieners. Shame on you. Amen to that. Adam and Eve is about God's amazin' power and his creativity. He created a man and a woman. The very first ones. Before Adam and Eve there was no peoples—just animals and birds flittin' around. Then God created us. You Andy. You Ricky, and you Spike honey. His word is to be rever-ed."

"What's rever-ed?"

24

"Obeyed. God's word is sacred." She searched our blank eyes. "It is to be learned. And remembered." Andy shrugged. "Yes, remembered and followed." She paused and mumbled, "This ain't gonna be easy. So, you might as well go and play."

Six

Georgey was a hardheaded, practical woman. She refused to move into our house like some "shifless nigger"—her words, not ours—working only days, no weekends. She had her own little house twenty minutes away. She had her own friends, her own life, and her own church. Somehow she had been married to somebody who wasn't around anymore (and no one ever asked). She had a son named Leon who was in the Army, stationed in Germany.

She came from the Bahamas and worked for Dad's family from the time Dad was 15. After Dad and his brother Gordon went to college, Georgey worked only periodically for the family, preparing social dinners, serving cocktails, and cleaning up afterward. She must have done some incredible things and made a huge impression on Dad's parents for Mom and Dad to commit us to her care—in her own way. Likewise, Dad's family must have made a huge impression on Georgey for her to commit her life, her faith, and her soul to our family. Many lines were drawn, I was told, before Georgey agreed to be part of our family—many that went beyond her feelings on punishment and discipline.

In just a short time with us, Georgey became the guard, the captain of the ship, the referee, and the enforcer. She quelled every practical joke we tried, discovering our stash of rockets, matches, a Bunsen burner, knives, and birds' fecal sacs in water-filled pie pans. It was as if she'd been through this before. She won a dozen arm-wrestling competitions against Andy and me. Against all odds, she became the moral fiber of our family.

We had Georgey every weekday. After Andy and I left for school, Mom picked her up to care for Spike and then went to the school where she taught. Dad took Georgey home after the dinner dishes were put away. Often Andy or I would go along for the ride, feeling safe in this different world while the car glided along, listening to Georgey and Dad.

"Doctah," she began during a ride to her house, "I knows this cartin' me back and forth is hard on you and the missus. But it gives me my own sense of pride. Don't need to mooch off a white folks like some ole slave with no place to go. And I got three fine boys to care for and love. How grateful I is to your fambly."

Dad smiled pleasantly as if he were hoodwinked, but knowing she was brown-nosing made him feel special. And there, I determined, was the secret to their relationship—she knew that he knew that she knew.

"I was thinking today about what our town was like when Gordon and I were young," Dad said.

"Yessir?"

"The biggest difference was that in those days nobody talked about it."

"Nobody talked about what, Doctah?"

"The racial"—he waved his hand looking for the right word—"atrocities, I guess would be the best word."

"Maybe for you. But I don't know what that fancy word means."

He glanced over at her to make sure she wasn't playing with him.

"Evilness, wickedness."

27

"Atrocities," she repeated. "I'll use that."

"Nobody really talked about the racial wickedness that existed in our town."

"The whites might not have, but my people sure did. Lordy, Lordy, 'member when Amos Sutcliffe washed ashore down on the river? He was beaten and shot several times. All the white folks claimed they didn't know who he was or who done it. One ole fella said he was eaten by wild dogs down on the canal someplace."

"Yeah, a wild dog with a .38 caliber pistol," Dad said, glancing in the rearview mirror to make sure I wasn't listening. "I vaguely remember that. He was nameless. There was something else going on behind the scenes, wasn't there? No mention in the paper."

"Whites, back then, Doctah, didn't need a reason to kill us Negroes. But yur right; it weren't reported in the newspapers or talked about on the streets like it is today."

"Do you know what happened to Amos?" Dad asked.

"Only that he had a 16-year-old daughter who had a child who never turned Negro, if ya knows what I mean."

"So old Amos went after the white guy that—you know."

"Yes, sir. As far as I knows."

We drove quietly through the colored neighborhood, not concerned for our safety, not out of place. Dad knew it well. Most of his patients lived here.

"This cigarette lighter work?" Georgey asked, pushing it in.

"Hasn't in a long time."

"Why'nt you buy one a them fancy Zippo lighters white folks use?"

"I'm not fancy white folk." He handed her a book of

28

matches. "Here."

She struck a match and read the matchbook flap, " 'Fox Burlesque. Exotic Dancers.' You still givin' them girls shots?"

"Yep."

"What kind of shots, Dad?" I asked from the back seat.

"Never mind, son." He glanced at me in the rearview mirror. "Here we go, Georgey. Door-to-door service." He pulled up to her house, walked around to her side of the car, and opened the door for her. Don't forget your cane."

From across the street and deep in the shadow of a porch I heard a man's voice.

"Evenin' Doctah."

"Lovely night, Zeke," Dad said, helping Georgey up her steps.

"Yes, it is. Yes, it is," in a teeter-totter rhythm.

That was the first time I heard Zeke's voice, but it was as familiar as that musical tune in your head you can't trace.

* * *

That night through the radiator pipes, I heard about a woman named Evie Jackman, one of Dad's patients. She wasn't well— running a fever, in uncomfortable abdominal pain, and had developed skin sores on her pelvis.

"A pelvic inflammatory disease," Dad declared.

"Poor woman. I just adore Evie."

"I know you do," Dad said. "I've known her husband Ed since high school."

"I hope you fixed her up, Wayne. You're such a wonderful doctor. Is it something serious?"

"If she hadn't visited me when she did, it could have been serious."

"My goodness. What in the world was it?"

Dad paused. "Advanced gonorrhea."

The room was suddenly quiet as I heard Mom gasp. Then the bed creaked. Dad lit a cigarette and I could hear the matchhead on the rough side of the matchbox, hear it ignite, hear the inhale.

"Oh, Wayne. Are you telling me Evie Jackman got this from Ed? Oh my God, this is from that Negro stripper, isn't it?"

"The Queen of the Congo. Yeah. This is the first one. Ed has always been active in racist things. He spends a lot of time at the Neighborhood Club on the outskirts of town. Four more to go."

"Does she know?"

"Not exactly. I made up a story and gave her a heavy dose of penicillin. Told her she shouldn't have any intimate relations with Ed because her ulcerations appeared highly contagious, and that Ed needs to come in and see me as soon as possible."

"Could it be something else?"

"Absolutely not. I've seen gonorrhea many times. I'm a doctor, you know."

"Oh, poor child. She probably thinks it's her fault."

"She doesn't know it's gonorrhea yet. I didn't tell her, specifically. Ed will have to do that. I'll make that absolutely clear when I see him. Either Ed tells her, or I will. And then I'll need to see Evie a couple more times."

"I hope she leaves him, that bum."

Seven

Zeke, nodding his head and mumbling—"Yes, it is. Yes, it is."

Georgey's neighborhood was an older, more established block of families. Six houses, a numbered cross street, six more houses, another numbered cross street. On the streets sat tarnished cars—big old Buicks, Lincolns, and Cadillacs with rusty bumpers, stuck windows, and broken antennas, listing to one side like an old man with a bad hip—all paid for; credit was only for whites.

Her house was small, like a toy building block with a roof, but as heavy looking as a sunken boulder in a cowfield. All brick, it had one floor with a prominent porch in front supported by brick columns. Dad called it a "bungalow." Her neighborhood consisted of similar bungalows (all with porches) no more than spitting distance apart and exactly 15 feet from the sidewalk—a full Monopoly board. The back door opened to a trash can, a rickety wooden fence, and a creepy alleyway where cats killed rats and dogs ate them both late at night. Bungalow after bungalow lined the streets as orderly as stitches on a wound; block after block followed until the white section of town. There everything changed—the look, the smell, the feel—like closing your eyes in Kansas and waking up in Oz.

Directly across the street from Georgey lived Mr. and Mrs. Zeke (he was Zeke, she was Zeze). Their porch smelled like a gym locker. They were old with big red smiles, purple gums, and blood-shot eyes. "Mr. Zeke"—as I was told to call him—was suspicious of me. Gruff and narrow-eyed with flexing jaw muscles, he sat on his porch when the weather was warm, waiting to pounce. Georgey told me how to ac "Now, darlin', when you sees ole Zeke lookin' at ya over the tops of   his ole glasses— the way he does—you says, 'Ga mornin', Mr. Zeke, sir.' You says it so he can hears you. You waves proud-like and you smiles."

"I don't wanna do that, Georgey. He's scary."

"No, he ain't. Zeke and yur daddy is real good friends, go way back. Now, child, you jes' do what I tell ya. If ole Zeke says, 'Mornin' back to you—if he do—then you proudly walks across the street and shake his hand. Don't shuffle yur feet and look down. Stand up straight like you was a proud man. 'Nice day, Mr. Zeke,' you say. And then you shakes his hand. He'll warm up to you like a baby kitten."

"Do I really have to do that?"

"If you wants to get along with colored folks, you has to do what I tells ya. Colored folks are physical—huggin', slappin', kissin'. They needs to be touched. Rules of the colored neighborhood."

"But Georgey, what if he hits me?"

"He won't."

I wasn't sure I wanted to get along with colored people, much less Mr. Zeke. He didn't like me one bit and he didn't hide his feelings. Actually, he didn't like white people, except maybe my Dad. He was impatient and quick to blame, and I lived in fear of him yelling at me. But he yelled at most people—the mailman with the sweat-stained mail bag ("Hey, goddamned letter man, quit stealin' my money!"); the policeman Johnson ("Hey, Johnson, whyn't you arrest some a them goddamned white folks?"); Reverend Williams from Georgey's church ("For chrissake, Reverend, half them people is stealin' from the offerin' plate and you ain't doin' nothin' 'bout it."); even his paperboy

Arkie—especially Arkie—calling him a "damned sawed-off nigger."

Next door to Georgey were Reginald and his wife Marjorie, as comfortable and quiet as two mice in a church basement. Neat, clean, orderly. Reginald—not Reggie—had razor bumps on his cheeks—bad ones—and Marjorie wore freshly pressed and colorful head rags. Their life, according to Dad, was "as tranquil and predictable as the curve of an egg."

On the other side lived Sonny and Ann Sue. He worked in a barbershop downtown, cutting the hair of wealthy, white people. His chair was on the main floor of Dad's office building, and many white businessmen would stop in for a morning shave before work, wearing dark suits and starched, white shirts. White people never made appointments with Negroes; they just showed up. That morning shave was a luxury and Sonny would perform, sharpening his straight razor on the strop with a flourish, lathering and agreeing. "Yessir. Yessir. A wonderful day. Yessir." He cut Dad's hair every other Tuesday after lunch. "Yessir, Doctah, yur lookin' mighty good, I say. Uh-huh."

Ann Sue was a seamstress and I never saw her without a silver thimble on her thumb. It belonged to her grandmother, I learned. Her grandmother was a slave from South Carolina who dressed like a boy so she wouldn't be sexually abused by her master, but when her master found out she was a woman, he shot her point-blank in the forehead for lying. Then he dragged her dead body into the woods and raped her.

"Can you imagine?" Ann Sue asked. "Rapin' a dead girl?"

I couldn't even think about it.

Ann Sue said she kept the thimble on her thumb for two reasons—so she wouldn't forget her heritage or where she left the thimble. Ann Sue and Sonny had a son who lived in Miami and married a Cuban girl. A silver-framed photo sat on their coffee table signed, "All our love, Carmencita and Robert."

Then there was Georgey's best friend, Miss Tildalayhu, who lived a block away with her sick mother. They met at the Church of the Holy God just down the street. Miss Tildalayhu was always dressed for church and I can't remember a time she was without a hat—broad-brimmed and curled up (to hold pencils, hairpins, and paper clips) with colorful satin headbands, often garnished with flowers, even lace. A big woman with heavy, high-heeled shoes like stumps connected to ankles, she was the color of a worn saddle. Her eyes, sad and grateful, were often closed when she sang, her long eyelashes resting on her cheeks like a butterfly at rest. Georgey said she had the most beautiful voice "in the whole wide world and that includes everone." Miss Tildalayhu's house was precisely like Georgey's—brick bungalow-style with a porch where you could watch the sun set over the homes across the street.

Those were her immediate neighbors—the ones I got to know well. The others were whispers I heard and eyes of suspicion I felt, because a white kid visiting a colored neighborhood on a regular basis was not a popular idea.

"We don't cotton to you bringin' no white boys here," a woman from down the street said to Georgey. "This is our part of town. Don't their momma know how to take care a them? We got enough troubles without white boys snoopin' 'round here."

"Yeah, snoopin' 'round then callin' the Klan."

When the sun went down, the families sat in the darkness of their porches, cigarettes aglow, backlit by the cold, blue-white glow of a black and white television set from their living rooms, talking with each other, laughing, the sounds of mock surprise like a coven of early morning crows.

"Zeze. Zeze. I says, Zeze," amid the gaggle.

"I'm listen', Georgella."

"Who was that handsome young man I seen you with yestaday?"

"I ain't tellin'. He jes' couldn't take his eyes off a me, could he?"

Zeke chimes in, the bass part to this operetta, "Good luck to him, I says. Gooood luck."

Laughter in four parts spreads across the porches.

Then Zeke adds, "Actually, that was Delia's son, Willie. He go up there to the Negro High School—Crispus Attucks."

"Ouee! Ain't he gonna bring pleasure to one a them sassy girls," Ann Sue exclaims, her silver thimble sparkling from her thumb.

"Shame on you, Ann Sue."

"Yes, ma'am. Shame on me, but ain't he?"

Eight

Arkie lived on the edge of Frog Island, the poorest colored section of town. He was about my age, closer to 13. Taller—but then everyone was taller than me—his voice had begun to change and a faint shadow of a mustache was shading his upper lip. His mother made him go to the Church of the Holy God and take part in the youth group there, but they didn't call it that; it was Christian Education Time (CETime). They walked the mile to church because they couldn't afford bus fare. Arkie delivered the afternoon newspaper to Mr. Zeke and stared at me a lot like he was real tough, until Mr. Zeke told him to teach me how to play basketball or he wouldn't take any more newspapers. Old Mr. Zeke held Arkie by the arm like a raggedy doll and dragged him across the street to Georgey's house, where I sat doing my social studies homework for Monday.

"What's your name, boy?" Mr. Zeke asked.

"Arkie, sir," he replied.

"Arkie, this here is Whitey. I hear you one great basketball player for such a young nigger." He scrunched his mouth and tasted his teeth. "Here, shake his goddamn hand. Gwan, do it."

We did, feigning pleasantries while not looking at each other. Then Mr. Zeke held Arkie with one hand and me with the other and steered us to the alley behind his house.

"You boys go out back and shoot some baskets. There's a old ball back there I done found. Put some air in it for ya. Arkie'll show ya how."

An old, red, basketball rim with a few strands of net dangling in the breeze was nailed to the top of Zeke's garage door in the alley.

We were away from colored eyes.

"Why that ole man call you Whitey?" Arkie asked, shooting the ball. Swish.

"Don't know. My name's Ricky, not Whitey."

"So, Zeke callin' you Whitey don't make you mad?" Swish.

He threw me the ball. I dropped it. "You should be mad if a colored call you Whitey."

"Why?"

"You just should. I'd be mad if you called me nigger."

"Georgey tells me to act proud around Mr. Zeke no matter what he says." I dribbled the ball and lost control as it squirted off my sneaker toe.

"You sure don't belong around here," he said, picking up the ball. Swish.

"I know. I don't like it here."

"Then go home." He tossed me the ball. I missed it.

"Can't," I said, picking up the ball and throwing to Arkie.

"Why not?" Swish.

"I messed up real bad at school, flunked a bunch of courses, so I'm supposed to spend Saturdays at Georgey's house studying until my grades get better."

"Why ain't you studyin' then?" Swish.

"Georgey says I need a break from time to time. You get good grades?"

"Almost straight A's. But I study real hard." Swish.

"I don't like to study."

"Well, one thing for sure, you don't fit in around here." Swish.

"Why not? 'Cause I'm not good enough?"

"No. 'Cause yur white." He dribbled between his legs and passed me the ball.

I caught it. "So?"

"Stand right here," he said, pointing to a spot three feet in front of the basket. "Hold the ball like this; fingers on the seams."

"Like this?"

"No. Spread yur fingers real wide. That's better. Now look at the basket, not the ball. Aim it and throw it up there."

It rolled around the rim and off.

"I dunno, Whitey. You jes' look dumb shootin' that ball."

"My name's Ricky. You're not Zeke."

"Whitey," he taunted, leaning his jaw toward me.

"Better not say that again."

"What you gonna do about it, Whitey?"

Without thinking I swung and hit him with every ounce of strength I could muster, while tears sealed my closed eyes. It was an explosion from within, uncoiling a need to make up for years of being out of place—too small, too young, too dumb, and now too white. With all my weight I stepped into that swing and round-housed him, connecting to the side of his face with frightening accuracy and knocking him back three feet to the ground and against an old garbage can. Dizzy from the physical effort, I stumbled and started to fall but stopped myself by stepping on his face—hard. He was motionless for an instant and then began to cry, blinking his swelling right eye.

"Ohh. Ohh!" He struggled holding his face. "Ohh."

"You shouldn't have called me Whitey," I said, posing in a boxer's stance, ready for Round 2.

He blinked, trying to get me into focus, his face scrunched up.

"You OK?" My fear turned to tears and snot.

"No, ohh. I never been hit in the face before. Ohh, it hurts real bad. Think you broke my head wide open. Can you see my brains?"

"No, not yet." I held my pulsating hand, hoping I wouldn't have to use it again. I couldn't stop crying.

"You know," he said, standing up, wiping his nose, and blinking his right eye. "Yur ass is grass. You gonna get killed by my friends."

"Yeah. Probably." I cried, not really ready for what was next, and Arkie cried, standing in the alley. Few sounds—sniffs, moans, hollow sounds. Two sore kids with snot on their faces and tears on their cheeks.

"Ain't you scared?" He blew his bloody nose to the side with his thumb.

"Yeah. Real scared." Impending doom lingered.

He looked around, wiping his face with his shirt. Then he handed me the ball. "Better try again."

I put my fingers on the seams, watched the rim, and threw it. It didn't go in. It didn't go in the next time or the next or the next. I cried harder each time I missed, because I wanted it to go in so badly—more than anything—and I knew I was going to get beat up by a bunch of colored kids like I read about in the Hardy Boys books. I was too damned short and skinny to do anything right. Soon I would die.

"Oh shit," I screamed. "Shit, shit, shit!"

39

Arkie dragged a large garbage can in front of the basket and tipped it upside down. "Get up on this. I'll hold it." His eye was purple and swollen shut, his nose continued to bleed and he wiped it, smearing blood and snot over his face.

I was two feet from the rim, threw it, and missed again. Cried some more.

"You're the worst damn basketball player in the whole world. Not cause yur white. Not cause yur short. You jes' plain stink. Yur lucky you ain't a nigger." He began laughing.

It suddenly became funny—the invisible lid over the basket, Arkie's snot and blood-smeared face, his swollen eye. I laughed too, wiping snot from my cheek.

"Yeah? Where'd you get such a stupid name as Arkie? Sounds like a girl's name. Arkie-girl."

"Shows how dumb you are. It's short for Arkansas; that's one of the states in our union. Yur so dumb you didn't know that." He laughed.

"I'm so dumb I know the capital is Little Rock. Next state east is Tennessee—double n, double s, double e. Nashville is its capital. Named after General Francis Nash." All that studying—for the first time it paid off.

"Well, la-de-da for you. My name's Arkansas Emanuel Johnson. My momma's from the state of Arkansas. My daddy's name was Emanuel. I never met him. My new daddy's last name is Johnson. OK?" He wiped his nose again.

"Sure." I continued laughing.

"What you laughin' at?"

"You. You oughta see yourself. Your eye's closed and you got blood and boogers all over your face."

"Yur lucky you don't got a mirror, Mr. Know-it-all." He picked up the basketball and shot it. Swish.

"Sure hasn't hurt my aim. What's yur name? I forgot already."

"Ricky; Richard Eli Stoner."

"Sure got a long way to go, teachin' you basketball, Ricky." Swish.

That was the first time we played basketball—the first of many times. I never improved drastically, but I did learn all the right moves and looked better than I was. Arkie was smooth. He could fake me out so bad that it felt like I had one leg shorter than the other; then he'd effortlessly glide by me, take a couple of big steps, and lay in the ball, brushing the bottom of the net with his fingertips. Most always he carried a basketball, sometimes dribbling it as he talked, never looking at it. He didn't need to— the ball knew where his hand was.

Nine

"Long, long time ago," Georgey began, "they was an old guy, name of Abraham—they called him Abe jes like one of our presidents. From him came you and me."

"How's that possible?" Andy asked.

"Ole Abe lived over there where Jesus was from, but way 'fore Jesus was born, thousands a years 'fore Jesus. Abe's wife was Sarah. She was a real nice lady, but poor Sarah couldn't have no babies, couldn't have one, even though God promised her she would have one. God kept promising this to Sarah and Abe until they was gettin' pretty old."

"Didn't Abe know how to do it?" I asked.

"Some ladies just can't have babies, darlin'. It's a medical thing. Yur daddy would know about that."

"Hmm," Andy pondered.

"Well, Abe and Sarah wanted a baby so bad, and they was gettin' on in years—long in the tooth, that is—so they used one of their slaves to be the mother and Abe to be the father."

Andy gasped. "Isn't that against God's laws, Georgey?"

"Not back then—many thousands a years ago, 'fore Moses and the Ten Commandments."

"Huh."

"Does Dad know about this?" I asked.

"Course he does. Now Abe and the slave woman had a baby boy. His name was Ishmul. Part Negro 'cause all slaves was

42

Negro. Then God decided it was time for Sarah to have the baby he promised her. This one was a white boy. His name was Isaac."

"And you say this Sarah woman said it was all right for Abe to—you know—do it with the colored lady?" Andy asked.

"Honey, the world was really different back then. This is God's word. It's in the Bible." We listened.

"So Ishmul and his momma—Hager was her name."

"Hager?" Andy repeated. "The Negro lady?"

She nodded. "They moved to Africa and started the Negro race."

"Really?" Andy asked. "That's where colored people came from?"

"Is that true, Georgey?" I added.

"As sure as I'm sittin' here. God didn't want no trouble so he promised Ishmul that he would grow up and be the father of a great nation. That's the way God put it—father of a great nation. And that Isaac, Ishmul's younger brother, would grow up and be the father of another great nation."

"Georgey, what color was this Ishmul boy?" Andy asked.

"He was colored—my color."

"But his daddy was white."

"That's right, darlin'. When a white person and a colored person have a child, their little child is colored."

"Always?"

"Sho-nuf. It's like chocolate milk. You have white milk and you adds chocolate. What you get?"

"Chocolate milk," Andy said.

"Course you do. So, if Ishmul was the son of Abe, and Isaac was the son of Abe, and the Bible tells us we is all chilluns of Abe, you know what that means?"

"Hope it means this story is almost over."

43

"Well, it don't." The look, once more. "It means that you, your momma and your daddy and all your friends are related to me and Leon and all my friends. We is all God's chilluns related through Abraham. Hallelujah and amen!"

Often, Georgey referred to herself as a nigger.

And we were not niggers.

Even though she told us, we knew we were not supposed to say "nigger." When she said it, we would cringe because Dad did. I think she liked to see us cringe. The way Georgey said it seemed innocuous—even charming—but it set the stage. "This ole nigger says" or "You watch yourself or this ole nigger'll get you." It was her word, not ours.

Most often, she described people in general by their color, but in a nonjudgmental way. She told the story of how she broke her leg when she was a little girl living in the Bahamas. "This buck nigger rolled a huge pickle barrel off a tobacco platform onto my leg. He took me into town and some white doctor set it, set it crookerd." I visualized a very big, colored man carelessly rolling a huge barrel onto her leg and an unemotional, sloppy, white doctor setting it, probably smoking a wet stogie and whistling while he patched her up.

Her stories weren't all bad. For instance: "My nigger Uncle Fiddledoo and his quadroon wife, Dede. She couldn't have no children until Fiddledoo peed on a live electric wire. Lord a mighty! They had eleventeen chilluns afore he died at 80. It woked up his do-whinkus real good." Her stories were as real and vivid as a new picture book.

Ten

Basketball was important to me because I wasn't any good at it. I knew I would get better—Arkie said so. I just needed the chance. Once I came home from a pickup basketball game in our white neighborhood before it even started. There were 11 boys and we picked two captains instantly, who picked four teammates each. I wasn't chosen. I cried all the way home, burst through the front door, and ran straight to my bedroom. Soon my door opened and I felt Georgey sitting on the edge of my bed. She began softly rubbing my back. I told her what had happened, sobbing and sniffling.

"Oh, child," she whispered, "I knows life is so unfair. All this will change. I promises."

"Oh, no, it won't," I blurted. "I'm always the shortest. Andy said I was shorter than the basketball."

"Oh, you's gonna be fine, a strappin' big man real soon." She put her arms around me and held me close. I cried hard that day. Then she said, "Jes' you remember one thing."

"What's that?" I asked, snot streaming down my cheek.

"This old nigger loves you more than anybody . . . loves you from the inside out. You, Ricky darlin', fill my heart with happiness more than any of them big, dumb, basketball players. You, my child, is special—so very special."

I cried some more while the entire idea of the basketball game drifted away and dissolved into nothing, like a drop of ink dissipating in a bucket of water. I could smell Georgey's presence as comforting and homespun as fresh warm milk from a barn and feel her huge, soft arms, light as clouds. And I heard that word again, nigger.

"Why do you say that word, Georgey?"

"What word's that, darlin'?"

"You know."

"No, I doesn't."

"You said"—and I whispered—"nigger."

"That's what I is."

"But Mom says it's a swear word. Arkie says I'm not supposed to say it."

"Hmm . . ."

She was quiet. I could feel her thoughts scratching through the air for an answer. "It's our word. When white folks use it, it's bad, so we use it to be special."

"Still the same word," I said.

"Yep. Spelled the same but means differnt. It's kinda like a sheriff's badge. Only a sheriff can wear it. If you ain't a sheriff and you wears it, it's bad."

"So, it is a swear word."

"I don't really know, darlin'. It's a bad word for whites to use 'cause they means it in a bad way, but it's an alright word for us coloreds to use 'cause we is proud of who we is."

I remember that conversation because I had heard people talking about the treatment of Negroes by bigoted whites. I heard white people hiss the word "nigger" between clenched teeth, saw pictures of police hitting Negroes with clubs, spraying them with mace, beating and kicking them. Friends of my parents said Negroes were more like animals than humans—dirty, stupid, and slow. "If the coloreds don't like the way they're treated, they should be put on a boat and sent back to Africa." That kind of talk would absolutely send Dad off a cliff and onto his platform providing the medical, spiritual, and social rationale for the equality of the races. Anyone left standing after one of Dad's orations could only agree, agree wholeheartedly. The Stoner family was against racism.

I learned to hear the word "nigger" and react to it differently, depending on who said it. I never heard Georgey use any swear word or vulgarity and, according to Georgey's rules, no one in our family was allowed to swear, not even a "damn."

Georgey and I went downstairs to the kitchen.

"Have a cookie, darlin'."

I grabbed two.

"Jes' one."

She put her hand on my head and prayed, "Jesus, yur so busy teachin' this boy his greatness. I pray that he knows what yur doin'. And God don't get angry with my Ricky for eatin' a cookie while this ole nigger is prayin' for him. And my best amens go to you."

"You said it again."

She hugged me and then said, "How many 11-year-olds were at the basketball game?"

"Dunno."

"Well, think."

"Uhm, maybe, lessee, besides Baxter and me?"

"And Baxter's almost a year older'n you."

"So?"

"So, here's what's gonna happen. I predicts that by the time ever one of you is 18—you included—you'll all be 'bout the same size. This is true, so help me God. I also predicts that the next time this happens yur brother will be feelin' so bad about this time he'll pick you to be on his team. Then you'll show 'em."

"You think so?"

"I knows so. Zeke say that young Arkie boy'll teach ya."

Eleven

Baby Shuli lived on Frog Island near Arkie. She was a year older than I and had freckles—dark brown freckles on light brown skin like a chocolate chip cookie—on her nose and cheeks, and she had large puckered lips that unfurled and turned pink when she smiled, and she smiled a lot. Her best friend was Tiny Marcella, who was 12 and had a goofy overbite and large black lips. "Yes" became "Yeth" and "Sweetie" became "Thweetie," and words like "Ostrich" and "Sarasota" became spit.

Tiny Marcella was built like a small, dark purple rubber ball with huge, white eyes that looked like saucers and giggling smiles, puckers, and oohs. She wore little girl dresses that often got wedged in the crack of her butt and she followed Baby Shuli the way a dust ball trails a broom.

Every day after school Baby Shuli and Tiny Marcella helped the women at the church, checked in on Miss Tildalayhu's mother, and delivered Ann Sue's hemming, darning and stitching around the neighborhood. They were always busy, always moving, always laughing and smiling. Tall and skinny with teeth too big for her mouth, Baby Shuli was clearly the leader and spoke to everyone cheerfully. Tiny Marcella was always running about three feet behind her—puffing and pulling her dress out of the crack of her butt.

"Afternoon, Miss Zeze, Mr. Zeke. How's my favorite couple today?" Shuli would ask.

"Yoo hoo! Good to see you, Mr. Reginald."

Tiny Marcella waved with her fingers, "Hi, thir."

"God loves you today, Miss Georgella," Shuli said.

Zeke said Shuli was the happiest danged girl he'd ever seen. "Somethin's wrong with her. No one's that happy. Pro'bly carries a butcher's knife under her skirt. And that other little girl—what's her name—can't be much bigger than a speck a dirt. What's wrong with her ass anyway, that she keeps pickin' it?"

"Nothin,' you rotten ole man," Zeze said. "The cheeks of her behind is maturin' quicker'n her other parts."

"Well, that ain't right, goddammit. Young girls is 'sposed to become young women evenly, not butt first." And then he chewed his teeth.

Baby Shuli wore dresses that spun when she turned and I saw her white panties several times. She saw me looking and bounced her eyebrows, skipping away in big strides, flailing her arms. She raised her skirt so I could see her bum, singing, greeting. That gave me a new feeling deep inside somewhere—I wasn't sure where. Something was happening to me because I kept remembering the look in her eyes and the flash of her sizzling white cotton panties.

* * *

Arkie leaned a ladder against Zeke's garage so he could get up to the rim of the old basket. "Found this in the janitor's room at my school," he said. A used basketball net encircled his arm as he climbed up. "Put yur feet down there so the ladder don't slide out."

He carefully unhooked the few strands of the old net that were hanging there, dropped them on my head, and hooked the new net to the rim—not really new, but at least a complete net.

50

"Told Rozelle Thorpe we had us a private basketball court and no one knows 'bout it."

"Who's Rozelle Thorpe?" I asked.

" 'Bout the greatest basketball player in the world."

"Never heard of him."

"That's 'cause you is white."

"You're full of crap." I tossed him the ball.

Swish.

"You know Crispus Attucks High School?"

Swish.

"Of course," I said, shooting and missing.

"He's a freshman there. Prob'ly be the best player since Flap Robertson."

"You know him?"

"'Course I do. His mama sings in the choir. I told him 'bout Mr. Zeke's court."

A few weeks later Arkie showed up with Lil Roy, not Rozelle Thorpe. Lil Roy Daniels—the fattest of all fats. Always had been, he said. He was born fat. His dad was fat and his mom was fat. He had a much older sister and she was fat, too. Fat Betsy, she was called. Little Roy said it was hereditarial. Arkie said, "It's cause y'all eat like an entire starvin' country."

* * *

"Georgella says you is almost 13 years old, boy," Zeke said. "When I was 13, I worked. Had to. I helped my daddy shine shoes down to the train station."

"Yes, sir," I answered.

"Looked up the skirt of a fancy white lady and got my head beat against a stone wall for it. Yep. 13 year old, I was. Busted my head damn near open, they did."

"They?" I asked.

"A bunch of white fellas. Maybe four. The white lady stood back a bit and pointed at me and said I was the one. 'That dirty little colored boy,' she called me."

"What'd yur daddy do?" Reginald asked.

"Told me to run. 'Run, Zeke,' he says. 'Run for yur goldarned life.' I didn't know why I should run. Hell, never saw anything 'cept silk and shadows. But they grabbed me and dragged me down the stairs and hit me and kicked me and smashed my head against the wall. Called me names I can't say in mixed company. One of 'em was laughin' and pissed all over me. Made the other fellas laugh. Then they left me there to die. Tweren't a thing my daddy could do about it. Still got a scar right here. See?"

"Bet you never looked up another white woman's dress," Reginald said.

"I never looked at another white woman, period, never let 'em see me lookin' anyways. Yessir, back in them days it was dangerous bein' a nigger."

"Still is, Zeke," Reginald said. "Still is."

"You can't understand that, boy," Zeke said to me.

"No, sir," I said, as respectfully as I could. I was certain five men wouldn't drag me into a basement and beat me up if I accidentally looked up a woman's dress.

Sonny said, "If you done that today in Mississippi, they'd hang yur ass."

"Sonny's right," Reginald said, shaking loose a cigarette. "It's worse today than 50 years ago."

52

That story angered me, and even though I didn't care for Mr. Zeke, I felt compelled to explain my feelings.

"Mr. Zeke, sir. If anyone would do that to you today, I'd stop them. I know I would. My daddy would be furious. He'd find out who did it and they'd go straight to jail."

The conversation stopped. Zeke lit his cigarette. Then the three of them looked at me and at each other.

"You run along, boy," Zeke said. "Gwan, find that Arkie friend a yurs."

Then fear and nervousness echoed through the backyard as I wandered off. Whispers of "You shouldn't be talkin' that way 'round the white boy. Apt to get in trouble."

"Yeah, yeah. I furget with him. Seems like he's one a us."

* * *

For the rest of that school year Arkie and I spent every Saturday—and many weekdays during the summer—sitting in the pitted and pot-holed alley behind Zeke's house. Often Lil Roy showed up, but not Rozelle. Georgey always made sure I did some homework before Arkie arrived after his paper route (Zeke's house was the last house he delivered to). Sometimes—if Georgey was watching—we acted like we were grilling each other on geometry formulas. Most times we played mumblety-peg until I broke the blade of my pocketknife, shot baskets, had hopping and crawling races, and long-distance spitting and pissing contests. We laughed, whispered, and told lies.

He taught me how to cup my hand, put it under my armpit, and squeeze down hard and fast, making a farting sound. Pump farting, they called it. I could do it better than anyone. Me—

53

Richard Eli Stoner—at 12 and one-half years of age, the best pump farter in all of Indianapolis.

We also had a collection of Coca-Cola bottles that we kept on the windowsills of the garages lining the alleys. On the bottom of each bottle was the town where it was made. Most were Indianapolis, but as time went on, we found many other towns.

As long as my grades were good and I was—as Dad would say—"a model citizen," my parents felt there was no harm in cultivating friendships in a colored neighborhood—a risky decision back then. Georgey, though, carried a look on her face that weighed heavily with suspicion, wondering whether the cards really disappeared or went up the magician's sleeve.

Twelve

It was one of those hot Indiana days in the year of the cicada, their chorus droning out their screechy, repetitive call. Cats lay dormant in shadows. Even birds sat still, hoping for cool air. Arkie, Little Roy, and I had just finished a contest to see who could walk the farthest while barefoot on the sidewalk—fighting stinging pain so unbearable that a year's worth of calluses would shred as we'd race to the garden hose for relief.

Little Roy had a collection of old, beat-up jackknives that he'd brought—two in each pocket that jiggled randomly—but there was so much going on with his body jiggles that they were raging to be free, like loose tomatoes in a paper bag. We made a drawing of Hitler on the garage wall and practiced throwing the jackknives. Little Roy was precise, flipping the knife just one rotation and sticking it in Hitler's heart. Arkie did a baseball windup and hurled the knife sidearm, but it never stuck until he cut out the fancy stuff. I followed Little Roy's lead and worked hard for accuracy—like throwing darts. The last one landed dead center in old Adolf's crotch.

"You live over on Frog Island, too?" I asked.

"Not me," said Little Roy, putting his shoes on—or at least *trying* to put his shoes on, because his stomach got in the way of seeing his feet.

"Me," Arkie said. "I is a Froggy. So's Baby Shuli."

"Not Marcella; she lives just this side of Crown Hill Cemetery," Lil Roy said.

"Rozelle's a Froggy," Arkie said.

"I've never been there. You think they'd kill me?"

"They? Who you think 'they' is?" Arkie asked, winking at Little Roy.

"Coloreds."

"They is me, man."

"You think the coloreds would kill me?"

"I don't think they'd be happy to see you. Man, you are the whitest lookin' white boy I ever seen. You'd glow in my neighborhood."

"Mine, too," Little Roy replied, checking the bottoms of Coke bottles lined on Sonny's garage windowsill—Terre Haute, Bloomington, Fort Wayne—and polishing them with his shirt.

Arkie sat on the ground, holding his basketball in his lap, trying to "palm" it with one hand—pushing his hand down hard, using his upper body, then pulling his hand up slowly, hoping the ball would stick to his palm. "Damn!"

"You play basketball on Frog Island?" I asked.

"Yeah. Kinda. My neighborhood's different though." Arkie tried it again—"When's my hand gonna grow?"

"How different?" I asked.

"Is your hand bigger'n mine? Hold it up here."

I did. It was much smaller.

"Well, my neighborhood's dirty," Arkie said. "I guess that's how I'd describe it. That how you'd describe it, Roy?"

"Yeah, dirty. Kinda," Roy said, spitting on the bottom of a bottle and wiping it clean. "Terre Haute."

"Lots of angry folks out there," Arkie said. "It's easy to get yourself smacked for doin' nothin'. Big kids think it's fun to hurt little kids. Really. Ain't that true, Lil Roy?"

"Yeah."

"That why you come here so often?" I asked.

"Lemme see your hand, Lil Roy," Arkie said. "Wipe yur spit off it first."

"Nothin' wrong with my spit."

"Just do it."

It was the same size as mine, blowing my theory that Negroes had disproportionately large hands.

"I come here mostly 'cause my momma volunteers at the Church of the Holy God where Miss Georgella goes. Little Roy's momma, too."

"Yeah," Little Roy said. "Daddy goes there sometimes. Not lots."

"Not my daddy," Arkie said. "'That's woman's work,' he says."

"Neither one of my parents go to church," I said, wondering why. On Sunday, Dad liked to read. He'd have several cups of coffee in the morning before breakfast and read the Sunday paper cover to cover, funnies too. Mom practiced her piano instead of prayer. I wondered if it was because of the difference between coloreds and whites; coloreds believed in Jesus because it made them feel better about being discriminated against, and whites didn't believe because they didn't need to. We were the top of the food chain.

Arkie continued. "Reverend Williams likes kids to be playin' up there to the church. There's a bunch of us Froggies that plays there on some days after school when the weather's right. Reverend Williams got me my paper route here and give me my own basketball. He says someday soon we gonna have a real basketball court at the church."

"Is the church that big?"

"No, stupid. There's a real big playground area next to the church with one old rim on a plywood blackboard."

"Soon it's gonna be almost a full-sized court with a basket at each end. The Rev says he's workin' on it," Little Roy said.

"You could play with us if you want," Arkie said.

"Yeah, Arkie says you ain't too bad."

"It's dangerous for you, Ricky. Some big ole buck nigger might kill you."

We laughed. Arkie picked up a stick, pretending it was a knife and holding it to my throat.

"Oh please, Mr. Colored Man," I pleaded. "Don't cut my throat or my friend Mr. Arkie Johnson will sneak into your bedroom at night and CUT OFF YOUR WIENER!" I screamed.

Arkie and Little Roy shrieked. "The colored man's wiener?" Arkie cried.

"That'll teach him," I laughed.

"Cuttin' off his wiener is only gonna make him madder."

"You can handle him, Arkie," Little Roy said. "Ricky and me'll be playin' ball. You glue his wiener back on."

Playing basketball with colored guys and living to talk about it would be great. They'd be dunking the ball and dribbling behind their backs like the Harlem Globetrotters, all patting me on the back for trying hard and risking my life.

"Think you'd take me to Frog Island?" I asked.

"Nope," Arkie said, with no hesitation. "Think you'd take me to Golden Hill?"

"Are you kidding?"

What followed was our first planning day: How to get a blonde-haired, blue-eyed, white boy to Frog Island and back—alive!

Thirteen

Saturday. It rained and I snooped around Georgey's house, looking at assorted old, faded, black and white photographs of palm trees with Negro children peering from beneath festoons of palm fronds, their eye whites like pearls in the moonlight, their bare feet tucked in dirt. Eleuthera. Florida. A colored man in an Army uniform: "To Momma. With love, Leon." Very white, faded white. A footstool inscribed with Miami, USA. Cigarette burns on furniture like liver spots. In contrast was a photograph of Dad and his brother Gordon taken at DePauw University in front of the Beta Theta Pi fraternity house in their pressed, white linen slacks, dark sport jackets and ties. "Soigné," Dad would say.

Through the sheets of windless rain that afternoon, Georgey's neighbors gabbled loudly on her porch about the plight of the Negroes and how it might be safer living in Africa and being hunted by lions. They told stories of slave grandparents, of rumors of abuse. Ann Sue's grandfather was a white landowner in South Carolina; that's why she's lighter than Zeke, she said.

"Zeke, though, is 100 percent Negro," Zeze said, poking her husband. "No white blood runnin' through those old purple veins. He's black as a Halloween cat, 'cept the bottoms of his feet, and he hides 'em in his shoes."

"Yep. Black as the ace of spades, I am," Zeke added, standing and waving. "Black as the crack of a colored man's butt."

"Zeke! For cryin' out loud. You watch your language."

"Gotta run down to Elwood's for a minute," Zeke said, walking out.

"Y'all come over and have some Coca-Cola," Zeze said.

"OK, but we have to come back here to hear Miss Lillian Stoner on the radio."

Georgey and her neighbors ambled over to Zeke and Zeze's house to smoke and talk about men. Little Roy, Arkie, and I stayed and made prank phone calls. We called drugstores and asked if they had Prince Albert in the can. If they said they did, we told them, "You better get him off. There's other people who want to use the crapper." Then we hung up, laughing. We sure showed them.

That one grew old quickly. So we called bars and asked them to page Harry Balls. Most bartenders mumbled something about stupid-ass kids and hung up. But it was Muggsie's Tavern where the bartender shouted, "Harry Balls! Phone call for Mr. Harry Balls!" People hooted in the background.

Baby Shuli arrived through Georgey's back door, wet from the rain.

"Found a Coke bottle."

"Where from?" Arkie asked.

"Springfield, Illinois."

"No thanks. Already got Springfield. Where's Marcella?"

"She ain't well."

"What's wrong with her?" Little Roy asked.

"It's just that time of the month."

"What time is that?" Arkie asked.

"Oh, you men," Shuli huffed. "She's menstratin'."

"My sister Betsy does that but she don't stay home."

"Well, Marcella's different. Lots of things is changin' for her. She's also workin' on her speech impediment."

"Menthratin' and thpeech impedimenth," Little Roy mocked.

Shuli quickly changed the subject. "Let's play cards."

The ladies returned from Zeze's and gathered in Georgey's living room to listen to the radio. It was time for "Thirty Minutes of Music with Louise Waring and Lillian Stoner."

MUSIC
(Chopin Etude)
ANNOUNCER
(music down and under)

Good afternoon, ladies and gentlemen, and welcome to an hour of fine classical piano, the music of Louise Waring and Lillian Stoner, two of this country's finest pianists, trained by the great artists of Europe and New York. How fortunate we are to have them not only play for us but tell us about the music, its meaning, why it was written, how we can better appreciate it. So, without further ado, let me introduce Lillian Stoner.
APPLAUSE

"That's Ricky's momma on the radio," Georgey said to Zeze. The ladies smoked cigarettes and puffed out soft clouds of hominess, talking about men and food, but mostly men, stupid men. The world was full of them. Didn't make any difference what color they were.

61

"She sure is one famous lady," Miss Tildalayhu said. "Ricky, your famous Momma's on the radio."

We were in the dining room playing cards—Arkie, Baby Shuli, me, and Little Roy. We played Fish. Arkie said it was a colored person's card game. From the radio came classical piano, filling the rooms with sound other than gospel music and a loud-voiced preacher damning everyone to hell. Classical music seemed to turn Georgey's house into something it wasn't.

Little Roy couldn't figure out how to play Fish, and Arkie smacked him on the back of the head.

"You sure are one stupid nigger," he said.

From the living room: "You watch yo mouf in there. There's a white boy with you."

"Ricky's all right with that, aint' you?" Arkie asked.

"Doesn't bother me, ma'am."

From Zeze in the living room: "Jes listen to that. My, oh my. She sure can play that piano."

"Use that ash tray, won't you, darlin'," Georgey said.

"Can Miss Stoner play church music?" Miss Tildalayhu asked.

"I reckon when you're that good you can play any kind a music," Ann Sue replied, twirling her silver sewing thimble. "You ever hear her play church music, Georgella?"

"Can't say I have."

"She'd be just as good at church music. I can hear that," Miss Tildalayhu stated with certainty.

"How can you tell that?" Georgey asked.

"It's how a piano player strikes the key, producing an honest sound. Honesty is always the clearest, the best."

"Yes, ma'am. Honesty's the best policy, they say," Ann Sue chimed.

"Honesty? Now how do that sound?" Georgey asked.

"It's like the lead voice in a choir."

"The loudest one?"

"Oh no," Miss Tildalayhu said. "Could be a very quiet voice, but strong. It's the truest voice in the choir, the one that carries everone else. Don't have to be loud. If Jesus sang, his voice would be honest. Trained ears can hear it."

Then it went quiet in the living room. I could imagine them all nodding and flicking their ashes.

I heard a match strike. "Why thank you, Reginald," Ann Sue said.

From the dining room: "Go Fish!"

"How'd you learn to play this game so good?" Baby Shuli asked me.

"I been playin' Fish since I was six or seven."

"Yur jes lucky," Arkie said. "It don't take no skill to play this stupid game."

"My deal," Lil Roy said.

Then from the living room: "Speakin of music," Georgey started, "anyone here 'member Harvey Johnson?"

"Can't say as I do," Reginald said.

"Name rings a bell," Zeze mumbled.

"He was the guy who played the saxophone at the Fox Theater."

"Yep," Zeke said. "He was one damn good player. Even played once with Duke Ellington's colored band. Rumor says he was mulatto or somethin' like that."

"Yep, he was, now that I remember. He went to Shortridge High School and hung 'round with white folks. I don't think any whites knowed."

"That's chocolate milk for ya," said Reginald.

"Yeah. Not proud of his heritage. Shame," Zeze said shaking her head. "Shame!"

As Lil Roy dealt, I was searching for what I remembered about the Fox. The only thing that came to mind was the Queen of the Congo, and that was forbidden territory to discuss.

I heard Ann Sue's voice. "White mulattos, like that Johnson fella, come from a white momma and Negro daddy."

"Bet he was quadroon," Zeke said. "Who was his daddy?"

"Dunno," Georgey answered. "His momma and Harvey moved up here jes before the war. She never married again. Cleaned houses and such."

"Yeah, I knew who he was. I cut his hair from time to time," Reginald said. "I never knowed he was mulatto or quadroon. Just knew he could really play that saxophone. Man, oh man, he could make the Fox Theater jump."

"And them girls take their clothes off real sexy like," Zeke said, gasping dramatically.

Lil Roy looked at me. "You ever been to the Fox?"

"Nope. Not old enough. How about you?"

"How about Lil Roy, you say? Man, he not only old enough, he ain't white enough."

"That's right, Ricky. The Fox is not for colored folks," Baby Shuli said, as if she knew everything in the world.

And from Zeke in the living room: "Played in dance bands as well as the Fox. Why you askin'? What happened to him? I thought he was still workin' there."

"He died last week," Georgey said, speaking of Harvey Johnson.

They drew on their cigarettes in silence and exhaled respectfully. A kind of sadness set in.

"How'd you know?"

64

"The doctah. 'Parently he'd been dead for a while. Sittin' in a chair with his saxophone in his lap. Doctah said he really looked awful. Swollen face, eyes open."

"Poor man. What'd he die of?"

"Doctah say it was a sexual disease. Go-nór-ia, or somethin' like that."

"Well hell, if I was hangin' around them strippers ever night and I was unmarried . . . ," Zeke added quickly.

"You better say that," Zeze blurted.

"Well, how much temptation can a man take?"

Arkie's voice got my attention. "Ricky, how come your hair sticks straight up like that? Looks like my toothbrush."

I remembered the word "go-nór-ia" or "gonorrhea," as Dad called it. It had something to do with the Queen of the Congo.

"Hey, Rick," Arkie said.

"What?"

"Yur hair. Why's it stick up like that?"

"I dunno. It just does."

"Mine won't do that," Arkie said, pulling his hair up.

"That's cause you're colored and Ricky's white," Baby Shuli said, looking at me with her incredibly large, round, brown eyes.

Arkie walked around behind me. "Mind if I touch your hair?"

"No, go ahead."

"Ain't this something!" Arkie said, running his fingers around my head. "I push that hair down and it pops right back up. Looky here. Boing! See!"

Little Roy came over and felt my hair. Even though he was younger than me, he had a deep voice. His fingers smelled bad, like old underwear. "You sure has white skin."

"May I, Ricky?" Baby Shuli asked, running her fingers through my crew cut. "Feels so soft." Her eyes searched mine.

From the living room: "What's goin' on in there?"

Little Roy said, "We're all feelin' Ricky's hair. Feels jes like mowed grass."

Zeze added, "I don't think you children should be treatin' Ricky like he's some kind a strange little animal, scratchin' him and all."

I said, "No, ma'am. It's all right," even though I felt awkward, like some strange little animal.

"Sure," Arkie said. "Feel my hair. Go ahead. It's real different, ain't it?"

I did. I felt Arkie's and Baby Shuli's and Little Roy's. It was similar to poodle fur, not hair at all. White people said it felt like a Brillo pad, but that was because they never felt it.

The living room conversation had become awkward, as if Georgey had told everyone to end the discussion of Harvey Johnson.

"Miss Tildalayhu, you was talkin' 'bout honesty in music. Well, that certainly would be my Miss Stoner. Miss Waring's too interested in flirtin' and braggin'. She ain't got no honest nothin'."

"Oh Georgella, yur showin' favorites."

"Miss Tildalayhu. How's your momma?" Ann Sue asked.

"She's about the same, Ann Sue. Thank you for askin'."

"Reginald and I pray for her ever night."

"Yes. We all have Miss Alice in our prayers," Georgey said.

"Thank you and Hallelujah. My poor, poor momma's mind is leavin' this earth. Just yesterday I found her beautiful Easter hat in the ice box."

"My goodness gracious," Zeze said, laughing. "In the refrigerator. Can you imagine?"

"And if I don't lock the doors, she surely will be wandering the streets in her nightgown, calling out for Carlton. God rest his soul."

"Amen to that."

I was staring at Baby Shuli, her freckles. "I didn't know colored people could have freckles," I said to her.

"Sure can," she beamed. "You like 'em?"

"Yeah, I do. A lot."

That afternoon in the kitchen, Baby Shuli kissed me when no one was looking—I mean adult-like kissed me, on the mouth. Pressed her hips against mine, put both arms around me, tilted her head and kissed me, her mouth slightly open. It was a soft kiss. Wet. Passionate, I suspected. In retrospect I count the number of seconds that this embrace took—three. That's a long kiss, especially for a 13-year-old.

"There," she said, as if it were a duty she had forgotten to perform in the past, like picking dandruff off someone's shoulder. I stood bug-eyed and thoroughly aroused. My hips pressed back, even though I didn't tell them to.

Fourteen

A different Saturday. Eighth grade had started and I was back at Georgey's—I liked it better than my own neighborhood, where there was always a challenge. Arkie and I sat on the back steps of Georgey's house, bouncing a basketball off the fence and catching it on its return. I showed him a Coca-Cola bottle from Anderson, Indiana.

"Man, where you comin' up with these valuable bottles?"

"In a neighbor's garage."

"Is Anderson further away than Louisville?"

"I'm not sure. Maybe my dad's got a map. I'll check."

"You know, you can call me nigger if you want," he said matter-of-factly, chewing on a twig.

"I won't."

"Why not?"

"Well, don't really know." I couldn't even say the word in front of him. "Just not right for any white person to call a Negro that."

"Yeah, but you ain't really white. I call Willie Rice a nigger. He calls me a nigger."

"Who's Willie Rice?"

"A nigger friend of mine. You'll meet him today."

"That's 'cause you're both colored."

We bounced the ball back and forth off the fence some more. I studied how Arkie held the ball, how he threw it.

Little Roy came through Georgey's back door. "Hey, Ricky."

"Hey, nigger," Arkie said.

"What're you doin', man? What's this nigger talk?"

"I was tellin' Ricky he could call me nigger if he wanted to. He won't."

"I don't think he should."

"What do you know? Lemme hear you say nigger, Ricky," Arkie said.

"No."

"Please. I know you can do it. N-I-G-G-E-R," he spelled.

"No."

"Purty please."

"Come on, Arkie," Little Roy said. "Don't be stupid."

"He can't help that," I said.

Georgey opened the door behind us. "So you boys should be headin' to church now. Reverend Williams is expectin' ya. Should be fun paintin' the lines for the new basketball court. Zeke said the new hoops went up yesterday."

"Miss Georgella, will you tell Ricky to please call me a nigger?"

"No, I most certainly won't. Why you want him to?"

"Just 'cause he says he won't."

"Honey, Ricky's right. As close as you boys are, yur still different, like Ishmul and Isaac."

"Who they?" Arkie asked.

"Ricky'll tell you."

"Oh no. Another Mr. Smarter-than-thou lecture from the white boy."

"I think they was in the Bible," Little Roy said.

"Good for you, Roy Daniels," Georgey commended.

69

"When you 'spose we can shoot balls?" Arkie asked.

"Soon as the paint dries, I hear tell."

"Who else gonna be there?"

"Dunno," Georgey said.

"Do we have to walk down the street?" I asked. I always sensed discomfort from just about everyone in the surrounding area with "Georgella's White Boy" in the neighborhood—feelings of anger, puzzlement, and suspicion. The older coloreds pretty much told me I didn't belong by their closed windows and empty porches. "It ain't right. No good'll come of it."

"Nah," Arkie replied. "We'll cut through Mr. Zeke's yard and up that alley. We won't see a spook for three blocks. Then we'll race to the next block. How 'bout spook, Ricky? Can you call me a spook?"

Little Roy got up, shaking his head. "You know, Arkie, yur gettin' on my nerves."

"Mine too," I said, crossing the street to Zeke's house.

"Mornin' Mr. Zeke," I said.

"Sir," Arkie said.

"Mr. Zeke, sir," Roy said.

"Whitey," Zeke replied. "You little niggers be good."

We rushed along the side of his house and out Zeke's back gate.

"See?" Arkie said. "Zeke called me a nigger."

"Shut up."

* * *

By now I felt I belonged in Georgey's neighborhood—belonged as much as Sonny belonged in the barbershop or the shoeshine "boys" belonged in the lobby of Dad's office building. Still, if

70

Arkie and I wanted to explore without creating trouble, we did it by way of the small alleys running parallel to the streets. Rickety, old garbage trucks bumped and rolled along, swerving to miss the potholes. The alleys in that part of town all ran north and south, crossing over the roads. It was as easy to find your way around as on a Monopoly board—alley, street, alley, street, alley, street. Georgey's house was Go. The church was three streets and three alleys west then two streets north. We knew we could make the trip without anyone seeing us, ducking behind fences if anybody approached. It was exciting—this hide and seek game—adding to the allure of playing in that neighborhood.

The Church of the Holy God was a big, stucco, Gothic church that was bright yellow with white corner blocks, a large, green, double front door, and shutters of the same color. A light blue, painted dome with a gold cross sat on top. The church sat loudly in its surroundings, front and center. Next door was what Georgey called a playground—a poured concrete field larger than a full-sized basketball court. It lay in the heat of the summer sun and the bone-chilling cold of the winter nights, slowly cracking from lack of use and maintenance. Young girls sometimes jumped ropes and boys played catch there, but not often enough. It was simply an unused idea, like cars on cinder blocks and like idle promises.

Recently, when the Butler University Fieldhouse was refurbished for the state high school basketball finals, volunteers from several surrounding neighborhoods had rescued two fine basketball rims and backboards. And there they sat as the resident pastor put the finishing touches on a dream he had for the local high school kids, or kids of any age.

* * *

71

Reverend Oswald Williams was an intense, colored man in his early 40s with a receding hairline that added ten years to his age. He was a nodder. His head perpetually bobbed, sometimes subtly, sometimes emphatically, but always nodding. His upper lip was covered with a thick mustache—a smiling throw rug. Smiling and nodding, touching, hugging, and encouraging, he never forgot anyone's name and always thanked people. No wonder everybody loved him.

One Sunday in church he announced, "When God called me to this church, I knew I was where I was supposed to be the minute I saw the playground 'cause children are supposed to play on it. It was a sign that our church would prosper because of the children. Just like Jesus ministerin' to the children. Here it was. But sadly it's just a giant slab of concrete that shows I ain't doin' my job for our children. As long as there's more concrete than children, it ain't no playground. I want to see babies and boys runnin' and girls jumpin' rope and high school kids playin' basketball, all that stuff."

Little Roy, Arkie, and I emerged from the alley across from the church and ran into the playground. A hush fell over the crowd like a large exhale, as if a new dog had come into the neighborhood, one that was totally different from any of the other dogs—a white one, a symbol of nothing good for anyone there. An intrusion. Me.

I had no idea it would be like this, seeing a dozen young children and teenagers, mothers pushing broken-down baby carriages, Reverend Williams and a few adult men; Sonny, I recognized. Big high school kids. I saw Baby Shuli and Tiny Marcella in a cluster of girls. Everything was frozen in time. Me and Them.

Reverend Williams greeted us enthusiastically, corralling a half dozen teens and preteens. "OK, everone. Gather 'round here for a minute. Want you to meet a very special friend. This is Rick Stoner. His family has known Miss Georgella for many years and he spends a lot of time in our neighborhood."

"Mostly with me," Arkie said. "Ricky's my friend. He's white, you know."

"Ricky's good," Baby Shuli said, walking into the crowd of boys. "He's a friend of mine, too. Known him forever."

"And mine," Tiny Marcella said. She looked different— thinner, more mature, a couple of bumps in her shirt. Dad called it puberty. It was happening to everybody but me. But she still had her lisp.

"Yeah," Little Roy said, patting me on the back.

The boys slouched, shifted from one foot to the next, looked down, then at the church. An air of hostility came over the playground. I was uncomfortable and tried to put my hands in my pockets but they didn't fit.

Tiny Marcella stepped into the crowd. "Yeah, come on you guyth. Ricky'th here to help. Can't you thee that?"

"Yur right, Marcella," Reverend Williams said. "He's here to help. It was my idea. So, I want this work team to introduce yourself and shake Ricky's hand."

"Man, this is gonna be awful," Arkie said, holding his head, looking skyward.

"Arkie," Reverend Williams warned, pointing sternly.

The first to introduce himself was "Arnold." His voice was low like Zeke's and he was older than the rest, heavyset. He shook my hand without making eye contact. I felt like if he had a weapon, he would have used it.

73

"Rozelle." Well over 6 feet tall, skinny as a pencil with a long neck and huge Adam's apple, Rozelle shook my hand and patted me on the shoulder. Smiling with more gums than teeth. "Heard a lot about you from Arkie."

"Nathaniel Larimer Wilson. They calls me Nat, Nat the rat." A round of quiet laughter followed.

"Nat the brat," Baby Shuli added.

"I'm Willie. Arkie says you is OK."

"Of course, he's OK," Reverend Williams said, a lazy booger on his mustache. "He wouldn't be here if he weren't. He can paint lines as well as any of us 'cause we're all the same in God's eyes. Black, white, yella, all the same. Tall, skinny short, fat."

"Hear that Little Roy? Yur the same as us in God's eyes—thin, good lookin'."

And so we organized the task of painting lines. Exactly three inches wide, measured with yardsticks—each of us had our own. We drew the lines with blackboard chalk and used 2 x 4s as straight edges. Then Arkie and Nat meticulously painted them black. Arnold, Little Roy, Willie, and I drew the free throw lines and the circle around them with chalk. With his back to me and going out of his way to avoid eye contact, Arnold drew a small keyhole on the pavement to show us the shape and distances. His teeth clenched and I could see his jaw muscles working.

Several other boys gathered on the edge of the playground, eyeing me suspiciously, while Reverend Williams spoke to each one, nodding and patting them on the back.

"The free throw line is 15 feet from the basket," Arnold said. "Roy, you measure that and mark it. Willie and me'll draw a 12-foot circle around it." Then I was alone, a white dot on black paper, standing while everyone else talked to each other.

That moment, for however long it took—maybe two minutes while it felt like two hours—was awful. If I weren't white it wouldn't have been so bad, but being white and being excluded made me angry. Then Willie came over after he finished drawing the keyhole and we looked past each other for a while.

"Arkie says you beat him up once."

"I hit him once. Didn't beat him up," I said. "We're friends now."

"Yeah. That's what he says. Where you go to school?"

"Crooked Creek."

"You in the seventh grade?"

"No. Eighth."

"That school's way up north, aint it?"

"Yeah."

"You go on one of them school buses?"

"Yeah."

"My daddy says that we is all gonna be put on school buses and sent across town to white schools."

"Why?" I asked, unable to understand the point of going to a school that wasn't nearby.

"Teach the whites and the Negroes to live with each other, he says."

Arnold overheard our conversation. "Yeah, and Oreos like Roy's daddy's gonna get us all killed."

"Who's killin' who over here?" Reverend Williams asked, approaching the four of us.

"Lil Roy's daddy. My momma says we need to leave ya'll alone," Arnold said, looking intently at me.

"And who is ya'll?" Reverend Williams asked.

"You know, the whites. Him."

"No, sir, Mr. Arnold Turner. God wants us to live together, together in peace, to learn more about each other. Little Roy's daddy, Mr. Squiggy, is doing a very special thing for the colored people in this town. Equality will only come for us 'cause a man like Mr. Squiggy Daniels. And, yes, he risks his own physical well-being on issues of racial equality every day."

"My daddy graduated from college last year. He gonna graduate from law school next year and be a lawyer," Little Roy said.

"A lawyer?" Rozelle asked. "Didn't know colored folks could be lawyers."

"My granddaddy was a lawyer. We can be anything whites can be, Daddy says."

"Lil Roy's right, gentlemen," Reverend Williams said. "Mr. Squiggy been workin' at the trolley car company almost fifteen years now. Went to night school for ten years. And he will finish law school next year at thirty-five years of age."

"Yeah. Daddy says bein' equal is tough for our race."

Reverend Williams added, "And the time is now. It has to start someplace, sometime. Now." He paused. "Now, Arnold."

I looked at Little Roy. Then everyone looked at me. I was the white one—the antagonist, though at that time I had no idea what that meant, just the awkward feeling of being on the opposing side, the minority. Defensive.

As we worked, Arkie tried joking and Reverend Williams forced some lame, small talk with me, stupid conversations. Rozelle, too. Arnold was not happy, gravitating over to several, older high school kids who stared at me with their hands in their pockets— whispering, pointing, taunting—animals marking their territory. Out of the corner of my eye I saw one give me the finger. It scared me. Arkie and I gave each other the finger when we played basketball, but this was different. This one had a sneer and jutted chin, slitted eyes.

"Hey, Whitey!" someone suddenly yelled from across the playground. "Kiss my black ass!" The high school kids erupted in laughter. I was afraid to look up.

Reverend Williams went berserk, racing across the playground and yelling at two colored teens backstepping into a crowd and disappearing. "Go on! Get outa here! No room for that kinda talk! I don't want to see you around here again. Ever! Go on!" He reached into the crowd and grabbed one teenager by the back of his shirt, pushing him and shoving him into the street. "What's yur name?"

"None of yur fuckin' business," the boy said, running down the street. "Go home, asshole honky!" he screamed over his shoulder.

"Oh, my goodness, Ricky," Reverend Williams said. "I am so sorry. So very sorry. I prayed this wouldn't happen."

Arkie came over to me. "Come on, Ricky. Let's go."

Baby Shuli stood shocked, hands to her mouth, tears wetting her chocolate chip cheeks.

"No," Reverend Williams said. "I'll drive you back to Miss Georgella's. Come with me."

I stood alone, as alone as I had ever felt. Surrounded by people, yet dreadfully alone. Afraid and with no place to go. My emptiness turned to anger—"Leave me alone!" I screamed. "I hate it. I hate you all."

A hush came over the crowd and then a reply, from Arnold: "Now you know how we feel, honkey bastard."

Arkie spun around in sudden rage. He charged Arnold, who was several inches taller, and pushed him in the chest with both hands. Arnold fell over backward and Arkie leaped on him, pounding his face with both fists. "You stupid nigger!" he screamed. "Don't ya ever call him names." The crowd converged around the fight and came forward to pull Arkie off of Arnold, holding Arnold so he wouldn't go after Arkie.

I bolted and ran down the alley, sobbing—across one street in front of cars. A colored man yelled at me, "Go home, Whitey!" I heard Reverend Williams yell at the man, "Shut up, you stupid nigger." The playground had imploded. I kept running, the thoughts racing in my hea. Why couldn't I have friends like Andy? Regular friends? White friends? Why did I need to be here? I never wanted to come back here again.

I stopped in the alley at Zeke's fence and turned around. No one had followed me. I was relieved and wanted to be alone. I crawled over the fence and sat in the quiet of Zeke's tiny backyard, my back leaning against the fence. I was tired of crying, tired of running. Didn't want to talk to anyone. Just wanted to be alone. Zeke was listening to a baseball game on his radio. Nanny Fernandez hit a triple—my favorite player. Someone ran by breathing hard, then headed back up the alley. I felt safe tucked against the fence.

Ann Sue called out to Reginald. "Reginald. Reginald! Where are you? Georgella, you know where Reginald went?"

I sat, knees pulled to my chest, thinking about Arkie and the rest of "them." I should have stood up to Arnold, called him a nigger. I didn't need Arkie fighting my fights for me. Who does he think he is?

"Zeze, is Reginald over there with Zeke?"

A fly landed on my arm, looking for a comfortable place to settle, moseying around like an old, six-legged, colored man. Tic-a-tic-a-tic-a-tic-tic-a. Back and forth, scratching one leg with another, he suddenly flew away.

"Whatchu doin' here, boy?" came the gruff voice of Zeke from his back stoop.

"Nothin'," I mumbled, holding my knees.

"Hmm. Nothin's good, sometimes."

"Yeah."

All at once we heard Arkie running down the alley, calling my name. I looked up at Zeke. He put his finger to his lips.

"Mr. Zeke, sir," Arkie said breathless, "you seen Ricky? I lost him."

"Nope. Not around here."

We heard Arkie's breathless pace as he ran back up the alley.

Zeke shifted his gaze back to me. "Ya don't look too happy."

"I'm not."

"You and Arkie have a fight?"

"No. Not really."

"Things didn't go well up to the church, huh?"

"Guess not."

"They get on ya 'cause you is white."

"Yeah. I never should have gone."

"Hmm. Told Georgella it was wrong. Goddamned women." He sat on the top step of his stoop, long legged, shook out a Camel, and lit it. "Injuns are ahead 3-2."

"I heard."

"Who's yur favorite player?"

"Nanny Fernandez. Third base."

"Mine too." He paused, looking for something else to say. The score changed to 4-2. "Got somethin' over here for ya," he said, pulling a Coke bottle from under a chair.

"Cincinnati. Ya got anything further 'n that?"

79

"We got a Louisville."

"Well here," Zeke said, handing me the bottle. "I'm not sure which one's further." I turned the bottle over, running my finger over the letters. "You don't smoke yet, do ya?" he added.

I looked up at him in disbelief. He was smiling, all red-gummed and yellow.

"Me?" I asked.

"No one else here."

"'Course I don't smoke. I'm only 13."

"Here." He handed me a cigarette. "Go ahead. I think yur old enough."

I took it and put it between my lips like a Popsicle. He lit it for me. I puffed.

"Smokin's good for ya sometimes when yur angry. Gotta be careful you don't breathe in right away. Jes enjoy the puffin' at first."

I puffed again and smoke got in my nose, making me cough, making me inhale, making me cough.

"Oops. There ya go. Try not to breathe in that smoke. And yur gettin' the end of yur cigarette all wet with yur lips. You know what the white folks call that?"

"Call what?"

"When you gets yur cigarette all wet on the end."

I coughed again. "No."

"Nigger-lips. They say, 'do not nigger-lip your cigarette, Judy.'" He imitated the high voice of a white woman, pursing his mouth and tilting his head effeminately.

I laughed, then coughed, then laughed again and gagged.

"Nigger-lips?" I asked, still coughing.

"Yep. You ask yur daddy. He'll tell you. Tell him you and ole Zeke smoked together and you nigger-lipped yur butt." He smiled real big and messed my hair. "Yur a good boy, Rick Stoner. A real good boy. I'm proud to call you my friend. I wished I had me a boy like you. I'd be damned proud."

"Thank you, sir," I said, coughing, suddenly realizing I had said the word "nigger" and it didn't sound like an insult. And Zeke had called me Rick instead of Whitey.

"Now why don't you go on over to Georgella's? Don't you tell her you and me smoked. She'd have my ass."

"I won't."

"Be careful when you stand up. You'll be dizzy, yur first time smokin' an all."

I stood up, blinking my eyes and holding onto the fence. Then I regained my composure, rubbed my cigarette out with my shoe (like I knew what I was doing), and walked to Georgey's house—coughing, blinking, big strides, listing, queasy. I could feel Zeke's smile all over my back.

Fifteen

Monday after school I grabbed a cookie in the kitchen. Georgey carried a large clothes basket outdoors to hang on the clothesline. Spike was playing his violin in the living room. Mom came home early from school and was accompanying Spike on the piano. It sounded different—Spike played violin as if he knew what he was doing, but he was only eight. I never knew what I was doing at that age.

"Ricky darlin'. Can you give me a hand with these sheets? Bring along another cookie."

I followed her outside.

"You know," Georgey said, clothespins in her mouth. "I spoke to Reverend Williams after church yesterday. Everone's talkin' 'bout what happened Saturday. There's a real sadness fillin' our hearts."

"Should be."

"Specially Arkie. Yur whole gang is sad."

"They're not my gang. I'm white. I got my own gang."

"That's foolish talk."

"Not anymore."

"You know, Arkie told me you was the brother he never had."

"He did?"

"Yes, he did. And that's a big deal that a colored boy and a white boy could be best friends. Sounds to me yur purty special."

"Huh." I didn't want to hear it—colored propaganda. Spike's violin and Mom's cadence took center stage in my mind. A perfect, clean sound, uncluttered, allowing my mind to think. I still didn't have a perfect, clean anything.

"You can't stay mad fur ever."

"You wanna bet?"

"Well then, you is gonna become that bigoted white boy they thought you was. All right then. They was right. You ain't a bigger man than they is."

More colored propaganda.

"So, Arkie, Baby Shuli, Lil Roy, and Marcella are jes a bunch of dumb niggers?"

"I didn't say that."

"No, you didn't 'cause you don't believe it for a minute, do you?"

"Not really."

"Listen carefully: You knows what yur s'posed to do when a horse bucks you off?"

"What?"

"S'posed to get right back on that horse. Show him you is braver and smarter than he ever knowed."

I didn't answer her right away because I wasn't sure what she meant.

"Let's sit fur a minute," she said, as she eased herself to the ground. Quiet covered the luffing sheets. Mom was praising Spike inside. There was no more music. I couldn't understand what Georgey meant.

"You don't mean you think I should go back to the church?" I asked in disbelief. That thought was furthest from my mind.

"I do mean that. Go back, honey. Tell Arkie you wanna play ball on that court."

"Are you crazy?"

Mom came outdoors. "Hi, honey."

"Am I crazy? Not a bit," Georgey said "You can either be a scared little boy or a brave man. Yur choice."

I didn't answer. Mom sat on the grass with us. Quiet. Georgey wouldn't let go of me with her eyes.

She continued. "Everone warned David not to mess with Goliath, but he was brave, and he knew God would protect him. I knows God will protect you. But I don't know how brave you are."

"Did I hear you correctly, Georgey?" Mom said. "Did you just tell my son to go back to your neighborhood?"

"I did," Georgey answered, shaking her head and holding my hand in hers.

"Are YOU crazy?" Mom's voice ramped up an octave. "My son was just attacked by a bunch of . . ." The word couldn't come out of her mouth.

"What word ya lookin' for, Miz Stoner? Nigger?"

"I'm not looking for any particular word, Georgey. I'm trying to save my son's life. Something that you are not doing."

"And I is tryin' to turn him into a man; not some little boy who was taunted and insulted by other little boys. This is an important time for Ricky. God builds character during these times."

"You know," Mom said. "I'm getting pretty tired of you thinking that your God and your Jesus are going to protect my

84

children!" And Mom stormed over to her car and drove off in a huff.

I heard my heart beating. For the first time in my thirteen years, I knew my mother was wrong.

"Child? It's yur decision."

"What am I supposed to do?"

The idea of going back was a nightmare I didn't want to have.

"You jes tell Arkie you wanna play basketball with them boys. That'll scare 'em half to death. They'll have a respect for you that you can't imagine. More importantly, you will have a respect for yourself that will last forever. Thinks you can do it?"

"I dunno, Georgey. I don't think so."

"Think about it, honey. You out there on the court, head held high. Many boys watchin' you, wonderin' how you got the courage to come back. Those boys will become yur friends. They'll respect ya."

"The truth is those guys will probably be wondering if I've got a brain in my head."

"I don't think so. You go bravely. You tell 'em when they makes good shots. You kid with 'em when they don't. You and that Arkie boy make a good pair. I hear you jokin' out in the alley."

"You do?"

"Lordy do I, and God forgive me fo listen' to that language. Sound like a couple of liquored up sharecroppers." A huge smile unfurled and her eyes lit up.

"Now I gots one more thing to say to ya: I loves yur momma with all my heart. As much as I loves you and all the other Stoners. I feels deep inside that she will be the greatest of ya'll with a sensitive and giving heart. I know she's mad at me

85

right now. But I also know she'll get over it. Because this"—she raised her hands—"this situation about you becoming a prideful man scares her. She will understand. Jest needs to go for a fast drive."

The sheets wafted slowly in the breezeless air, not even disturbing a chickadee perched on the clothesline. A swirl of an aphid hatch caught our eye. Georgey put a blade of grass between her thumbs and blew on it. It sounded like a distant horn, moaning.

"How'd you do that?"

"You never done this? Watch." Repositioning the grass, she took a deep breath and slowly blew between her thumbs. Mom would have called it a French horn—B flat. Dad would have called it an eager bull elk. It was a haunting sound.

"Here, you do it, too." She searched for a blade of grass that was thick and broke it off. "Give me your thumb." She laid it carefully on my thumb. "Now put your other thumb over it. Make sure the grass is tight. Now you blows right into that opening." She blew on her grass and the sound happened. Then I blew a lower sound. It was background music to an ancient chant.

"The trumpets of Israel, callin' to ya, Lord," she whispered.

We continued; low breathy sounds blending harmoniously.

"Know who taught me that?" she asked.

"Who?"

"Yur daddy. Once after a Boy Scout camp. Reckon he was 'bout sixteen."

"My dad?"

"You bet. Ole Buster Stoner. He wasn't as good a student as you is fast becomin', but he knowed more worthless information than anyone, and, sho nuf, he memorized stuff like 'Little Orphant Annie Come ta Our House ta Stay.'"

"By James Witcomb Riley," I added.

"You is right. Buried right over there in Crown Hill Cemetery, he is."

I didn't go to Georgey's neighborhood the following Saturday. Later that week Arkie called to tell me that someone had walked on the lines before they were dry and tracked black sneaker prints everywhere. There were no apologies and no remorse—it was time to get back on the horse. So Saturday Dad drove me to Georgey's on his way to the hospital.

"That was some brawl week before last," he said, lighting a cigarette.

I opened my window. "Yeah."

"Georgey told me the whole story."

"She did?"

"Yep. Ozzie even called my office on Monday."

"Ozzie?"

"Reverend Williams—Ozzie. He was angry and mortified. He was certain nothing like that would ever happen."

"Yeah. I was scared."

"I would have been scared, too. It was a brave thing you did. I'm proud of you."

"I didn't do it 'cause I was brave. I just thought me, Arkie, and Roy were gonna paint lines and have a bigger place to play ball. Arkie bugged me to help. Then there was this Arnold guy and another older kid who Arkie jumped on and Reverend

Williams lost his temper. Someone walking down the street called me a honkey bastard. It was a real mess."

"Yep. Sure sounded like it," he chuckled.

"It wasn't funny, Dad."

"I'm sorry, son. I know it wasn't funny then. But so ironic in retrospect. Here are all of these people who suffer from discrimination, discriminating against you. And so now you're going back."

"That's Georgey's idea."

"Smartest thing you will ever do. Now every person in that neighborhood will see you as a terribly brave white boy who is not afraid to stand up for what is right. Now you represent something good. Good always prevails, but rarely on time."

"You think so?"

"I most certainly do." We rounded the corner onto Georgey's street.

"Dad? Do you think colored kids and white kids should have to go to schools across town?"

"Frankly, I don't. It seems like an unnecessary thing to do. Neighborhood schools seem fine to me. But that's me."

"Yeah. I could end up at Crispus Attucks."

"You certainly would stand out there." His cigarette hung from his lopsided grin.

We pulled up to Georgey's house. Dad waved to Reginald and Zeke, flicked his cigarette out the window, and drove off. I watched the old Plymouth listing to one side until it turned the corner. Then I searched the street for Dad's cigarette butt. Finding it, I held it up for Zeke to see.

"Bone dry," I said.

"The doctor knows what he's doin'. He sho do."

There was hardly anyone at the church, just a janitor pouring some liquid into the cracks on the court and a couple of mothers with kids in carriages. Arkie and I shot baskets with Rozelle, Nat (the Rat), and Little Roy—the five of us joking and cheating. I made the loudest farting noise with my hand cupped underneath my armpit. The infamous pump fart. No one could do better.

"You makes louder farts 'cause you ain't got no hair under there," Little Roy said.

"That has nothing to do with it," I said. "I'm just a better farter than you."

We stood beneath a rim, pumping our arms, making obscene noises and laughing.

Rozelle could easily grab the rim but couldn't get the basketball over it enough to dunk it. Arkie could touch high on the net, as could Nat. I was an inch short of the bottom of the net. Little Roy couldn't even jump out of his sneakers. No one talked about whites or coloreds. We played HORSE, then Russian Roólette, as they called it. We stood in a line, facing the basket just four feet away. First Little Roy shot and hit. Then Arkie shot and hit. I shot and hit. Rozelle, too. The game was simple. The first time you missed you were out. Same shot, nothing fancy. Sudden death. Have to play fast. After the third round Little Roy missed. Two rounds later I missed. That left Arkie and Rozelle. They shot and made it 10 more times. Back and forth. The pressure became intense but neither of them broke. Swish, swish, swish.

Reverend Williams came out the back door with Marcella and walked over to me. "Yur all right, Rick Stoner. One brave young man. I'm so very glad to see you back. Yur message is noted by everone."

"Me too," Marcella said.

"OK man," Rozelle shouted. "This ain't even fun no more." Swish.

"You can always forfeit," Arkie said. Swish.

Nat took a long look at Marcella, squinting. "Man, that girl lookin' good. How old she getting' to be?"

"'Round thirteen," I said.

"That ain't gonna happen," Rozelle said. Swish. "How 'bout this. We each take one more shot. From the free throw line, this time. If we both hit it, it's a tie." He reached in his pocket and pulled out a nickel. "Here Ricky. Flip it. I'll call it."

"Why can't I call it?" Arkie said.

"Hell, I don't care," Rozelle said. "You call it."

"I don't wanna call it," Arkie said, grinning. "You call it."

I flipped the coin. Rozelle called "heads." It landed heads.

"OK. Shoot," Arkie said.

"No. I won the toss, man. I get to decide. You go first. This is it. Winner take all. Give it everthing you got."

"Suit yourself." Arkie shot.

And he missed.

Rozelle smiled. "My daddy taught me that."

"Taught you what?" I asked.

"If you wants to win, mess with their head. Make 'em think."

We sat on the steps of the church trying to figure out what Rozelle meant—trying to figure out if Rozelle knew what Rozelle meant.

Finally Nat said, "Glad ya come back, Rick. Must a been hard to do."

"Yeah. Me, too," Rozelle said, who walked like he was in slow motion—a wide gait, rolling shoulders, and holding the basketball in one hand the way I might hold a melon.

Over time Arkie and I had come to know where we were geographically when we were at Georgey's house. Fifteen blocks north and five blocks west of us was my house. Frog Island and Arkie's house were ten blocks south and three blocks west. We talked about going to my house or Frog Island without being seen by anyone. We'd cut through backyards to the towpath along the canal. South would take us to Frog Island; north to my house.

North was much more dangerous because of the Silver Gun Patrol. Rumor had it that they were a group of white men who wore guns—six-shooters—strapped to their legs like cowboys and heavy, black boots with metal heels. A crudely painted sign down near the canal read: "PATROLLED BY THE SILVER GUN PATROL. TRAVEL AT YOUR OWN RISK." We decided that going to Frog Island would be safer and shorter.

* * *

"This way to yur house," Arkie said, pointing north up the towpath of the canal. "Frog Island is the opposite. This way," pointing south. "The canal runs into the river about a mile south, then we'd have to follow the river. That's really creepy."

"Who do those jokers think they are?" I asked, throwing a rock at the sign.

"Yeah," Arkie said. "Postin' some big sign like that, claimin' this land for their own selfs."

"Yeah, claiming it with pistols, rifles, and knives."

So we went back to Georgey's with impending adventure in our minds.

"Next Saturday," Arkie finally said. "Let's do it. We'll flip to see which direction. Yur house or mine."

"Swear to God?"

"Swear to God. Don't tell no one."

"No one. Shake on it."

We did.

Sixteen

Two weeks passed. It was Mom and Dad's seventeenth wedding anniversary. We had lunch at the country club across the street from our house, a short walk across the golf course. Andy, Spike, and I had to wear neckties. Knowing her boys and knowing how tight she was with money, Mome hid our neckties so we wouldn't soil them and she wouldn't have to buy new ones. She hid them under her underwear. (We'd never look there.) Neckties, pressed slacks, and sport jackets.

The manager of the club prepared a special flower arrangement for our table. Baxter's parents, the Moriaritys, and other friends of Mom and Dad drifted in as if they hadn't been invited, but they were part of Dad's crafty surprise. Mom teared up and Dad smiled. Their friends had jokes to tell about Dad and adulations for Mom. This was our life, rich with variety, humor, and love.

Our waitress that day, named Emma, was a long-time patient of Dad's. She was huge and round with a teetering waddle that bounced the flesh high on her hips.

"Now which one a you boys is Ricky?" she asked, smiling with a space between her two front teeth big enough to easily slide a pencil through.

"I'm Ricky, ma'am."

"Well, well. I'm Li'l Roy's momma." She put her hand on my shoulder. "I am so sorry about what happened a few weeks ago at church. I just don't know what to say."

"We're all over that," Dad said.

"I'm fine, Mrs. Daniels. Those things are bound to happen."

"And this is my oldest, Andy, and youngest, Spike," Mom said cheerfully.

They said "nice-to-meet-cha," also cheerfully.

"Ricky's talked about Little Roy many times," Dad said.

"Little Roy's not so little," I joked.

"His daddy called him Little just 'cause he weren't. Even when he was just borned," Emma said. "But then Squiggy ain't so small either."

"Squiggy's about three or four years younger than me," Dad said. "I remember him when he was Arthur. Just plain ole Arthur Daniels."

"Doctor, you don't," Emma said.

"I do. Ask him. The story goes that he had the worst penmanship in public school number three. Teachers couldn't read his writing because he was left-handed and dragged his hand across the paper as he wrote. Like squiggly smudges, they said. That's where he got his name."

"My goodness, Doctor. Ain't you somethin'?"

Dad asked, "How's Squiggy doing?"

Emma rolled her eyes. "Not good, doctah. We was thinkin' about callin' you a week ago. Squiggy said, no."

"Tell him to call me if there's anything I can do."

"Oh, thank you, doctah."

Dad nodded and Emma reverted to our pleasant waitress.

After lunch we walked home across the golf course. Dad found a golf ball and decided we would have a contest to see who could throw it the farthest.

"Ladies first," Dad said, handing the golf ball to Mom. She wound up, took a running start (in her high heels), and unleashed her best throw. Unfortunately she let go of the ball late and it ground into the fairway three feet in front of her. Her second attempt went haywire, way to the side. Lack of finger control, Andy pointed out.

She picked up the golf ball and handed it to Dad. "Am I wrong or was Emma hesitant to talk about Squiggy?"

"Very hesitant," Dad said. "Squiggy's been around awhile working for equality for coloreds. Squiggy will make a great lawyer for his people,"

"Why is the issue of Squiggy so secretive?" Mom asked.

"Squiggy works closely with the NAACP—the National Association for the Advancement of Colored People. Colored folks—especially colored folks at an all-white country club—keep those things under wraps. My turn."

He wound up and heaved a great throw. I didn't think I would be able to beat it.

"Not bad, huh? Should have tried out for the Indians."

"Maybe the Sioux," Andy said.

"I'll get it," Spike said, racing to recover the golf ball.

"Yeah, Squiggy's what this town needs," Dad said. "The Negroes in our city need good legal representation, ethical legal representation. We have colored lawyers but most have been corrupted by our bleached-out white lawyers. Your Uncle Gordon calls most of the colored trial lawyers the Oreo Bar."

"Why's that?" Andy said.

"You ever eat an Oreo cookie?"

"Sure."

"What's it look like?'

"Well, it's a small round cookie."

"What color?"

"Black."

"What's inside?"

"Some good, sugary cream stuff."

"What color?"

"White."

"Black on the outside and white on the inside, right?"

"Yeah."

"That's like many of the successful colored lawyers, black on the outside and white on the inside. Squiggy calls them the Oreo Bar because on the outside they appear to be on the side of the colored people. But on the inside they are supporting everything the white lawyers tell them to."

"Why would they do that?" Mom asked.

"Fear. Not to mention money, power, prestige. It's amazing what morals are compromised when money is waved. We haven't really had any real strong Negro representation since Squiggy's grandfather, the last Daniels lawyer. He fought the Klan in the 1890s. Squiggy's father wasn't a lawyer, but he was on the city council and butted heads with the best, lost a subsequent election and was eventually drummed out in favor of an Oreo member of the city council. He died that same year."

"Sounds like the Daniels name is poison to most of the white people," Mom said. "Not our friends; the other white people."

"That's right. There is a secretive—and very active—Klu Klux Klan in our town. They're nervous about Squiggy. He's a decorated soldier; Purple Heart from somewhere in the Pacific.

Served his country well. Worked his way through college. Has a lot of clout with the NAACP, an unusual amount. I think he's being groomed by a Dr. Martin Luther King down in Georgia. If King gets involved up here, our radical white population will not sit still."

"What can they do? It's legal, isn't it?" Mom asked.

"Absolutely. Legal and necessary. It's happening all across the country. Eventually our government will have to enforce equality." He paused, then said, "I'd rather finish this contest. So Lill, you be the contest official, not a participant. You run ahead and mark each of our throws."

"Great idea."

She removed her high heels and ran until she got to Dad's golf ball, where she marked his spot with one of her shoes. Spike threw next, not as far as Dad but surprisingly good. He even surprised himself and he was happy. Spike never did things to win; he did things to have fun and with a perpetual smile on his face. Andy and I were different. We did things to win. Mom put her other shoe near Spike's spot, giving him an extra five feet.

"Way to go, Spike-o," she yelled.

He raced across the fairway to join her. Two very visible red shoes lay on the course. It was my turn.

"Your turn, Ricky," Andy said.

"Let's flip to see who goes first," I suggested. "It's only fair."

"I'll flip," Dad said. "Andy calls it."

He flipped the coin.

"Heads," Andy said.

It landed tails.

"OK, little brother. Go ahead."

"No. I won the toss, so I choose who throws. You first."

"You sure?"

"Yeah," I said. "I need to see how far I have to throw it."

"Hmm." He scrutinized the distance to Mom's shoe resting on Dad's mark and looked at me. "You're sure?"

"Yeah, go ahead. Give it everything you got."

He wound up and threw the ball as hard as he possibly could—perhaps even harder than he possibly could—wincing and gritting his teeth. It went high rather than far, just barely to Dad's mark. Not his best throw. Spike marked it with one of his shoes. Two red high heels and a loafer lay in the fairway, with Mom ruining her nylons and Spike limping in one shoe.

Spike came running back with the golf ball—still wearing only one shoe—and handed it to me. Quickly I uncoiled and threw the ball past Andy's. There was a lot of teasing that day. Dad said the fairway rained with good fellowship. He lit a cigarette and I warned him not to nigger-lip the butt. Mom was appalled, never having heard the expression.

"Nigger-lip the butt?" she whispered, cringing, as if sucking on a lemon. "I don't think we should be talking that way."

Spike asked what it meant and Dad and Andy laughed. I told the family about my first cigarette with Zeke and Rozelle's "psyche job" on Arkie. I remember that time so clearly because it was the first time I was on a par with Andy and Dad. I wasn't a skinny little kid who could do nothing well. Not anymore. Substance would be Dad's word for it. Swish would be mine.

Seventeen

It was cold as a witch's tit, and the wind pounded against the down in our winter coats. The sign read:

THE SILVER GUN PATROL
NO TRESPASSING
THIS PROPERTY
IS PATROLLED AND PROTECTED BY
THE SILVER GUN PATROL.

Other people had scribbled insults on the sign—new words for Arkie and me to add to our vocabulary. "Kill homos," the scribbling read.

"What's a homo?" Arkie asked.

"Not sure," I said. "It sounds Italian."

We looked down the length of the canal until it veered lazily behind barren oak trees and disappeared, its water moving like warm molasses. A red flannel shirt, half submerged, inched by an empty pack of Chesterfields. A pair of old jockey shorts lay on the bank, dirty and ripped. No birds nearby. A raw wind. My mind grew fuzzy as we looked from the sign to down the towpath. It would soon be too late to change our mind.

"Heads we go to Frog Island. Tails we go to my house."

I flipped a nickel and it landed tails.

"I figure it's about three and a half miles," I said. "It's the third tunnel."

"What's the third tunnel?"

"The third tunnel is under our street, the street I live on."

"How you know that?"

"Dad told me once."

"How we gonna know?"

"I'll know. We can see our house from the canal."

"I brought a knife," Arkie said, reaching into his back pocket and producing a kitchen knife with black electrician's tape on the handle.

"Oh, good. We can spread butter with that," I said, pulling out Andy's new Boy Scout knife. "We'll stab with this and spread their guts around with your knife."

"You know, this ain't funny. This is serious stuff. We could die out here."

"I know. Wanna go back?"

"I ain't no chicken."

We stood quiet, looking everywhere except at each other.

"Ready, set, go!" I started first. "Come on."

We ran crazily, listening to our feet, gasping for air, stopping to catch our breath and spit, then running some more.

"You sure about these tunnels?"

"Sure, I'm sure. Heard Dad talking about them several times."

We passed another sign that said the same thing. Someone had written, DUMB NIGGERS, KILL THE JEWS. We ran farther. Then we saw the first tunnel, dark and fifty feet long. Out of the corners of our eyes we saw some scurries in the leaves and trash, but then nothing. Before entering we stopped to catch our breath again, looking through the entrance to the other side. The light glared bright white in the distance as an an ice-cold wind blew through the tunnel. We heard our breath echo in the concrete archway. The tunnel smelled of urine and mold, and

100

crumpled paper bags with empty whiskey bottles were scattered along the edge. Old paint peeled from the ceiling, held in place by generations of spider webs. A dead rat lay at the entrance near a pile of moldy feces.

Arkie reached into his pocket and pulled out his knife. "Let's go."

The walls were covered with vile graffiti—racial slurs by whites against coloreds and coloreds against whites—most of which we couldn't read because it was too dark. The artwork was obvious: crude drawings of genitalia and sexual acts, a dead person hanging from a tree. Arkie's white eyes glowed with fear in the darkness and we raced to the other side, to sunlight.

"That's number one," I panted, standing at the tunnel exit, leaning over, hands on my knees.

"Two to go."

"I didn't see any Coke bottles."

"Peoples that comes here don't drink Coca-Cola— straight whiskey." The echo of our voices in the tunnel behind us was ominous, like talking with a metal bucket over your head.

We tucked our knives back in our pockets and began running to the second tunnel. It felt like we were running forever. My side began to cramp and I had to stop. Leaned over, gasping. Arkie was gasping too, looking everywhere.

"How much further?"

"I don't know," I answered. "I've never done this before."

"Let's go slower or we just might die of tiredness, rather than murder."

"OK. Let's sit for a minute," I heaved.

"Ya know, my daddy told me never to go down to the canal. He said stay away from it. Been some strange things happen down there."

101

"My Dad said the same thing." We looked around as we talked, on guard. "People have disappeared down here."

"Think we oughta head back?" Arkie asked, unsure.

"You scared?"

"A little. Not really though."

"Me neither." My voice cracked as my neck tightened. I felt for my knife.

"My daddy is part owner of a gas station downtown," Arkie said, beginning to walk.

"Which one?" I asked, turning around and looking over my shoulder, thinking I heard something.

"It's a Phillips 66 station right on the main road to town. Can't miss it. The gasoline makers, they give him a uniform to wear, same as the white owners wear." Arkie picked up a rock and tried skipping it on the water. "Little Roy's Uncle Benny is Daddy's partner. They used to work on the milk trucks at Flannigan's Dairy. Hardly paid 'em anything. Then Mr. Squiggy pulled some strings and got 'em the Phillips 66 station. Not many gas stations owned by coloreds, ya know."

"Little Roy's father, Squiggy?" I asked. "I met his mother at the country club one afternoon."

"Yeah, she'd been there awhile they say. They fired her 'bout a month ago."

"What for?"

"They said she done stole some silverware."

"Little Roy's mother? Stealing silverware?"

"Oh, she didn't steal nothin'. Daddy says it's just the way white folks act when they thinks coloreds is getting' close to bein' equal. Miss Emma knew it was just a matter of time after Mr. Squiggy got written up in the newspaper for standin' up for supportin' colored folks' rights."

"Wonder if my dad ever buys gas at your dad's gas station."

"Probably not. Not a lot of white folks buy gas there." He looked around, his eyes growing bigger. "Maybe we ought'a pick up our speed again."

"Yeah."

We jogged. Soon we saw another tunnel off in the distance.

"Number two," I said motioning.

"Yeah. Let's not stop. Keep on going."

"OK."

Just before the tunnel we heard voices and swearing coming from the woods on one side of the canal. It was right then that we fully grasped the reality of our situation—like going to watch a war movie and then realizing it wasn't a movie at all. It was real. Should we race back to Georgey's neighborhood? Should we run for it, heading to my house? We stared at each other, eyes bugging, breathing hard.

"How much further to your house?" Arkie asked.

"Dunno. I told you, I've never done this."

"Come on, man. We gotta do something. They'll kill us."

"Maybe we should swim across the canal," I suggested.

"I can't swim," Arkie said.

"You can't swim? Everyone can swim."

"Every white person can swim. You go to a swimmin' pool. We can't. 'Sides, we'd freeze to death."

The voices got louder and then we heard it—a gunshot. Sharp like a slap in your ears and jawbone. It rang noiseless in our imagination. Then the voices were yelling and swearing as they moved closer.

"Quick!" Arkie exclaimed. "Down the bank! We can hide in them bushes."

We slid down the bank of the towpath and wormed our way into a dense covering of evergreens and debris—old rags, liquor bottles, and dead leaves blown beneath heavy shrubbery. The voices grew closer.

"Cover yourself with some leaves," I hissed. "They'll see that red coat easily."

I rubbed dirt on my face and adjusted some branches to cover us, just as I heard footsteps ten feet away. My breath stopped as a hush settled.

We saw the first person walk by us and scamper up the bank. He was tall and skinny and wore a leather jacket and Army cap with a large, silver gun medallion. Two others followed, both in leather jackets with "Silver Gun Patrol" painted on the back; all wore pistols. The last one took a leak right close to us, then lit a cigarette. I was close enough to see the steam and smell the urine. I could see the silver ring on his black, leather boots.

"Hold on," he yelled to the others. "I'm tired. Wanna sit and smoke for a sec."

He scratched and clawed his way up the bank and sat on the path looking into the woods, just over our heads.

"How bad you hurt him, Jimbo?"

"Not real bad. Sure as hell taught him a lesson."

"If he were a jiggaboo, he'd be dead."

"That's for damn sure. Don't think he was queer. Do you?"

"No, he weren't queer. He was just watchin' birds with them binoculars."

"Think them things is worth anything?"

"Doubt it."

"We could'a throwed him in the canal just like Jake did. Let 'em drown."

"They never did find that kid, did they?"

I tried to breathe lightly, not moving my shoulders or chest. Slow inhales. Slow exhales. I squeezed the pocketknife in my hand. Moving only my eyes, I glanced at Arkie under a pile of leaves. He met my stare and closed his eyes, wincing in pain. It crossed my mind that this could be the end. Dad would find us drowned in the canal with our brains blown out.

The four men sat on the path, smoking. The one with the Army cap seemed to be the leader, because he doled out the orders. The others nodded and swore and spit. Then they left, heading away from the direction of my house toward town.

"You OK?" I whispered.

"Am I OK? Man, I was about to die. You probably would've gotten off with just having yur fingernails pulled out. We gotta get outa here."

We scrambled up the bank to the top of the path, ran through the second tunnel, and headed toward the third tunnel—the one that ran under the street in front of my house—as fast as we could go.

"You know that one guy who was talking about throwing a nigger in the canal? The fat one?" Arkie asked as we ran.

"Yeah, so?"

"That colored boy was Darnell Young, friend of Rozelle's. Two years ago he drowned in the canal. That's what everone said. 'Cept he drowned with his face all beaten up."

"That's scary stuff, Arkie. Don't think you should tell anyone."

"Yeah. Better off left as is or I'll be the next to drown."

"Yeah."

We slowed to a fast walk. The tunnel was straight ahead.

"Here's the last tunnel. It looks familiar. Come here," I said, entering the tunnel. "Let's read some of this stuff."

"Hey, I wanna get outa here, man."

"My house is just up the bank here and over the bridge. I know where I am."

We walked into the tunnel, letting our eyes adjust to the darkness. A golf club lay bent over an empty pack of Pall Malls— reminded me of Dad. Crumbled newspapers, an open box of wooden kitchen matches.

"Hey, Arkie. I found some matches." I struck one. "They work."

Arkie took several. "Can you do this?" He lit the match with his thumb nail then lit a rolled section of newspaper.

I tried it several times. Arkie was reading the walls. In red paint one read, "Written with the blood of a dead whore." Our panting breath glowed orange and gray in the firelight and shadows.

"Whore?" Arkie asked pronouncing the W-H like WHISTLE. "You s'pose he meant hore? Never knew you spelled it with a W," Arkie said.

"Me neither. Thought it was H-O-R-E. S'pose they don't know any better?"

"Dunno. They're pretty dumb."

"Look at all the names of girls," I said, lighting another rolled newspaper section and moving along the wall that was covered with threats, crude drawings of naked men and women having sex. This was the place where men bragged about the people they killed, the women they raped. A feeling of uneasiness and fear came over me and saliva pooled in my mouth. I was anxious to get home.

"Look at this one," Arkie said, squinting at some graffiti. "This girl's got a telephone number. It says, 'Mary Lou wants you.' S'pose she's colored or white?"

"Hmm, don't know. Could be either. Let's call her and find out. What's the number?"

"'Wabash 6742. Mary Lou wants you. For a real great piece,' it says. You think she wrote it?" Arkie asked.

"Could have, but that means she charges. Probably a whore, with a W."

"We'll have to call her and find out."

"All right, boys," a loud voice from the mouth of the tunnel yelled. "Hold it right there."

It was a policeman. He approached with his pistol out of the holster and aimed at me.

"What are you doing here?" he shouted. "Move outa here into the sunlight."

"Officer, I'm Rick Stoner," I stuttered, my voice an octave too high and the words rapidly falling from my mouth. "Over there. I live right over there. House at the top of the hill."

The officer looked at Arkie. "Who's this?"

I answered quickly. "This is Richard. He's, uh, an exchange student visiting us from uh the Bahamas, Eleuthera."

"You boys shooting guns down here?"

"No, sir," I answered. "I swear. Swear to God."

"You the doctor's boy?"

"Yessir."

"What's your father's name?"

"Wayne, sir. Wayne Stoner."

"Your address?"

"1333 West 38th Street."

He eyed me carefully, then Arkie. "Well, you're crazy to be down here, especially the colored boy. We been hearing some shots fired. There's a band of crazy kids that roam around here. Call themselves the Silver Gun Patrol. They post signs like they own the place. You better get back home. Don't ever come down here again. Understand?"

"Yessir," I replied.

"Thank you vedy mooch, officer," Arkie said, with some kind of an accent, more Russian than Bahamian.

We worked our way up the hill to the street that crossed over the tunnel and canal. The officer returned to his squad car, watching us in his rearview mirror as he drove off.

"Man, oh, man," Arkie said. "I've had enough close calls today. Think I'm gonna go dig me a hole and crawl in."

"Me too." We checked to make sure the policeman was gone. "You never learned to swim?" I asked, as we headed up the hill to our house.

"My daddy put me in the river once, but I was scared."

"Why not learn at a public swimming club?"

"Man, yur just dumb. Coloreds can't swim in water that whites swim in."

"Why not?"

"Whites thinks we is dirty, my momma says. Hell, some places will drain an entire swimming pool if a colored swims in it."

"Really?"

"Sure 'nuf. Benny—that's daddy's partner— says the swimming pool issues is 'bout to change on account a Mr. Squiggy."

"Why Squiggy?"

108

"He knows the laws better'n most white lawyers. Once he's a official lawyer he gonna sue the town to let us swim in pools."

"That's crazy, Arkie. Colored people can't sue white people."

"Why not?"

"Well . . ." I thought for a moment. "I dunno . . . 'cause you're colored."

"Yur as dumb as the rest of you people."

"Hey, look at this," I said, picking up a Coke bottle alongside the road.

"Where's it from?"

"Hmm. You're not gonna believe this, Arkie."

"Tell me. Where's it from?"

"Morgantown, West Virginia."

"West Virginia? Lemme see that."

I handed him the bottle.

"Great find. Let's not lose this," he said putting it in his back pocket.

Eventually we could hear classical music filtering through the woods. Mom and Aunt Weeze were practicing.

"Man, oh, man," Arkie said. "That's them playin' their pianos. Sounds like their practicin' in the forest. Pretty creepy."

"If Dad's not at home, Mom's gonna be mad."

"Whyzat?"

"Well, she's gonna have to take us back to Georgey's."

"You mean you never thought of that till now?"

"No. Maybe we should go back on the canal towpath."

"Are you crazy? Man, those Silver Gun Patrol guys are out there waitin' for another nigger to drown."

"Oh yeah. Jeesh!"

"For a white guy, yur sure are dumb, Ricky. We're in trouble no matter what we do."

"Sorry."

We were approaching our house.

"That yur place?" he asked, stopping at the driveway.

"Yeah."

"Holy crap. That's a palace, not a house."

"I got two other brothers and a mom and dad."

"Hey. I got a mom and a dad and me, and we could fit in yur toilet."

"What was Mary Lou's number?" I asked.

"Wabash something or other. You really gonna call her?"

"No. You are," I said.

"Not me, man. 6742."

Dad was home and quite disgruntled with our choice of things to do that morning. But he was always calm—a calm disgruntled. He suggested we quickly and quietly get in his car and he'd return us to Georgey's. But that wouldn't work either. I was home. Georgey would be looking for me. Just Arkie needed to go back.

"You guys had lunch?"

"No. I'm starved. Arkie is too."

"You guys fix peanut butter and jelly sandwiches, three of them. Three milks. I'll call Georgey and make up a story. Then we'll all go to Frog Island."

"Ohh, Doctor Stoner. I don't think you wanna go there."

"Arkie, my friend, I go to Frog Island regularly. I've got a number of patients out there. I have never been bothered by the colored community. They have always been polite and grateful to have a doctor come to their house, more grateful than most of my white patients. Do you live close to the Burns?"

"'Bout two blocks away."

I began putting peanut butter on the bread. "You mean we're gonna die on Frog Island? Eaten by the savages?"

"You're gonna die on Frog Island. Not me. I live there," Arkie said.

"We'll all die together," Dad said. "Milk's in the icebox, Arkie. I'll call Georgey."

"You know who the Burns are?" Arkie asked me as Dad left the kitchen.

"No."

"Mr. Burns got out a jail 'bout a year ago. He killed some guy who tried to stab his son. They're a tough bunch and yur daddy takes care of 'em?"

"Guess so."

"They ain't got no money. How they pay him?"

"Dunno."

Dad returned to the kitchen. "We're OK. I told Georgey I picked you guys up because I needed some help moving a fence post."

"What fence post?" I asked.

"Don't know," Dad said. "I'm glad Georgey didn't ask."

"You gonna get switched for lyin'," I said, imitating Georgey.

"White lie," Arkie said, smirking. "I can't tell one 'cause I ain't white."

"You two are too quick for me."

After lunch we squeezed into Dad's Plymouth.

"What's this?" Arkie asked, pointing to Dad's medical bag in the back seat. "You goin' somewhere?"

"That's my medical bag, Arkie. I take it with me when I call on patients."

"You said you was a doctor."

"I am."

"My daddy is part owner of his own gas station."

"That's great, Arkie. Where is it?"

"On Northwestern Avenue and Third Street."

"I know that station. A Phillips 66. I buy gas there from time to time."

"Wilbur Johnson's my daddy. His partner is Benny Daniels."

"That would be Squiggy's little brother."

"You know him?"

"Oh yes. Squiggy and I have known each other for quite some time. So, your father is the tall good-looking one."

"He's the tall one. I'm the good-lookin' one."

Dad looked at Arkie in the rearview mirror and grinned. "You must know my humble son, Rick."

"Also better looking than his father," I added.

"Arkie says Mr. Squiggy is gonna sue the town to let coloreds swim in pools."

"Wouldn't surprise me a bit. It's against the law to ban Negroes from public swimming pools. Once Squiggy learns the politics of the City Council—and he's learning quickly—he'll chop their legs off."

"Chop off their legs? Really?" Arkie asked.

"That's just an expression—a figure of speech—, my friend. Once he learns the ins and outs of the law, he'll bring racial equality to this town. There are many white folks supporting him and his wife, Emma."

"Like Dad," I said.

"Like Jim Moriarity's family and hundreds of other white people."

"Moriarity?" I asked.

"After Emma Daniels lost her job at the country club, the Moriaritys hired her to help manage and clean their huge house."

I expected Frog Island to be over a bridge that led onto a dark, dirt path with lean-to shacks. Instead, Frog Island was a gradual process from low-income houses to poor folks' homes. Stoplights ceased to exist at one point and telephone poles and streetlights listed, being they were last on the city's list to repair. Old cars lined the streets, many without tires, and some on Coca-Cola cases. The roads were paved but years of neglect had left them looking tired, in some spots giving way to dirt entirely. Old sycamores lined them, with their speckled bark reminiscent of Shuli's freckles. The houses were very small—smaller than Georgey's—and made mostly of wood and tarpaper.

We drove silently down the main street (called "A Street") until Arkie told Dad to turn left.

"It's that red house on the right," Arkie said, clearly uncomfortable with his house.

Dad pulled over and let him out. "I certainly enjoyed meeting you at last," Dad said. "I've been hearing about you for several years. Rick's really fortunate to have a pal like you." Dad held out his hand. Arkie shook it.

"Thanks, Dr. Stoner. See ya, Rick."

Dad and I were quiet on the way home. Finally he said, "That was a mistake."

"A mistake? What mistake?"

"Taking Arkie home."

"Why?"

"It was like rubbing his nose in his own poverty."

"I don't get it."

"I know you don't, son. But just think how he must have felt. He comes to our house, slate roof, brick turret with a living room big enough for two grand pianos. Three cars in the driveway and a kitchen bigger than his house. People feel embarrassed when they feel inadequate, even when they're not. We should have been perceptive enough to know that, kind enough to respect his poverty. Yes, I said respect his poverty. We were lording our wealth over him unknowingly because we weren't sensitive enough."

"So, what am I supposed to do?"

"Nothing. It's the next time that will show your character."

Eighteen

"Mary Lou wants you" it said, embellished on the concrete wall of my mind. For a great piece called Mary Lou. "A great piece" filled my imagination from the inside out like a cranial balloon, inflating until there was no room for another thought. Only Mary Lou. I saw her as colorless, luscious, and wanting, destined to be the first woman I would "go all the way" with. We would be in love. Tears would flood our eyes as we lay in bed, embracing after a night of heavy lovemaking. Me and Mary Lou. I was in love with a woman who existed on the wall of a tunnel. I wanted to go back and touch the writing. For a great piece. Maybe there was something more, a hidden message, a hint at what was to come. I returned to the tunnel with a flashlight one afternoon. There it was, Mary Lou wants you. For a great piece, Mary Lou B. That's it. B. Her name was Mary Lou B. I could find out where she lived and hitchhike to her house, hold her in my arms, and make out with her. I tried to explain this to Arkie—this infatuation, this seeming reality—but Arkie howled with laughter.

"Come on, man. She's a name on a wall. Don't exist."

What if she wanted to meet us? What if she asked how old we were? What name should I use? Rock or Tab? Too white. Arkie would know.

The time was right when Georgey walked down to Miss Tildalayhu's house to help her with Miss Alice and we were alone. Prince Albert in the Can and Harry Balls were games for children.

"I can't remember her number," I said.

"Wabash 6742," Arkie said instantly.

"How'd you remember that?"

"Six times seven is forty-two. You call her."

"I thought we agreed you were gonna do it."

"We never agreed on anything. You're the one who's crazy with this Mary Lou thing. I think it's all purty stupid."

"What if she's colored?"

"How you gonna know?"

"She'll talk like you."

"Huh." He thought for a second. "So you should start out talkin' white and be ready to shift into colored talk if you have to. And Ricky, what if she's colored? What you gonna do then?"

"I have to see her, Arkie."

"Yur crazy." He handed me the telephone.

"What am I going to say?"

"You'll know. Hurry up 'fore Miss Georgella comes home."

I dialed the number and it rang.

Then a woman's voice answered. "Hello?"

"May I speak with Mary Lou?" I asked politely, my voice at a lower register than normal, a 30-year-old register.

"This is her speaking," she answered. I covered the mouthpiece. "White," I whispered to Arkie. He winked and gave me the thumbs up.

"Mary Lou," I started. "I have to know something." My mind collapsed.

"Who is this?" she asked.

"Mary Lou, are you a great piece?"

116

Arkie grabbed his head in disbelief, eyes bugging from his head, mouth open, tongue out.

"Oh, God," she said, mournfully. "Why? Why do I get these disgusting insults? I never . . ." She began sobbing. "I never did anything to deserve them. One of these days my children will know about that horrible writing, wherever it is. I pray to God that it gets erased." She began crying. "If you believe in God, you'll erase it."

"I . . . I'm . . . ," I mumbled.

"Please don't call anymore. Please don't give my number to anyone. Oh, please. I beg you."

I quietly hung up.

"Well?" Arkie asked, big smile, head nodding.

"Well, nothing. Somebody was playing a prank on her. She ended up crying and begging me not to call her again. Asked me to erase it. Asked me if I believed in God. That was awful. Man, I feel terrible. Never should have used the word 'piece.' That was wrong."

"One of the wronger things you done. You spendin' too much time thinkin' 'bout sex."

"Me? You're the one that starts it."

We looked at each other silently. "Let's shoot some baskets at Zeke's," Arkie said.

"Good idea." We ran across the street to Zeke's alley.

That afternoon was troublesome for me. I kept thinking of Mary Lou and the emotion that came through the telephone. I visualized a very troubled woman with children and felt her worry.

Neither Arkie nor myself wanted to face what had just happened. It was time to change the subject.

"That ole Zeke, he's some mean sombitch," Arkie said.

"Yeah, he sure as hell can be."

He started laughing. "Man, you sure sound funny swearin'. I been meanin' to talk to you about that."

"You think so?"

"White folks gotta learn to swear. Coloreds know how. It's real smooth. Comes natural to us."

"So, what the piss do you think I should do?"

"What the piss? Man, you said, 'what the piss.'"

"So?"

"Sounds like yur tryin' to swear."

"I was."

"That's yur first mistake. Never swear on purpose. And never use the wrong swear word. Like you said, 'What the piss?' I'm fourteen, man. I never heard anyone say, 'What the piss?' Colored folks don't use the word 'piss.' That's a white man's word. Whites also use the f-word a lot. Reverend Williams says only colored trash use that word. We just swear. The f-word is ugly." He shook his head as if I were some kind of a moron. "I'll help you. This swearin' thing's tough. Don't worry. Now before we begin, there's just a couple of rules when swearin'."

"You sound like some college professor," I cut in. "This is about swearing, not physics."

"As I was saying before the dumb white boy interrupted, one must remember the two rules to swearin': One we covered— the f-word. Never use it. The other rule is never use the Lord's name in vain. Keep the God word away from vulgarity. Those two rules will help you to become a good swearer, not a dirty swearer. OK?"

"Aren't you a damn friend."

"Wrong! Wrong! Wrong! First of all, there's no need for a swear in that sentence. It's like yur showin' off. Secondly, you say 'ain't' not 'aren't.' You should say, 'you ain't no friend of mine.' See? Smooth as silk. No need for a swear."

I threw him the basketball. "Will you just shut up and shoot?"

"Say, 'Shoot the damn ball, man.'"

"Shoot the damn ball, man."

"OK, Mr. White Boy." He stepped back from me and launched a jump shot that clanged off the rim. We both raced for it, yelling. I shoved him into some metal trashcans, grabbing the ball from his grasp and dribbling to the basket for an easy layup.

"How'd I do, Mr. Colored Boy?"

"Better. You look good but yur still the worst basketball player in the whole damn world—black, white, yella, green. Don't make no difference. You stink up a basketball court."

"You say."

"Yeah, I know." He slapped the ball out of my hands, grabbed it, stepped back, and started launching another jump shot. I leaped toward him, blocked the shot, then grabbed the basketball and ran down the alley with Arkie in hot pursuit.

"Hey, Arkie," I yelled. "Thought you was supposed to be Mr. Basketball."

"I'll Mr. Basketball yur ass." He tackled me and we rolled into someone's garage door laughing. Out of breath. Speechless.

We waited for the silence to settle. "You ever smoked a cigarette?" I asked.

"Sure. Many times. Have you?"

"Yep. A couple a months ago. Zeke and I smoked in his back yard."

"Zeke?"

"We did. He pulled out a pack of Camels, offered me one, and told me I was old enough."

119

"Oh, that old man's gonna get his ass in trouble."

"Only if you tell."

"Don't worry."

"You know what nigger-lipping is?" I asked.

Arkie hooted. "Nigger-lippin'? Course I know what nigger-lippin' is."

"Zeke says it's what whites say when they get the cigarette wet on the end."

"That ain't true. It's a nigger word. I know it is."

"Well, I guess I nigger-lipped my cigarette."

We chuckled as we locked the picture in our imaginations.

Arkie said, "You know, they say Miss Georgella is a holy lady."

"Yeah. She is," I agreed.

"I'm scared a her."

"Why's that?"

"Not real sure. It's like she knows, ya know? Maybe she could send me to hell if she felt like it."

"She's not that holy. You send your own self to hell if you're bad."

"Yeah, and I am bad. I use swear words."

"So do I."

"Yur prob'ly worse, 'cause you don't use 'em right."

"Huh."

"I lie."

"Me, too."

"I stole that basketball net a year back. 'Member the one we hung?"

"You didn't."

"I did."

"I stole a girlie magazine from a drugstore."

"Really? A dirty magazine?"

"Yep. Naked pictures, almost naked."

"Well, yur really gonna go to hell."

"You'll meet me there."

Arkie sat on the basketball looking intently into my eyes. "Get ready for this."

"What?" I asked, the suspense building.

"The other night I seen Miss Shuli Wright undressin' in her bedroom."

"You did? Baby Shuli? What'd you see?"

"Everthing."

"Everything?"

"Ever-blessed-thing—hair, nipples, everthing. And she sure ain't no baby. Not no more."

"Oh, my God. You're the luckiest sombitch in the world. Tell me what every part looked like."

Nineteen

One of Mom's shortcomings was her inability to say "No. Sorry, I'm too busy. No. Absolutely can't fit it in. I have a full-time teaching job and three young boys." That "no" gave birth to the two-piano team of Waring and Stoner. The owner of WFBM radio heard them and begged them to try—just try—a couple of radio broadcasts. Mom said no. Aunt Weeze said they'd love to. When the next person asked Mom to help out with little Sarah who needed someone to teach her advanced piano, Mom said, "No. Sorry, I'm too busy. No. Absolutely can't fit it in. I have a full-time teaching job and three young boys, a weekly radio show, and just too many private concerts. Just not enough hours in the day." But little Sarah was very talented, probably better at nine years old than most adult piano teachers in the city, so Mom said she could cut back on her teaching hours to fit Sarah in.

Actually, Mom cut back on us.

Little Sarah was a more gifted pianist than Spike was a gifted violinist. Very soon we could see the effect that her talent was having on Spike, who was reaching out to Mom to show her his progress, everything she had taught him. Demanding her attention, crying, practicing harder. But Mom had found a new outlet: She had found herself when she was nine—the prodigy. She would be Walter Piston and Arthur Rubinstein, and Little Sarah would become the young Lillian—Mom. Slowly Little Sarah took precedence over the family, and once again we returned to unfettered chaos. Andy and I were not aware of the depth of the damage. We had our own lives.

Everything seemed the same until Georgey announced that she would be leaving.

Quitting.

Georgey.

It was as sudden and impactful as President Eisenhower announcing war with Korea. Only worse.

Georgey told Andy and me that she wasn't feeling well and her legs just didn't seem to want to carry "my old body to the basement for the manglin' iron, then upstairs for sweepin', then to the second floor to make ya'll's beds." She told us in sadness, with misty eyes. She didn't seem anymore crippled to me than she already was. Andy wanted to know what happened. It was worse than Mom leaving.

Mom told us that we were old enough to take care of ourselves. "Goodness gracious! Andy, you're almost fifteen and Ricky, my goodness, you're twelve. You don't need a nursemaid."

First of all, I was thirteen, and secondly, Georgey wasn't our nursemaid. All three of us felt injured. Something was being left unsaid. We knew that Mom had made a big mistake and all the smiles we saw were simply pasted there like Mr. Potato Head.

Dad defended Georgey's decision, saying she might need an operation to straighten her right leg. Since "Danny and the pickle barrel" incident when she was sixteen, her other leg had been working harder and her hip was lopsided. Dad found a walker for her, temporarily, and lots of aspirin. Spike ran away. You should have seen him curled up next to the golf pro shop, wailing. Mom cried. Damn her. I knew this was the result of the argument she had with Georgey.

123

Dad took Georgey home that night. It was softly raining. I asked if I could go with him, and he said no. I wasn't there, but I knew what was going on. I could imagine. I could hear the tires on the street and feel the wind through the car window. Both Dad and Georgey are smoking, not talking, their cigarettes smelling of stress. Two shadows riding along in his Plymouth. He pulls up to her house and they sit in the car, heads moving—first him then her, then him then her. Soon Dad gets out, walks around to open the door for her, but he is too late, she's halfway out. No one else has held the door open for her. He stands like a colored doorman.

"You bring my walkin' cane?" she asks.

"Hey, Doctah." The low quiet voice of Zeke rolls.

"Zeke," Dad loudly whispers, waves into the darkness.

They say things at her doorway. She calls him "Bussie darlin'." Questions. Hard talk. Dad nods. Georgey touches his arm tenderly, the same way she has often touched mine. They speak quietly, so no one can hear them. Then Dad puts his arms around Georgey and holds her the way I might hold Santa Claus.

Twenty

After a couple of weeks it was clear—the plan wasn't working. Mom made Franco-American spaghetti from the can with Wonder Bread and oleo; Andy, Spike, and I tried making our beds; Dad wiped the dishes. The broom and the Hoover stayed in the closet. The mangling iron ceased to mangle. Then Mom burned the toast for our chipped beef on toast and watered down the cream sauce (to save money).

Two weeks later Mom announced, "Georgey has agreed to fix dinner on Fridays and Saturdays. I think after a week of my cooking, we will all cherish Georgey's meals." We looked at her. "Don't you agree?"

We nodded politely. Dad, too.

When Georgey came to work that first Friday, it was like Christmas. "Georgey's back!" announced Spike, racing through the house. She tried to stay in the kitchen, which was a mess—spoons in with forks, flour bags open, waiting for grain moths, jelly smeared on the refrigerator door, dirty dishes in the sink. The skillet used for her chipped beef dinner still had globules of aged milk growing fuzz from its surface. Dust balls rolled freely in the corners of the dining room. She said nothing. Sucked her teeth. We knew it wasn't going well.

Until Gloria Hufnagel—a 23-year-old student at the Indianapolis School of Beauty. Mom was delighted when the school's owner, who did Mom's hair for half the price of a fancy beauty salon, suggested that the Stoners provide free room and board to a deserving student in exchange for cleaning, ironing, folding clothes, and putting things away. It wasn't full time.

Gloria Hufnagel was from Fort Wayne—glossy, dark hair, always immaculate; dark eyes with heavy mascara and fine, thinly plucked eyebrows like all the girls at the beauty school; a perpetually sweaty forehead; and tall high heels that made her walk funny with shortm, bumpy steps, teetering like a model on a runway. We didn't know much about her except that she was genuinely interested in becoming a hairdresser, and she was from a poor family, one of ten children. There was something mysterious about Gloria, something in the air like an unfamiliar scent that you can't quite figure out. You weren't sure whether it was good or bad, probably good. She shook your hand with both of hers. I never had anyone do that to me before, clasp my right hand in her two hands. Instantly you wanted to be her best friend. And Gloria looked deep into your eyes like Dr. Frankenstein. She was all right, I felt, except that when she walked in those high heels, her thighs rubbed together and her nylons made an uncomfortable sound like sliding fingers on guitar strings.

Mom loved her. So did Spike. Gloria called him "Spikey" real cute-like and listened to him play his violin. Told him how good he was. She mussed his hair a lot as if she really cared, but I don't think she did. Dad looked embarrassed around her. Too many bubbles, I think. Andy was polite but wasn't comfortable with the two-handed shake. Wasn't sure a woman should even shake a boy's hand in the first place. That first Friday when Georgey met her, she looked at Gloria with a puzzling frown, the way a lioness eyes a hyena. Aloof and wary. And, if possible, warm and loving. Mom said that perhaps Georgey was jealous.

126

"Jealous? Georgey?" Dad scoffed. "She doesn't have a jealous bone in her body."

Gloria made beds every morning and dusted before she walked up the street to catch the bus. On the surface it wasn't a big change in our routines. Mom moved Little Sarah's piano lessons to our house, and Spike sat quietly in Dad's den during Sarah's initial instruction, figuring out how to kill "that little snot-nose." Gloria returned at dinnertime. Anything she fixed was better than canned Franco-American cuisine. On Friday and Saturday, Georgey fed her in the kitchen. I heard her ask Georgey, "Do you think the Stoners would mind if I ate with them?"

"I think you're better off in here," Georgey answered. "Let the fambly be the fambly."

As Gloria cleared our dinner plates for dessert, she asked how Dad's day went, then Mom's, standing in the doorway, balancing plates, still talking until Georgey called her—nice-like. "Come on, darlin', dessert's gettin' cold."

Georgey knew this was new for Gloria and would require a time of adjustment. She told Dad, "When you buys a new dog, and ya already got six dogs, that new dog's gotta figure out where she belongs in the peckin' order. It's easier on the six dogs that been together. Harder on the new dog."

We gave Gloria the guest room on the first floor. It opened onto the hallway to the kitchen. She had a radio that played the latest tunes on "Hit Parade" and decorated her room with pictures from *Modern Screen* and *Movie Mirror* magazines. The faces of Ava Gardner, Jane Russell, and Marilyn Monroe, mixed in with Frank Sinatra, Tony Curtis, and Howard Keel, stared from her walls. It was to study their hairstyles, she told me. Made sense.

"You might consider letting your flat top grow longer on the sides, and train it back with a brush," she said one evening. "You're getting old enough to wear a more mature style now. I'll pick up a couple of small brushes from school and teach you how to do it."

She often sat in Dad's den with me and Spike after our homework was done, watching television, talking about movie stars and how they lived. Andy wasn't interested in movie stars. He read his summertime reading list and worked on Boy Scout projects. Andy had turned into "the class grind." If he didn't have something to do, it meant he must have forgotten something. Gloria told me that her father was a drunk and a slob. They never had any money, and all the children worked after school to pay the rent and groceries. I felt sorry for her. It was a very tough life. When Mom and Dad were out for an evening, she rewarmed some of Georgey's cookies for us before bed.

Andy went to the prom in June. His first. He wore a rented tuxedo and borrowed Dad's red, silk cummerbund and bow tie. And, too, Dad's high-gloss, formal, slip-on loafers, just a bit too large, flapping at the heel. Gloria fixed his hair. He looked ten years older—half-closed eyes, furtive glances, one of Dad's cigarettes dangled from his mouth. Except his face looked like an advanced case of measles, pot-holed and ruddy. When Gloria suggested a small dab of makeup to hide the red-tipped welts, Andy turned cold and walked away. There were some things you couldn't talk about with him. Zits was number one.

Mom and Dad drove him to pick up his date. They would pick him up at 11. In the meantime, they were at a friend's house playing bridge.

I called Arkie.

"Zits? That a white word?" Arkie asked.

"Must be. A lot of guys get them in their teens. They're like pimples, bad ones."

"We get razor bumps. That's what we call 'em. Razor bumps. But coloreds get 'em from shavin'. Our whiskers come in curlin' and sometimes grow back into our skin. Then we shaves 'em, it bleeds, and a bump forms. Look at ole Reginald. One of the worst cases of bumps I ever seen."

"You shave yet?" I asked Arkie, struck with this growing up kind of conversation about pimples. I rubbed my soft chin, trying to imagine what whiskers would feel like.

"Yeah. As soon as you starts gettin' fuzz on yur chin and lip, yur s'posed to shave it. It makes 'em grow in thicker. Like cuttin' a lawn. My daddy told me a few months ago I should start. Comin' along real fine now. Ole Amy Dalrymple's gonna be sorry she don't pay me no attention."

Gloria came in to ask me if I thought Mom would mind if she tried a little mascara from Mom's vanity dressing table. I nodded. She mouthed a thank you and went into Mom and Dad's bedroom.

"Which one's Amy Dalrymple?" I asked. "I ever meet her?"

"Probly not. She don't go to church. She and Marcella Ames is good friends.

"Tiny Marcella? How's she doin'?"

"Man, I never seen such a change from little girl to woman. Not Tiny Marcella no more. This been a big year for her. The fat's gone and her girl parts been replaced by woman parts, with a capital W. She's still shorter than you were last year."

"You think coloreds mature faster than whites?"

129

"Don't know 'bout that, but ole Marcella shed her fat and grew herself a couple of real big titties."

"No."

"Shore as I sit here. Seems like overnight."

"Marcella?"

"Marcella Ames, too young even to go to Crispus Attucks High School. When's the last time you seen her?"

"I don't know. Lessee, a couple of months, maybe longer. I remember she wasn't with Shuli because she was on the rag."

"Yep. That was part of it. Lost a lot of weight. Wears her hair different like."

I tried visualizing her but couldn't turn the fat, little, colored girl with a lisp into a woman.

"Maybe I should start shaving early like you, Arkie, might make it grow," I said, certain a beard was at least a century away. I was still waiting on significant pubic hair. I didn't see myself as mature enough to be in a group of kids well into puberty.

Spike was practicing his violin. He was getting very good. Eight years old, and the sound echoed the ironed confidence of a seasoned maestro. He no longer searched for the true tone—it was there under his fingers and stroked by the bow. I watched him in his bedroom, sitting in a chair, back straight, violin tucked abruptly under his chin, head down, holding it like a lance in his neck. His eyes were closed and he hummed as he played, right hand quivering to create a perfect vibrato. The music came forth, pouring like dusty sunlight from an opened curtain. Mom said it happened as a result of Little Sarah.

"First the bud," she said, "then the fertilizer—jealousy—and then the glorious bloom." This was a win from Mom's point of view, to be balanced against the loss of Georgey. Spike would have adamantly felt otherwise—that the cost of his creativity was far too expensive. He missed Georgey more than any of us. To lose love for the sake of creativity was a loss far beyond his scope.

I wandered back downstairs to say goodnight to Gloria. She didn't see me as she sat facing the oval mirror at Mom's vanity dressing table like at a piano keyboard, the keys being fingernail polish; perfume bottles capped by small, squeezable orbs; etuis holding needles, thimbles, and small pearl earrings; crystal containers filled with face powder and puffs. She had removed her blouse and wore only a brassiere. She examined herself in the mirror—a poseur at work—trying on Mom's pearl earrings, tilting her head. She tried different perfumes by putting a small dab on her fingertip then running her finger slowly down her neck and between her breasts. Leaning her head back, she stroked her neck softly, closed her eyes, touched the edge of her breasts. I stood slack-jawed and dry-eyed, unable to move. My head lowered from heaviness. I couldn't hold it upright. Gloria continued, eyes closed, head back, tracing her fingers along the edge of her brassiere, over her nipples, back and forth. I knew I shouldn't be there, but my feet were stuck in lust. She moaned softly. "Oh baby," she whispered. Spike called from upstairs. Gloria jumped and grabbed her blouse. I skittered away like a frightened mosquito from a skin pore, still wanting more.

The next morning we heard about the prom. Andy and his date learned how to do the jitterbug. He promised Mom and Dad he would teach all of us.

"Don't forget me," Gloria chimed from the kitchen.

Gloria brought two brushes for my hair from the beauty school. "Palm brushes," she called them. She sat me in a chair and showed me how to use them. "Tab Hunter uses these to train the sides of his hair, just like you should. You must wet it

131

down regularly then brush it dry. As your hair grows, I'll cut the top and shape the sides." She leaned over brushing the sides back while I looked helplessly down the front of her blouse.

"Are you looking down my blouse?" she whispered, playfully.

"Uh." I couldn't think of an answer. "Yeah. Sorry." I closed my eyes so I wouldn't look.

"It's alright to look. But you can't touch. Not now. But maybe when you're a little older. We'll see." She kept brushing my hair. "There. That looks great. What do you think?"

"Yeah" was all I could say.

I could never look at Gloria the same way as before. She became vulnerable to me, fallible, an object of lust. Like scenery rearranged in a play, the friendship scene had moved to the background.

"Someone told me that it's just as easy to fall in love with a rich man as a poor man," Gloria said one evening, skimming *Movieland* magazine. "I'm gonna find a rich one and do whatever I have to do to snag him."

"Like what?" I asked, curious.

"Anything. I've got a girlfriend who got pregnant by a man who owns a Ford dealership. She drives a Cadillac now and wears a mink coat."

Getting pregnant for money didn't really register with me. I was more interested in what happened in order to get pregnant. The cause, not the effect. My mind was filled with images of Jane Russell, her blouse unbuttoned, and Gloria, touching her breasts with perfume.

Twenty-One

Most Saturdays I still went to Georgey's house. Dad dropped me off two blocks away on his way to the hospital. It wasn't dangerous anymore. After almost two years I had become the rumored white boy that was "one of us, Ole Doc Stoner's boy," and that neighborhood had become part of my life. Sometimes it was just Arkie and me in Zeke's alley. Every once in a while, I'd sit on Georgey's or Zeke's porch doing my homework and listening to outlandish stories. Other times Arkie and I went to the Church of the Holy God and shot baskets with Little Roy, Rozelle, Willie, Nat, and others. Never Arnold.

The church was also where I learned to dance the jitterbug, but the difference between my version and Andy's was the difference between a white jitterbug and a colored jitterbug—the difference between "I like you" and "I love you."

The Penguins were four colored men with conked hair who sang "Ice" to heavy rim shots and electric guitars. It went like this:

(deep bass, sliding low)
Uhm-be-leh-lo-leh-lo
(lead singer)
I went to see a little girl the other night.
I only saw her twice.
I put my arms around her waist and squeezed her tight.

She starting melting like a piece of ice.

It was a new kind of music. Frank Sinatra, Perry Como, and the Hit Parade were no longer on my wavelength—stupid music with no emotion. Doo-Wop was the music of the alleys behind Zeke's house that wound in and around the neighborhood and up to the Church of the Holy God—colored music, speaking in the language of the streets. It played through old plastic radios via disc jockeys like Moondog and blared from 45-rpm record players.

Hey Senorita, why don't you call me on the line?
If you do that baby, every little thing will be fine.
Oh, sweet momma, oh.

Impossible to stand still and listen to, the fast songs were steamy; the slow songs were filled with luscious love and romance. The first time I heard the Penguins sing "Earth Angel," I knew I would never be the same.

Earth Angel. Earth Angel. Will you be mine?
My darling dear, love you all the time.
I'm just a fool, a fool in love with you.

Many of the high school girls from Attucks practiced dancing at the church and dragged their boyfriends from the basketball court to the basement, where a record player sat stacked with 45s—"Bip Bam," "Money Honey," "Shake, Rattle and Roll," and many others. Baby Shuli was a freshman and mingled with the high school cheerleaders, who practiced at the church because the town wouldn't put up the money to build a gymnasium.

My first dance partner was Shuli, but over time she became hands-off for everyone. She was spoken for, but her guy never showed up at church. My second partner was Tiny Marcella, and we were made for each other. She was small and had spent most of her life in the shadow of Shuli, who had taught her how to dance, how to wear makeup, how to fix her hair. And boy, could she dance! Puberty had transformed her into a curvaceous teenager with an overbite and oversized breasts, but she was still the same Tiny Marcella, still followed Shuli around—always there like a faithful holster—still called me "Sweetie"—the lisp was gone—and she put her arm around me. She was perfect for me and I loved dancing with her.

* * *

"I can't believe there are still drinking fountains that coloreds can't use," Dad said, folding the newspaper and laying it on the floor. I was memorizing animals of Australia for a geography quiz. "Separate crappers, separate cemeteries, and even separate Bibles for Negroes on which to swear an oath."

Georgey poked her head into the den. "I's ready to go when you is."

Dad kept his train of thought. "There's still an unspoken exclusion from many restaurants and public libraries in our town. And Gordon told me last week that many parks in the southern part of the state post signs that say, 'Negroes and dogs not allowed.' What are these white people thinking? Negroes and dogs!"

"You gonna end up with burnin' crosses in yur front yard," Georgey piped in. "It's one thing to love yur fellow man; it's another to do it real loud. If a kitty purrs long enough, you'll scratch its head. If'n it growls yul shoot it."

"Are you suggesting I keep my mouth shut?" Dad asked.

"I is suggestin' you just purr," she said. "I thinks ya'll needs to be careful 'bout the amount of time my Ricky spends with coloreds. Not sayin' he shouldn't be seein' his colored friends at all. Not sayin' that. But he needs white friends, too."

"So, if Ricky has three colored friends, he must have three white friends?" Andy teased.

"And Georgey, my goodness," Dad said. "You need to get busy. Get out there and make some white friends. Your segregated friendships are out of balance."

That I had become part of her life pleased Georgey, and she accepted the burden of mothering in this unusual social arrangement. She fixed lunches for Arkie and me—peanut butter and jelly sandwiches, jezapebas they were called, plural with an "s" because that's the way you ate them, and Campbell's hot tomato soup, from the can with milk. The only way to eat it. I learned that Arkie's diet was different than mine. His family ate squirrel neck bone (that they had trapped in their backyard) and rice (because it was inexpensive). Arkie and I had dinner at Georgey's once. She fixed Goolagomba, as she called it: shrimp, fried rice, turkey necks, and okra stew with pig tails. "Lots a thises and lots a thats," she said. I never learned what the ingredients were until much later, when soul cooking had become fashionable. Most colored folks had their own Goolagomba recipes, different than Georgey's and driven more by lack of

136

money than food preference. The Stoners, too, had our own Goolagomba made by Georgey—hash made from leftovers and "lots a thises and lots a thats" with buttered Wonder Bread.

Twenty-Two

I told Arkie about Gloria and his eyes bugged large and he hooted. Then Arkie and I overheard a conversation between Georgey, Zeke, and Zeze.

"Always connivin' to raise her position in the fambly," Georgey said.

"That's white trash for ya," Zeke said. "Goddamned white trash."

"The doctah's too smart for that," Zeze added.

"I knows. And I knows I shouldn't be gossipin'. Think what Jesus would say."

"Sounds like He'd be purty goddamned suspicious, too."

"Maybe so. Maybe so," Georgey said.

"Now what about them earrings you saw that girl wearin'? Was they Missus Stoner's?" Zeze asked.

"Don't really know, but I would swear they was. The doctah bought 'em for her. You know he loves to buy her jewelry. Probably his only vice. I seen 'em a lot. Gloria wears 'em only when Missus Stoner ain't around."

"That's 'cause she thinks you is just another dumb nigger," Zeke said.

"You know where Missus Stoner keeps her jewelry?" Zeze asked.

"I do."

"Check it. See if they's there."

"Oh mercy, Zeze, I couldn't do that. That's un-Christianlike."

"That's nonsense, Georgella," Zeke added. "If that white girl got one piece of jewelry, she got more. Don't smell right to me. How can this lady be so great if she's robbin' yur folks blind?"

I found it difficult to put Gloria into perspective, but eventually another image came into focus. I thought of Shuli, who was being raised in a much poorer family yet would never stoop to common burglary, much less getting pregnant just for money.

When I told Andy about Georgey's conversation with Zeke and Zeze, he nodded as if he knew.

"She's a little crook," Andy said. "Georgey used to get after me for leaving money in my pockets. She always took it out and put it on my dresser. I still leave it in my pockets. I know I do. But I haven't seen a penny in the past few weeks. I probably wouldn't have thought about it except I cashed my last paycheck and lost it."

"You sure you didn't misplace it?"

"That is not my style, brother. Money and me don't separate easily."

I knew he was right. Andy was super organized and always hung up his pants, put his dirty laundry in the hamper, put the cap on the toothpaste, even cleaned his desk before he went to bed. I never did that. Those details took too much time.

"I'll tell you something," he said. "You know that red dress of Mom's, the one with the wide, black belt?"

"No." I tried remembering, but I couldn't remember anything that Mom wore—to me Mom was a mother, not a fashion model.

"Well, I'd swear Gloria had it on last Saturday when she had that date. I saw her put her coat on over it."

"Are you sure?"

"I wasn't sure until you told me about Georgey's conversation with Zeke. Gloria and Mom are exactly the same size."

We decided to check Mom's closet. Her red dress was hanging there.

"Doesn't mean she didn't wear it," Andy said.

Georgey spoke with Dad one Saturday night while we drove her home. "You know, Doctah. Gloria ain't what we thinks she is."

"I know," Dad said, eyes on the road, appearing preoccupied but not.

"You know?" Georgey asked.

"Yeah. I think she's a snitcher and an overt opportunist. I've been missing change off my dresser, then dollars, then an old gold tiepin that belonged to my father. I'm pretty sure it's her. But she's clever."

"Should we call the cops?" I asked.

"Oh, no. We're not going to do that. We're not going to tell Lill, either."

"Andy's missing a paycheck, you know."

"He told me."

"And I swear that Gloria has Missus Stoner's pearl earrings that you give to her a long time ago."

"Didn't Zeke tell you to check her jewelry box?" I asked.

"She keeps them in that little glass case on her vanity," Georgey said.

"Did you look?" I asked.

"I just can't bring myself to do that. God told me they ain't there."

"I think God and I will check it carefully," Dad said.

Mom was shocked. Surely everyone was mistaken. She was an interesting woman, my mother. She could understand why Chopin could be a "rabid—and abusive—womanizer," but normal people were puzzlements to her. It never dawned on her that Gloria could be dishonest. Reluctantly, she agreed that something had to be done, so the following Friday night after the dishes were done and Mom and Dad were having a cup of coffee, Dad asked Georgey and Gloria to come into the dining room.

"Gloria," Dad began, "We seem to be missing things. Some things are unimportant, others are more important. Do you know what I am talking about?"

"Me?" she said furrowing her brow. "What do you mean? You don't think I took anything, do you?"

"I do," he said calmly. His eyes stuck to her face.

I looked at Mom. She was scared. She had that look on her face like a member of a firing squad about to shoot someone—ready, aim . . .

"Gloria, we're all going to go to your room and check out a few things," Dad said. "I'm sure you won't mind."

"Be my guest," she shrugged.

Spike whispered to Dad on the way through the kitchen, "If you think Gloria stole things, I can promise you she didn't. No way." Spike and Mom were always on the same wavelength.

Dad patted him on the back like rewarding Fido.

In Gloria's room Dad asked her where her jewelry box was.

"I don't have one," she answered.

Mom opened her top dresser drawer expecting to find it there. Just crumpled underwear—panties and bras. She closed the drawer, then frowned, blinked her eyes, and opened the drawer again, like looking into a pond expecting to see a fish but not seeing one until you looked away. "Wait a minute. This is my brassiere," she said, holding it up and examining it.

"No, it isn't," Gloria said.

"Of course, it is. I bought it last month and couldn't find it recently. I thought this small red band on the strap was quite nice. This one looks very familiar, also."

"I'm sure you're mistaken, Missus Stoner. A lot of women wear bras. You're not the only one."

That kind of sanctimonious comment could get to Mom—make the hair stand up on the back of her neck. I anticipated we'd see more than the discovery of used underwear.

"You're making me very angry, Gloria," Mom said, opening all her dresser drawers. "My sweater. Look." She held it up.

"My mother gave me that when I graduated from high school," Gloria said.

"And bought it here in Indianapolis at Ayers Department Store? See the label?" Mom said.

Andy shook his head in wonderment.

"What else?" Dad asked.

"Nothing else," Gloria said. "And furthermore, I am incensed. Humiliated that you people would accuse me like this. I've never—"

"Gloria," Georgey asked, "where is Missus Stoner's pearl earrings? The ones I saw you wearin' last week."

"I have no idea what you're talking about."

Andy opened the closet. "Anything in here belong to you, Mom?"

Mom looked through the racks with Georgey. "I'm not sure. I don't think so."

"Missus Stoner. Here's your red high heel shoes. Doctah?"

"You're right," Dad said.

Then Georgey did the strangest thing I had ever seen her do. She lowered her head and began whispering to someone. Back and forth. Shaking her head. She reached into the back corner of the closet, pulled out a large box of laundry detergent, and handed it to Dad. It was filled with small change and bills, Dad's tie tack, Mom's earrings, cuff links, a ring, someone's watch.

Gloria blamed it on her rotten life, her drunken father, and the insensitivity of rich people.

"Doctah," Georgey said, "I is ready to go home."

The following morning Mom helped Gloria pack her belongings, gave her one of our suitcases, and dropped her off at the bus station. She gave her $50 for bus fare and incidentals. Mom's biggest disappointment was that Gloria never apologized, never thanked her for the $50, never looked Mom in the face. "How do you forgive someone like that?" she asked.

And that was the last of Gloria Hufnagel. Yet, as always in our family, the humor in it persisted.

"If she would have stolen one of Georgey's brassieres," Dad said, "she could have packed all her belongings—and ours— in it. Would have saved us giving her one of our suitcases."

"I don't know, Doctah. Peoples would rob ya'all blind if I wasn't plugged into Jesus."

Twenty-Three

Aunt Weeze was much flashier than Mom. She wore a lot of makeup and flirted unmercifully with wealthy men. Scorned the rest. "She got more red paint on her mouf than a new Cadillac car," Georgey would say, followed by, "Mercy sakes."

It didn't seem to bother Aunt Weeze's boyfriend Sid (the guy with the massive comb-over). When she played the piano she raised her hands dramatically with her fingers poised (and painted), and often—too often—she shook her hair as if it were in her eyes, but it was covered with so much hairspray that a Saharan windstorm couldn't have ruffled it.

"In terms of foolish dramatics, she puts Liberace to shame," Dad declared.

Mom, on the other hand, was an undramatic workhorse who knew precisely what she was doing. She didn't need histrionics or hairspray, and how she looked was incidental to how she performed. Her beauty showed through her music. She still had her hair done at the local beauty school (sans Gloria) and clipped her unpainted nails short, so they wouldn't make noise on the piano keys.

During their practice sessions Mom's execution was so perfect that Aunt Weeze always did what she suggested, but in a crowd Aunt Weeze led everyone to believe that she was the superior artist and controlled the quality of sound from Waring and Stoner. (After all—one need not say—it was Waring and Stoner, not Stoner and Waring.)

As the radio show progressed, the producers urged Mom to be the primary spokesperson. Whenever Aunt Weeze spoke, it was mostly about herself, New York City, Central Park in the spring, the Rockettes, and famous names like Leonard Bernstein and Gregory Peck. The show's restructuring set Aunt Weeze off something awful, but it boiled down to Mom having to do the bulk of the speaking or the show would be canceled—a fact that scared the heck out of Aunt Weeze.

Andy and I were never comfortable around her because she was always sighing in dissatisfaction, followed by a heavy "tsk." Whenever Mom and Aunt Weeze were together, the air became tense—kind of like being in a yard full of dogs circling each other while everyone's waiting to see what's going to happen. Who would bite first?

Fortunately, Aunt Weeze only came to our house on Saturdays and Georgey rarely had to deal with her. Andy and I often drummed up the vision of Georgey switchin' Aunt Weeze—bent over the arm of a chair, dress up, girdle pulled down, those gadgets that connect the nylons to the girdle askew—and getting the crap beat out of her for vanity, lying, adultery, stealing, and "not believin' in our Lord Jesus Christ."

The first—and last—time Mom got testy with Aunt Weeze was when Mom asked Spike to play the violin for her. Spike proudly stood erect as he played, chin down, steadying the instrument. I was surprised at how much better he'd become. Aunt Weeze wasn't listening and rolled her eyes. Finally she said with a pained smile as she dismissed him, "That's very nice, Spike." After he left the room she turned to Mom and said,

145

"Looks like you've got your own little Jack Benny." Smirk, smirk, chuckle, chuckle, wink.

Mom shouted, "What?"

"Well, you know," Aunt Weeze patronized, "he is still learning, Lillian."

Mom calmly said, "Louise Waring." But then she became angry. "You say some of the stupidest, most insensitive things I have ever heard. When it comes to my family, that's where I draw the line, and you just crossed it. Jack Benny is a joke. Spike Stoner is not. That comment pretty much ends our relationship. You and I are through. Get out."

Aunt Weeze began apologizing profusely, falling over herself with feigned remorse. I was upstairs but could still hear Mom.

"Here's your coat. Get out. Go on."

I heard Mom's deliberate feet marching around the room, stomping, getting madder.

"Lillian, please. Let's not . . ." The piano bench rocked, tipped over, and crashed on the floor. "Don't Lillian—please."

Now Mom was screaming. "I'm done with you, Louise Waring! I'm not kidding. Find someone else."

"Lillian, I am so very sorry. Please forgive me."

"Go home. We'll talk about it some other day, maybe never."

I was still upstairs, but Spike was hiding behind the curtains in the dining room.

It grew strangely quiet. Maybe Mom killed her, I thought. Wouldn't that be neat! I'd help her bury Aunt Weeze. I'm sure Spike would. We'd drag her into the backyard—each of us grabbing a shovel—dig a deep hole, and toss her in.

Then I heard low wails—moans, sobs, screams of sorrow. I had to find out what was going on. At the foot of the stairs, I could see into the living room. Mom's piano bench was still tipped over and somehow had ended up ten feet from the piano. She was standing over Aunt Weeze, who was on her hands and knees, sobbing at Mom's feet and holding her ankles, wailing. Mom stood rigidly, hands on her hips and fire in her eyes. It was unlike any emotion I had ever seen from her.

"Oh, Lillian," she sobbed and pleaded, her mascara running down her face. "Oh, Lillian. I haven't been myself lately. I am so sick. My life is miserable. Ohh! Last night I decided to kill myself but, ohh, I . . . I just didn't know how." She cried louder, kneeling at Mom's feet while gazing up at her, the most sorrowful expression I had ever seen. "Oh, Lillian, please help me. I am so sick. My body hurts. I'm about to lose it all."

I ducked behind the entranceway and held my breath as Aunt Weeze continued sobbing and wailing and begging for help. I wondered if she truly was dying. Maybe cancer. I peeked around the corner. Mom slid down on the floor and had her arms around the hysterical Louise Waring. She certainly wasn't going to kill her.

"Louise, please try and get ahold of yourself. You can talk to me. There, there."

"Oh, Lillian. I am such a miserable person and now it is too late."

"It's OK, Louise. What's wrong with you?"

"Well, ohh, Lillian. You will hate me if I tell you."

"Do you have a physical sickness?"

"Oh yes, ohh. It will ruin my life."

"Louise, you can talk to me. Look at me." Mom lifted Louise's chin and looked at her face. She looked like something out of a horror movie—blood-red lipstick smeared over her mouth, mascara encasing sunken eyes. The two of them sat on the floor like little girls at play.

"Oh, Lillian." She buried her face in her hands, smearing everything that was already smeared. "Lillian, I have a severe pelvic inflammatory disease that wasn't treated on time, and now . . ."

"Are you seeing a doctor? I'm sure Wayne can help."

"Oh God, no! Please, and you must promise me that Wayne will never know. Never! Please! You must promise."

"OK, Louise. I promise, but what is so bad about a pelvic disease?"

"It's gonorrhea, Lillian. Do you know what gonorrhea is?"

I could hear Mom's jaw hit the floor. My eyes bulged in disbelief.

"Gonorrhea? Oh, um, yes, I know what it is."

"I know. See? You think I'm a whore, don't you?"

"No, Louise. I don't. Please. But, um, isn't it treatable? Like with antibiotics?"

"On most people. But you have to stop it early. Apparently, the disease got stuck in my womb before I noticed any symptoms."

"Did you get this from Sidney?"

"Oh, I don't think so."

"You mean there were others?"

"Yes. Others. Several," she sobbed. "I am such a bad person."

"Louise, if it wasn't Sid, won't you give it to him?"

"No. He never wanted to have children. So he always wore one of those . . . things."

"A prophylactic."

"Yes. Lillian, am I a slut, a dirty, old slut?"

"No dear. Not at all. So it's only possible you got it from someone who wasn't wearing one. How many do you suppose there were?"

"I don't know, Lillian. My doctor, Ned Cuthbert, asked the same question. I couldn't answer him. I was so mortified."

"You'll need to contact them, otherwise they can infect others.

"Oh God, Lillian. What will I do?"

"I think you need to calm down and concentrate. Think who they might be and do the right thing. Call them."

Aunt Weeze covered her eyes. "I can't call them all!"

"Why not?"

"Well, five of them are married."

"Louise. Louise. Dear woman. I'm sure Dr. Cuthbert is going to take care of you. I feel your pain and your sorrow. I am here for you." She stood up, lifting Aunt Weeze with her. "You need to go home and get in bed. Take your medication and we'll put Waring and Stoner aside until you're feeling better."

"Oh, Lillian. I know you want to quit our partnership. I don't blame you. But you and our music is all I have left."

"You have Sidney and a very active social life, Louise. It'll be fine. We'll just take a couple of weeks off. Get yourself straightened out, and we'll be back on the air."

"Oh, thank you, my friend. I don't know how I could exist without you."

Mom began guiding her out of the living room. I ducked behind a large potted plant in the hallway as they walked by.

Twenty-Four

"Wayne, you're not going to believe what I learned today. Let me get you a beer and let's sit down."

Twenty-Five

Waring and Stoner had been off the air for three weeks when *Look* magazine called to do a feature article on the duo. Mom knew that would get Aunt Weeze out of bed, so she put the details of the interview in her hands.

The interview was held at our house. I went to Georgey's. Andy went to a Boy Scout meeting. Spike stayed at home and wore a necktie.

The man who wrote the article was Justin Fotheringham from New York City. He hired a local photographer to take pictures of the team playing the two big concert Steinways in our living room—Aunt Weeze showing much more leg than Mom and an extra layer of rouge. I don't think Mother had a chance to say much that afternoon; Aunt Weeze talked about herself constantly, laughing and complimenting Justin the entire time. Justin must have seen through her though, because when the article came out three months later, it featured more about Mom and her background, her relationship with Arthur Rubenstein, her rigorous work ethic, and how she balanced her career with "three children, one a blossoming and extremely talented violinist with an unparalleled détaché—bow stroke." He described Mom as "a natural beauty. No false flourishes or heavy makeup. Not extravagant. She has her hair done at the local beauty school." I was quite puzzled to imagine my mother as "a natural beauty."

We came to find out that Justin was both a respected critic and an accomplished pianist himself. Dad said he was also a homosexual. My brother and I called them queers, but not to their face. I guess it was just another private word like nigger.

Aunt Weeze felt the article was demeaning to her character, blamed it on her sickness, and threatened to sue *Look* Magazine, but she never did. (She was always making life-ending threats.) The Indianapolis School of Beauty gave Mom a free perm. Dad commented that, in many respects, Aunt Weeze was like our old sitter, Gloria.

Georgey, however, was concerned that more fame would draw Mom further away from us boys. While fixing dinner she told Mom, "We been through this before, Missus Stoner. The boys need more of you. I'm a little worried."

"I'm not sure I understand."

"Ole Zeke said to me the other day that Ricky was gettin' to be quite a nigger."

Mom stiffened. "What?" (even though she knew what). "My goodness," she sputtered, blinking in recoil, "why would he say a thing like that?"

"'Cause he's beginnin' to think and react like a colored boy. And he ain't. He needs more a you and less a me." Georgey put her hand lovingly on Mom's arm. "Miz Stoner, my how I loves you," she said, looking deep into her eyes, "but you is the momma and I is the maid. You needs to get involved in Ricky's life."

Mom froze—staring at Georgey, blinking her eyes, hearing something she already knew but wasn't willing to accept. Mom looked at her career the way a drug addict needs a syringe. She could rationalize her way around anything that might get in the way of that piano bench, those keys. Her fingers rooted out the sounds of her being. Intellectually, she knew what she should do. Umbilically, she couldn't walk away—the cord was too strong.

Georgey knew how to deliver different kinds of messages effectively, and a lot of what she said was hyperbole—most often humorous rather than critical. We'd learned to let it filter through our brains like a silly radio show. But when it was time to say things very important, Georgey would get face to face, hold you with her eyes, and speak simply: ". . . gettin' to be quite a nigger . . . needs more a you and less a me . . . you is the momma, I is the maid." There was no doubt what she was trying to say. Mom's New England upbringing and accent, her expertise in classical music, often rubbed Georgey the wrong way. You could see it in how Georgey stiffened her resolve and how quickly Mom could move in and out of tears.

That night, Mom ate dinner while blinking back tears, something my father could never handle. Emotion was a monster from which Dad ran. He built a fire in the den that night, smoked a cigarette, drank half a beer, and read the *Journal of the American Medical Association*.

Mom must have thought that time would take care of adolescent developmental issues because, once again, little changed. Her practice schedules remained the same. Her radio show required the same amount of preparation and planning as before. She continued to work with Little Sarah, who was truly gifted and brought out the genius in Spike—two geniuses in one house smiling, tilting their dramatic little heads, blowing their noses into linen handkerchiefs, washing their hands before they played. "Clean hands on clean instruments," Mom said. Sarah and Spike would occasionally perform duets without music, by ear, extemporaneously.

Smiling with big eyes like a ewe in pasture unable to identify her own lambs, Mom looked at Andy. Andy would "baa" and she would blink tenderly. She'd ask me how things were going, curious about where I was spending my after-school time. "How's Archie?" she asked more than once, mispronouncing Arkie's name. Though she acted all interested, it was a veil I could see through.

Her music was the blood in her veins and it guided her every move. Her boys could not replace it. Nor did we try. Spike had his violin and, of late, a harmonica. Andy had Andy. Dad had Dad. Mom had Chopin et al. And I had Georgey's neighborhood.

Since Georgey's comment to Mom, I began to spend less time at her house; Georgey encouraged me to play in my own neighborhood on Saturdays. She didn't insist, just suggested it a lot. I was aware of her worries about me. I didn't know anyone else who spent as much time with colored friends as I did. Zeke said I shouldn't be bragging about it.

Arkie had honed my basketball skills to where I had become as good as most other white guys my age, except Jim Moriarity, who stood several inches over me and had a soft set shot from the key. He lived in the biggest house in Golden Hill and had four skinny sisters with knees like ball joints—all taller than me—five children and eight bedrooms, as quiet as a half-empty honeycomb. The Moriaritys were different. Mrs. Moriarity did all the cooking and took pride in it. Jim's father built a basketball court next to their garage that was bigger than Baxter's.

Some random thoughts about our neighborhood: There were several girls my age who thought I was "cute." They were stiff Barbie dolls compared to Shuli or Marcella. One day I clearly won a fight with Jake Stapperd and he actually said "I give." From then on, I was feared. Expansive lawns, big basketball courts, paneled basement family rooms. I didn't need to go to Georgey's, but I missed her neighborhood—the chaos of it—small, smoke-filled rooms that smelled of people, not furniture polish; cluttered alleys; people yelling across the street at each other; fire-and-brimstone sermons on scratchy old radios. I missed teasing Arkie and hiding from suspicious colored people. I especially reflected on specific events that were burned into my memory as pivotal happenings—basketball with Arkie, Shuli kissing me, nigger-lipping the butt, dancing with Marcella, near death on the canal—the stuff of my daydreams, the thoughts that rocked me to sleep at night. Me, a white kid.

That fall I started high school.

Twenty-Six

I had four major problems as I approached my freshman year in high school: My voice was too high, I had no hair under my armpits, a growing spurt (which Georgey promised) left me plucked-chicken skinny, and I never had money. The physical problems, I was told, would all go away. The money was mysterious. It was elusive, in sight everywhere, but it always belonged to someone else. When I received money, it seemed to disappear. It'd vanish like a coin in a magician's hand. Dad called it "pocket change," but it never stayed in my pocket. I'm certain Mom and Dad talked to me about money management, but I don't remember any of those conversations. Dad was an easy source for an occasional dollar or two. When he asked what I had spent it on, I had no idea—some pencils? A Coke? A haircut? It never added up to the dollar or two he had given me. Georgey gave me money when Mom or Dad wasn't around, but soon she began asking questions about what I bought. Getting money from Mom was agonizing.

"Mom, I need some money."

"What for?"

"We were thinking about biking up to the Dairy Queen after we play basketball. I'd like a strawberry malt."

"How much will you need?"

"I don't know. A dollar?"

"I'll give you 50 cents."

"Come on, Mom. Fifty cents? What if I want something else?"

156

"Then split a malt with Jim. He doesn't need a whole one either."

Eventually Andy convinced Mom and Dad to give me an allowance like they gave him when he started high school. Two dollars each week, Sunday afternoon. Dad's pocket to mine. Malts were 50 cents, candy was a nickel. Got my hair cut every other week. One dollar.

* * *

Baxter was the oldest neighborhood kid in our high school freshman class. Eleven months older than I, he should have been a sophomore but was sick for a year. His mother had a big fifteenth birthday party for him. Boys and girls.

After he opened his presents he asked, "Who wants to play basketball?" Every boy raised his hand. Baxter appointed himself as one of the team captains, Jim Moriarity was the other. They flipped a coin to see who would choose first, and this was always a big deal. Who would be the first pick?

"I'll take Rick," Jim said. I remember walking over to Jim and patting him on the back, filled with such confidence and recalling that distinct episode of running home to Georgey three years earlier, crying. She was right. I grew. I was unaware of how much I had grown.

During the game one of my teammates was left unguarded with an easy shot. I yelled out, "Shoot the damn ball, man." It had a tinge of a colored accent, just like Arkie. Swish.

As I walked home from Baxter's birthday party that afternoon, Zeke's comment haunted me. I was getting to be "quite a nigger," equally at ease in Georgey's neighborhood as Golden Hill. I accepted the fact that colored people were different from white people. Just different—not worse, not better. Colored people didn't worry about the same things as whites. Being white meant thinking for tomorrow. Being colored meant thinking for today. I was more reckless with Arkie than I was with Jim or Baxter or Andy. The last time I was at Georgey's, Arkie rubbed burnt cork over my face and hands and pulled a stocking cap over my head. After I worked on my style of walking, we traveled around the neighborhood unnoticed until Little Roy saw us and called me "a painted nigger." He spit on his hands and rubbed my face while I shrieked until the white showed through. That never would have happened to a colored boy in Golden Hill.

Georgey smiled when I told her that I was chosen first, inflating her big brown cheeks and patting my face with flour-laden hands. "I'm so proud a you, darlin'. When bad things happen to us, we pray. When good things happen, we should pray, too, givin' thanks."

"I'll do it tonight."

"God's a busy man. We'll do it now." She had her hands on my arms so I couldn't walk away. "Thank you, great giver of miracles, for the blessings you has bestowed on this here child. Amen."

"That's it?"

"Sometimes you just has to throw out a quick one. He likes 'em short and He likes 'em long. He's busy, you know."

I walked out of the kitchen with flour on my cheeks, in my hair, and on my shoulders.

Andy noticed me and smiled. "Georgey must have made you pray."

"How'd you know?"

158

"You're covered with her holiness," he said, dusting the flour from my arms.

Twenty-Seven

In late fall I was measured for the freshman basketball team. "Five feet and seven inches plus," the school nurse said. I wondered how that happened. The year before I was barely five feet tall. I still was quite a bit shorter than Andy, but Georgey said, "You jes' got started with the growin' thing. You'll be taller than Andy 'cause you prayed for it. Now you gotta get some meat on that skinny body. I'll pray for that, too, while's I make larger helpins for you."

That same year, with no fanfare, Andy got his driver's license. It was just like him. He did things quietly, the way they were supposed to be done, without the noise and complications I would have made. I don't remember Dad congratulating him or Mom beaming with pride. I didn't know anything about it until one day he pulled into the driveway in a 1933 Ford four-door sedan rust bucket with no front bumper. He never talked to me about buying a car, much less getting his driver's license, but then maybe he did. I wasn't listening too much back then.

I remember those times well—out of touch like the old man who talks about the war he fought in Europe, but doesn't think about the war he fights within. A lot was changing in my life, both inside and out. My body was undergoing a major upheaval—not just that I grew six inches in one year, but my voice was cracking and producing some weird sounds, and pubic hair, at long last pubic hair. Then there was my mind and what I thought about how I looked (I had mastered Gloria's dual hairbrushes), who liked me, what was cool. And girls, mostly girls. I was no longer in control of Ricky Stoner. I was totally oblivious about Mom's career, or Georgey, or Spike—that he actually could play a harmonica as well as the violin—and Dad. I didn't even know Andy had a part-time job bagging groceries after school. That's how he had made some of the money to buy his car. Where was I?

Shortridge High School was integrated because our confused town insisted on it. Yet a mile away was Crispus Attucks High School, for Negroes only. To add insult to injury, Cathedral High School, an all-Catholic white school, was between Shortridge and Crispus Attucks. Indianapolis—integrated with its own segregated schools.

At Shortridge, coloreds and whites had lockers next to each other, attended classes together, and played sports on the same teams. But we drove separate cars, ate lunch at separate tables, went to separate dances, and whites kissed whites while colored kissed colored. Since there was a good Negro high school nearby, most whites would have preferred that the coloreds go to a colored school. Most Negroes in our town agreed, but the political pressure for integration was so great that many colored children had to attend Shortridge.

There was a lack of qualified teachers at Crispus Attucks, and classroom size was at a maximum. Further, the Library Fund, according to Dad, never reached the school. It was authorized by the city Board of Education but was never made available. The white politicians said the colored educators had squandered it away, and the colored educators said they never got it to squander. It sounded like an argument on a basketball court—He double-dribbled. No, he didn't. Yes, he did. No, he

161

didn't. The town newspaper supported the white politicians, pointing fingers at the colored school administrators and librarians.

The Shortridge parking lot was segregated, though not openly. The colored students who had cars parked on the street. Compared to many of the cars in the parking lot, Andy's was below cool. Dad was right. It was a jalopy. Even Dad's Plymouth would have been better. That never bothered Andy.

The coolest car was owned by the quarterback of the football team, Mike Dunbar. It was a 1949 red Cadillac convertible with red and white real leather seats, tightly fitted fender skirts, wire wheels, chrome lake pipes and loud duals—glass paks. Always washed. Always waxed. Permanent highlights like eye glitter. I often stared at it longingly, imagining myself driving to a football game with my arm around one of the varsity cheerleaders. Mike was pretty cool himself, with his well-manicured Balboa (short flat top with long sides, combed to a ducktail in the back) lathered in grease, tight jeans, white socks, weejuns, and a thin, white belt he buckled to the side—enough to the side so one would know it was purposeful, not sloppy. His manner was confident and direct. Everything in Mike Dunbar's life was purposeful. I watched the way he walked—bigger strides, more authoritative. I copied it, even added a little swagger of my own. He winked at people, too. That was cool. Winking without making a face was a studied gesture I practiced in front of the mirror, but my wink seemed to involve my cheek, the side of my mouth, and my ear.

Girls, unlike money, were plentiful. They roamed the halls in bobby socks, pastel-colored sweaters buttoned in the back, pop beads, and bouncy hair. Jim Moriarity introduced me to Karen Coolidge from his Spanish class and friends with his girlfriend,

Polly. Karen Coolidge was beautiful, perfect for me. She had blonde hair, a ponytail with a pastel bow, and a certain mannerism that was the sexiest thing I had ever seen—a toss of her head, a furtive eye-only glance at my entire body, a way of folding her arms under her breasts when we talked, bringing my attention to them. She loved my hair and how—thanks to Gloria—I had trained it to go back on the sides without grease. "Oh, it's so cool," she would say, running her fingers through it. I believed she was right.

There were many unspoken rules about dating in our high school, and an annoying one was that the boy always carried HIS girl's books to her class. And when he did, he was expected to ask her out on a date within a reasonable time. It would be rude not to—a violation of an unspoken rule.

"So, what are you doing on Saturday night?"

"Oh, nothing."

"Wanna see a movie?"

"Sure. Which one?"

"I don't know. Whatever's playing."

Some more about rules: The boy always paid. The boy's parents drove. The boy had to knock on the girl's door and chat with her parents until she arrived. The boy had to be charming and solicitous toward the girl's parents. The boy could put his arm around the girl in the theater or hold her hand, but no heavy making out—"swapping spit," they called it—unless you sat in the back row. Only certain types of girls sat in the back row— girls whose names were written on tunnel walls by the canal. I imagined Mary Lou sat back there when she was younger. Karen Coolidge sat center in Row 6. I kissed her on many occasions and she kissed with a matter of urgency—very hard with a tooth-breaking closed mouth, lips squenched, eyes shut tight, grimacing

163

like she was holding the cheeks of her butt tight. Then she'd push me away as if she had gone too far with a pained shame-on-me face.

"We have to stop," she'd say, preening and adjusting, fear in her eyes, doing something she was expected to do, not something she wanted to do.

I wasn't aware we had started.

Karen's father was a World War II veteran and manager at the power and light company. Inside the front door of their home was a framed purple heart from the Battle of Corregidor. The Philippines. 1945. Beneath it was a framed, silk, 8 x 10-inch patch with an American flag, and in French, Thai, Lao, Chinese, Korean, and Japanese, it told the reader that the wearer is an American aviator who is in distress. An enemy of the Japanese. "If you protect me and return me to my government, you will be reimbursed," Mr. Coolidge translated it for me.

"That was the war to end all wars," he told me. "The next war will be our Savior Jesus Christ, coming to earth and ridding us of Communists and slanty-eyed yellow people, Buddhists and Negroes. Might not happen in my lifetime, but I'm sure you'll see it."

Karen and her little sister rolled their eyes as if they were tired of hearing about it, while Mrs. Coolidge sat on the plastic-covered sofa making squeaking noises with her thighs as she thumbed through *TV Guide* and *Movieland* magazine.

"Yeah," Mr. Coolidge continued, "I feel sorry for your dad."

"Why's that, sir?"

"Socialized medicine. It'll be the end of rich doctors. The government will tell him who his patients are. They'll give him coloreds as well as whites. And he'll be flat-ass busted, sticking thermometers up the butts of old Nigras and Gooks."

"Martin!" Mrs. Coolidge exclaimed. "Watch what you say."

I often rode my bike to Karen's house after school so we could practice new jitterbug steps that I had learned from Marcella at the Church of the Holy God, but after the Nigras and Gooks comment, I didn't want to tell her where I learned them. There was always someone else there—one of her friends or Mrs. Coolidge. So much structure—records, supervised dancing, and silly games—I thought I would scream. When would I ever be able to slow dance with her in the dark—just Karen, me, the Penguins and my hot breath on her neck?

When I got home from Karen's house, Georgey was still there. There were still-warm cookies stacked on tinfoil, and I still had to pray in order to get one.

"Lord, thank you for my family, my home, and Georgey's cookies. Amen."

"How's what's-her-name?" Georgey asked.

"Karen," I said, muffled by chocolate chip.

"That's a beautiful name."

"She's a beautiful woman." I liked calling her a woman. It made me sound older. More mature.

"She as good a dancer as you?"

"How'd you know I'm a good dancer?"

"Baby Shuli and that little fat girl, what's her name, says so."

"Marcella and she's not fat anymore, Georgey. You oughta see her. Va-va-voom!"

"I can wait," she said sarcastically.

165

"Those kids at the Church of the Holy God are the best dancers—by far. That's where I really learned."

"Well, you was born with music in yur veins, darlin'. More so than most peoples."

"Except Spike."

She nodded her head. Spike was amazing. "'Cept my Spikey."

I reached for another cookie, feeling like there was some substance to my life and that I was going somewhere—a great jitterbugger with a great haircut.

"So, this Karen, tell me about her."

"Well, she's really pretty and has a great figure. I'd say she's the most popular girl in the freshman class."

"Then you must be the most popular boy."

"Could be."

"Look at how the Lord has blessed you. Do you remember bein' so small and cryin' in poor ole Georgey's lap and prayin' that God would make you taller?"

"Oh Georgey. I was going to grow anyway. God had nothing to do with it."

"Oh, you was gonna grow anyway. But you growed a whole bunch and you got real handsome. And you is just started. I knows it. Growin's one thing but God gave you more. God does that. Now He wants to see what you is gonna do with it."

"Like what?"

"Like being kind and helping others, being patient with those not as fortunate as you. Look at yur daddy. He spends a lot of time helpin' folks. Most often not chargin' for his work."

"Well, maybe when I'm his age I will too."

She put her hands on my shoulders and looked into my eyes. "God wants you to start thinkin' 'bout it now. Yur a young man, not a little boy no longer."

I looked at her, though I had nothing to say. She brought a conversation to a simple end—an open mouth, a blank stare. It made the conversation easier to recall.

"Now come here and give poor ole Georgey a hug."

Twenty-Eight

Dad returned home late Friday night. Mom said he was at the hospital until 2 a.m., and this morning he had to go to a meeting downtown because of some kind of legal thing related to his being at the hospital. Andy had to be at work at the grocery store; Spike was in the living room working on his violin vibrato—eyes squinched shut, chin down hard on the instrument; and I was going to Karen's house at lunchtime, hoping we might find some time to dance alone, maybe more.

"Morning," Dad said, walking past us and out the door. "Gotta get the newspaper."

He returned, reading the paper as he entered the door. "Well, it wasn't front page news, but it made page 3."

"A new girl at the Fox?" Andy asked half-jokingly.

"Far from it. This has to do with Little Roy's father."

"Squiggy Daniels?" I asked. "Isn't he a lawyer for Negroes?"

"Well, in a sense, yes. He's more accurately a lawyer for human rights, for equality."

"God, Dad. You sound like Reverend Williams."

"Well, yesterday Squiggy represented the NAACP and Frog Island to improve the sewage system there. God knows they sure need it. He called my office and asked if I would testify about the health risks of people living in that horrible slum, and I told him I'd be proud to. Well, typical of our bigoted town, an all-white sewage commission was formed and they were supposed to draw up plans for Frog Island and several other neighborhoods."

"Let me guess," Andy said. "They somehow forgot about Frog Island because it is all colored."

"Worse than that. The commission did draw up plans and was ready to present them to the Board of Health. Naturally, someone was needed to represent Frog Island, so Squiggy showed up, dressed in a nice coat and tie, a satchel under his arm with plans to include Frog Island in the project. Duncan Boyd from the NAACP was with him, as was I. A lawyer from town met us at the door—Tommy Stanton, a 6-foot-11-inch, sanctimonious, racist jerk—and said that Squiggy's initial letter included the replacement of burned-out street lights, an area of improvement not under the jurisdiction of the Board of Health. Well, that self-righteous jackass declared at the doorway that the petition to include Frog Island was not valid, all because of the street lights. Even Judge Jones backed Tommy and told Squiggy his petition would be taken under advisement and should be submitted next year.

"After they turned down Squiggy's admission to the hearing, Squiggy lost his self control," Dad said, shaking his head. "The police started to forcibly remove him from the building when he hit one cop in the face with his briefcase. Then there was quite a fight. Five cops and several other white people beat the living crap out of him. I took him to the hospital. Squiggy had broken ribs, lacerations on his face, his right eye was almost poked out of the socket, and two fingers on his left hand were broken. He will be released this morning and taken to the county jail. The town has charged him with inciting a riot and assault and battery on members of the police department."

169

Mom put Dad's eggs, toast, and strawberry preserves in front of him. "I'm so sorry, Wayne. That's just awful. Horrible."

"You know, son, the next time you see Little Roy you need to tell him how embarrassed you are for our race. Mark my words, Squiggy Daniels will become a major citizen in the equalization of our races."

"I will, Dad."

"Here's the bottom line to this episode. One that you, Ricky, can understand better than any of us. Those plans drawn up by the town engineers show a rerouting of the sewage pipes around Frog Island, leaving that area to function like a private leaching field, are disastrous. That means Arkie, Baby Shuli, what's-his-name—Rozelle—and several of my already sick patients will be exposed to more sewage and more infections."

Squiggy was in jail for two months before lawyers for the NAACP could get him out. Then he lost his job at the trolley car company.

Twenty-Nine

After Andy got his driver's license, Georgey wouldn't ride with him for a while. She couldn't believe that he knew how to drive a car.

"He's still just a baby, Doctah."

Eventually, Dad had to put his foot down. One night he had some reading to catch up on and told Georgey that Andy would be taking her home in his "new" car.

"Andy?"

"Yes. Number one son, Andrew Stoner," Dad said calmly, trying to put an end to the conversation.

"Doctah. He's too young to be drivin'."

"Sixteen's the age. He got an A plus on his test." An exaggeration. It was a pass or fail road test, but Dad needed to enhance Andy's abilities.

"He may have got a A plus on his test, drivin' around some parkin' lot in yur car. Drivin' me home is different."

"No. He passed his driver's test in his own car. He's been driving now for a couple of months."

She didn't miss a beat. "Drivin' me home through that dangerous colored section of town could get him killed, as sure as I'm standin' here."

"Then Ricky will go along, too, sort of a bodyguard. That'll be you, pal," he said, pointing to me.

I snarled and growled.

"I'm too big for that car," she said.

"You fit well in my car. Andy's is larger."

"Then maybe you'd like to drive Andy's car," she said.

"Good idea. I might take it to work tomorrow." He winked at Andy.

"Well, I guess I just has to walk home."

"Through the white neighborhood on one leg? Why, you'll be killed as sure as I'm sittin' here." It wasn't often Dad could get the edge in one of Georgey's arguments.

"Well," she huffed, walking into the kitchen and still talking, "if we all dies, you got nothin' left."

"Are you calling my wonderful wife and youngest son nothing?" Dad smirked.

Eventually, Georgey got over her fear of driving with Andy. She found things she liked about the car, for instance, the way Andy's doors opened from the front. They were called "suicide doors" because of the danger of them flying open—the wind catching them and ripping them off their hinges and sucking the passengers into the street. Andy didn't mention that, nor did I. Dad wouldn't have, either. The running boards made it much easier to get in and out of the car. Over time she refused to ride in Dad's car because, she said, Andy's was much more to her liking. She rode in the front seat with Andy, proudly sitting and looking straight ahead like a queen in a parade. I sat in the back with my window rolled down, my arm hanging out, sleeve rolled way up, and hair blowing in the breeze. Real cool.

"Quick now. Where's the horn?" Georgey asked.

"Right here," Andy showed her.

She beeped. Miss Tildalayhu was standing at the bus stop in her straw, wide-brimmed hat with the fuscia band and her bright yellow dress.

"Hi, Georgella, "Miss Tildalayhu called, waving.

172

"Why, Miss Tildalayhu," Georgey answered. (The light was red.) "Where you headin'?"

"Waitin' for my bus."

"No you won't. Not as long as I has a breath a Sundays. You get right in the back seat here. We're on the way to my house. We'll take you home." Miss Tildalayhu leaned down and looked in the car. She had never met Andy before. "This here is my boy, Andy," Georgey said in sing-song voice. "Missus Stoner's oldest."

"Very nice to meet you," Miss Tildalayhu said.

"And you remember Ricky."

"Oh, my goodness, yes. You certainly have grown up, Ricky. Gettin' to be quite a handsome young man. My goodness."

"Thank you, Miss Tildalayhu." A car beeped at us from behind. I opened the back door, which opened just like the front ones—four suicide doors.

"My, isn't this nice," she said. "I hope I'm not taking you out of your way."

The light was green. "Hey. Get that crate movin'," the driver behind us yelled.

"Not at all, Miss Tildalayhu," Georgey said. Then to Andy, "She lives just four houses north of me."

Several cars beeped their horns. Miss Tildalayhu cast a shaking index finger their way. "I listen to your mother every Saturday," Miss Tildalayhu said, sliding in next to me. "She is the most talented pianist I've ever heard."

The beep again—an angry beep. Georgey opened her door and stepped out, squinting at the driver behind us. "You just wait, young man. Nothin's more important than lovin' yur neighbor. We is on our way."

She slid in her seat.

"We're very proud of her," Andy said.

Georgey put her hand on Andy's arm. "And Miss Tildalayhu knows good music. You should know that she has the finest singing voice in all of America, the voice of an angel. She leads the choir at our church."

"Why thank you, Georgella. What a kind thing to say."

"We needs to get Missus Stoner and Miss Tildalayhu together."

"Do you suppose Missus Stoner could play the piano for me while I sang? Help me with my voice?"

"Would you like me to ask her?" Georgey said.

"Oh, my goodness. I would be so honored." If a colored woman could blush red, she blushed. I could hear it in her voice and feel a rush in the air, like an open window.

"I will too, Miss Tildalayhu," I said. "I'll talk to Mom for sure."

"Thank you. I would appreciate that." Miss Tildalayhu had a humbleness about her so appealing that it was like one of those kittens you wanted to take home.

The next morning at breakfast, Andy told Mom and Dad about picking up Miss Tildalayhu and was about to ask Mom if she would help her.

Dad interrupted. "Let me get this right," he chuckled. "You and Ricky and Georgey picked up one of Georgey's friends in the colored section of town, driving a 1933 Ford jalopy?"

"So?" Andy replied.

Dad started laughing, wheezing, coughing. His eyes watered.

"Let's picture this scene," he said.

"Really," Mom said, putting her hand on Dad's arm, laughing, "two white teenagers in a jalopy with their dates."

"who were . . . ," Dad interjected.

". . . two older, overweight, colored women," Mom said. "I'll bet Northwestern Avenue had never seen that before."

Andy added, "I sure felt awfully safe."

"You certainly were."

We totally forgot our promise to Miss Tildalayhu. Things like that happened often in our family—important things getting lost in humor and lightness.

Thirty

In my freshman year, Andy was awarded the Eagle Scout badge of the Boy Scouts of America. He was a junior. Mom, Dad, Spike, me, and Georgey attended the ceremony. There were only seven Eagle Scouts in the entire town. The scoutmaster asked the seven fathers to come on stage and pin the badge on their sons. Then he said, "I think these boys deserve a real pat on the back from their dads, don't you?"

The audience applauded while five dads put their arm around their sons and one hugged his. Dad couldn't do either. He shook Andy's hand awkwardly. Mom shook her head, while tears wet her cheeks. They were sweet tears and sad tears—sweet ones filled with pride for her son, sad ones for her emotionless husband. Dad was one step short of being an amazing man, while Mom was used to perfection. After all, an F-sharp can only be F-sharp, nothing else.

Andy worked harder than anyone at everything he did—bagging groceries, athletics, even his grades. He studied all night when he had to, and it paid off. But he wasn't without his own demons, one of which he couldn't hide—his acne. For two years he and Dad had tried everything. It was so awful that he was almost disqualified from one wrestling match because his face was bleeding so badly. He spent a lot of time in front of the bathroom mirror, washing his face and putting medicine on it. With each new medicine that Dad gave him, he'd say, "This should do the trick." Finally it did, but his face had permanent craters—like convex razor bumps—by then.

In many ways Andy was a stoic like Dad. But Andy was human, whereas Dad often seemed above it all. When Andy got jilted by Sonia Cryspman—dumped for a guy without zits—he ended up in his bedroom crying his eyes out, cursing the entire high school and swearing at God for giving him acne. Mom was there. She told him how unimportant it was and about some guy who dumped her when she was a sophomore. In ten years, she said, Sonia would wish she had never dumped him. Mom used her signature line that day—-"the race is to the finish line." I heard it many times and privately wondered what the finish line was. If it was death, I didn't want to be in that race.

Georgey told Andy that many years ago she, too, became angry about some things that happened to her. Felt it was not right, unfair. "How could a loving God hurt the children who loves Him so much? We think it all has to make sense. But God's ways go 'round us, making sense for some peoples but not for others. This Sonia girl thing is terrible. I sees you sad and it breaks my heart; yur sadness hurts me deeply. And, 'cause Sonia brought you this sadness, I'm angry at her."

She softly rubbed his back and continued, "But I don't think God is. I think He's molding a special man out a you. Look at the great things you done, and yur jes 16. Look at how you help yur brothers and yur momma and daddy. Look at the happiness you bring to yur fambly and to me. Andy, child, you is the strength of this fambly. You is the rock. Sonia what's-her-face is a speck in yur eye. She ain't good enough for you. You has to be patient and wait for the queen. You'll find her. She'll be comin' along soon."

Andy was a very mature sixteen, and he knew Georgey was right. His pride had blindsided him for a while. Emotion was a dangerous thing.

"You're right, Georgey," he said, wiping his face. "But it still hurts. It's embarrassing."

Georgey nodded in agreement. "It is. But that goes away."

"I'm OK. Mad as hell but OK."

"I'm mad, too." She put her arms around him. "You know, huggin' you is exactly like huggin' yur daddy. We called 'em armless hugs. Like huggin' a pencil. I had to teach that boy to put his arms around me. You understand?"

Andy laughed. "I understand, Georgey." He put his arms around her.

*   *   *

Georgey refused to attend Andy's wrestling matches in high school. She said if she saw some boy hurting one of her boys, she'd run out there on the floor and switch his naked behind. "Lord forgive me, but I would."

Dad went often. Mostly though, Andy went with the team or someone else's family. He never said it bothered him, even though most of the other boys' families were there, cheering and hooting. Andy was like that, just like Dad. Unemotional. Focused. I went a few times with Dad and screamed my lungs out.

His junior year, Andy wrestled in the city championships against a boy from Crispus Attucks. The gym looked and sounded different than it ever did before, and tension gripped us like a tightly wound wet sheet. Colored faces with white eyes on one side of the gym stared across the large mats at white faces and red noses. Many whites whispered slurs and assumed the coloreds were figuring out how to kill them—the prevailing

178

rationale from what I could tell. Dad and I felt differently. We were out of place on both sides.

It was a very close match with just one point separating Andy from winning. All he had to do to tie was escape the other boy's grasp, but he couldn't get away. The colored wrestler was glued to him as Andy twirled and rolled.

The colored section cheered. There were many racial comments and loud slurs coming from the white section, and an older man in the front row had the audacity to say, "Kill him, Andy. Shake off that nigger."

After the referee raised the colored boy's arm as the winner, Andy shook his hand warmly. "Great job. I just couldn't get away from you. You're too tough."

"Thank you." The colored boy was taken back. "What's yur name?"

"Andy Stoner."

"I'm Nelson Jones. Maybe next time."

"I hope so, Nelson." Andy said, patting him on the shoulder.

I stood up and screamed, "Way to go, Andy!" He looked into the stands and saw me and Dad and waved.

A bullnecked, flush-faced man with a red bulbous nose like the fat end of an enema injector sat in front of us. "He didn't need to congratulate a nigger."

"I think he most certainly did," Dad said. "The colored boy was better than him this time."

Andy wasn't sad or mad that he lost. That wasn't the way he was. He would just have to work harder.

Thirty-One

The highlight of my freshman year, 1954, was being invited to become a member of a prestigious high school boys social club that had been around for decades—the Corpse Club. My Uncle Gordon was a member. Dad was never a joiner, and neither was Andy. Generations of stories about the savagery of Corpse Club's initiation drifted through time, building the image of unusually strong-charactered Midwestern men. One rumor spread that a pledge had drowned trying to swim across White River during a winter initiation. Another pledge class had to beat up a colored hobo near the train tracks. And another told of the tarring and feathering of a homosexual.

My time of pledging was comparatively easy. Weekly, the pledges had to kneel into a chair backwards, knees on the front of the seat, head against the back, holding your testicles. The active members had Corpse Club paddles with which they pounded our butts till we bled. We felt it was worth the pain so we could wear a small gold pin—a skull with rubies as eyes—on our shirts or sweaters. Only six to ten pledges per year, thirty-five members total—the white, Christian, social elite of Shortridge High School, as American as one could be. I was proud.

Mike Dunbar was asked to be my pledge father. His pin was worn by Patty, a blonde cheerleader with big loose breasts that moved a half a second after she did, quietly colliding to keep up . It was alright to stare at the pin, slowly. She told me I had the coolest hair in Shortridge. I brushed it back with my fingers. "Coolest hair—Rick Stoner."

Mike was an all-state quarterback on the championship football team, a member of the Blue Devil Student Council, and owned the red Cadillac convertible that glowed in the Shortridge parking lot. I was envious of everything he had and considered myself lucky to have him as a friend and pledge father. I told him so one day in the parking lot.

"Let's go for a ride, pal," he said.

"Pal," I repeated in my head. I'm his pal. I nodded my head.

"You drive." He opened the driver's side door of the Cadillac.

"I don't have a driver's license."

"We're just gonna drive around the parking lot."

"I don't even know how to drive."

"Driving this baby is a snap. Put it in 'D'—see it here? And press this pedal slowly. Can't afford to wreck this beast." He winked.

"Are you sure? Wow. That's great."

"Before you start, make sure she's in park; that's the 'P' there. Then turn on the key. Give a slight pump on the gas pedal."

I turned on the ignition and started the car.

Rumble, rumble, rumble, rumble.

"Feel that power?" he asked.

"Yeah. Cool."

"I call her my great beast. Let's put the top down. I'll do it. You release that lever up there. I'll release mine." He pulled the knob for the top and it whirred, lifting away from the windshield magically like an opening bloom on a flower, and folded back on itself. Everything did what Mike ordered.

"Is this the radio?"

"Sure is. We need some sounds, don't we?" He turned it on and immediately the right music played. Subtle rock and roll—*Hey nonny ding dong, alang alang alang, boom ba-doh, ba-doo ba-doodle-ay*—

"Now take your foot off the gas pedal, slide it to the brake pedal and pull the gearshift into Drive, slowly."

Oh, life could be a dream (sh-boom). If I could take you up in Paradise up above (sh-boom).

"Drive?"

"That's what 'D' stands for. 'P' is Park."

"So 'R' is Reverse. This is my brake, right?"

"Right. Go ahead. Let's cruise real slow like we're at a drive-in and the chicks are really hot." He reached over and put his hand on my leg. It felt good.

If you would tell me I'm the only one that you love. Life could be a dream sweetheart.

I pressed slowly on the accelerator pedal and we inched forward at walking speed. Mike acknowledged people with a casual hand motion—a relaxed point with his index finger—and a wink. He tilted his head, raised one eyebrow, pointed, and winked.

"Hey, Dunbar."

"Hey, cat man," he acknowledged quietly. "You know my pledge son, Rick?"

"Hey, Rick."

I pointed and winked. "This is so cool, Mike," I said lightheadedly. This was everything I ever wanted, the car, the acclaim. I was there, under the tutelage of the master himself.

Hello, hello again, sh-boom and hopin' we'll meet again. Boom ba-doh, ba-doo ba-doodle-ay.

People looked. I pointed and winked. People stared. Mike pointed and winked. We winked. I was so cool. I began to get an erection. Really.

* * *

There were six in our Corpse Club pledge class, bonding like brothers. Jim Moriarity and I were from the same neighborhood. The rest were scattered around town—the young Shortridge elite—all wearing pastel-colored, V-neck sweaters over white T-shirts, jeans, and Weejuns.

Mike's family held a pledge party for us at their home—the six of us, plus Mike and the president of Corpse Club, and Mr. and Mrs. Dunbar. Dad drove Jim and me to the party, up a long, circular driveway to a large house with pillars and manicured gardens. Dad was appropriately smug. "Very nice," he said, as if praising a rookie.

I was impressed. I couldn't help not being so. Mike's red Caddy was parked in the front circle along with a green Jaguar convertible—forest green, it was called. I noticed the steering wheel was on the passenger side.

"Looks like Christmas," Dad said.

"Christmas?"

"Red and green cars."

Several pledge brothers were clustered around the cars with Mike and his father, a big man with a blonde pompadour and his thin belt worn to the side.

"Well, well, Wayne Stoner," Mr. Dunbar said, approaching our puffing, faded-blue Plymouth sedan.

"Bob," Dad said, "so good to see you. What a magnificent spread you've got here."

Jim and I got out of the car. I couldn't wait to see the Jaguar. Dad was happy with his dusty old Plymouth—the outside sun visor slightly atilt like his lopsided smile—you could tell.

"Would you like to come in, Wayne? Caroline would love to see you."

"No thanks, Bob. I've got house calls most of the day plus rounds at the hospital."

"The hospital? Hope it's no one I know."

"Funny you'd say that, Bob. It's Sarah Atchinson's mother. A sizable stroke. Not sure how she's going to pull out of it."

"Oh, my goodness," he said, reaching into his back pocket and pulling out a small pad. "I'll put her on my prayer list. And this afternoon Caroline will send her some flowers. Nice lady. Brenda Atchinson. Methodist Hospital?"

"That's right. I know she will appreciate hearing from you and Caroline."

Dad returned to his car and the blue Plymouth chugged down the driveway like the final scene in a Charlie Chaplin movie.

"I went to Shortridge with your dad and your uncle," Mr. Dunbar said.

"Dad mentioned that. Said you were one of the greatest athletes Shortridge ever saw."

"That's very nice of him. It's not really true. I did play football, though not nearly as well as my son."

Mrs. Dunbar looked like a movie star—Dorothy Malone in *Battle Cry*—with her heavy makeup, long eyelashes that she batted slowly, fluffy pink sweater sporting Mr. Dunbar's 25-five-year-old Corpse Club pin, and a black, tight skirt. She looked tired and had a distant look in her eyes—looking but not seeing, waiting for something to end or wondering in anticipation—unfocused and preoccupied.

We ate on small tables around the back patio; cheeseburgers, french fries and Coca-Cola served on plates of porcelain leaves with runny pickles. "A lunch for champions," Mr. Dunbar said. Before eating he said grace, holding his wife's hand. "Lord, Father, we thank thee for thy blessings upon this house and these fine young men. We pray also for thy healing of Brenda Atchinson, who recovers as we speak at Methodist Hospital. In the name of our Savior, Amen."

During lunch he carefully talked to each pledge brother. "I remember your uncle Gordon very well," he said. "As I'm sure you know, he was a Corpse Club member and a president. That prepared him well as a lawyer."

The Dunbars were different than the Stoners—like Mickey Mouse was different from Zorro—both heroes, one pretend. I thought about that as I ate on glossy porcelain. My family was different than most families. "Artsy" was one word that came to mind. Artsy and unstructured. We had more options than other families, more fun, too. Mom would never wear a pink fluffy sweater or heavy makeup. We never polished our cars, and we didn't own a sprinkler. Our "things" were breakable, and most often broken. But broken for good reason. We were Mickey Mouse.

"Gentlemen," Mr. Dunbar began. "Don't know how many of you have ever shot clay pigeons. If you have, raise your hand."

Two pledge brothers put up their hands.

"Clay pigeons," Mr. Dunbar continued, "have been used by serious bird hunters for at least a hundred years, honing their marksmanship skills. They are sometimes called skeet. Here is what they look like." He held up a six-inch clay disc. "I thought it would be fun to go out to the back field and try our hands at it."

This was the stuff of English barons. We walked across an early winter wheat field to a mechanical slingshot that hurled the skeet.

Mike was first, shooting with a spotless shotgun and talking while he aimed and shot.

"You get your gun up and at the ready," he said. "When Dad lets the skeet go, you pick it up as fast as possible. But you don't shoot until you're just ahead of it. Watch.

"Pull," he shouted, and the pigeon was released. He followed it for three seconds then pulled the trigger. The skeet disintegrated. "Don't jerk the trigger, pull it slowly."

"Aim fast. Pull slow," his father said. "That's the rule of bird shooting."

Each of us tried it—hitting few, missing most. After several spent boxes, Mr. Dunbar sat down in a collapsible, canvas safari chair and asked us to join him.

"I would like to take a couple of minutes to just congratulate all of you for honoring this great old club," he began. "My father was in one of the first pledge classes of Corpse, 1897. It was quite different then. Shortridge was entirely white, but the Negro population was growing. Many families were concerned about the caliber of education at our school, feeling the intermixing of the two races would negatively affect education and, therefore, prohibit the good white students from finding suitable colleges. Corpse Club in the '20s became very involved in efforts to separate Negro curricula from white, to allow a greater focus on the white students. It was partly because of this great club that politicians were forced to provide an all-Negro high school for this town—Crispus Attucks. The coloreds were happy and the whites were, too. So, you boys are part of history. Since our nation is presently struggling with unrealistic racial situations, we must pay heed to our forefathers and what they fought for. We must be strong and listen to our heritage."

I sat silently, listening to his message yet unable to understand exactly what Mr. Dunbar was saying: good for the coloreds, good for the whites? I was confused. The others were also. I wasn't the only one. Glancing over at Jim, we shared a weak smile.

"So, let's head back to the house and tell my beautiful wife what a wonderful lunch she prepared for us."

At home, Dad asked how it went. I told him about shooting skeet, driving in the Jaguar, and Mr. Dunbar's vague lecture on race.

"What do you think his feelings are about the Negro population?" Dad asked.

"Not real sure. He's for them, I guess."

"You guess?"

"Yeah. For them but kinda concerned about them. I dunno. Nice family though. They pray a lot. Georgey would like that. He was an Eagle Scout. Andy would like that."

"Bob was an Eagle Scout three years after your Uncle Gordon."

"He said that. Yeah, they're an alright family. Just different."

* * *

As our initiation continued to the Corpse Club continued, we endured a cold February "Hell Night" with a minor beating. Then, in an attempt to confuse us, we were blindfolded and driven in circles, eventually arriving several miles outside of town at the same location where the club always ditched and beat their pledges—the property was owned by the Northside Neighborhood Men's Club, an exclusive retreat for wealthy men in our town. The clubhouse was a pristine log cabin overlooking a man-made pond, and the inside was said to be elegant—bearskin and zebra rugs, mounted animal heads, leather sofas, white linen tablecloths, polished silver, and cut-glass decanters. The club offered fine wines supplemented with carefully prepared dinners. The men and women members served it; a humbling kind of thing. The members were bonded by a similarity of interests—fishing and hunting, skeet shooting, the Indianapolis 500 race, the Indianapolis Indians, and politics. Who would be the new mayor, the new governor? Who would be the power brokers of the town? It was an all-white-only club, clearly one Dad was not asked to join. Many of the Corpse member families belonged.

It was also the place where active Corpse members could come and park with a date and drink beer without being hassled. Far from the nearest road, it was behind a cornfield in a stand of gnarly sycamore trees and its only access was a dirt tractor path through the cornfield. Most of the pledges knew the location well. In fact, Jim and his pledge father had taken two girls there for a bonfire and tried to get them drunk. The girls outdrank them and Jim got sick and vomited.

On Hell Night, we were ready with our own plan. Jim's father drove one car and Dad drove another and parked 100 yards up the road with their lights out. I could see Dad's cigarette glow. After we were blindfolded and tied to each other, the members raced off in their cars. We began laughing after they left. I had one of Little Roy's pocketknives to cut all of our ropes, and Dad and Mr. Moriarity drove across the cornfield, picked everyone up, and drove them home.

"I'll promise you one thing," Jim said. "We sure as hell are going to change the location for ditching next year's pledges. This was too easy."

Thirty-Two

March was the start of the 1955 Indiana high school basketball championship season, and even though Martin Luther King, Jr., was embroiled in racial struggles, Senator Joseph McCarthy was exposing communists, and there was talk of a Russian-assisted takeover of South Vietnam, the front pages of newspapers throughout the state were filled with basketball stories. We had our own colored high school—Crispus Attucks—and it was rumored to win the state championship this year, having lost in the finals the year before. The newspapers followed every move the team made—each player, each game. As the all-colored, segregated high school was aiming for the best in the state, the hysteria rolled as Attucks beat one team after another. Photographs and stories of each of the players built the frenzy as the town rallied behind "its colored team." As each game neared the end, the Attucks cheerleaders—wearing white sweaters with a black letter "A" on the front (a topic of great humor for the well read)—started singing "The Crazy Song," a haunting, vaguely disrespectful chant to a Cab Calloway melody. Where most schools' cheerleaders would be screaming well-worn cheers, Attucks started singing and the fans joined in.

> *"Hi-de-hi-de-hi-de-hi;*
> *Hi-de-hi-de-hi-de-ho*
> *Skip, bob, beat-um.*

That's the Crazy Song!"

The second verse drove the nail home.

"Central thinks they're rough.
Central thinks they're tough.
They can beat everybody.
But they can't beat us."

The death of Albert Einstein was the only national newsworthy event over that two-month period, but in our town even that was relegated to page two.

Attucks meant more to my family than most because of our close association with Georgey's neighborhood. Arkie and Little Roy were there as a freshman. Rozelle and Baby Shuli were sophomores.   After Attucks won the state championship, the town slowly returned to normal. Once again, the coloreds weren't welcome in white restaurants. They had to sit in the balcony at white theaters and swim in the river, rather than public swimming pools. Negroes could only go to the city amusement park on certain days and had to drink from separate drinking fountains there. Not much had changed after all.

A month later, Mike picked me up when I was hitchhiking home from basketball practice. His car was beautiful as it cruised up to me and stopped. He winked. "Hop in, pal." I winked back.

"Goin' home?"

"Yeah. If it's out of your way, just get me close and I can walk."

"Oh, no. When you wear that sacred pin, you're my brother."

"Yeah, that means a lot to me."

191

"You still dating Karen what's-her-name?"

"Coolidge."

"Nice ass. You getting anything?"

"Well, not much," I mumbled, wondering if I should lie or tell him the truth—nothing.

"Sometimes with a virgin you have to be firm. You're the man in that relationship you know." Low radio sounds of doo-wop and the wind in my face. "Even the Bible says that the woman has to do what the man says, to obey him. I think it's Ephesians that says: 'Women should regard man as they regard the Lord.'"

"It says that in the Bible?"

"Absolutely. Ask your father. Dad says he's one of the brightest men in town."

"My father?"

"That's what Dad says. And your mother is one of the best pianists in the country."

"That she is. Ephesians, you say."

"Yeah. You might want to memorize a couple of sentences, so she knows you're religious. Girls give in faster if they think you've got God on your side." He laughed and slapped me on the chest like his pal. "Once you get through all those crinolines, the rest is easy. She'll start breathing real heavy and then she won't be able to say no."

"You sure?"

"It takes time, Rick. You have to be persistent. It took me awhile with Patty. I even had to force her legs apart that first time. Man, she cried. Now she loves it." He removed his wallet and pulled out two prophylactics. "Here ya go, brother. These'll prevent any unnecessary little Rick Stoners from running around."

"Oh, wow. Thanks, Mike. Cool," I said, anxious to show it to Moriarity. I don't think Andy had ever seen one either.

"You have to give me all the details."

"I sure will, Mike. Thanks a lot."

"I tell you these things 'cause you're my brother now. It's private, between you and me. OK?"

"Sure. I wouldn't tell anyone, Mike." My mind was struggling with how to put it on, who puts it on, when—in the actual process—does that happen? Does one size fit all?

"I wanna show you something else," he said, pulling into the grocery store parking lot. He reached under his front seat and stopped. "Since nothing we say goes any further than this car. Just you and me, a club brother and his pledge father. OK?"

"Sure." I thought maybe some dirty magazines or photographs of Patty without clothes—black and whites—would be fine.

He pulled out a double-barreled, sawed-off shotgun. The handle had been shortened and shaped and the barrel was 10 inches long. "Beautiful, huh?"

I looked around to make sure no one was looking. "Yeah. Really cool."

"Here, hold it." He handed it to me.

"Not loaded, is it?" I asked, fearful that he might want to show me how it works.

"Oh, no. I got shells in the glove compartment." He reached across and opened it, pulling out a handful of shotgun shells. "See?"

"Cool." I handed back the gun.

"I'm ready for niggers." He winked at me.

"Niggers?" I whispered, hoping I had misunderstood.

"Niggers."

Something deep inside sent an alarm. A myriad of voices and images of Georgey, Zeke, Zeze, Sonny, Ann Sue, of Arkie, Marcella and Baby Shuli ran through my head—the smells, the specialness of the neighborhood. Suddenly I was torn—my world becoming divided and more complicated—as I was faced with looking into a door I never anticipated opening. Should I tell him I disagreed, that I had spent more time playing with colored kids than white ones? He was a junior. I was a freshman. He was popular, had a great car and a beautiful girlfriend. That was everything I wanted. The thought occurred to me, maybe he was right.

He sat stroking the gun and nodding. "Gonna name this baby Princess. Yep, Princess. You like that name?"

"Cool," I said, ashamed that my standards were so watered down that I couldn't believe in anything. Dad's words of injustice, Ishmael, Zeke's smile, Georgey's hugs, and Ann Sue's silver thimble poured over me in desperation.

"My dad told me that several years ago there was a Nigra at the Fox Burlesque. You know the Fox?"

"Yeah," I said, feeling fear and a tension in my neck—like knowing a loose snake is on the floor in a dark room.

"'The Queen of the Congo,' she called herself. Seems she was taunting a bunch of men in the audience. They took her out back, raped her silly, and sent her home. Taught that nigger a lesson she'll never forget. I'd like to find me some pig meat one day, just give it a try once. There's one in my chemistry class I'm working on. Dad says the entire nigger community has never forgotten what the whites did to that whore. They're plotting a way to get even. So, we gotta be prepared. That's why I named this Princess."

194

I nodded my head as best I could, but I couldn't look at him. Even my peripheral vision was vibrating with the image of this high school hero—loved by everyone, never unsure, oozing confidence, always polite—now in direct conflict with the last decade of my life. Could I have been wrong?

Thirty-Three

"Georgey," Dad called from the dining room where we sat.

"Yes, Doctah." We could hear her fumbling around in the kitchen, searching for her cane, and grunting. "Always callin' me. Come here. Go there. Lord knows why I loves him so much." Her voice was just loud enough to be heard. Dad grinned.

"Guess who came to see me today?" He pushed back his chair as a smile spread across his face.

"Now how am I s'posed to know?" Georgey said from the doorway. "I ain't no Houdini."

"Miss Tildalayhu."

"I knows that," she said, one arm high on the jamb. "She's not feelin' well. Her momma's drivin' her batty. I told her to come see you."

"A very nice woman, she is," Dad continued. "She was quite a famous singer."

"Did she sing for you?" Georgey asked.

"Oh, no. That might have been a little disruptive in my waiting room. She brought along a scrapbook though, filled with newspaper articles and photographs about a very accomplished gospel singer named Matilda Lee Hughes."

"Sounds almost like her name, don't it?" Georgey said. "Miss Tildalayhu. Matilda Lee Hughes. You think they could be the same?"

"I know they are the same."

"I can see how we got confused," Georgey said.

"She was raised in New Orleans and moved to Chicago," Dad said, "and sang with a famous gospel group headed by Mahalia Jackson."

"Mahalia Jackson?" Mom sputtered. "Is that true?"

"Who's Mahalia Jackson?" Andy asked.

"The greatest Negro singer in the whole-ever wide world," Georgey said, sitting down at the table with us. (Our dining room table sat six, one on each end and two on each side, so there was always one extra chair for Georgey.) "And if you ever heard Miss Tildalayhu sing, you'd know she was just as good as Miss Mahalia Jackson. My goodness. She never let on."

"She's that way," Dad said. "According to many of the newspaper articles, she and Mahalia Jackson sang duets and toured the city's churches and surrounding areas with the Johnson Gospel Singers."

"I just knew she was good. Miss Tildalayhu. Matilda Lee Hughes." Georgey sighed. "How wonderful for her."

Dad continued, "I have the scrapbook in the car."

"Missus Stoner," Georgey said, "Miss Tildalayhu said she would like to sing with you sometime. She'd be terribly honored. Do you think . . . ?"

"That's right," I said. "Just last week she asked if Georgey and I would talk to you about it. We forgot."

"That's why she gave me the scrapbook," Dad said, getting up from the table. "I'll go get it. It is most impressive, Lillian."

"Oh, goodness," Mom said. "I would have no idea how to play that kind of music."

197

Georgey put her hand on Mom's arm. "It looks like you'll just have to learn. No one else on this planet got as much talent as you does. Why, you got more talent in your little finger than a room full of Miss Mahalia Jacksons."

"Mom playing Negro music?" Andy asked.

"Negro gospel music," Georgey emphasized.

"Mom can do it," Spike said seriously.

"Aren't I busy enough?" Mom replied.

Dad handed Mom the scrapbook.

In that din of silence as Mom perused the meticulously glued scrapbook, much was happening in her mind. Gospel music was an assault on Mom's creativity, an assault on her childhood, on her training. Music sung by the uneducated. That we were even interested in it—or might prefer it—was an assault on her life's work.

"I am not colored," she suddenly blurted. "You can't make me colored."

"Oh no, no. We knows that Missus Stoner."

"Classical pianists," Mom paused, thinking, "are the whitest white people on the planet."

"That don't mean nothin'," Georgey said. "They ain't fit to wash yur laundry, darlin'."

"Georgey," Mom said, "I remember studying piano with a very famous pianist, Walter Piston, who told me that Negroes were incapable of being classical pianists, something about the anatomy of their fingers."

Dad guffawed. "Walter Piston knew as much about anatomy as I know about the music box of a Steinway."

"Now wait a minute," Georgey said. "Jes' stop it! You bof forgets what's goin' on here. God give us Miss Tildalayhu. She ain't done with His purpose for her. God give us Lillian Stoner.

She ain't done with God's purpose for her either. You and the doctah is arguin' about whether colored folks can play the piano. We is talkin' 'bout God, not colored folks' fingers."

"But Georgey, your kind of music is not inside me. It's just not there. You must accept that."

"'Nonsense. It ain't there cause you won't let it in. You thinks you is better than colored people's music. You is too proud a bein' white."

"I look at it differently," Mother replied stiffly. "Miss Tildalayhu is a colored woman from the churches of Chicago. I'm a white woman from Radcliffe College of Cambridge, Massachusetts."

"You know, Mom," Andy suggested, soothing the conversation, "maybe your talent is bigger than just classical music."

"Ain't children wonderful? Andy jes might be right. Your fancy music is like a stone in a creek that ya steps on to get to the other side, a higher ground."

Mom sipped her coffee silently, thumbing through the scrapbook. "Here's an interesting name: 'The Five Blind Boys of Mississippi.'"

"I listens to them on the radio."

"Miss Tildalayhu sang with them once. And Ethel Waters! Oh, my goodness. Miss Tildalayu sang in a backup group with Ethel Waters. Can you imagine?"

Mom pushed back her chair and watched her potatoes. Dad lit a cigarette and a soft film of smoke rose over the dinner table.

"You know," he said, "I think I might have a half a glass of beer."

Was it possible that Georgey knew Mom had more depth in her than just classical music? More greatness? Georgey always *seemed* like an unguided ship in a tempest, floating unphased through the storm. Saying things without really understanding. Yet with a husband like Dad and three restless boys stretching Mom's resolve, Georgey must have known there would have to be more.

Georgey shuffled back into the dining room with Dad's beer. "If you can do this—this gospel thing—darlin', you will be givin' to the glory of God, not to the memry of Walter Pistol, or whatever his name was."

"Piston," Dad said.

"Nonsense," Mom uttered, slowly closing the scrapbook. "Thank you, but nonsense. Could I have a refill of water, Georgey?"

* * *

Over that summer, interspersed with the quiet beiges and men's-room-green tablatures that spoke languages of the high-brow literati—"Pour Une Infante Défunte," Scriabin, pianoforte, zwei Klavier, "Prelude for the Left Hand" (pour le gaucher), Herausgegeben von Ruthardt—strange-looking pamphlets landed on Mom's piano bench. Now there was sheet music like "It is Well with My Soul," "Precious Lord, Take My Hand," "Follow the Drinking Gourd," and "Peace in the Valley." There were photographs of Mahalia Jackson, Ethel Waters, and other Negro singers.

Slowly, when she thought no one was listening, Mom tried those songs, her efforts sounding insincere and like fake laughter at a cocktail party. She even tried warming up with Scott

Joplin sheet music. We rolled our eyes. One night we listened to a record of Mahalia Jackson singing, accompanied only by a piano.

"Hear that piano in the background?" Mom asked, lifting the phonograph needle and putting it back. "I can't do that. That music and this sheet music"—she waved it off the music stand—"are two different things. The pianist on that record is improvising. This," she said, picking it up from the floor, "isn't Negro gospel music. Some white transcriber wrote this." She thought for a minute, and we wondered how she knew.

Lifting the needle again, she started it back at the beginning. Then she sat at the piano reading "Go Tell It on the Mountain" and, as the record started, Mom started. I thought it was going quite well, just that Mom's timing was off—she wasn't hitting the notes at the same time as the recording, and she wasn't hitting enough notes. Shaking her head, she stopped.

"Missus Stoner," Georgey offered, "your feet ain't movin'. Colored folks listen to that music and we can't keep still, movin' our bodies, our arms, clappin'."

"It's not necessarily Negroes, Georgey," Dad said. "Lots of country music and jazz have strong beats."

"Well," Mom huffed, "you are certainly a big help, telling me everything I'm doing wrong."

Dad and Georgey fell over themselves with apologies. "Just trying to help."

"Well don't, dammit!"

So we listened to Mahalia sing—all of us keeping time to the music—while Mom had her feet glued to the piano pedals out of spite, motionless.

It didn't take long before she blurted, "I don't like it. I can't do it. I'm too damned white! Case closed!" She stormed out of the room.

No one argued. We heard with our guts just how white she was. Teaching Mom to play Negro gospel music would be like teaching Mahalia Jackson to hold her breath for two days.

Thirty-Four

Miss Tildalayhu served breakfast and lunch downtown at Sandborn's Restaurant six days a week. It was the only place where you could see her without one of her glorious hats. The first time I went there with Dad, I walked right past her because she looked so different—like Wonder Woman in street clothes.

She traveled to work by bus (first locking her mother in the house). Her porch was exactly twenty steps from the bus stop, and she got off the bus twenty steps away from the restaurant. Our house was two full blocks from a bus stop, but when she came to our house she insisted on walking rather than allowing mother to pick her up. She marched proudly through our white neighborhood, a domestic in everyone's mind who saw her except her own. At that moment she was a lady, a musician, honing her skills. "No," she said proudly, "I love a good, brisk walk."

And Miss Tildalayhu of Chicago, Illinois, insisted on paying Mom for weekly "voice lessons." Two dollars. At first Mom tried to wave it off, but then she accepted it and secretly gave it to Georgey to give to the church.

* * *

After the first time that Miss Tildalayhu heard Mom talk—heard her voice— she knew that Mom had perfect pitch, that unique ability to hear any note, sung or played, and know which note it was and whether it was exact—not a little flat or a little sharp, but exact. As perfect as a sound must be to shatter a goblet, or that moment when an autumn leaf knows to let go or a perennial knows to bloom, precision was Mom's ear. Often when the wind howled through the windows of our house, Mother would say "D-flat," and if we ran into the living room and hit the D-flat key on the piano, it was exactly the same as the wind noise. Hmm. Miss Tildalayhu heard Mom talking on the radio and knew by the sound of Mom's voice that her tonal ear was perfect. At that point it wasn't important that Mom know gospel music.

She once said to Mom, "A white person's voice is cleaner, truer, than a colored's voice. As Miss Jackson used to say, 'God gave us so much soul we're a little short on self-control.'" Mom liked that line a lot. She used it to describe Aunt Weeze.

Spike, too, was impacted by Miss Tildalayhu's musical spirit. She taught him how to bend a note on his violin, an effect used in blues guitar where the performer actually stretches the string over a fret, making the sound slide into a flat or sharp or in between. But it was never done on a violin until Spike Stoner perfected it at eleven, to no one's amazement. And his harmonica, she said, was capable of bending notes by using facial—mostly lip and tongue—muscles. Many gospel groups had harmonicas in the background. Mom tried it by wincing, rolling her lips, and turning her head. Miss Tildalayhu, too, made the most comical faces. It took Spike several months before he could do it, and do it well.

* * *

Mom was "Mrs. Stoner" and Matilda Lee Hughes was "Miss Tildalayhu," two mutually respectful artists learning from each other. There was also a growing affection between them because both women were having fun. Being creative ceased to be hard work for Mom. Once, after a particularly moving rendition of "Amazing Grace" when Mom began improvising, Miss Tildalayhu and Mom were both brought to tears. Mom shouted, "Oh Matilda, that was absolutely beautiful! Beautiful! Moving!" Her exclamation was so loud that I left my room and sat on the bottom step of our stairway, listening.

"Praise the Lord!" Miss Tildalayhu said. Then she sat on the piano bench next to Mom and held her hands. "You are so kind, Lillian. So helpful. So inspiring. I feel God's presence is with us."

Mom didn't know what to say. She felt it also but wasn't sure if it was God's presence or last night's meatloaf.

After that, they were Matilda and Lillian.

"Do you feel music, Lillian? Inside?"

"Oh, yes, especially Chopin," Mom said. "I feel he wrote with me in mind. I don't really need the music. It's here now." She touched her heart. "It all goes from my body through my fingers to the keys."

"Yes, yes. Hallelujah! Me, too. I know what comes next, if you can understand that."

"Exactly." Mom looked around to make sure no one else was in the room. "I sometimes just wrap my arms around myself and play the music in my head. It sounds perfect there."

They both nodded their heads like two little girls talking about their dolls.

"The heavenly knowledge," Miss Tildalayhu said.

"The what?"

"The heavenly knowledge, Miss Mahalia used to say. The sounds you hear so deep and so perfect no one could duplicate it."

"Do you hear it?"

"Oh yes, but it's someone else's voice singing, not mine. It's Miss Mahalia's voice."

Mom nodded. "I understand that, Matilda. When I play your gospel music—when I play it right—I hear someone's voice singing with me."

"You do? Is it Miss Mahalia's?"

"No, Matilda. I hear your voice. Pure and clean like a newly tuned piano."

The next week's voice lesson started with a spontaneous prayer by Miss Tildalayhu.

"Heavenly Father," she began, taking Mom off guard, "prepare our talents. Bring out the greatness of our sister Miss Lillian Stoner. Let it flow through this room and pour over bof us so that we can glorify Your holy name. Oh, yes. Glorify! And as always, great God, we ask this prayer in the name of your Son, sweet Jesus Christ. Amen."

And from the kitchen came a loud, "Amen. Amen to that, sweet Jesus!"

"Lillian, would you mind if I took my hat off while we practiced?"

"Not a bit, Matilda."

Soon they became Tilly and Lilly.

* * *

"Lilly, are you surprised how well we work together?"

"I'm amazed, Tilly. You bring out things in me I didn't know were there."

"And you do the same to me."

They stared at each other smiling, waiting for the next great thought.

"Lilly, do you know anything about the great white pelican?"

"A singer?"

"No. No. It's a magnificent bird."

"Oh, a pelican. Yes."

"A certain kind of pelican, Lilly, the great white pelican. It's the state bird of my home, New Orleans, Louisiana, where I was born."

"No, I don't know anything about pelicans."

"Well, the great white pelican is a giant of a bird with a wingspan of almost 10 feet. It's one of the largest birds in the world."

"Ten feet? Really."

"More important, Lilly, it has such powerful wings that it can fly higher than any other bird. To watch that beautiful white bird circle so high, so gracefully, and then dive into the water is a sight few can understand unless they have actually seen it."

Mom was on the verge of wondering what Miss Tildalayhu was talking about.

"Here's the point, Lilly. The great white pelican is all white 'cept for the very tip of its wings," she said, tracing her fingertips with her thumb. "There, a few black feathers grow. That giant bird needs the black feathers 'cause they is stronger than the white feathers; allows that wonderful bird to rise to even greater heights but those black feathers are too coarse to let the bird get off the ground. They needs bof."

207

Just like us, Tilly. Just like us," Mom said.

"Yesterday I was rememberin' my daddy tellin' me about the great white pelican and knew it was a sign from God. Talkin' to bof us."

Mom stood up from her piano stool and slowly, uncharacteristically, put her arms around Miss Tildalayhu. "Thank you," she said.

* * *

Mom was changing. You could hear it and see it in her performances with Aunt Weeze. She began reflecting her music emotionally—moving her upper body, getting closer to the keys, encouraging her raging hands and fingers, attacking the keyboard one minute and caressing it the next. It was like eating with your hands rather than with silverware. Mom learned to be visceral from Miss Tildalayhu, so totally focused when she practiced that she unknowingly made faces, frowns, closed-mouthed jaw drops, and winces. I laughed at her stupid faces, but she had moved into a different zone. She was quicker to praise Aunt Weeze, quicker to hug her boys, quicker to laugh out loud than before she met Miss Tildalayhu, and her attitude about everything was mellowing.

Georgey said it was Jesus Christ entering Mom's life.

Mom said it was just fun and nothing else counted.

Dad said it was Andy's turn to drive Georgey home.

Zeke saw it, too. He said Mom was "brownin' up."

Thirty-Five

It was September and I had just started my sophomore year. Driving south on the main road into the colored section of Indianapolis in the 1950s was like opening the curtains for Hammerstein's *Showboat.* Suddenly everyone was colored.

First white folks in cars, white folks on their porches, white folks walking down the street. Quiet, orderly. The Dairy Queen, the hardware store, and the Texaco gas station made up a demilitarized, integrated block. Then it was colored in cars, walking down the street, sitting on their porches. Bigger than big, dirtier than dirty. All the Dairy Queen wrappers from the white section blew south and settled against gutters and storefronts. Busy. The music was behind the scenes. Early doo-wop. We drifted in so often—Andy and me and Georgey—that we knew the music. Knew the lyrics. Knew members of the cast. I can't remember a routine drive to Georgey's with Andy, one where I might have dozed off. Georgey talked about the Bible, her neighborhood, and food. Of late, she talked about Martin Luther King, Jr., how he was going to change everything in this country. I didn't see how that was going to be possible, but I never said anything. The Dunbars seemed to be the majority in our town.

My family was busy with school, athletics, dates, music, and medicine. So often when we dropped Georgey off, I spoke to Zeke. Had to. "Hey boy!" he shouted. I knew the drill—walk across the street onto his porch and shake his hand. "Good to see you, Mr. Zeke. Miss Zeze." I nodded politely and hugged Zeze, her cheeks warm and soft, always soothing. I waved to Reginald and Marjorie. When I saw colored kids my age, I always mentally compared them to Arkie. A week without Arkie was like a week without peanut butter and jelly—something was missing—so we talked on the phone frequently. We talked about school and his new girlfriend; Hanna was her name. I wanted to meet her. We talked about Karen, and I couldn't imagine her meeting Arkie. Karen was too white, too stiff, too glued together, not pliable. Hanna would be completely different. We talked about integrated high schools versus segregated, and we were both interested because we heard about discussions in Washington to get rid of segregated schools. Get rid of Attucks?

"Man, I like goin' to school with colored folks. There ain't no racial stuff at Crispus Attucks High School for colored folks."

"Well, you just wait," I said. "The government's gonna make Negroes and whites equal."

"They might try. But my daddy says it'll never happen. We got colored colleges, colored high schools, we crap in colored toilets, we marry colored girls."

"And I'm stuck with a colored friend," I interjected.

"Well, that's integration for ya."

Thirty-Six

A month had passed. From the window of Andy's car, I saw Arkie standing on the street corner with a couple of schoolbooks under his arm. As a young, 6-foot-tall, colored man who looked just like Arkie Johnson, his soft features were now hard carved. He had turned the corner on manhood. I was surprised.

"Hey, Arkie," I yelled from the backseat window.

He turned around, looked, and scrunched his forehead. Two white kids in an old car and a colored lady. "Hi, honey," Georgey said.

I got out of the car. "Man, almost drove by you. You look so serious, and you grew again."

"How long's it been? A few weeks?" he asked. "Evenin', Miss Georgella."

"This is my brother Andy," I said, walking him over to the car.

Andy held out his hand. "Nice to finally meet you, Arkie. I've heard a lot about you over the years. Stories of stories."

"Uh oh. I'm in trouble."

"Not at all. You guys have had a lot of fun together."

We looked at each other with lopsided smiles. "That we have," I said.

Arkie and I had moved beyond race. Zeke was right. I was becoming "quite a nigger" and I didn't even know it. Our friendship had grown stronger than any color barrier that could have separated us.

"Yur brother, here," Arkie said. "He play ball?"

"I do," Andy said. "But I couldn't make varsity, so I'm on the wrestling team."

"Tell you what," Arkie said. "I'm s'posed to find two more guys for a game tomorrow at church. If yur not busy, it sure would liven up the court, eight coloreds and two whites."

Andy winced. "I dunno, Arkie."

"I guarantee yur safety. Ricky knows the court better'n most of the neighborhood. Reverend Williams is always there. Rozelle, too. Willie, Nat. Hey, and Little Roy is playin'."

"How's he doing?"

"Good. Been eatin' lard and whipped cream for six months."

I looked at Andy. "Whadda you think? You wanna risk your life?"

"That's stupid, man," Arkie said. "You ain't riskin' nothin'. We'll just have fun. Play some good ball."

I looked at Andy again. "Come on."

"Sure," he shrugged. "We'll do it."

"Two o'clock."

* * *

I hadn't been to the Church of the Holy God playground since Spring. It looked like it had grown up, just like the rest of us. On Sundays the playground was sparsely populated with small children, parents, strollers, and old people sitting on benches in browns and grays, smoking unfiltered cigarettes and stubbing them out with worn shoes. On Saturdays, when the weather was

212

warm, it was all basketball and had been since Roy, Arkie, Rozelle, and I painted the lines a year earlier. Bicycles surrounded the court, some standing, others without kickstands lying down like sleeping metal creatures.

Now teenagers crowded the area. A 45-rpm record player's tangled extension cords ran across the ground and were plugged in through the church window, and some colored girls in pink full skirts, white socks, and sneakers were jitterbugging and giggling. Tough-looking colored guys lingered in drifting pockets, sleeves rolled to their armpits—some smoking Camels or Chesterfields—and wore tight jeans. Andy and I slowed down to park. "I don't think so, Rick," he said. "This isn't what I expected."

"Me, neither," I said, remembering a much more solitary, isolated court. But the sounds were friendly—the doo-wop music, high-pitched laughter, and bouncing basketballs sounding like snapping fingers.

"Hey, Ricky!" we heard. Arkie raced into the street waving us down.

"This is kinda scary, Arkie," I said. "I don't think . . . ."

"Yeah," Andy added, "I thought this was just a small pickup game."

"Oh, come on. It'll be fine. The Reverend Williams is always here. He refs the game."

Andy looked at me. "I dunno."

"I guarantee your safety. I swear. We need you 'cause it's too late to find a couple more guys. We got the court from 2:30 till the Attucks cheerleaders take it over at 3:30."

Reverend Williams came over to the car. He wore a sweat-stained, short-sleeve shirt, clerical collar, and old sneakers. "Hey, Rick. Good to see you again."

"Thank you, sir." We shook hands.

He looked at Andy. "Welcome to our church basketball game. I'm Reverend Williams and I know who you are. You're Andy. There's a third, right?"

"Yes, sir," Andy said, stepping out of the car. "Spike."

"Plays the violin. Miss Tildalayhu says the harmonica, too. Yeah, I know. I feel like I've known your entire family for years. Georgella talks about you all the time. Ricky helped us paint the lines here and has blessed us with his presence on many occasions. Isn't that right, son?"

"I have."

"Well, I want you boys to play ball with us. I'm serious. This is a marvelous opportunity for our community to share with you our commitment to fair play and our love of Jesus Christ."

I smiled diagonally, uncomfortable with his overt Christianity, mild though it was compared to Georgey's. I didn't expect the message to be so loud. This was basketball, not Sunday school.

"Come on," Arkie said, putting me in one of his friendly headlocks. "Besides, you gotta meet Hanna. Hey, Hanna," he yelled, motioning into the crowd of girls milling around the music, not watching us when we looked, watching us when we didn't. I saw Marcella and a couple of other girls I had danced with at the church. One broke and ran toward us, head lifted high with an open-mouth smile and eyes round with laughter. She felt like the music from the record player.

"Hi, Ricky," she said at full skip.

"See?" Arkie said. "See what I mean? Beautiful, ain't she?"

"Don't embarrass him, Arkie. What's he supposed to say?"

"He knows."

I smiled pathetically. She was tall, with a long, graceful neck and happy teeth she couldn't hide, even though she tried. Dad would have used one of his favorite lines on Hanna—"a presence to be reckoned with." She seemed older than Karen, older than white girls her age. She wasn't raised to be beautiful and popular, but to exist and thrive. "Are you really a bad basketball player or is that another one of Arkie's stories?" she asked, twinkling.

"Hi, Sweetie," Marcella said, putting her arm around me. "You growed some."

"Think so?" I asked, as Andy approached. "Hanna, Marcella, this is my brother Andy."

Andy did some nice-to-meet-yas, staring at Marcella's breasts.

"Where's Shuli?" I asked.

"Around here someplace," Hanna said, tucking her bra strap under her blouse.

"Hey, I know you," a voice said from a nearby cluster of boys. "Yur Andy Stoner."

Andy looked hard, picking a bee from a hive, then smiled. "Nelson Jones?"

"Good memory."

"You playing?" Andy asked.

"I am now."

"This is my brother Ricky. Nelson's the guy who beat me in the City Wrestling Tournament last spring."

It was Hanna and Nelson who made the difference—the reason we stayed.

The gathering crowd milled and moved like jelly, looking for a corner to settle in. More people joined Hanna and Arkie, while others drifted back to the shade of the church and a giant, old sycamore tree half stuck in uprooted concrete. I spotted Reverend Williams' line-painting crew from a year ago, sans Arnold, the troublemaker. Andy and Nelson were talking about wrestling. He felt better about the situation, rolling his eyes in a forgiving manner and shrugging his shoulders. Andy wasn't on his turf, but he was always eager to learn.

"This'll be fun," he winked.

Little Roy had packed on more weight, over 200 pounds. He was heavier than I was, at 140 pounds. He still smelled, and he sweated a lot. Sweated before the game started and stunk by the end. But Little Roy had a great outside shot, a 30 footer. And he never clutched. Arkie was lyrical on the court. He and Rozelle were the best—Rozelle, though much taller than Arkie, was not as effortless in his style. Reverend Williams split Andy and me up so it wouldn't appear to be colored versus white. Arkie, me, Roy, and two others: one named Buster—Buster Blackie—and Jude. Rozelle had Andy, Willie Rice, Nat, and Nelson Jones.

The game got serious, as good games get, with some confidential cursing and muffled growls in the battle over ball ownership—who stepped out of bounds, who shoved, double-dribbling, watch yur mouf, boy. Nothing out of the ordinary. As the intensity and emotion built on the court, more kids gathered, cheering. It was an out-of-the-ordinary event—two white kids playing ball in a colored crowd. But the game really was Rozelle versus Arkie. The crowd seemed to be evenly split and loud. Hanna led cheers for our team, and Marcella led them for Rozelle's. These weren't tried and true high school cheers like "Two Bits, Four Bits, Six Bits, a Dollar," given by cheerleaders whose hair never moved. These were real cheers for heroes of the streets by the kids who lived there. More like songs than cheers— finger-snapping, thigh-slapping, foot-stomping cheers.

"Hey Baby.
(clap, clap, clap)
Let's get hot.
(clap, clap, clap)
Can't not hear ya.
(clap, clap, clap)
I say I can't not hear ya.
(clap, clap, clap)
Go big Arkie, Beat, Beat, Beat 'em up!"

First Hanna and her crowd, then Marcella and her crowd.

At one point Rozelle held me by the back of my pants as I raced for a layup.

"No fair!" I yelled. "Come on, Rozelle. I had that one."

"What?" Rozelle said. "I didn't do nothin'."

"You grabbed my pants, for cryin' out loud."

"Cryin' out loud? Who'd say such a stupid thing as 'cryin' out loud'?"

"Me. Come on."

"Hey, Rozelle. I seen you, man," Arkie said, chestin' up to him.

"Come on, give Whitey a free throw," Buster said.

Reverend Williams ran into the argument. "Who called him Whitey?" he asked. "We won't tolerate any of that kind of talk. Ya'll know better. I'm sorry, Rick."

"I didn't mean nothin' by it," Buster said. "You know that."

217

"No, no. That doesn't bother me at all," I answered. "Whitey's fine. Rozelle's just working us."

"Sure," Arkie said. "When Rozelle can't play basketball, he plays psychiatrist."

"Zeke calls me Whitey. It's just a name to me, Buster."

"If it bothers Ricky, he'll let you know," Arkie said.

"Yeah," Roy said. "He's Whitey 'cause a his hair and his skin. All white milk ain't bad, ya know. You can fool with Ricky. He's OK."

"Well, OK, but give Rick the ball. One free throw," Reverend Williams ordered. I missed it. Rozelle poked me on the way up court, smiling.

"You big goon," I said.

Andy hit an outside jump shot. They were up by six points.

"Way da go, big Andy. Way da go," clap, clap, Marcella cheered, followed by her crowd, "Way da go, Big Andy. Way da go," clap, clap.

"Booga, Booga bad boy.
Hot time star.
Lay it in the bucket, babe.
Specta-cu-lar."

"Timeout," Buster called, motioning to Reverend Williams.

"No timeouts," Andy said.

"What's the timeout for?" asked Reverend Williams.

"We needs to regroup. We're behind."

"All right. A 30-second timeout."

We huddled around Buster. Hanna and Marcella were trying to outscream each other with "Booga, booga, bad boy" cheers.

"We need tighter defense," Buster said. "Hip bumps on Rozelle, grab at the ball. Jude, you gotta get in the game. Come on!"

"Yeah," Arkie said. "Real tight defense. And this." He took off his shirt.

"What'cha doin?" Little Roy asked.

"Psychological stuff, like Rozelle would do. Don't argue with me. Shirts off."

We stripped off our T-shirts and tossed them in a pile on the sideline. Hanna did a spontaneous "T-shirts is off" cheer. "Booga, booga, bare boy." Little Roy threw the inbound pass to me and jiggled down court—belly, breasts, spare tire, everything out of control, slapping around. Andy whistled.

"Watch out!" Rozelle shouted. "Chocolate Jell-O on the court."

"Number seven!" I yelled, holding up four fingers. There was no number seven. I had just made it up.

"Number seven," Buster acknowledged. "Over here, Whitey."

Everyone stared at Buster. I threw a fast pass to Arkie for an easy layup.

"I thought we weren't allowed to call Ricky 'Whitey,' " Nelson said.

"Shut up and play ball," I said, slapping the ball out of his hands and passing it to Buster for another quick two points.

"Hey, Reverend Williams," Rozelle said. "They ain't allowed to take off their clothes like that."

"No rules 'bout that. But I'm still not comfortable with the Whitey thing."

"You know, Reverend. You said the word "Whitey" more'n anybody so far. I think we should get a free throw," Arkie suggested.

"Yeah. A civil rights free throw."

"I just might give you a technical foul unless you boys don't stop using racial language. It can get out of hand. Understand?"

"OK," Buster said. "Their ball."

Soon the game was tied at 30-30. The next basket would win the game. Reverend Williams called timeout to diffuse some of the emotion. Most of the kids had quit doing what they were doing and came over to watch. I was certain we were going to win. We had Arkie. Buster and Little Roy were hitting their outside shots, and Jude and I were tenacious on defense.

During the timeout, Hanna and most of her friends started the Crispus Attucks High School victory cheer, "The Crazy Song."

"Hi-de-hi-de-hi-de-hi
Hi-de-hi-de-hi-de-ho
Skip, bob, beat-um.
That's the Crazy Song!"

I had heard that cheer the year before when Crispus Attucks pulled ahead of another high school team during the state basketball championships. It was haunting and known to infuriate competition, especially white competition. Rozelle was fired up during the timeout and made up his own second verse, which everyone joined in.

"Arkie thinks he's rough.
Arkie thinks he's tough.
He can beat everbody.
But he can't beat us."

Everyone on the playground sang despite Hanna's objections, because Arkie was more fun to tease than Rozelle. Andy took the inbound's pass and spotted Rozelle racing to the other basket. He heaved the ball full court and Rozelle slam-dunked one final layup, making it 32-30. It was the first time I'd ever seen that happen while I was on the court. At 5'8, the rim was two stories high to me and unreachable. Rozelle was reserve varsity at Crispus Attucks. He told us there were four players on the varsity who could dunk without a running start.

"They just stand there flat footed and jump high enough to dunk the ball into the basket. One was named Oscar Robertson. He was 6'5—my height—and not the tallest player."

We looked for our T-shirts. Marcella found mine.

"Look how white you are, boy!" she cried, pulling my T-shirt over my head.

"That's why we're called white. Where's Shuli?"

"She said she was gonna be here. Sorry you missed her."

"She all right?"

"Sure," she said, looking up at me. "You and me could be trouble, ya know." She ran off, turned back, and looked at me smiling.

I thanked Little Roy, Jude, and Buster, thinking about Marcella's comment. Tiny Marcella.

"You can call me Buster Blackie," he said, putting his shirt on. "Yur all right."

"You too," I said.

Reverend Williams made the two teams shake hands—funny handshakes, floppy handshakes, hair mussing, and lopsided grins. He thanked Andy and me—as in a sermon—for the courage we had in setting an example that whites and coloreds could get along just fine—his words. I had no idea or inclination about "setting an example." If I did, I probably wouldn't have come. Neither would Andy. "This is not Selma," Reverend Williams said. "Our town, even though it is still segregated—and that saddens me—encourages coloreds and whites to attend all kinds of events together. You are both welcome here anytime. Am I right, boys?"

"Yes, sir," Roy said.

Positive mumbles emanated like weak handshakes.

Arkie had Rozelle in a friendly headlock, giving him noogies.

"Hey, Rick. There's Shuli."

"Shuli?"

"Hey, Shuli. Come here," Arkie said. "Look who's here."

She came over cautiously, different than Arkie, whose every emotion shown clear. Even different than Hanna and Marcella. Shuli seemed suspicious. Cloudy. Hesitant.

"Baby Shuli?" I asked, smiling at my good friend.

"We ain't called her Baby Shuli in a while," Little Roy said. "She don't look like no baby, do she?"

"No," I said, except she was still Baby Shuli to me. But now she was Shuli, just plain Shuli—bobby socks, crinolines, pink sweater, and a baby blue ribbon in her hair. "You look real good, Shuli. It sure is good to see you."

222

"Seems we all growed up." She smiled awkwardly as if she wanted to leave. "Well, I gotta get back over there. We're dancin'."

"Yeah. Can I watch?"

"If that's what you wanna do."

I turned to Arkie as she walked away. "What's up with her?"

"Her boyfriend's that big mean-lookin' cat with the red T-shirt. He's a fighter, Ricky. She don't wanna get him jealous. You don't either."

"Maybe Andy and I oughta leave."

"Yeah, I think we should anyway," Andy said. "It sure was fun. Never been in a game like that."

"Dancin' Al's here," someone yelled. "DANCIN' AL!"

"Ya can't leave. Dancin' Al's here," Arkie said.

Everyone's attention focused on a colored guy with conked hair who was wearing pink, baggy, pegged pants with a gold watch chain that hung from his belt to his knees and swung from side to side as he walked. Big strides, shoulders rolling, lips puffed, smiling from coast to coast.

"Stay a couple a more minutes. Al's one cool cat."

Someone turned up the record player and a circle formed around Dancin' Al. A tall, skinny girl who couldn't keep still clapped, danced, and sang into the middle. Couldn't wait to dance. Hoppin' to the music. Yeah! Yeah!

Such moves. Dancing spontaneously, improvising, neither knowing exactly what the other was doing until that last split second when their bodies rhythmically got in sync. Spinning. Kicking. Twirling. Dancin' Al moved from one partner to the next. When a girl started dancing in the surrounding crowd, he simply moved over to her. All spontaneous, never rehearsed.

223

Everyone else clapped to the beat of the music. I totally forgot I was out of place. As often as my eyes drifted across the dance area, I saw Shuli, and she was looking at me.

Then "Maybellene." Chuck Berry singing. The music grew.

"Oh, Maybellene, Why can't you be true?
Oh, Maybellene, Why can't you be true?
You started back doin' the things you used to do."

Dancin' Al danced into the crowd—watch chain swinging, shoulders hunched, hands up, conked hair solid, all teeth—and came back with Shuli.

"A Cadillac rollin' on the open road
Nothin' will outrun my V8 Ford."

She was alive again, looking just like the Baby Shuli I knew. Big smile, large brown eyes. Hoppin' good fun.

"Cadillac doin' 'bout ninety-five.
She's bumper to bumper rollin' side by side."

It was like he wound her up then let her go as Dancin' Al drifted to another girl—Hanna this time—hopping in place, clapping her hands.

"Me, Crazy Al! Me!" yelled Marcella, skidoodle dancing into the circle.

Shuli stayed momentarily, dancing by herself. Then she pointed, motioned me onto the dance area, and I joined her. I didn't think or hesitate. I was in the groove. Gonna dance my brains out. YEAH! YEAH!!

* * *

Later that day Andy said I really looked great and all the kids were clapping and saying, "Go. Go."

I say "later that day" because the last thing I remember about Chuck Berry and "Maybellene" was this big, angry, colored guy in a red T-shirt busting onto the dance area. He hit me once in the side of the face, blasting sparks and bright streamers into a sea of blackness. I fell, then he kicked me in the face. No pain. None. And that's as much as I remember. Andy said he kicked me several times before he was dragged away, yelling that I was a honky son of a bitch trying to "get on my girl." I didn't hear that.

I awoke in the hospital that night with my head wrapped, held in place by some contraption and humming "Maybellene."

"First thing I saw that Cadillac grille
Doin' a hunered and ten gallopin' over that hill.
Offhill curve, a downhill stretch,
Me and that Cadillac neck by neck.
Maybellene."

Andy, Mom, and Dad were sitting beside the bed, and Mom's face was wet with tears. I tried to talk but couldn't. A sharp pain held my mouth closed. Dad handed me a wet facecloth. "Here, keep your lips moist with this, son. Don't try to open your mouth. It's wired shut. You really got yourself beaten up."

225

"Might be quiet around the house for a change," Andy added. I tried a smile. Even that hurt. "He was some mean sucker, that guy. After he started kicking you, I jumped on him. So did Arkie, Rozelle, Roy, the Reverend Williams, and a bunch of others. By then he'd stomped on your face. We pulled him away and he was screaming and kicking. I sure learned how to stream together filthy cuss words."

"Who was he?" I mumbled.

"Name was James Barrett," Andy said.

"Barrett?" I asked, grimacing.

"Yeah. He's Shuli's boyfriend. Cops got there just after we got you in the Reverend Williams' car and were heading to the hospital. That kid was dangerous, just like Arkie said."

"Now I want you both to listen to me," Dad said, in his best calm voice. "You boys didn't use good judgment in the first place. You never should have gone. You're white. There's too much going on in this country racially, especially now. That whole issue is a smoldering powder keg. And you boys need to stay away from it."

"Dad's preaching integration," Andy said.

"Well," he rolled his shoulders, "I may be preaching common sense."

"How long like this?" I asked, between clinched teeth.

"Six weeks," Dad said. "Now . . . ." He paused to think. "Hear me out. We won't say a word to anyone about this."

"Why not?" I asked, imagining a hero's welcome at Shortridge.

"Not yet." Dad continued. "I spoke to Reverend Williams an hour ago. Tomorrow morning we'll talk about it. Tomorrow morning before the Reverend Williams preaches. Before the police come here to get a statement from you, Rick."

"Why?" Mom asked.

"What's going on?" Andy.

"I'm not sure yet. Rick, don't talk to anyone tonight, under any circumstance. I'll have the nurse give you some pain medication. Tomorrow morning early, we'll talk. The recovery will be painful but you'll make it. You'll eat and drink through a straw. Probably miss a month of school. That's a bigger issue. In the meantime, you're a patient here for a week. Get some sleep, son. Do what you're told."

"I brought you a few comic books," Mom said, "and some magazines." She patted my shoulder and kissed me.

"Really cool fight," Andy said, rolling his eyes. "Wish you could have seen it."

"I mean it, Andy. No talking, no bragging. Nothing."

Before drifting off I thought about what Dad had said, about the fact that we never should have gone to the playground. I didn't feel that way. Keeping us away from the colored people didn't seem to be a solution; it was more of an irritant. But that was because I had spent a lot of time in the colored community. And Dad, for the first time, was bleaching out—siding with whites.

I don't know how long I slept but a nurse woke me, jiggling some tubes connected to my arm. It was dark. The machines around me blinked tiny specks of snow in moonlight, making the room glow. She saw my eyes open.

"How you feeling?"

I didn't know the answer to the question. "Maybellene?" I mumbled.

"No, Dorothy."

* * *

227

Early the next morning, after I sucked my breakfast through a straw, Dad and Andy returned with Georgey and the Reverend Williams.

"You're a brave man," Reverend Williams said.

"Why's that?" I mumbled.

"If I woulda seen that big buck a comin' at me, I woulda run so fast nobody catch me."

We laughed. It hurt. Georgey softly rubbed my shoulders.

"I never saw him, sir. I was too busy watching Shuli and dancing."

"Just as well." He put his hand on my arm. "This event can be bad for our community, Rick. Before the fight, I praised the Lord for the courage of you and Andy. Never in the far reaches of my mind did I think something like this could happen. Now I'm afraid we are gonna hafta deal with the newspapers and the politicians as well. God just ain't speakin' to me right now. It's like he hung up on me. I don't know why, and I don't know what to do."

We looked at each other in silence, like waiting for the sun to come out from behind a cloud. I was waiting for Georgey to say something, something that would fix everything. She didn't—just furrowed her brow and looked at Dad, who puckered his mouth and bounced his eyebrows.

Andy asked, "How is anyone gonna know?"

"Police report," Reverend Williams said. "It was filed that afternoon, after everyone had disappeared."

Dad asked, "Did they arrest the Barrett kid?"

"Not yet," Reverend Williams said. "They're still tryin' to find out who did it for sure."

Silence again.

Dad said, "I've been thinking about this a lot."

"What do you mean, Doctah?" The Reverend asked.

"Andy's right."

"Andy's right about what?" Georgey asked.

"Last night I had an idea just before the police called the house," Dad said cautiously. "What if no one did it? If it was an accident, it wouldn't interest anyone."

"Where you goin' with this, Doctah?" Reverend Williams asked.

Dad rubbed his eyes under his glasses and pinched his nose. "What if there wasn't a fight after all?"

"But there was," Andy said.

"Aren't you the one who just said, how are they going to know?" Dad asked. "What if Rick—say—collided with the pole that holds the basket, at full speed, driving for a layup? And all the kids there got in a flap trying to help him." He paused, thinking.

"But he didn't," Andy said.

"Confusion set in. A big crowd formed around Rick." Dad continued. "Somebody said, 'fight'—'cause that's what kids do—and it just got out of control. There never was a fight."

Quiet flooded the room. Georgey stroked her neck and picked her teeth with her tongue. Searching eyes bounced from Andy to Dad to Georgey to Reverend Williams to me.

"My son, Rick, slammed into a telephone pole that held a basketball backboard and broke his jaw. That is the image we must all put in our heads."

Still quiet. I heard a nurse blow her nose from the hallway and footsteps like raindrops passed down the hall. The room tingled with breathing and wondering—headshakes and scratches. Reverend Williams walked a slow circle— as a dog

229

would do before lying down—head bowed, chewing his moustache.

"Furthermore," Dad continued, "it was an integrated, social basketball game, something only Indianapolis can do. Andy was on one team, Ricky was on the other."

"That part's true, but Dad, everyone there knew there was a fight. You couldn't miss it." Andy said. "There had to be at least fifty people there."

"The police don't know that for sure. Reverend Williams, are you familiar with the name Emmett Till?" Dad asked.

"Every colored person in the United States is, Doctah."

"I'm not," I said between clinched teeth.

"You're not colored," Andy said.

"Zeke thinks I am."

"Hush," Georgey said, holding my hand, brushing her thumb back and forth.

Dad continued. "A few months ago there was a colored boy named Emmett Till—same age as you, Ricky. He was visiting his family in Mississippi. They say he whistled at a white woman—much less controversial than dancing with one. He was kidnapped, brutally beaten, one eye gouged out of his head and shot several times. His dead body was dumped in a nearby river. All that for whistling at a white woman. Murdered."

"Did they catch the guys?" I asked.

"They certainly did. Two white men. One was the husband of the woman. They were arrested for the murder, all but admitted it. Joked about it but lied on the witness stand."

"Justice was served," Andy said.

Reverend Williams said, "Justice was not served, Andy. They was tried by an all-white jury, found innocent, and let go. Walked. It underscored the fact that whites can kill Negroes and

230

Negroes can't do anything about it. A horrifying comment about this country."

I remembered Reginald's comment about it being safer among lions in Africa than being colored in this country.

"The reason I bring this up is simple," Dad said. "Here's this white kid that gets beaten up badly by a colored kid just for playing basketball in a colored neighborhood. Do you think the white community in this town is going to sit still for that? There are still Ku Klux Klan members here that are left over from their heyday in the '30s. There is a lot of racial tension that is just sitting, waiting for something to ignite it. Something just like this."

"We supposed to lie?" the Reverend asked.

"Through your teeth," Dad said, slowly to emphasize the point. "All of us. Never backing down. The police will probably be here sometime this morning to talk with you, son. They called the house last night and wanted to discuss what they called 'the fight.' I told them I wasn't aware of a fight, only an unfortunate playground accident. Rumors will swirl. We need to change the story as quickly, completely, and adamantly as we can. I'm certain most of the kids at the basketball game have already told others."

"You can bet this story has permeated that entire neighborhood," Reverend Williams said.

"So, the question is this: Can we stop it?" Dad said.

"We need to get Arkie and Rozelle and Roy and have them help," Andy said.

"I can speak to Arkie this morning, Rozelle and Roy, too," the Reverend said. "Every boy who played I will speak to, personally. I will go to their homes, talk with their parents.

"I must call Squiggy Daniels this morning—Roy's father. I'll call him from my office after we leave here. Maybe he'll meet me there. I'm sure he's deeply concerned."

"That's right," Georgey said. "Talk to him 'fore he develops his own plan."

"I called him last night," Reverend Williams said.

"What did he say?" Dad asked.

"Surprisingly calm, like he'd given up. He'll be interested in your story, doctor."

Georgey stood up and walked behind Dad, putting her hands on his shoulders. "This lyin's all right," she said, knowingly. "Sometimes we has to do wrong in order to do right. Just like God. Sometimes He allows bad things to happen, so He can do good things."

"You right, sister. Good can come out a this," the Reverend said, not entirely sure of his statement.

"We is gonna need to get more than Arkie and Rozelle and all them boys who played basketball," Georgey said. "We needs to talk to Shuli girl and Marcella and that dancin' boy, everone there. They's gotta understand that this lie can save lives."

"I'll start with Arkie," Reverend Williams said, gathering his composure. "I'll lay it at his feet before church. No, I think I'll go visit his family right from here. We can make this work. All of us."

"Lord, guide us," Reverend Williams whispered, quieter than he expected. He cleared his throat. "Lord, guide us. Give us the wisdom to make this seemingly wrong thing right. Reach Yur wondrous hands down into our community and move our minds and bodies like men on a chess board, puttin' us where we is s'posed to be. We knows that Satan is the opponent here, and we

232

knows he's clever. But You are the one great and powerful God. You will lead us and protect us. So we put this—this situation—in Yur hands. Amen."

I heard Dad talking with the nurse on his way out. "I notice the accident report here says 'fight.' It wasn't a fight, just a horrible accident. You'll need to change that. Don't want the hospital accused of misinformation, do we?"

"Oh, no. Thank you, Doctor. What did happen?"

"Rick went in for a layup at full speed and smashed into the pole that holds the basketball rim."

"Ouch!"

"I'll say. He oughta look where he's going."

"Kids."

By the time a policeman came to my room, it was afternoon. I had slept through their first attempt to see me. I was nervous but heavily medicated, with my mouth wired shut. I still had that contraption—Dad called it a halo—holding my head steady. The sergeant wanted to verify a fight. I told him I wasn't aware of any fight, just a heavy telephone pole I hit at full speed then blacked out. I asked him if he knew whether my team won or Andy's.

"Are you sure?" he asked.

"'Bout what?" I mumbled.

"The telephone pole."

"I should know." And feigned sleep.

The next morning Mom and Georgey showed up. I was sucking on my straw. Two nurses had removed the halo and I had a pulsating headache like a clock pendulum striking the sides of my head. Georgey brought me a Bible. Mom was dressed for school.

That morning I saw Mom and Georgey through different eyes—a little older and a little wiser. Two completely different women—a Radcliffe-educated, New England, classical pianist and a Bahamian holy woman—both mothers to me. I was alright with the idea of that. On one side was Mom's driving ambition, her immense creativity, and her blindness to reality. Yet somewhere in the back of her psyche was an awareness of what she should be doing. She did know but couldn't face it. On the other side was Georgey's selfless devotion to our family, her overwhelming spiritual drive, and stuck-in-the-earth fundamentals. Georgey knew how "her boys" should behave. There was no doubt in her mind. She knew what was missing, and she knew how to tell Mom and Dad. But could Mom and Dad believe a 50-year-old colored woman with a third-grade education? Each of these women was growing because of the other. Both were in pain because of that growth. At fourteen I didn't understand the complexity of that relationship; that kind of understanding could only come with time and retrospect.

Mom sat on one side of the bed, rubbing my hand and arm. "Oh, Ricky. I'm so sorry. I didn't even know what you and Andy were doing, where you were going. This is my fault." She sputtered. "If I were only a better mother. If I . . ."

Georgey put her hands on Mom's shoulders. "You hush up, darlin'. This had nothin' to do with you. This was God tapping all us on the shoulders, showing us what's important. Tellin' us how to act. Teachin' us through His lessons, painful lessons. I knowed the boys was gonna play ball with Arkie and some friends. It seemed fine 'cause it was at the church playground. Reverend Williams is always there."

"You think?" Mom was empty, vulnerable. For two days she had beat herself up for everything, looking and hoping for someone else to accept some of the blame. Her fingers of guilt, in her mind, pointed heavily at herself.

Georgey still had her hands on Mom's shoulders. She put one hand in mine. It was warm, like love. "I'm gonna pray now, you two. So, listen up." She spoke quietly.

"Dear God, comforter of all, most lovin' One, we is confused about what's goin' on. We needs Your compassion. We'd like to know where You is takin' us, how we is s'posed to feel. Our hearts is broke but our faith is strong. Heal this wonderful child. He is my boy. Use this tragic happenin' to bring him closer to You. And Lord, bless my sister, Missus Stoner, here. Soothe her wonderful giving heart. Show her Your way to calm her spirit. Come to us now, Great One. Be with us in this room. Start Your healing now as I touch the ones I love. Make my hands Your hands. I pray for Your attention. I know I got Your love. You are so wonderful but You are mysterious. Teach us Your way. And almighty God. I pray for the Doctah and Reverend Williams and Andy and little Arkie that this terrible thing that happened will not spark a bigger fire. Enough peoples are being hurt already. And I asks this plea and blessin' in the name of Your wonderful son, sweet Jesus Christ. Amen."

A shade of silence fell over the room. Then the vent cover on the heating duct came loose and rattled, opening our eyes.

"God just came in through the heating duct," I mumbled.

Mom put her head on Georgey's hand that held mine. "Georgey, Georgey, how you seem to shape our lives. I wish I understood it."

"That's God workin' in our hearts. Lovin' us from the inside out. Hallelujah!"

Georgey left the Bible on my bed with several strips of paper as bookmarks, mostly about David and how he overcame all sorts of things. "Some words you should read." All I could do was wink. It hurt to do that.

On Tuesday morning the pain arose in harrowing fashion. My teeth, my jaw, my temple—they all hurt. Dad and Mom visited in the morning, and I took a pain pill and went to sleep in the middle of our conversation. It was quiet when I awoke. I wondered what was going on with Dad's story. Did Andy and Reverend Williams get to enough people? What was going to happen? I picked up a comic book. Plastic Man. I loved Plastic Man and began reading it. I never got to page three. Not interesting. I was living in a different reality. Fantasy would have to wait. I longed for it, falling asleep with a straw in my mouth.

* * *

I dreamed I was jitterbugging and Chuck Berry was there, saying "Go, cat, go!" I heard "Maybellene" over and over, echoing like the reverberation of an empty garbage can tipped over my head. I was restless from pain and in and out of reality, but Chuck Berry was always there. He is so cool. One cool cat man—the way he plays that guitar and duckwalks across the dance floor. I danced with Baby Shuli—the happy Baby Shuli. I could smell her strong perfume like Miss Tildalayhu's. Ouch! Can't roll on my side. What was that guy's name again? James. James what? Barrett. I could still smell Baby Shuli. I heard her voice from another dream.

"Ricky, Ricky," she whispered, "I'm so sorry."

"Ouch." I opened my eyes. She sat by the bed, her head on my arm. When I put my hand on her head, she looked up at me—wet freckles on shiny cheeks, eyes overflowing, slippery upper lip.

236

"Baby Shuli?" I asked.

"Shh," she whispered. "I had to come. I had to apologize. This was all my fault."

"My jaw's wired shut. Can't talk too good." I blinked hard to clear my eyes and wiped them with my hand.

"I know. You don't need to talk. I'll talk and then I gotta go for I get caught."

"You don't need to apologize. Arkie warned me to stay away from you. I didn't think that guy—what's his name—Barrett was that crazy. I guess I was asking for it."

"No. I was so happy to see you. I felt such happiness when I watched you play basketball. You were still horrible," she smiled, "but you look so good bein' bad. Just like Arkie says."

"Hurts to smile. Don't make me smile."

"Sorry. I'm really sorry. When I told James I knew you, that we were old friends, he got real mad. Didn't think white folks should be in a colored neighborhood. I told him you was different. He started swearin'. Said all whites is the same. Then Arkie called me over. I couldn't say no. I just wanted to say hi and go back to James. Maybe go home. No harm done. Then Dancin' Al came and everone started havin' so much fun. And I watched you gettin' so worked up, bouncin', clappin'." She squeezed my arm. "Just like a blonde-hair, white-skin colored boy. I couldn't help but laugh, so when Dancin' Al moved on, I wanted to dance with you more than anything. It seemed all right. Oh, Ricky," she started crying. "I don't know what to do."

"It's alright, Shuli. I'll be fine in a few weeks." My "Fs" were difficult and I salivated as I spoke. I wiped my lips with a Kleenex.

"It's not aright."

"As long as no one knows it was a fight, it'll be alright. You know that, don't you?"

She wiped my mouth. "Oh, I know that, Ricky, but there's more to it."

"Dad says if it gets out that there was a fight between a colored and a white, it could cause a riot. You heard the story of Emmett Till down south and how he got murdered by white folks."

"Yeah, Arkie's told everone 'bout that. So has Reverend Williams." She paused. "It's James."

"What about James?"

"He's gone, Ricky. No one seen him since Saturday. Run off somewhere."

"Well, that's probably good."

"Ricky." She shook my arm.

"Ouch! Careful. What?"

She put her head on my chest and sobbed.

"What? What's happening?"

"I'm pregnant, Ricky."

"Pregnant?" It seemed like such a strange word. Inappropriate. It didn't belong with the word Baby Shuli—the one with the cotton underpants. Teddy bears don't get pregnant.

"Yes," she said.

"You sure?"

"Absolutely. And I'm scared, really scared. James is the daddy and I know he don't want me. Momma's gonna kill me."

"Oh God, Shuli. Oh, God. I am so sorry." I rubbed her back. We stayed that way for a while, our minds racing, hers going in one direction—motherhood—mine in another—sex. This was the stuff of adults. I didn't consider myself one. Shuli was a real woman, carrying a real child, holding me like I was an

238

adult. Pregnant women don't wear cotton underpants, have footraces, play hide and seek. How did "pregnant" get in there? So far from Plastic Man, where all I had to do was turn the page. I was fifteen, feeling years older.

She was gone when I woke up and I wondered if she were ever there at all or if it were a dream—such a thin line between "is" and "perhaps." "Pregnant." I said the word over and over. "Pregnant." I wondered what it really meant. Pregnant. A child. A 16-year-old mother. I blinked hard and squinted, trying to put it into perspective. Will she go to school? What about the prom? What will her friends think? Then I thought deeper. What would it mean to me? A child. I couldn't imagine becoming a father. How could Shuli become a mother? Her name was Baby Shuli. My friend, my playmate. The girl with the white cotton panties. A dream I once memorized. Now she would be Mother Shuli in soiled, cotton-print dresses and heavy-healed shoes. Soon to bloat and frown. Sex with James. That was easier to understand than motherhood, responsibility, raising a child, teaching him or her lessons of life. "Are you kidding?" I said aloud. "This isn't real. This is crazy." And sleep enveloped me again.

* * *

"Sure was nice of you to go to a hospital near my house," Arkie said, pulling a chair up to my bed.

I reached for my bottle with the straw in it—the only form of food I could eat. "Want some?"

"It's brown, man." He shook it. "Got small lumps in it. I'd never drink anything that looks like canal water. How you doin'?"

"I'm fine. Still a little swollen and sore here," pointing at my right eye and jaw.

"Can't you eat?"

"Yeah. Through this. Got wires in my mouth so I won't open it."

"Lemme see." He leaned forward and I tenderly pulled my cheek away from my gums. It hurt.

"Careful. Can you see 'em?"

"Will you look at that. Whoa. Man, yur breath smells really bad. They got anything here for that?"

"Really?"

"I'm not kiddin'. Like you ate the butt out of a dead dog or somethin'. Might need to sip some gasoline through that straw. 'Bout the only thing'll help."

"Oh, man. My girlfriend might come visit me."

"She won't stay long. Ouee!"

"You're kiddin'."

"No. Serious."

"Shuli was here yesterday," I said.

"Yeah, I told her where you was. Hope you didn't mind."

"No. Not a bit. Is everyone straight on what happened?"

Arkie sat cross-legged at the foot of the bed. "Everone. Everone knows the story. Most of 'em are scared 'cause of all the news about Emmett Till and the other bad stuff happenin' down South. This thing is goin' through school like a crazy man. One story—like a rumor— is about James stompin' on your face. The other is about you runnin' into the telephone pole. Folks would rather believe the telephone pole story."

"Is it true no one knows where Barrett is?"

"It's true. Rozelle done talked to his momma. Told her the new story. Made her feel better. He's got an uncle in Chicago, his momma said. Rozelle thinks he's there."

"You know about Shuli?" I asked.

240

"Know what?"

"She's pregnant."

"She what?" His legs uncoiled and he jumped to his feet. "Pregnant? Oh, my God, man."

"Yeah."

"James?" He paced the room.

"Yeah."

"She just turned sixteen a couple of weeks ago. What she gonna do?"

"Don't know."

A concerned look came over his face. "Her momma know?"

"Don't think so, Arkie. Can you hand me that water mug?"

"This one? Here, I'll put yur canal water over here." He shook his head. "Really love that girl, like my sister."

"Yeah, me too."

"Gonna be tough on her momma. They live with Shuli's gramma in a house 'bout the size of yur kitchen closet."

"Wish I could do something for her."

"Ain't nothin' to do." He looked around the room. "When you get outta here?" he asked.

"Tomorrow."

I slept fitfully that night, thinking about Shuli—thoughts strong like windstorms in my mind, swirling in dark futility. I imagined her in her house and telling her mother—her mom and her sitting on an old mohair sofa in the half dark, wrenching their hands, tears pouring down their cheeks in streams. How would they move forward and survive? With a sense of futility I realized there was nothing I could do.

Pregnant.

Momma Shuli.

The next morning after Dad picked up Georgey, they stopped at the hospital.

"My boy looks better each day I sees him," she said.

"He's certainly quieter. We might consider keeping his mouth wired shut permanently."

"Funny," I muffled.

"I have to coordinate your release for this afternoon. I'll be back."

Dad left and Georgey began organizing my clothes.

"You know Baby Shuli." A statement, not a question.

"Course I does. I don't know her mama well, but I hear she's real nice, too. Why?"

"Shuli's pregnant."

"Oh, mercy." Georgey's eyes never left the bureau drawer. She shook her head slowly. "How'd you find out?"

"She told me herself yesterday. The father is that guy who hammered me."

Georgey smacked her lips and moved her head slowly from side to side. "Gonna be tough for her and her momma. James is the boy's name, from out on Frog Island. He done run away to Chicago after the fight."

"How did you know that?"

"Whispers travel real fast. But I didn't know the poor child was pregnant."

"I'm not sure anyone knows. I think I was the first."

"Mercy, mercy," she said, then whispered, "Help this poor child, Lord. Mercy me."

"So, what'll she do?" I asked.

"Well, God will provide." She sniffed and wiped her eyes with her sleeve. "Oh, my. Well, it's different for coloreds than for whites." Folding my T-shirt.

"How's that?"

She looked at me with her ginger eyes. "Colored girls is raised to be mommas. White girls is raised to be wifes. Havin' a baby and no daddy happens more with us. Don't make it any easier. And it don't make it right." She wagged a final finger and pulled a tissue from a nearby box, wiping her eyes. "It's all so close now. My oh my, Lord."

I sat silently, watching her lay out my jeans, socks, belt, and weejuns.

"Did that happen with you, Georgey?"

"It did, darlin'. Long, long time ago. Before I worked for your daddy's fambly. I was Shuli's age, maybe younger. We lived in Eleuthera down in them Bahama Islands. My momma was dead. My daddy didn't have time to be a nursemaid, so he put me on a boat to Florida to be with my Aunt Clorina. That's where my son, Leon, was bornd." She smacked her lips. "Long time ago that was. Hand me that Bible, will ya?"

"Sure."

"D'ya read any of it?

"Sorta," I lied. "Where's Leon now?"

"He lived in Germany for many years. That's where he was stationed when he enlisted in the Army. He was 'round 18."

"Is he still there?"

"You certainly is nosey, but I'll tell you 'cause yur daddy and yur Uncle Gordon knows. About ten years ago Leon come home. He was in bad straits. Real sick, no money. I prayed real hard as my boy laid in bed. Finally, God told me to call yur daddy for help. Together we fixed up Leon. I did the prayin'

243

part, Doctah kept stickin' needles in poor Leon's behind. Then he worked for yur Uncle Gordon in Bloomington while he got hisself straightened out. He's doin' real fine now. A fine job with a fancy hotel in Chicago. He's the doorman there. I gets Christmas cards ever year. He calls ever once in a while. Visits from time to time. He accepted the Lord Jesus as his savior. What more could I ask for?"

"I'm glad he's OK, Georgey."

My father and his brother, I thought. Just like me and Andy and Spike. Uncle Gordon and his family lived about an hour south of us. He was very different from Dad in many ways—different but similar too. He, too, was quiet, unemotional, and stepped in without conditions and did what he had to do.

I tried to visualize Dad as a young boy like me. We probably wouldn't have hung around in the same social circles. Likely he was more like Andy—quieter, willing to stay in the background. Yet this is the same man who one day slugged some guy on the street corner for making an inappropriate racial remark to Georgey.

"You're a good boy, darlin'," Georgey said, drying her eyes with the back of her hand and exhaling a deep sigh of resignation.

"Dad—he's pretty cool, isn't he?"

"Real cool. Does he know about Shuli?"

"I didn't tell him."

She washed her hands in the room sink and dried them on the towel. "Don't tell no one I washed here. I'd get in trouble."

"Isn't that dumb?"

"I s'pose so." She folded the towel silently. "You Stoner men. I swear. Yur daddy, yur Uncle Gordon and yur granddaddy was that way, followin' the Great Commission. You'll be jes' like 'em. Jesus said when you do good—really good—you don't tell no one. If you brags or even want your name known, the good you did is sorta washed away by pride. Some day yur daddy might tell you about Leon. Don't you ask him."

"What's the Great Commission?"

"Jesus said to love yur neighbor as you loves yourself."

"Can you help her?" I asked.

"Shuli?"

"Yeah," I said. "I don't know how 'cause I'm pretty young."

"Yur gettin' older mighty fast. I can pray that God will tell me what to do."

I sat up in bed and thought about how different we were—Georgey and I. How would I react if Mom died and Dad sent me somewhere else to live? Or if I got someone pregnant and had to care for the baby. What would I do? How cloistered my life was, how well protected.

"What if He doesn't?" I asked.

"Then I ain't s'posed to meddle. God'll be at work on His own. Ya gotta believe."

Thirty-Seven

By late afternoon I was due to check out. My duffle bag was packed and I sat on the bed, X-rays in my lap, waiting for Dad. I heard somone walking down and the hall and I recognized the sound—Mike Dunbar. Unmistakably it was Mike. He wore little metal plates on the heels of his favorite loafers, the cordovan ones with polished Indian Head pennies. It sounded like the Gestapo approaching. The plates—clickers, we called them—complemented his swagger, his smile, and his wink. I breathed a sigh of relief that my earlier visitors, mostly colored, had departed.

"Hey Rick," he said, entering the room, "you look like you're ready to get out of here."

"Hi Mike. Yeah, Dad's gonna pick me up anytime now."

"Oh, I'm sorry. I would have been more than happy to bring you home. Should a called me."

"Dad's got other patients here."

"Got you wired, huh?"

I nodded. "Awful nice of you to visit."

"Dad told me, when I turned 16 and had my car, I should begin visiting friends who are hurting. Besides, we're brothers. Remember?"

I nodded.

"Are you in pain?"

"Yeah. I'm due a pain pill."

"Dad says hi. We prayed for you at dinner last night." He put his hand on my shoulder and looked in my eyes. "We're gonna get the niggers for this."

Recognizable words fled from my mind. Just a jaw drop—that didn't drop— was all I could muster.

"What are you doing playing ball with them, anyway? They're niggers. You're lucky to be alive. Now today is not the time or place for me to tell you what I've been hearing about you and your affiliation with coloreds in this town. We'll talk about that later. I just hope you've learned your lesson. You can't trust jigg-a-boos. They'll warm up to you, get to know you, then kill you. It's happening all over this country. My dad's got research and statistics. Large groups of colored men—mostly mulattos—down South are teaching methods of eliminating the white race. And white people are strangely disappearing across America, so much so the F.B.I. is investigating it, but quietly." I sat dumbfounded, words escaping my grasp. He continued. "They don't want the press to get a hold of it for fear of a major race war. They call these missing white people *los desaparecidos*—the missing ones—because they began disappearing first in South America. In the meantime, colored women are flaunting their stuff at white men, making them have sex, like that Queen of the Congo at the Fox. Then they get pregnant and bring another mulatto into the world—part of the colored race but smarter because they got white blood in them. Part chimpanzee and part man. These are scary times, man. You've gotta be on guard."

I had developed a bitter taste in my mouth and my head throbbed, not from pain but from anger—or was it confusion? I had to wonder if Mike was right. What if the Negroes were plotting to get rid of the white race, just like Hitler tried to eliminate the Jews ten years earlier?

"Mike, I've got a horrible headache. Can't really talk about it now. I'm on pain pills and they're making me sleepy." I lay back on the bed.

"Oh sure, I understand. We'll talk about it later." He pointed at me. "Think about it. You almost became one of those *desaparacidos*. That close." He showed a narrow space between his thumb and index finger.

And that was when Dad walked in. Mike turned around with a pleasant expression of confidence and amiability.

"Doctor Stoner, so good to see you again. Mike Dunbar." He reached his arm right out and forward, shaking Dad's hand warmly. I could always tell when Dad was impressed, as he was now. Mike was a big, good-looking, outgoing, young man filled with confidence.

"Good to see you again, Mike."

"Thank you, sir. Just stopped by to pay my sympathies and respect from everyone at the Corpse Club and especially from me and my family."

"Well, that's real nice of you, Mike."

"So, I'll see you when I see you, Rick."

In the car Dad said, "Something about that boy bothers me. I know he's your friend, but he's as smooth and dangerous as a water moccasin. As transparent as his father."

"He stopped in the hospital to tell me that my accident was part of a worldwide plot to eliminate the white race."

"Doesn't surprise me in the least."

I told Dad about the mulattos and the "missing ones" and how we should never mingle with Negroes.

Dad drove quietly for a few minutes. Then he calmly said, "That is the single most outrageous pile of crap I have ever heard. Ever since Hitler, the white supremacists have been

248

paranoid. They prey on the stupid and the insecure who gravitate toward any overt emotional trauma. If there is one ounce of truth in that hysterical concept, I'll—I don't know— I'll eat my hat. I'll eat your hat, too."

"Dad?"

"Yes, son."

"Remember the Queen of the Congo?"

He looked at me suspiciously. "Yes. Why?"

"I think I know who one of the guys was that raped her."

"You do? Who?"

"Mike Dunbar's father."

"You know, son, in high school Bob Dunbar was voted Most Popular. He was a great athlete, good looking. Just like his son. Always had the best of everything, the shiniest, the newest." He paused to let the similarity sink in.

"Here's what you don't know: He was pretty high up in the Klan ten years ago when white people bragged about it. He's probably still secretly involved. I know he's in the Northside Neighborhood Men's Club. If Bob was not there—and I'm sure he wasn't—he knows who was."

"Why do you think he wasn't there?"

"Bob's too smart. He's deeply religious and a serious member of the Klan. To many members the Klu Klux Klan is a spiritual group, not an impulsive, violent, and racist one. That poor young lady in the alleyway of the Fox said several men wore white hoods. Knowledgeable clansmen wouldn't desecrate their robe during a rape."

"Like a priest's robe, uh?"

"Yep. The Queen was brutally beaten and raped by a bunch of thugs. I sewed up a six-inch gash from her mouth to her ear and listened to her cry. I felt really sorry for her. And I must admit that Bob Dunbar did go through my mind. But a burlesque show on the edge of a colored neighborhood is not where you'd find Bob. Those men—and we know several of them—were neither religious nor bright.

"Mike told me the story. Didn't tell me it was his father. Said his father told him. But it was one of those stories that no one knew unless they were there."

"I had completely forgotten that you and Andy knew about that."

"Mike really hates coloreds. He carries a sawed-off shotgun in his car. Told me it was for niggers—his word."

"How did that make you feel?" he asked, shaking out a Pall Mall.

"Really uncomfortable."

Dad lit his cigarette and inhaled. "It might be time that you stay away from him. There isn't one positive thing about that family."

"I will. Before he told me about the Queen of the Congo, I thought he was the coolest cat in high school."

"I'm sure he is. And it's a sad statement of our times that people agree with you. Stoners, though, are not cool cats. We drive old, dirty Plymouths."

"And Mom doesn't own a fluffy pink sweater."

"Thank God for that."

I had nothing else to say.

Thirty-Eight

Gospel music happened to Mom like fluency in a foreign language happens to certain people. First she learned the vocabulary and verbs, then she learned the accent, then she practiced it until something in her brain clicked, and then it took over. She had become bilingual—snap!—just like that. It happened early one morning during her warmups. Bimusical. Suddenly I heard a spontaneous finger roll—a vamp—with a distinct rhythmic beat and a few bars of "Precious Lord"—just before Chopin—followed by a "Hallelujah—yes!"

Mom had turned colored.

* * *

"Lilly," Miss Tildalayhu said, standing at the piano and carefully removing her lovely hat, "would you consider helping me with the choir at church?"

Mom's immediate thoughts: No way, Tilly. Absolutely not. I teach. I give concerts. I have a weekly radio show. I have a piano student. I give voice lessons to you. I have three boys that, according to Georgey, need more of me. I can't take on one more thing. After the Gloria Hufnagel disaster I have learned to say no.

No.

*   *   *

The church was packed. This was a very special day—a white woman would accompany the church's blessed voice, Miss Tildalayhu. Dad, Andy, Spike, and I sat to one side trying to be inconspicuous—like an elephant in the bathroom. Women wearing brightly colored dresses that barely touched their heavy ankles and straw hats with colorful felt bands and giant hairpins outnumbered men three to one. The few men were as indistinguishable as a clone of aspen—black suits, pressed, white shirts, and dark neckties. Little girls with tightly braided ponytails held by pastel ribbons ran in and out of the service, dressed in frilly short dresses or flowered prairie dresses and white ankle socks with lace cuffs. Far different than the Presbyterian Church just three miles away. A different world.

Reverend Williams rose slowly from his chair by the choir. He looked tired, whipped, struggling to smile. The happenings of the past six weeks had taken their toll. "Galloping rumors," he called them. But many of the colored community knew what really happened on the playground. They knew that their pastor had lied to them for a good reason, but it was still a lie with no real explanation. The Reverend Williams knew he had to talk to his flock and explain why God said it was alright to lie.

"It is the Lord's purpose," the Reverend Williams said, deep into his microphone, letting the sound resonate. "His plan!"

"The Lord's plan," the congregation repeated. "Yes! HIS purpose."

"To love one another."

"Yes!"

"Our brother Martin Luther King STRUGGLES down in Alabama. He KNOWS the Lord's plan."

"Praise the Reverend King."

"There is such INJUSTICE in the world. So many travails. BAD SITUATIONS; a world of tensions, yes! And frustration. VIOLENCES and UP HE-VE-AILS. We don't know which way to turn."

"Which way," from the congregation.

"Yes!"

"Help us, Jesus."

He carried his Bible in one hand, a finger marking the reference for his sermon.

"This mornin' I want to talk about . . ." He paused. "LYING. L-y-i-n-g. Lyin'. Now I want you to bear with me as I get to that subject."

Occasional "Yes" from the congregation and whispers of anticipation. They knew.

He lowered his voice. "Rahab . . . I say, Rahab."

"Rahab."

"Do you know of Rahab?" Reverend Williams asked.

"From the Bible."

"God's Holy word."

"Yes!"

"RAHAB WAS A PROSTITUTE." A gasp. "Yes. A prostitute in the time of Joshua and ya'll know what Joshua fit." He smiled.

Laughter then, "Joshua fit the battle of Jericho."

"Yes, Jericho. Joshua was to lead the Lord's army into the PROMISED LAND by way of Jericho."

"Hallelujah!"

"But there was many obstacles and travails. You see, Jericho had its own king. The people even had their own Gods, false idols. Before Joshua advanced against Jericho, he sent two spies into the town to check out the situation. To get THE LAY OF THE LAND. Now where do you think those spies stayed?" He held his Bible high.

"It says here in Joshua 2, verse 1." He opened the Bible, put on his heavy, horn-rimmed glasses, and read, "They arrived at an inn operated by a woman named RAHAB who was—and it says right here—'a PROSTITUTE!' Joshua's spies stayed at a HOOCHIE-COOCHIE HOUSE. Well, some army folks within the town learned that two spies from the LORD'S army were frequentin' Rahab's Inn--RAHAB'S HOOCHIE-COOCHIE HOUSE. Before the town's army got to her place of establishment, she hid those spies. She stuffed 'em under some brush on her roof. She risked her life because Rahab believed that THEIR GOD WAS THE SUPREME GOD OF HEAVEN. Let me repeat that. She risked her life because Rahab believed that their God—JOSHUA'S GOD, THE GOD OF MOSES—WAS THE SUPREME GOD OF HEAVEN. SHE KNEW."

"Praise the Lord!"

"Right here in her heart, Rahab knew," he said, patting his heart. "Yes, Rahab knew. And when the town's officials asked where the spies had gone, SHE LIED. RAHAB TOLD A KNOWING LIE."

"Yes. She lied." A voice from the congregation said.

"She said, 'They left not too long ago.' They left the hoochie-coochie house and had headed back on the road out of town, 'right down there,' she said. The spies were SAVED BECAUSE RAHAB LIED." He paused and wiped his forehead with a handkerchief. "She lied to further God's plan and purpose. Let me say that again. SHE LIED TO FURTHER GOD'S PLAN AND PURPOSE. SHE LIED." He tucked the Bible under his arm and slowly walked the width of the church platform, his head down in deliberation. He smacked his lips. Then he turned to the congregation and said, "Sometimes God asks us to do things we just don't understand. But if we believe in our God, and we know we are furthering his purpose, then we do what we believe is best. Rahab lied to protect God's army. She became one of God's children and was mightily rewarded by God." He slapped his Bible closed.

"Hallelujah!"

"Yes."

"Rahab, the prostitute, became an ancestor of our Lord, Jesus Christ. Rahab is the great, great, great, great, great, great grandmother of our Lord Jesus Christ."

"Great, great, great."

"We, too, will be rewarded whenever we act to further God's purpose."

"Yes."

"You see, God wants us to love one another. Each of us to love each of us. It is what the Lord wants."

"Tell us, Lord!"

"Speak to us!"

"He wants us to love our brothers. Love 'em colored and love 'em white," the Reverend said.

"Yes!"

"To love our brothers no matter what color our skin is. Do you hear me?"

"Hallelujah!"

"Hallelujah!"

"Hallelujah!"

"Hallelujah!"

"Yes!"

Reverend Williams spoke deep into the mike, "It is the Lord's desire."

"Amen to that."

"To love one another."

"Yes! Amen, Reverend Williams."

"This mornin' we got the blessins of the voice of Sister Miss Tildalayhu to help us praise the Lord's name today."

"Yes. Praise her name, Lord. Lord Jesus."

Mom sat at the piano, her back to the congregation. It was time to give Miss Tildalayhu a chord.

"Lord, plant my feet," Miss Tildalayhu sang, "on a higher ground."

"In each of our hearts it must be our desire to be like the Lord," Reverend Williams shouted. Then he looked at Mom and winked. God's word was given. I could feel the excitement in her mind and body as she released herself from years of musical discipline and surrendered her fingers to the piano keys mentally and physically. The introduction to the song was hers. Nine bars—heavy chords setting a distant rhythm for the music. The choir swayed from side to side as Mom played. She was one white woman in a Negro choir of fifty, with a colored preacher walking across the front of the church.

Mom motioned with her head and the choir sang, "It's my desire . . . to be like the Lord." Perfect enunciation, perfect rhythm.

Mom was beginning a journey into a new sound, becoming part of the music with improvised chords and notes that enhanced the emotion.

The choir continued, "It's . . . my . . . desire
To be . . . like . . . HIMMM."

256

Mom repeated some chords. This time they sounded even more rhythmic—like fancy garnishes on a $100 dinner plate. She watched the choir sway.

"It's . . . my . . . desire," they sang again.

To be . . . like . . . the Lord."

The choir swayed harder and some members raised their arms.

"It's . . . my . . . desire

To be . . . like . . . HIMMMM."

I could see a small woman from the front row, her arms raised high as she sang a single high penetrating note: "Himmmm."

Then Miss Tildalayhu stepped forward and leaned into the microphone. The opening sound of her voice sparkled so clear and bright that it was as if she were singing only to me—to my heart.

"It's my desire," she sang.

Mom's playing grew spontaneous, filled with emotion.

The choir responded, "To show that I care."

Mom again—becoming more soulful, more moving.

Miss Tildalayhu once again leaned into the microphone, "To be a friend."

"To reap my full share," the choir answered.

"Till the end," Miss Tildalayhu.

"Though it is so rare," the choir.

"To be a friend," Miss Tildalayhu.

The sheet music fell from the piano but Mom, her eyes closed, was unaware. She didn't need it. The music was inside her. Many of the women were in the aisles now, clapping and singing with the choir then silent when Miss Tildalayhu sang.

"You in my bosom."

The piano had become part of the choir—one unit of music. Mom's shoulders lifted as she looked at Miss Tildalayhu, who smiled and nodded, then sang, "To be a soldier."

The piano answered.

Then the choir, "For His great call."

Everyone, including Mom, sang, "To give my life as we believe. It's my desire. It's my desire to be like Himmmmmmm."

At the end of the song, the congregation was on their feet. Everyone. Even Dad. Reverend Williams stepped close to the microphone. "Now before the final blessing let me bring out our family back here now. Sister Beloved, OUR Miss Tildalayhu who wears the coat of many colors. And our SPECIAL DAUGHTER, Miss Lillian Stoner, bringin' our races together. Hallelujah for that and praise the Lord Jesus. And all God's people said . . ."

"Amen."

"Mornin' Ricky." Shuli glowed, walking out of the church. Someone said that a pregnant woman glows twice as bright with an extra life inside, and I could see it deep within her eyes—like four eyes looking back, a glowing candle with an extra wick.

"Miss Georgella," she said, as Georgey motioned her over.

"Come here, darlin'," said Georgey, putting her arms around Shuli softly, scooping up a bundle of love. "We is gonna fill you and that child with the love of Jesus. All us."

"Thank you, Miss Georgella. Thank you so much."

"If you walk this ole spook home, Zeke say he drive you to yur house."

"I'd love that," Shuli said. "Bye, bye, Ricky. Say hi to yur daddy."

Thirty-Nine

I was unhappy that Karen Coolidge never visited me in the hospital—no, I was angry. I thought that a guy's girlfriend should be by his bedside. She gave Mom a card for me that read, "Get Well. Love ya, Karen." Mom said that I shouldn't be disappointed. After all, Karen was just a girlfriend, not a wife. When I got home from the hospital, I saw a list of people who called or sent cards. Mom was first on the list. Andy added to it. Spike wrote his own name with the k backward. Georgey wrote "God." I think that was her writing. Baxter, Jim, Arkie, Marcella, Reverend Williams but no Karen. Buster Blackie and Willie Rice, but no Karen. Even Hanna, but no Karen.

Besides my family and Mike, the only people who visited me were my colored friends. Not Karen. After Shuli, Karen didn't seem like a flesh and blood person, but instead a paper doll with changeable clothes, always looking ironed. Always sitting on the shelf with her legs crossed. I never imagined her as a mother or getting pregnant. I thought about sex for a while—sex with Karen, sex with Shuli, sex with one of those girls in a girly magazine (the one I stole from the drugstore), sex with Mary Lou from the filthy tunnel wall. I wasn't sure I knew exactly how to do it, but at least I was ready, tapping my wallet and remembering Mike's gift.

Baxter dropped by after school one day, shortly after I got home from the hospital.

"Were you awake when they wired your jaw?"

"Nope."

"Cool, man. Cool."

The "white" side of the rumor was very much intact. Baxter described it well. "A basketball game in the colored section of town with Negroes from Attucks High School. Cool! You and Andy took your life in your own hands, man. I heard Oscar Robinson was there!"

"You mean Oscar Robertson?"

"Yeah."

"Who told you that?"

"Jim. Said half of the Attucks team were there practicing for next spring's state championships."

It hurt to laugh. "Not true, Bax. Just eight colored kids, Andy and me. The game was supervised by a colored minister and played in a church playground that I helped build. There were two guys who play for Attucks. One was reserve varsity. The other was JV."

"Still," he said, "colored guys from Attucks. Cool, man!"

"It really wasn't a big deal, Bax. It was like one of our basketball games."

"'Cept there were a bunch of niggers against you." His eyes bugged out big.

"Bax, I learned something real important out there."

"What's that?"

"Don't ever call a colored person a nigger. It's the worst thing you could say."

"Well, you know."

"No, I don't know. I'm serious. It's a way to really start trouble. It shows disrespect for an entire race."

"I'd never say it to their face. Geez, they'd kill me."

261

"I can't say I'd blame them. OK?" I surprised myself.

"Sure. Didn't mean to be bad or, you know."

"All right."

"You think I could play the next time?"

"I think that's a good idea. I'm sure many of the colored guys would like it."

"Can they come here?"

"No."

"Why not?"

"We'd probably lynch one before the game was over."

Forty

Since Gloria's demise, I had to revert to standard barbers working on my hair, my signature social statement. Dad recommended Sonny, who cut hair in his office building—Ann Sue's husband. He had no idea how to handle a long, blonde flattop brushed with two palm brushes, and it took two weeks to repair that damage. Then Mike's girlfriend, Patty, told me about Jake & Ed's Barber Shop on the north side of town near the Northside Neighborhood Men's Club, where we had Hell Night a few months earlier. It was wedged into a small strip mall where there was a drugstore with a lunch counter, a five-and-dime, the First National Bank, a dry cleaners and Jake & Ed's, shaded by a canopy that hung over a long walkway lined with wooden rockers. It was a bustling little mall where neighbors met, shopped, and napped.   Jake & Ed's, according to Patty, specialized in "flattops, Balboas, long pompadours, haircuts for cool cats." That's what she said and that's what it said in the window. They cut Mike's hair.

So, I hitchhiked north on Highway 491. The barbershop was packed—mostly men around Dad's age gossiping and talking loudly. The waiting area was also filled, so Jake (or Ed) asked me if I'd mind sitting outside in "our extended waiting room. Nice old rockers and I'll call you in a while."

I did some homework I had brought as customers left and others sat outside. The window to the barbershop was open, and voices from a few loud men, smoking and swearing around an inside table, got my attention.

"What a tough break."

"Yeah, he lost everything."

"It was the clap that started it all."

The clap? I startled. I wanted to turn around and look in the window.

"One of the worst cases I ever heard of. So, without knowing it, he passed it on to Marci. She got really sick and ended up in the hospital."

"Oh my God! What was he thinking?" another man asked. "If I contaminated my wife with VD, she'd take everything I own, move to Florida, and cut my you-know-whats off."

"Florida? My wife would point blank shoot my ass dead."

"Gonorrhea turns into syphilis if you don't take care of it early."

"That's what I heard."

"Then it was like the Lord was out to punish him: Marci left him, then the IRS went after him and eventually shut him down."

"Heard it was a nigger agent."

"Don't know about that. But, hell, he's lost everything. Moved back to Anderson with his parents."

"A real pity. Ned was a great guy. Had a swell family."

They lowered their voices to a whisper.

"A lot more to it than that."

"Yeah."

Jake poked his head out the door. "Hey, kid, you're next."

I thought of leaving, but went inside anyway. The men I overheard sat around a card table in the corner of the shop.

"I'm Ed," the barber said brushing my hair with his hands. "I'd kill for a head of hair like this."

"I'll say," Jake agreed, and everyone in the shop stopped talking and stared at me.

"You just need a real careful trim," Ed said.

I nodded as the group of men picked up their conversation.

"Heard a strange story from Jack Wallbrown last night at dinner," a gruff-voiced man said. "You know Jack. He's a downtown cop. Seems a white boy got injured down near Frog Island a while back."

I froze, staring straight ahead.

"What in the world was a white boy doing on Frog Island?"

"I guess it was a basketball game."

"That doesn't make any sense. A white boy'd have to be pretty stupid to get into a ball game with a bunch of niggers in a nigger section of town. Sounds pretty stupid."

"I agree, but Jack said it was a fight. A nigger beat the crap out of this white boy."

"A fight. Well, that's different."

"Niggers beating up one white kid?"

"Hold on, now. Jack said he had to change his report to say it was just an accident. Guess it wasn't a fight after all."

"What made him think it was a fight?"

"A fight?"

"Yeah, an eyewitness—a nigger preacher said so. Then the story changed."

You comb this with a brush?" Ed asked.

265

"Two palm brushes," I answered, terrified by the conversation from the corner.

From the other side of the shop: "What's the white kid say? The one that got hurt."

"He says he accidentally ran into the post that holds the backboard."

"That's absurd. Who is this kid, anyway?"

From Ed's chair: "You ever wear a stocking cap to bed at night? That'll train your hair real good."

My mind was confused. "Excuse me?"

"A stocking cap or a woman's nylon stocking. Wear it to bed at night. It'll really train your hair."

"I've never done that, thanks," I said. Still listening to the background, my neck tightened when I heard Dad's name mentioned.

From the other side of the shop: "Yeah, Wayne Stoner's boy," a man at the table said.

"Well, say no more. Doctor Stoner, this town's biggest nigger lover. He has a brother down in Bloomington, a lawyer, also involved with coloreds."

"The Doctor and his highfalutin' wife allow their boys to mix with coloreds."

From Ed's chair: "Who taught you to brush your hair this way?" Ed asked. I heard only snippets of the conversation from the corner as I replied.

"A girl I know at the beauty school—Gloria was her name." .

"Man, she knows what she's doing."

Then more from the other side of the shop: ". . . named Daniels. First name is Squiggy, a real arrogant nigger if there ever was one."

"Friend of ours in Bloomington told me Squiggy finished up his law degree down there. Might be moving back to town."

"We'll keep our eye on him. He'll make a mistake and we'll be there."

"I tell you, this town is slowly falling apart."

"You mean the nigger problem."

"Yeah. Jews, too. Someone was telling me that the Jewish Country Club's membership has doubled in the last two years."

"Don't your wives have things for you to do at home?" Ed finally asked the men.

"Just trying to improve our country," one answered.

"Well improve it somewhere else, will ya?"

The men nodded and smiled and walked out of the shop, talking about their church, a daughter in the finals of the spelling bee, the NAACP.

"Sorry 'bout that kid. Just a bunch of men from the Neighborhood Club. Every other week they come here for haircuts together and pollute everyone's mind."

I smiled politely.

"How's a buck sound?" Ed asked.

"More than fair," I answered.

Forty-One

Finally, Karen showed up. I checked the calendar—four weeks from the time of the accident. I tried calling her several times but she was always somewhere—cheerleader practice, drama club, 4H, class officers' meeting. Couldn't stay long, she said. Her mother brought her and waited in the car.

We sat in Dad's den.

"I'm so sorry about your accident," she started, shaking her ponytail into place. "How long before you get the, you know, wires taken out?"

"Next week," I said, hoping my breath didn't smell as bad as Arkie said.

"Well, it was so unfortunate."

"It was an accident. Things like that happen."

Silence enveloped the den. I watched her, not liking what I saw—pretty, but superficial; closed doors; falsies and girdles.

"I guess so," she responded. "Dad says you spend a lot of time in—what he calls—Negroland."

"Negroland. I never heard that." Something was happening. Like a lingering odor from an old dog on the floor.

"It's true, though. I hear your colored maid used to take you home with her."

"Karen," I interrupted, "what in the world are you trying to tell me?"

268

"Well, Mom and Dad think I shouldn't be going out with you. Especially since this happened."

"Mom and Dad, huh?"

"Well, it's not like we've been seeing each other a lot lately."

"Well, that's true. Sorry about my being in the hospital."

"You're being disrespectful."

"So we better start seeing other people. Is that where you're going?"

"Yes, Mom and Dad . . ."

"Going out with a greaser who plays basketball in colored neighborhoods does not look good for you?"

"You said it, not me."

"Let me walk you to the door."

We passed through the dining room and into the kitchen, where Georgey was making a meatloaf.

"Georgey, this is Karen Coolidge," I said. "Her parents want her to break up with me because I spend too much time with Negroes."

"How very nice to meet you, Karen," Georgey said pleasantly. "How attractive you look today."

Karen ran out the kitchen door. Leaped into her mother's baby blue convertible.

I stood silently watching the car drive down the driveway.

"You all right, darlin'?" Georgey asked after a minute.

"Never been better." It was a Chevy, that baby blue car, and matched the bows in her ponytail.

"She weren't good enough for my Ricky."

"I guess I never really knew her," I said, shutting the door.

"You liked what she was, not who she was. What she was, was popular and cute. Who she was don't exist yet."

"No Bible story for me?" I said.

"Nope. I'm jes' proud of my boy for growin' up the way he has—wires in his face and all."

Forty-Two

Attorney Arthur "Squiggy" Daniels drove a 1942 Ford coupe—lima bean green—and Little Roy called it "The Bean." It was cared for by his brother Benny, part owner of the Phillips 66 gas station with Wilbur Johnson, Arkie's father. For Squiggy, that car was a no-nonsense symbol of honesty, hard work, and no extravagance.

Those involved in civil rights in Indianapolis knew Squiggy. Mom and Dad's generation watched him progress from menial jobs to college and law school and read about his fiery outbursts, arrests, and involvement in civil rights issues. He once told Dad that he (Squiggy) was the most famous failure in town. He reminded me of a big brown sea lion with his massive bullneck with black creases and shoulders as broad as Indiana Avenue. He wore light brown suits, white shirts, and a red tie and, like his son Little Roy, he sweat profusely—light brown suits with dark brown sweat stains and a wet upper lip. He was three years younger than Dad, the same amount that Dad was younger than Uncle Gordon, and they went to Shortridge High School in the 1930s.

Uncle Gordon told Andy and me that Squiggy was an activist from a family of activists (a word Dad had taught us). His grandfather came to Indianapolis on the Underground Railroad, graduated from college and law school, and never left. He became the Negroes' Negro lawyer. Squiggy's father created an organization called Safe Havens in the early '20s, an underground information source for Negroes to combat the efforts of the Klu Klux Klan. He served on the city council until his death in 1942. That was when Squiggy and Dad started talking more often—first remembering old times at Shortridge, then discussing racial inequalities in town. After his father died, Squiggy immediately ran for his seat on the council.

"That election was a disaster," Dad said. "Squiggy had no idea about protocol or manners. He was just loud and forceful. That didn't go over well, so his bid was soundly shot down. That same year he was drafted into the Army, as was I. He returned from the war a different man. A Purple Heart. More patient, eager to learn."

"Did you shoot anyone in the war?" Spike asked.

"No, son, but I gave a lot of penicillin shots at the VA hospital in Mississippi."

He and Mom shared a look.

* * *

Squiggy was a fast learner and took heed to Dad and Uncle Gordon's advice that he needed to become a legitimate, ethical representative of his people, not an ill-informed hothead. He doubled his course load in school and began studying the Negro history of Indianapolis. He began writing and the colored newspapers in town ran his editorials on voting rights, public accommodations, healthcare, housing, education, and employment. Then the white papers began running condensed articles of what he had penned.

One piece showed that the population of colored people in our town increased by over 70 percent over a 10-year period and included a small class of Negro professionals—doctors, lawyers, teachers, and such—while the white population had increased by 28 percent. The article also covered the activities of the Ku Klux Klan and lynchings. That fine piece of reporting cost Squiggy his car—burned to a crisp and left smoldering in an alley. That is when he bought "The Bean."

It was of great concern to the Klan that the Negro population was growing so fast. They must have feared that the colored population would "gang up" on the whites, just as they had done to the Negroes. The white establishment pushed to be more effective—more political than physical—using any tactic to make sure that Negroes remained a quiet, subservient minority with no political power.

Because Dad seemed to be "in-the-know" regarding local politics and hobnobbed with the downtown lawyers and other professional men, he was a virtual storehouse of civil rights happenings and brewings in our town. Uncle Gordon knew the Oreo lawyers and the bleached-out white lawyers. They both saw a power in Squiggy that could help diffuse the racial climate in our town, but he needed self control. His eagerness to help and become involved was offset by a lack of what Uncle Gordon called "legitimacy."

As Squiggy contined to be rebuffed and ignored, his resolve intensified. His final "straw" was losing the right to represent the families of Frog Island who desperately needed a city sewage system. That was when he hit the guard at the courtroom door with his attaché case and spent two months in jail. When he was finally released, it was clear he needed a law degree and a big dose of patience.

"Have to learn to dot my i's and cross my t's," Squiggy said casually, one morning in our kitchen with Dad and Uncle Gordon.

"And keep your voice down," Uncle Gordon said.

"And no name calling," Dad added.

273

Squiggy slowly wagged his head, wiped a new tide of sweat from his forehead, and shook out a Chesterfield. "Got a light, Doc? Left mine in the car."

"Think so," Dad said, reaching into his shirt pocket and handing Squiggy a matchbox.

"The Fox Burlesque," Squiggy read aloud. "Remember that colored girl who they say was nearly killed there a few years back?"

"Now that's a vicious rumor, Squiggy. And it isn't true. I examined her. She was sick as a dog. Jerry and I put her on a bus."

"Wish I believed ya, Doc. I know you examined her and I know you and Mr. Jerry put her on a bus. But, just so you and Gordon don't think I'm stupid, I know her name was Celeste Arthur, and one of the guys that raped her damn near ripped the entire side of her face off. She's changed her name since then and I hear she might be back in town." He looked patiently at Dad and Uncle Gordon over the rim of his glasses.

"Seriously?" Dad asked.

"As far as I know, from someone who would know. And all them folks that mysteriously carried the clap are the ones who did it."

Dad looked at his fingernails and bit his lip.

"Mary somethin'-or-other," Squiggy added.

* * *

It was the little things that got in Squiggy's way. After he graduated from law school and passed his bar exams, he represented a colored hairdresser. She wasn't allowed to use the elevator in a hotel in order to reach her customer's room. He

274

sued the hotel on her behalf. The Marion County Superior Court ruled that because the hairdresser was not a guest of the hotel herself, she had no right to use their elevator. The score: City 1. Squiggy 0. Little things.

Squiggy sued the Applegate Ice Cream Parlor for refusing to serve a Negro customer. He lost the suit when the court ruled that an ice cream parlor was not technically an "eating establishment" and so was not covered by the civil rights law. Score: City 2. Squiggy 0. Little things.

"Dot my i's, cross my t's and think like the Klan."

And so it was on July 8, 1954, that attorney Arthur Daniels, on behalf of the citizens of Frog Island and the NAACP, filed a suit against the city of Indianapolis and the Indianapolis Board of Health for purposefully and willfully subjecting certain citizens to unnecessary exposure to disease and sickness and endangering the lives of the residents of Frog Island. It violated the Civil Rights Act of 1875 and the Board of Health bylaws that included equal treatment of citizens. He called for the removal of the present members of the Board of Health—all of them—and two members of the city council. Attorney Daniels would be assisted by Charles W. Copeland, Esq., attorney for the NAACP headquarters in Atlanta and endorsed by the Rev. Martin Luther King, Jr.—who personally agreed to appear at the court, if necessary.

The suit called for the immediate drafting of sewage plans and construction to begin within six months. It also called for free medical care for those citizens of Frog Island "so deemed to have been infected by the adverse conditions according to a registered physician of the town." Dad memorized that clause because he was that registered physician.

The legal action started out the way it always had: First, the lawyers for the town refused to recognize Squiggy on the basis that he was a "hardened criminal, having done time in a penitentiary." Second, the court ruled that the decision to bypass Frog Island had already been made. Case closed. Then the court banned the *Indianapolis Recorder* (one of the local colored newspapers) from attending the hearings on the basis that Squiggy Daniels was a reporter for them and his articles on racism in the town were inappropriate and inaccurate. Only the two white newspapers were admitted.

The night before the initial hearing, Squiggy and his team convened in our living room—Uncle Gordon, Dad, Squiggy, Dave Moriarity, and Charlie Copeland. They met to anticipate the court's attempts to block Squiggy's cases, especially the Frog Island issue. Squiggy's stint in jail was a misdemeanor and there was no law on the books banning an individual convicted of a misdemeanor—having paid his debt to society and being a member of the Indiana Bar Association—from suing or being sued. For that matter, there was no law banning any kind of criminal from representing any citizen, as long as the attorney was a member in good standing of the Indiana Bar Association. That one was easy.

The team knew that the attorneys for the town would claim the case was closed, but Squiggy had made certain that the judge's statement of "taking the issue under advisement in a year" remained on record, to show the case was still open.

That Squiggy was a reporter for the *Indianapolis Recorder* was hardly a point, since he was never paid by the paper nor punched a time clock. He was no different than the attorney for the town who had written several op-ed pieces.

Squiggy's research revealed that the owner of the engineering firm for the sewer project was related to the town manager. Furthermore, the original project was never put out for bid, leaving only one firm to engineer the effort—the manager's brother-in-law and member in good standing of the Northside Neighborhood Men's Club.

Squiggy's opening statement read: "I am here at the request of Dr. Martin Luther King Jr., who is aware of the injustices regarding the population of Frog Island. I have here statements from five physicians reporting on the health of the citizens of Frog Island. I have here the records of the construction on the sewage bypass, begun last year and now 38 percent over budget. The engineering firm is owned by the brother-in-law of our city manager. And I have here a petition signed by every single resident of Frog Island pleading for justice. Every single one of them. Pleading!"

The judge tested the waters. "Do you feel there are other—as you say—injustices that I should be aware of?"

"Is there a reason the *Indianapolis Star* is here and *The Recorder* is not?" Squiggy asked.

"It appears *The Recorder*'s credentials have been forged."

"How so, your honor?"

"It has been brought to our attention."

"By whom?"

"That information is not readily available."

"Your honor," Squiggy said quietly, "I am here with Attorney Charles Copeland from the NAACP headquarters in Atlanta. We have requested that reporters from *Time* and *Life* magazines attend this hearing. They are here. Mr. Johnson and Mr. Thorkilson—sitting in the back there. Everything that is said will be a matter of public record. Are you really prepared for this case?"

Finally, and after many threats by the judge and white lawyers, the court allowed that the sewage system would include Frog Island, as long as the city council members—less the manager—would be allowed to keep their seats.

Forty-Three

Every other month, Mom and Aunt Weeze—mostly Mom— invited the conductor of the Indianapolis Symphony Orchestra, Fabien Sevitzky, to critique their Saturday morning rehearsals. Those were the Saturdays that Spikey and I had to disappear. Some Saturdays I took him to Golden Hill; other Saturdays we went to Georgey's house. Mr. Sevitzky was flattered and over the years became a strong supporter of Waring and Stoner. In return, Dad and Mom were strong supporters of the Indianapolis Symphony Orchestra, and Mom plugged the symphony on her radio show. The town's symphony orchestra was gaining more exposure, more patrons, and bigger audiences. Waring and Stoner weres becoming a better two-piano team. Even Dad—he joked—picked up a few patients from the string section.

"Yep," he once said, "my patients include the string section of the Indianapolis Symphony Orchestra and the G-string section of the Fox Burlesque."

Mom didn't think it was funny. Andy and I certainly did. Spike knew only that the G-string was the first string on his violin.

* * *

During the depths of one of Mom and Aunt Weeze's struggles, Mr. Sevitzky and his wife came for dinner. Mom was considering ending the team and canceling the show. After she got over her gonorrhea, Aunt Weeze's continual pelvic problems aged her a lot and she became unsupportive and tired easily. Partnering with Aunt Weeze was getting to be too much—Mom was exhausted and unhappy. She felt speaking with Fabien would be helpful. He was never shy about expressing an opinion.

She insisted that Andy, Spike, and I join them for dinner, wear neckties—still in her underwear drawer—behave ourselves, wipe our mouths without being told, and not talk unless one of the Sevitzkys asked us a question. After dinner we would be excused. The wires were removed from my jaw, and I was cautiously chewing. "Especially," Mom added, "we don't talk about what happened to Ricky's jaw."

"Just an allergy to a 200-pound Negro's foot," Dad proffered.

The Sevitzkys were upper-class Russians, and Mr. Sevitzky was prone to excessive dramatics (such as wearing a cape with a red satin liner). An average Midwestern meat and potato dinner would be out of the question, so Mom and Georgey cooked an elaborate multi-course meal. All the best silver and crystal wedding presents came out of the closets and were dusted, washed, and polished.

Georgey served the meal silently, drifting from one place setting to the next like a breeze from an open window. They never noticed her—a crippled, 240-pound, colored woman serving dinner. Never noticed. She knew how to be invisible. I sat quietly listening to the sound of silverware and chewing.

"Lillian," Mr. Sevitzky said, after finishing his entrée, "I have noticed a new strength—a new exhilaration in your performance."

His accent was heavy with excessive guttural trills on his r's. Andy and I made eye contact. We wanted to chuckle, but knew better. Mrs. Sevitsky chewed quietly and swallowed hard. The wattle under her chin would not behave.

"I am very impressed," he continued. "It's bringing a new life to the team, propelling you further into what I feel is greatness. It seems that the two of you are getting along quite well."

"Well, Fabien, thank you very much. I . . . ," Mom responded.

"I was so impressed after our last gathering in your magnificent piano salon that I took the occasion to speak with an old friend; Neil Sarggison is his name. He is in charge of this year's American Piano Competition."

"How nice, Fabien. I . . . ."

"Well, quite frankly I raved about Waring and Stoner and asked the radio station to send Neil some recent tape recordings to listen to."

"You did? I . . . ."

"I did, without your permission because I didn't want to get your hopes up. Neil called me on the telephone the day before yesterday. From Los Angeles, mind you. California. On the telephone. He called to tell me that he was absolutely mesmerized by your performance of Mozart's 'Sonata in D Major.' He would be honored if you and Louise would fly to Los Angeles and compete in the 1954 American Piano Competition. Naturally they will pay all expenses."

Mom stopped eating and stared blankly at Mr. Sevitzky, her mouth open just enough to see her chewed potatoes lurking. Mrs. Sevitzky coughed politely and dug at her gums with her tongue.

"The American Piano Competition? Los Angeles?" She wiped her mouth.

"I knew you'd be speechless, Lillian. This is a great honor. Only ten two-piano teams in the entire country are chosen. It is a weeklong festival, two teams each night."

"That makes Mom one of the ten best piano players in the United States," Andy said.

"Well," Mom managed, "I don't know what to say. Thank you. Thank you, Fabien. So much. So very much." She paused, her eyes filling with tears, and she suddenly began to cry. "I'm so sorry," she said, getting up from the table and rushing into the kitchen, unsuccessfully grasping for composure. .

Dad reached his hand out and put it on Mr. Sevitzky' arm. "Well, this is obviously not what Lill expected."

"We know how hard she has worked," Mr. Sevitzky said. "Frankly, in the last few weeks her performances have been incredible, like a different person. A power quite perplexing, infusing the team with creative energy. I've never seen anything like it."

"Yes," Dad said. "Over the last few months, Lill has been . . . well, she has been learning a new musical . . . um . . . expression, might be the best word."

"How interesting," Mr. Sevitzky said. "Tell me more about it."

Spikey blurted out, "It's Miss Tildalayhu, sir."

"Excuse me?"

281

"A Matilda Lee Hughes has been working with Lillian on a new musical genre," Dad said, using the word "genre" as if it were a topic far above human understanding—GENRE, so to speak, as if it should have a fancy French accent.

"Which is?" Sevitzky persisted.

"Negro gospel music" fell from my aching jaw.

"Negro music?"

"That's right, Fabien," Dad said. "Negro gospel music. It has proven to be a real . . . um . . . motivational factor in her recent development."

Mr. Sevitzky's hairline mustache crinkled like scorched plastic as he tried to force a smile, but his disdain was so evident that his face became a wreck. Without checking, I knew in my gut that there was not one colored person in the Indianapolis Symphony Orchestra. Maybe one swept the floor after each performance. Classical music was the music of kings and queens—white ones.

* * *

The American Piano Competition was exactly what Aunt Weeze needed to be born again, rejuvenated. Enthusiasm and self-pride propelled her. The following week began a grueling schedule of rehearsals. Even though Mozart's "Sonata in D Major" lasted only ten minutes, there were hundreds of details to be ironed out. If it were only one piano, the timing would not be as big an issue as it was with two. And it was an international competition.

With Mother's newfound enthusiasm, she searched for more emotion in the piece. Clearly that would make the difference. "From here, Louise," Mother said repeatedly, hitting her stomach. "Play from here." Aunt Weeze felt they had enough

282

emotion and didn't understand where Mom was going. Listening to the argument, I could feel their frustration. It was like talking to two very sad people and asking one to be sadder. Mom's creativity was now coming from deeper inside her—Miss Tildalayhu had guided her to that spot spiritually. Meanwhile, Mom was dragging Aunt Weeze by her emotionless, permed hair.

Forty-Four

Mom went to Sunday school every weekend of her young life. She was dragged there, she recalled, gasping and dreading it. Her mother and father tithed their musical talents to the Congregational Church in Fall River, Massachusetts—her mother at the organ, her father in the choir. Because she was forced to go, Mom saw these classes as a punishment.

During high school she sat in church and worked on piano arrangements in her mind and by ear—studying, two hands on an imaginary keyboard. When she went away to college, she spent Sundays relaxing with her friends, not attending church. Sunday became a day when she didn't have to do anything. She could lie around and read the Sunday paper if she wanted. "It wasn't until I was twenty that I realized that Sundays were supposed to be a day of rest, not church," she said. It was also a good time for piano practice. Church was another obligation. Mom had enough of those.

Like Dad, she believed in God because she was supposed to. She was reverent and compassionate, bowing her head when others prayed. She took a Thanksgiving turkey to a poor family every year and wept when her mother died, wondering if she was "up there." But the deep spiritual thing was missing, and she was afraid to look for it because it might overtake her drive for success as a musician. She told Dad one evening that she could actually see how much better she needed to be as a pianist. She could visualize greatness—it was within her grasp. That left little room for God. She existed as if in a room filled with mirrors—too crowded with her own reflection to allow for any sunlight.

The mirrors began to disappear in her work with Miss Tildalayhu—Tilly—and her introduction to gospel music. Here was her sunlight. Tilly opened Mom's creative door and filled her soul with spiritual viscera.

To say Georgey attended the Church of the Holy God would be a gross understatement—Georgey was a part of the Church of the Holy God and the Church of the Holy God was a part of Georgey. On Mondays late at night, she swept and vacuumed the sanctuary. Wednesdays late at night, she gathered the "Welcome" cards left in pews by visitors. She sorted food in the food pantry to keep busy and always supplied the church with just-baked cookies, hobbling the six blocks from her home to there carrying a stained, brown, still-warm grocery bag.

Zeze and Georgey put "God's Money" in several pews. They put a $5 bill in an envelope. It said,

GOD'S MONEY.
This is for those in need.
If this isn't for you, put it back or give it
secretly to the one who needs it.
You help quietly, never telling anyone,
never expecting thanks from anyone
except our Lord Jesus Christ.

On most Sundays the envelopes remained full. They were thrilled when an envelope was missing.

Every half hour each Sunday and starting at 8 a.m., the church bells played a three-bar spiritual refrain followed—on the hour—by the appropriate number of gongs. Eight, nine, ten, and eleven. A two-hour, fire-and-brimstone service was then held—embellished with the best gospel music Indianapolis had to offer, thanks to Miss Tildalayhu.

We rarely saw Georgey on Sundays. "It is the day God rested. And hallelujah for that. It is the day we pour out our thanks to our Savior in His house."

The Stoners attended the Second Presbyterian Church on Christmas Eve and Easter morning. Twice a year. Dad said that church was "for some people and not for others." We were the "others." But Dad believed in God and he believed in his town, and everything flowed from that simple belief. He never proselytized or moralized, and he never said grace except on Thanksgiving (and then it was quick and sounded like one word—

BlessthisfoodtoouruseandourlivestothyserviceAmen).

He bowed his head at funerals and when anyone else prayed. Dad was a believer, but not a wearer.

I'm certain that Georgey tried to reach him during those younger years when she worked for his family. She still tried. But Dad felt fine about himself and his faith. Felt he wasn't missing anything. Georgey understood.

286

Forty-Five

It felt good to be going back to school, especially going back as a kind of hero. Everyone had heard about the basketball game—that is, Dad's version. Baxter and Mike praised my courage at a Corpse Club meeting. Jim Moriarity told the Shortridge basketball team. Someone dubbed it "the jawbreaker" and it stuck.

My math teacher said, "Having the courage to wander into a Negro neighborhood and challenge them to a game of basketball took a lot of guts for both Andy and Rick Stoner."

Several colored boys stopped me in the hall to shake my hand. "Proud to know ya." No one knew. It was the telephone pole, nothing else.

Mike sat in his car, idling, and beeped at me that first day back.

"Hop in, Rick. I'll run you home."

"Hey, thanks, Mike," I said, hoping we wouldn't get into another discussion about the Negro domination of the world and how we would have to "kill 'em all." But Mike was charming, so much so that he was like a magnet, attaching personalities to himself.

"Heard about you and that blonde icicle you've been dating."

"Yeah? Who told you?"

"Moriarity."

"Yeah, that wasn't going anywhere."

"The no-touch rule, huh?"

"Pretty much, I guess."

"Well, it was time. You've been dating her for a while. Time to put up or shut up."

"I'll say."

"Listen, I wanted to tell you that I think I might have come on a little too strong the other week at the hospital."

"I'm not sure what you mean," I lied.

"Well, my feelings about colored people sometimes get out of hand. Mom has told me many times that I'm narrow-minded when it comes to race. So, I'm sorry."

"Oh, that's all right, Mike. I understand."

"Dad's even worse, so I must come by it honestly. You see, my father was beaten up by a group of colored men when he was eleven—beaten up and laughed at. Dad has never let go of that memory. He's scary with it. Even Mom is wary of colored men. Dad says their eyes follow her like a lion watching a wildebeest. They can't stop looking at her. It's weird. Something about her scent, Dad says. Some have followed her. She's a little nutsy about it—can't say as I blame her. Dad told her to avoid shops or grocery stores where coloreds work. Especially to be wary of gas stations with colored attendants. They stare at her when they clean the windshield." He put his head on the steering wheel. "So, I come by it honestly. Sorry."

"I understand. Boy, that's real tough, what happened to your dad."

"'Nuf said. Now, Friday. What're you doin' Friday after school?"

"No plans."

"I've got a get-well present for you."

* * *

Friday after school was my undoing, and her name was Arlene. I don't know her last name. I never wanted to know it. I never told anyone about Arlene—well, not the truth. Her mother worked the night shift at the A&P warehouse in Zionsville and her father was long gone, working oil rigs in Texas, she said. So Arlene was alone in her family's rundown trailer with wasps in the eaves until her mother got home after midnight. Arlene's bedroom was just her bed. It had never been made. She said "hmm" a lot and kissed me with her mouth open, searching inside my lips with her tongue. I gasped with erotic excitement and began feeling her breasts.

"I hope you brought a rubber," she said, rubbing my crotch softly.

That was the trigger word: "rubber." That was when I realized this was not a page in *Movieland* magazine. I'd never heard a girl use that word and it sounded dirty. I reached for my wallet and pulled out the two prophylactics that Mike had given me.

"Here," I said, trembling.

She laughed. "You're the one who's supposed to wear it. You ever put one on before?"

"Not exactly."

"Here," she said, handing one back to me and tearing the other one open. "Put this one on." She unbuckled my pants and pulled them down to my ankles. "No, no. You're putting it on inside out. Here, let me. Hmm. You roll it on like this. Hmm. I've never put one on a guy before. Hmm. This is real exciting." She pulled her dress off in one quick motion—magical. Then she was

289

instantly all pubic hair, shaved legs, and small, jiggly, pink nipples. "Hmm. Come on lover boy," she said, pulling me on top of her.

I was not ready for Arlene—not any part of it. Sadly, her fondling was too much and it was over before it began. She laughed as I hurriedly dressed, embarrassed. Never covered herself or even kept her knees together.

When Mike picked me up, he giggled and asked how it went, winking.

"All right, I guess."

Arlene, though—I never forgot the excitement of her soft kisses and searching tongue. I never told anyone the truth.

Forty-Six

Dad knew that his concocted story of the playground accident would not be believed by many. He told me that lies breed lies— that they feed on exaggeration. Like the colored stripper story, if we could hold fast to our lie, eventually it would become the truth.

On many Sunday afternoons since the accident, Reverend Williams stopped by our house to check on me and talk with Mom and Dad. He had come to see Dad as a sounding board for rumors. It was a mutual relationship, because Dad was interested in the tie-in between the number of members of the church with ailments and the ill health on Frog Island.

This particular Sunday evening, there was to be a gathering of the church youth group to thank the Stoner family. It was clear by this time that my public involvement with the church neighborhood needed to be diffused.

"If it weren't dangerous," Dad said, "Ricky's friendships would be good for everyone."

"You're so right, doctor," Reverend Williams said. "That fateful basketball game—what do they call it now?"

"The jawbreaker," I said, pulling up a chair at our breakfast table.

"Jawbreaker. What a horrible name. Anyway, the jawbreaker sent a clear message to many of us that integration will be very difficult for coloreds as well as whites." He shook his head. "But this is Indianapolis, folks, not Selma, Alabama, not Money, Mississippi."

"Money?" I asked.

"That's the name of the town where Emmett Till was murdered," Dad said.

Reverend Williams continued: "I was hoping we could set a Christian example for this country that other northern cities could emulate, that we could be a leader in civil rights, rather than a participant in civil wrongs."

It was beginning to sound like a sermon, but that was the tone of the Reverend's everyday dialogue.

"It tells me that we need to lay low for a while," Dad said.

"Dad, are you saying that I can't see Arkie or Rozelle?"

"No. I'm saying we have to think carefully about where you are going to meet them and what you are going to do."

Andy entered the breakfast room. "I was in the other room listening to your conversation. Here we are struggling to create an integrated society—as you call it— and you people are talking about separate grounds. Isn't that the word Mr. Squiggy Daniels used—"separate grounds"—to describe segregation?"

"Sit down, son." Dad pushed a chair out for Andy. "I know it sounds hypocritical and I'm a little embarrassed, but caution should be applied. I don't want my family to be in danger or my house burned."

"No one wants that," Andy said. "But doing nothing in the eyes of the white community will send the signal of no change."

"Andy's right," Reverend Williams said. "The Stoners are in it. Everyone knows that."

"In it . . . ." Dad responded. "What is "it"?"

"The fight for racial justice," Andy said. "What do you call it? Civil rights. We are now in the thick of it."

We sat looking at each other. My jaw tingled as I realized that this was no longer a teenage thrill.

Dad said, "But we will be cautious. Reckless can hurt everyone."

"Yet rumors prevail and grow. A white boy was injured in a fight with a colored boy. Then someone added that the white boy had a gun," Reverend Williams said.

"And that's what I'm talking about," Dad interjected. "Rumors breed embellishments. That's what concerns me. That is why we need to go underground for a while."

"I'm resigned to the fact that these so-called rumors will persist," Reverend Williams said.

"Juicy stories stay like grape stains," Dad said.

"God forgive me for lyin', Doctah, but if I had to do it again, I would do the same."

"I would, too," Dad said.

All of us nodded our heads. Reverend Williams checked his watch. "Besides Ricky, who is comin' tonight?"

"Can Andy come?" I asked.

"I don't think so," Andy said. "It's your jaw. Let's keep it simple."

Dad checked my jaw. "Chew for me," he said. "Good." He applied pressure to my jawbone. "Does that hurt?"

"Yeah."

"Good. It should."

* * *

293

Fifteen teenagers were in the church basement—all familiar faces and warm hearts. When Reverend Williams and I walked in, I was met with a strong sense of belonging. Shuli hugged me each time Reverend Williams mentioned my name. She was "heavyin' up with chile," as Zeze said. Marcella hugged me too, because she was Marcella and she hugged everyone.

Arkie talked about how I punched him in the face the first time we ever met, our Coca-Cola bottle collection, hiding from the Silver Gun Patrol, and that I was the best friend he ever had. We ate hot dogs from paper plates and Campbell's pork and beans—some going outside, some eating on the steps. Marcella and Arkie and I went out to the basketball court until Hanna called him in.

We sat on a cold, concrete bench near the courts, cross-legged facing each other, our plates in our laps.

"Beans, beans the musical fruit . . .," I said.

Marcella chuckled. "You better not."

The sky was turning orange and the sycamore trees had aged to faded green and brown. Marcella's emerald eyes, as shiny as Mom's rings, held my gaze. Her matte black skin reflected in the shadows with deep, alizarin, crimson highlights—purples, mango—so much to see when the sun turns black to color.

"What are you looking at?"

"You."

"Why?"

"You're so dark, blacker than Zeke."

"Is that good or bad?"

"Oh, real good. I like it," I answered too quickly, self-consciously.

"That's OK, sweetie," she said. "I know what you mean."

"Arkie and I tease each other about looking white and looking colored. He says when I'm in this neighborhood I look like white sidewalls on a black car."

"Poor boy. Only brown as a store-bought football."

We listened silently to a football marching band rehearsing far off in the distance. I closed my eyes and inhaled the smell of early, burning, fall leaves still smoldering in small piles arranged along the street curb. Soon they'd turn to ash and wash away with the next rain.

"Fall's here. Don't you just love it?" Marcella asked, laying her empty plate on the ground.

I smiled, looking at her.

"What's so funny?"

"You and Shuli talk like a couple of old ladies."

"Old ladies? You mean you don't think about how beautiful it is? The smells, football bands, harvest moons?"

"I do, but not like you and Shuli and Georgey."

"Maybe it's 'cause we're colored."

"Maybe. I think about the homework I have to do, about this creep at high school who makes me real nervous. I think about buying a car, Shuli's baby."

"I don't know nothin' about white people, but it sounds to me like you're worryin', not thinkin'."

"You might be right."

"You should breathe in real hard and feel how good the smells of burnin' leaves makes ya feel. You should sit near a crick and listen to the rushin' water talk to ya."

"Long time ago I sat in a field with Georgey."

"Miss Georgella?"

"Yeah. We sat way in the back of our yard together and she taught me how to make grass sing."

"How do you do that?"

"Come on. I'll show you." We walked to a small patch of grass growing beneath a section of chain-link fence.

"Here's some," I said, sitting down and sorting through several blades of grass until I found a thick one. She sat next to me. "You lay one blade here on the palm of your thumb, then hold it there with the other thumb. See? Then you blow, like this." Like a musical refrain of a memory, the haunting sound filled the courtyard. The distant band had stopped. Birds were quieted.

"Oh, that is beautiful. Just beautiful."

"Georgey said it was the trumpets of Israel calling to God."

"My goodness. And I thought you was just another unfeelin' white boy," she chided.

I searched for another blade of grass and broke it off. "Here. Give me your thumb." I laid it carefully on her thumb. "Now put your other thumb over it tightly. Blow into that opening." She blew on her grass and nothing happened, only air.

"Watch how my mouth fits on my thumbs." I held out my joined thumbs and slowly put my lips to them, then blew. The sound returned as a haunting moan.

"OK, I got it now." She laid the grass between her thumbs and blew. Nothing. "Think it's 'cause I'm colored?"

I laughed. "Your palms are as white as mine. I don't think you're blowing right. Maybe too hard. Here." I held her hands in mine. "Keep the heels of your thumbs tight together. Let me do it with your hands." I placed my lips on her thumbs and carefully blew, lightly at first as the sound started. Our foreheads were touching. Breathing in, I accidentally touched the palm of her thumb with my tongue, tasted its saltiness. Hesitated. Swallowed.

296

I raised my eyes to look at her. They met and her breath quickened.

"You try it now," I whispered. "Blow softer until you begin to hear the sound."

"Here goes," she murmured, watching me as her lips touched her thumbs softly, puckered. Her eyes half-closed. The haunting sound began.

"Hooray for Marcella," I said, still quietly.

"Let's do it together."

I blew a lower sound.

"The trumpets of Israel," I said, remembering that moment with Georgey so vividly.

Marcella shifted to face me, cross-legged. She reached for my hands. "Oh, Sweetie, I am so hot. I know it's wrong. But honest to Jesus, if you don't kiss me soon I'm gonna melt right here. I don't wanna do nothing else. No grapplin', no breathin' hard. I just want to kiss you, just this once for sure."

"Kiss you." The words wrapped their legs around me—easy words that stretched into the hollows of my mind. Time seemed to stop as the words took effect, first with our eyes drawn to each other's mouth. I became droopy-jawed and my arm quivered. I imagined a sound in my ears like a faint violin section from afar. My breath stuttered. *Kiss you. No grapplin'.* She leaned her head back and wet her lips slowly, and my body rolled toward her as if I might fall, breathing in anticipation. I watched her lips relax as our mouths moved closer, as they opened and reached for me. Our mouths touched as softly as an early first snow might land in the palm of your outstretched hand. We savored that kiss for a long time there on that patch of grass, cross-legged still. No grapplin', but hearts racing in wild abandon. Our breathing gave away our passion. She slowly traced her fingers on my cheek, and then it was over.

She pulled her lips away from mine and they stuck to each other, as lips often do. "Goose bumps," she said. "Best kiss I ever had. Is that the way all white boys kiss?"

"I thought that's the way all colored girls kiss."

We looked at each other, wondering.

"Where could we possibly go from here, Sweetie? This is dangerous." We nodded our heads. We both understood.

My voice was only a breeze. "I know, but now I really want you more." I cleared my throat and wiped the wetness from my eyes.

"We better get back inside ," she said.

Forty-Seven

I was studying upstairs when the sound of Mom's piano spoke strangely—not like it usually did— with explosive gusto. She picked away at the scale slowly, one note at a time. I sensed her immense sadness and despondence and envisioned her in the living room, sitting on her piano stool with her hands on her thighs, staring at the keys for some reason. I didn't feel right going down to ask her what was wrong. Could it be about me? Guilt drove me to the top of the stairs, where I sat and listened. I heard her weep quietly and imagined her, through teared vision, dimly reading Steinway and Sons above the keyboard and wondering who Steinway's sons were. Wondering if they were ever in a hospital with a broken jaw. Wondering. Slowly she repeated the scale of C with her left hand:

C   D   E   F   G   A   B   C

Slow, dull sounds. Then down

C   B   A   G   F   E   D   C

Slowly, like it was her first time.

There was a lot going on in Mom's life, and nothing made sense to her. It was more than just me. I sat on the top step and realized for the first time that Mom was human. Images entered and exited casually through my mind: Andy, Spike, Dad, Aunt Weeze, Georgey, the American Piano Competition, Tilly.

C   D   E   F   G   A   B   C
C   B   A   G   F   E   D   C

The hospital, me. I could hear the voices in her head: "Even Georgey needs help. Could have been killed," the Reverend Williams had said. "Never should have been there in the first place," Dad said. "More a you and less a me," Georgey said."

She played faster.

C   D   E   F   G   A   B   C

Then down.

B   A   G   F   E   D   C

Slowly she wept, wiping tears away with the back of her right hand while she played with her left. Her mind pictured Los Angeles—or at least what she thought it might look like—lights, people in evening gowns and tuxedos. Frank Sinatra would be there, she thought. Ava Gardner, too. She and Aunt Weeze on stage.

C   D   E   F   G   A   B   C

Then down.

B   A   G   F   E   D   C

I quietly scooted down to the first step.

Georgey stood motionless in the doorway to the living room, holding up the door jamb with one arm, supporting herself on her cane with the other, as Mother wept uncontrollably. Slowly she made her way to her and softly touched her shoulder, startling Mom.

"Scoot over, darlin'."

Mom scooted over.

"Jesus told me to be here."

"Not now, Georgey. I think I've had enough of Jesus lately. I'm more confused than ever."

"I know you're confused. I feel it in my heart."

Mom exhaled and her shoulders sagged in exhaustion and defeat.

"I knows this is hard for you to believe," Georgey continued in a whisper, "but God talks to me."

"Oh, Georgey. God doesn't talk to anyone. That's silly."

"Oh, yes, He does. I hear His voice. Just hafta know how to listen. I ain't makin' this up. When we know Jesus and we lives like him, peoples can really hear God's voice—a small voice, way off. Some folks learn how to hear Him. It's like this here piano and you. You taught yourself how to hear its messages. Most folks can't hear what you hear—the small notes, the tiny changes. They think you is crazy."

With an understanding smile, Mom gently nodded. That was true. She could hear things in music few people could hear— the bass part in four-part harmony, the cello section in a full orchestra, even a cold piano.

Georgey continued. "I jes' hafta be in tune with God first. I practice all day and all night."

"I think it works for you, Georgey. Not me."

"Not yet, it don't work for you, and maybe never like me. But again, jes' like you and this piano, not everone can do it, but many peoples can understand and appreciate music just like folks can understand and appreciate God's word."

Mom shrugged.

"This mornin' as I was prayin', God told me—through a vision—that you would be sittin' here cryin', confused 'cause you don't know what to do. You don't really want to go to Los Angeles, but you spent yur whole life gettin' there. You don't want to stop bein' Miss Waring's partner, but you is growin' weary of her ways and yur havin' more fun with Miss Tildalayhu."

Mom looked at Georgey like she was caught in a lie. Georgey knew.

301

"You don't love playin' yur music no more."

"I never really loved it, Georgey," Mom blurted. "My mother forced me to be better than she was. Locked doors so I couldn't play with other children. Physically held me on the old, wooden piano stool until I started practicing. Practicing this . . .

C D E F G A B C B A G F E D C

"Now I'm good at it."

"You is the best, darlin'. Can't you see how God has singled you out to make you special?"

"No. This God you talk about has hurt me and confused me."

"This God is settin' you up to be greater than you ever thought. Now yur piano playin' is glorifyin' God, not glorifyin' Lillian Stoner. That's the whole point of life, glorifyin' God. And you can do it in such a wonderful way. Different from us average peoples. When you was in that church with Miss Tildalayhu, all a them folks in the choir, God and Jesus and Angels was thankin' you. And, Miss Lillian Stoner, you knew it. I was watchin' you. You was doin'—at last—what God had in mind for you. You knew it."

Mom nodded her head. "I did."

"Then you come in here and sits and thinks about Mozart's 'Sonata in D Major.'"

"My goodness, Georgey. How did you ever remember that?"

"I always remember important things. So, you was gettin' ready to start playin' Mr. Mozart's music, and it weren't yours no more. You done gone beyond Mozart last Sunday. You broke through God's door of greatness."

"Does that mean I can play classical music with more feeling and maybe enjoy it more?"

"I s'pose it does. God'll tell you. All you gotta do is listen— listen for a small voice deep in your head. It'll happen. I just knows it will."

They sat together quietly looking at the keyboard.

"Lotta choices here," Georgey said, pointing to the keys. "Eighty-eight I think you said."

"That's right."

"Now let's you and me sing. We never done that. How 'bout 'Precious Lord'? You knows it?"

"I does," Mom said, smirking.

A rhythmic piano introduction was followed by Georgey's off-key voice being straightened out by the knifelike accuracy of mom's perfect pitch—like sound straightening a bent lead pipe.

"Precious Lord, take my hand, lead me on, let me stand.
I am tired, I am weak, I am worn.
Thru the storm, thru the night, lead me on to the light
Take my hand, precious Lord, lead me home."

Effortlessly, Mom rolled out a piano transition originating somewhere near her heart, one leg going out to the side for rhythm in a very unladylike manner.

"Hallelujah! Praise the Lord!" Georgey exclaimed.

"Yes!" Mom answered.

Then together, "When my way grows dreary, precious Lord, linger near.
When my life is almost gone.
Hear my cry, hear my call, hold my hand lest I fall.
Take my hand, precious Lord, lead me home."

303

Georgey said, "Hear that, darlin'? When your way grows dreary, call on the Lord."

Then she spoke the last verse.

"When the darkness appears and the night draws near
And the day is past and gone.
At the river I stand, guide my feet, hold my hand.
Take my hand, precious Lord, lead me home."

With a wiser and warmer heart than I had just an hour before, I quietly tiptoed back upstairs.

Forty-Eight

Once I had been initiated, the luster of belonging to the Corpse Club slowly faded, as had the luster of Mike's car and Mike's girlfriend. Many other members shared Mike's racial feelings, though no one as openly or violently. In my pledge class, both Jim Moriarity and I were very aware of the racial tension in Indianapolis and at Shortridge, yet the average white high school student (and their family) rarely thought about any kind of racial problems. It was just the way it was—they were them and we were us. Because of my connection with Georgey's neighborhood, I knew that the colored population always talked about injustices and discrimination. For me, all of Georgey's neighborhood felt like my home too, somehow.

Jim got his driver's license in early November, so we drove together to club events. During one meeting, Mike gave an impassioned pep talk on the importance of being better at whatever we do. "We need to be smarter, get better grades, work harder in athletics, and tune our bodies. We need to examine our friends and test their loyalty. We need to keep the race clean."

I knew exactly where he was going with this. Jim glanced at me. He knew too. Most of the members were looking carefully at Mike—nodding, yet confused. I wondered how the club was divided—who agreed or disagreed but were hesitant to say.

Finally, I bit the bullet. "Mike, what are you saying?"

He looked sharply at me, mid-sentence. "You, my pledge son. You have become a traitor. A true Judas among your white brothers."

"What are you talking about?"

"You should know better than anyone in this room," he said.

"I should know what?"

"About niggers."

"You mean Negroes." Anger tightened my jaw and my resolve.

"You mean Negroes. I mean niggers. I hear a good friend of yours is a nigger." He folded his arms. Eyes in the room flickered like moths in headlights.

"That's true. Wasn't aware that's a crime."

"Only a moral crime."

"That's absurd, Mike. I've known Arkie for so many years, he has no color. The only difference between him and you is the color of your skin."

"Don't you ever insinuate that a dirty, filthy nigger is anything like me." He searched the room. "I am a member of the white race. We are the supreme *Homo sapiens*. We are being threatened by niggers every day. Most of you can't even imagine it. If we don't do something about it, they're going to take over the world. Breed into us. Dilute us."

My heart pounded. "What a hysterical pile of crap that is, Mike." I stood up and looked around the room. "Do all you guys buy into this garbage? Am I missing something here?"

A heavy quiet fell over the room as members looked away. Finally someone said, "OK. I think Mike might be a little over the edge."

"Me too, but Stoner, you say this colored kid is your best friend."

"I did. My very best friend. Is there something wrong with that?"

"Wrong?" Mike shrieked. "The kid's a nigger. He's related to a chimpanzee. He wants to take away our rights!"

"You know," I said, "Mike is certain that the colored race is conspiring to end the white race. He's told me stories about colored women luring white men into having sex with them, in order to dilute the white race."

Jim laughed. "Really?"

"Come on. Is that true, Mike?" One of the members asked.

"It is absolutely true. Case after case has been reported worldwide."

Mike's friend Todd jumped to his feet. "Mike's right. His father is working against our demise with loyal white men across the United States."

"That is just so much crap," Jim said. "I've checked that out in the library."

"I called my uncle in Bloomington," I added. "He's a lawyer and works with colored leaders as well as white ones all around the United States. No one seems to know about this except you."

"And other KKK members," Jim added.

"Ease up, Dunbar. That's dangerous talk. Calm down," someone said.

"That is their secret, gentlemen," Mike continued. "The niggers are keeping this a secret. That is exactly where this thing is going. Quietly, subtly, the jig-a-boos are eating us up."

"If it's such a secret in the colored community, how did you find out about it?" I asked.

"Yeah," Jim said, laughing, "maybe Mike is in the know because he's part Negro. You suppose?"

Mike's mouthed pursed and his eyes narrowed. Then he swung wildly at Jim, hitting him in the shoulder as they tumbled against the sofa, knocking a lamp off the table. Several members pulled them apart.

"OK," a member said. "That's enough. Not in here."

"Yeah, Dunbar," Jim said, smiling. "No coloreds allowed. Go home."

"Be careful, Jim," I said.

"Enough!" someone yelled.

"I'm OK," Mike said, pushing the hair out of his eyes and holding his hands up. "I'm just fine. You," he said, pointing to Jim, "you're not long for this world. As for the rest of you, your patriotism is now at stake. You will make your own decisions."

A member named Luke picked up the lamp and placed it quietly on the corner table. Another pushed the sofa back in place. Mike didn't move, holding Jim in his glare. "I don't want to have anything to do with a club that supports any part of the nigger cause. So, it's either me or Stoner. Take your pick."

"Stoner and me, for sure," Jim chimed.

Stoner and Jim and me," another member added.

Several more endorsed us, roughly half.

"That's fine with me," I said. "I'd much rather have a friend like Arkie than a sick, bigoted fool like you. He's ten times the man you'll ever become."

Mike smiled. "But he's still a nigger, you dipshit."

"And you're still an asshole, Dunbar," Jim shot back.

The room bristled and eyes darted from faces to the floor. Slight coughs and adjustments rippled. I was certain we were going to have a brawl—it was only a matter of time.

"You know," someone spoke, "I don't have a problem with colored people. Look what Attucks did last year."

"Really. And what they'll do this year. Those guys are great."

Three members left the room—a subject too ticklish to tickle. The rest clustered uncomfortably like two separate schools of fish. The room was quiet as we waited. Mike glared at everyone—drumming his leg with a pencil, beating most eyes back to the floor—then at Jim in wild rage. Long, hard, burning. The Corpse Club had lost its meaning, and so had Mike Dunbar.

From the time I jitterbugged with Shuli at the church playground to when I woke with my jaw wired shut, something had happened to me—perhaps something symbolic. That time of unconsciousness awakened a deeper part within of me. I had crossed the line between knowing what was truly important and what wasn't.

Finally, Jim spoke up. "Well, this sure was a great last meeting for many of us. I want to go on record as saying I don't agree with one thing Dunbar said. I never did like you, Mike. Never trusted you. I won't be back if I hear you're still a member." Jim looked at me. "You ready to go, pal?"

"I am."

Yet many stayed.

309

Forty-Nine

Mom and Aunt Weeze practiced hard through Thanksgiving and Christmas—three-hour daily sessions. Mom was confident, explosive. Still urging Aunt Weeze on, still encouraging her, still pushing her for perfection. But ever since her gonorrhea and the complications that followed, Aunt Weeze couldn't physically keep up with the musical level that Mom had set. She was afraid. She had too much wear and tear. She had never had to ratchet her talent up this high. But she would rather die than not go to Los Angeles.

The private school where Mom taught gave her a sabbatical to prepare for the American Piano Competition. Aunt Weeze prepared four piano shows of Christmas music for the radio show, which Mom politely declined—"It doesn't take two pianos to do 'Deck the Halls.'" That allowed Mom to continue her weekly voice lessons with Miss Tildalayhu and help her prepare for the Christmas pageant at the Church of the Holy God.

Because of the hectic nature of the holidays and Mom's preparation for the competition, Dad suggested, uncharacteristically, that we have Saturday morning family meetings to review and discuss our schedules. Mom sat at her piano. I sprawled out on the sofa reading an assignment for my sophomore English class. We were waiting for Dad, Andy, Spike, and Georgey.

"Honey," Mom began, "can you hear the difference between the sound of this note when I play it this way"—she played a single note—"and when I play it this way?" She played the same note again.

"One's louder than the other?" I guessed.

"Possible. Is there another way you could describe the difference?"

I got up and walked over to the piano.

"Sit here and watch how I strike the note." She hit the note quietly. "Now watch and listen." She struck the note differently, this time caressing it.

"The second time you had more feeling?" I guessed again.

Spike and Georgey arrived.

"Come on, Doctah," Georgey called.

Andy came downstairs, zipping his pants.

"A week from tomorrow is Christmas . . .," Mom said.

"And thanks to Andy and Rick, we have a tree," Andy interrupted.

"I helped too," Spike said.

"We have a Christmas tree that is sitting on its side in the driveway," Dad said. "Three strong boys need to bring it in and bring the decorations down from the attic. We will all decorate it. Mom and I are out almost every night this week at holiday parties."

"Wednesday and Thursday we won't be here for dinner," Mom added.

"Cheeseburgers and french fries!" Spike cheered.

"Everyone's Christmas shopping coming along?"

We nodded.

Mom turned sideways on the piano bench. "I need everyone's attention for a few minutes. Before you came in, I was thinking how different we are from other families, yet in many ways we are the same. We live in a house. We have each other. The man of the house—that's you, honey—"

"Hooray for Dad," Andy said.

Mom continued. "Dad drives to work each day. Three boys go to school. That's what most people see."

"You forgot Georgey," Andy said.

"No, I didn't. You see Georgey is where we start being different. Most people see Georgey as our maid, but she's not. Once she told me—and I'll imitate her— you is the momma, I is the maid. A statement that was not quite true, but it sounded great, memorable.

"I was doing this exercise with Ricky before the rest of you showed up. I played middle C like this." She struck the note. "Then I played it like this." She struck it again. "Ricky thought they sounded pretty much the same, except one was louder."

"I thought they sounded exactly the same," Dad said.

"To the average person they do sound the same, but to the trained ear they are very different. That's us."

"What's us?" I asked.

"To the average person, we are an average, upscale family, but there's a huge difference here that very few people can see. It's the feeling. It's the knowledge of the depth in our lives. It's our ability to hear the imaginary and make it real, to see through the shadows.

"I know this might be difficult for you to understand, but please stick with me. This is important. Last week Georgey told me she can hear God's voice—a faint whisper. I thought she was making it up, because I couldn't hear it. But I can hear the difference between these two notes." She played them again. "I hear that difference like Georgey hears God's voice. Loud and clear. Believing that Georgey can hear God's voice makes me believe there is a God. There's a depth of understanding that we as a family—Georgey included—possess. We are different from the rest. We are the Martians living on Earth. Something, someone is guiding us."

"So, what do we do, Lillian?" Dad asked.

"Yeah," Andy said.

"Yeah," Spike added.

"We follow the sounds in our hearts."

"What does that mean?" Andy asked.

"We do what we are being guided to do. Like lying about Rick's accident. We arrived at an agreement because we felt it was right. We felt it in our hearts. Georgey once told me that my playing the piano only glorified Lillian Stoner. It doesn't really help anyone in this family. It certainly makes very little money. For years I have played the piano from my head, yet Tilly has taught me to play music from my heart. That is when I began glorifying God with my music. And I didn't know it. I'm still not sure of the connection, but I know something is there."

We were getting restless. Each of our minds were formulating "To Do" lists.

"That's wonderful, Lillian," Dad said. "So, you must do more with Miss Tildalayhu."

"And less of classical music," Mom added.

"You can stop teaching that new little girl you're working with. What's her name? Sarah?" Andy asked.

"No," Georgey said. "Teachin' Sarah helps Sarah. Teachin' Sarah is good."

Mom looked at Georgey. "Georgey is right. The Sarahs of the world are important. It's the American Piano Competition that is not."

Wham! Just like that—a stomach-punching, body-wrenching statement.

It grew quiet, each of us taking it in.

"So, I'm not going to California. I'm going to withdraw from the American Piano Competition."

"What?" Dad shouted. "Lillian Stoner you absolutely cannot withdraw." Dad continued, sounding like a losing coach at halftime. "You are not a quitter. I will not . . . ."

"Can I go outside now?" Spike interrupted.

"Gloves are on the floor in the closet," Georgey answered.

"You're right, honey." Mom said. "I'm not a quitter. I asked myself, who would benefit from our going to L.A.?"

"Your career would benefit," Dad said.

"My career is not as important as it used to be, Wayne. You, Rick, Andy, Spike, and Georgey are more important than my classical music journey. My musical career is closer to Tilly Hughes. I don't need recognition. Louise does. I'm not interested in fame. Louise is. And I could care less about winning some silly-assed piano competition in Los Angeles far away from my family."

"Lillian, do you know what you're doing? What about Louise? Fabien Sevitzky?"

"I think Louise's health is failing. I don't know what other complications she could have with her sickness, but she's in a state of panic. She will welcome the news, and she can blame me. She can talk about how she was invited to the American Piano Competition and her partner just couldn't take the pressure. All of you are more important than Louise or Fabien or WFBM or the entire Indianapolis Symphony Orchestra. About a year ago, Georgey told me that Ricky needs more of me and less of Georgey."

"I did," Georgey said. "Spike, too."

"So, I'm going to make some changes—welcome ones. I want to use my music to help people, not to impress them. I want to be with my family and learn more about you, so I can figure out where I fit in."

"Ain't you the great lady," Georgey said.

"Thank you. So, what's most important is what our family can do to help others, rather than helping ourselves."

"Like what?" Andy asked.

"Well, like it or not, we have a stake in the Negro community."

"Like it or not?" Georgey challenged.

"We have made a good, yet costly choice, Georgey—Wayne's practice, Ricky's jaw, Miss Tildalayhu and the Church of the Holy God. . . ."

"Baby Shuli and the baby to come, Arkie, Little Roy's family," Andy added.

"And let's not forget people like Sue Moriarity," Mom said.

"Jim's mom? What's she doing?" I asked.

"She's having Tupperware parties."

"What's that got to do with helping the Negro community?"

"Well, Honey, white women around the country are learning about civil rights in a woman's environment—in a way familiar to many women—over coffee and chatter. Sue heard about it and began asking her friends if they'd like to come. It's a low-profile, civil rights information meeting. We're thinking of inviting Squiggy Daniels to tell us about Frog Island."

"We?" Andy said.

"I went to one the other week. You'd be surprised who was there."

"Why Tupperware?"

"Well, it's safer for many people to meet under the guise of a Tupperware party. Sue actually sells some plastic containers."

Dad chimed in. "What your mother is saying is that most people who are in favor of racial equality do so in a much quieter way than us. We're the exceptions. It's risky for whites to gather, especially further south. It's an underground effort and allows whites that might be nervous to play a more active role in their community's racial issues."

"I hope people like the Dunbars don't hear about it," Mom said.

"Most people know about the parties. I suspect the Tupperware Company is getting a little nervous. They're afraid of losing customers because of racial issues."

"It's a shame it's come to that." Andy said.

Mom nodded her head. ". . . that money is more important than equality."

"The more personal issue," Dad said, "is our immediate circle, especially Shuli."

"How's she doing?" I asked.

"She's quite well. I saw her last week because she's been fighting a cold. As Georgey would say, she's heavyin' up a bit."

"Kinda waddling like a duck with a sack 'tween her legs," Georgey added.

"She came to my office rather than my driving into Frog Island, though it was unnecessary."

"Shuli's momma ain't well," Georgey said. "I ain't seen Mary Clarisa in a while. She has a sister who lives out there,

316

too—Eloise, I thinks. Well, Eloise says that Shuli's momma been sick for quite a spell. Real sick."

"How is Eloise?" Dad asked.

"How do I know? I ain't no Houdini."

Dad grinned. Georgey often treated him like a younger brother. He continued, "Frog Island is a filled-in, old outhouse. I've been there when the entire area smelled like a backed-up toilet. There's a fine colored doctor with a lot of patients out there. I spoke to him not too long ago to find out how he treats many lingering things like croup, pleurisy, earaches, wounds having a hard time improving, eye ailments, diarrhea—lots of routine things that never seem to fully heal."

"What's this mean for Shuli?" I asked.

"Could mean nothing. There are many healthy families out there as well, just real poor. You've heard of the Robertson boys? I believe Oscar is the most well known in our city. His older brother Bailey will be playing for the Harlem Globetrotters. Big, strapping boys. Arkie and Rozelle are two more. I think many families actually build up an immunity to the diseases that permeate the area. Ninety percent of the Crispus Attucks basketball team was raised on Frog Island. They endured. So, I think Shuli and her child will be fine."

Georgey responded, "That ain't good enough. Ten percent for someone we loves. Just ain't good enough."

We sat in our living room, large enough to hold two grand pianos effortlessly. Soon we would put up the Christmas tree laying in the driveway—it was 9 feet high and an array of Christmas presents would be placed around it. And still there was room for two large sofas, numerous overstuffed chairs, and our annual Christmas open house. Because material comforts have always been there for us, I never imagined a life without them.

317

And although Georgey had told my brothers and me that we needed to focus more on the poor and needy, we had no burning desire to do so, especially me. Life was complicated enough without getting involved in the lives of the poor and needy.

* * *

December 19th was our annual Christmas open house. The party was lavish, which seemed peculiar after our discussions about what was important. Hypocritical. Dad loved it. He knew what it meant.

"Some hypocrisy is good, as long as it's mine," he said. Often it was difficult getting around his logic.

For Christmas of 1955, we decided we would invite our colored friends as well as our white friends, if they would come. That was a big "if." It was Dad's idea, and Mom thought it would be OK. We thought it'd be good for all of our friends—not just Mom and Dad's, but Andy's, Spike's, and mine, too.

"This will be a festive occasion, a snazzy Tupperware party," Dad beamed. "The Peaceable Kingdom at the Stoner house."

It was a test for our living room. Could we fit twelve members of the Church of the Holy God choir, along with six members of the symphony, the curator of the art museum, the ballet director, and eight close friends of Mom and Dad? Then there was Georgey, Miss Tildalayhu, Zeke, Zeze, Reginald, Marjorie, Ann Sue, and Sonny; Arkie, Rozelle, Shuli, and Marcella; Squiggy, Emma, and Little Roy Daniels; Jim, Baxter, and their parents from our neighborhood; and Andy with three of his friends.

By the time the party came around, Shuli decided not to attend because of her continual morning sickness. Sonny wasn't comfortable with it, saying, "I ain't no token." The ballet director was still in Europe. However, everyone else agreed to be there.

I think the reason it worked so well was because of the crowded conditions. Like a thick lawn we stood, virtually propping each other up. Many moved to the circular entranceway. Some stood on the porch with the door open, which drove Mom nuts. "We can't afford to heat the whole outside," she kept repeating.

Mom introduced Miss Tildalayhu as "my very best and special friend, an amazing talent, student of Mahalia Jackson, and servant of God." Then she introduced each member of the choir, making each one feel special. "Molly Hinkle. If ever an angel sang, Molly taught her. Momma Reynolds, as rich a sound as can be made. Rosa Mae. Oh Rosa, how we need your deep voice. Deeper even than Melvin's."

They sang Christmas carols and encouraged everyone to sing along if they felt like it. The music filled our house with such intensity, but it was the people's faces that struck me most. Myriad shades of skin from brown to purple-black to off-white. All eyes sparkling with happiness and peace. I could see that in each of us.

"Hey," Arkie said, following me to the kitchen during "Baby Jesus." "Don't you ask me to hand a drink to a white folk. I ain't no nigger waiter, you know."

"You sure look like one," I said.

"And the shoe do fit," Georgey added.

Georgey, Mrs. Morrison, and Marcella were in the kitchen, fixing new plates of hors d'oeuvres.

319

"That Mr. Saviskas man from the symphony loves our music 'cept he's afraid to show it. Here, darlin'," Georgy said, handing the tray to Arkie. "Pass this around out there."

"Miss Georgella, I ain't gonna pass around no food plate for whites."

"You too good for that?"

He thought for a moment. "Yeah, I'm too good for that."

"Was Jesus too good to wash his disciples' feet?"

"How many was niggers?"

"Don't know, but there was Jews, crooks, and prostitutes."

"Here, Georgey. I'll do it," Mrs. Morrison said, winking at Arkie.

"We got three big trays of goodies," Georgey said. "Thank you, Mrs. Morrison. Arkie, here's one for you. I'll take this one in."

That left Marcella and me in the kitchen, chopping celery, arranging olives on more plates, and feeling closer than we ever had. I watched her, knowing she knew I was watching, but I had nothing to say—no words, just Marcella, her breathing, shifting from one foot to the other. She wore low slippers—flats like the teenagers on *American Bandstand*—and a calf-length skirt made special just for her rear end. I wanted to scoop her up and take her to a giant bed somewhere, undress her slowly, and make passionate love to her. I wanted her more than a—well, let's see—a red Cadillac convertible with lake pipes.

"I feel yur eyes, sweetie," she said, her back to me.

"Yeah. Well, ah sorry. I mean, not really sorry."

She turned around smiling and leaned back on the counter with her elbows. "Is there someplace we could go and just make out for a while without being missed?"

"God, Marcella. You make me so hot I don't know how to think."

Loud laughter from the living room and we could hear the guests singing "Good King Wenceslas" to a variety of lyrics.

"Good King Wenceslas looked out
Deep and crisp and even . . ."

"Wait. Wait, stop!" someone interrupted. "You left out a verse."

"Which one?" Mom asked.

"It's 'On the feast of Stephen.' That goes before 'Deep and crisp and even.'" Then we heard the piano start again.

I was staring at Marcella's breasts.

"Well? Is there?" she asked again.

"What?" I murmured, not closing my mouth.

"Where we gonna go to? Right now, sweetie. I have to get my arms around you. Feel you up against me."

"Through here. Gloria's room." I took her hand and opened the kitchen door that led down a short hallway to Gloria's old room.

"Won't she be coming back?"

"Not anymore. She's moved out." I closed the door behind us and the hallway was dark. Not a speck of light. Dense dark. We stopped after only a few steps, standing close and breathing hard. We couldn't make it to Gloria's room. Our bodies reached out in passion.

"Kiss me like you did at church," she said as she moved closer, encircling my neck with her arms and pushing her breasts against me.

Her breath was hot and she smelled of perfume and everything good—of happiness and slow dancing, of steel paks idling on a country road. I held her face in my hands and brushed her lips with mine. She breathed hard and searched my mouth with her tongue.

"Sire, he lives a good league hence
Underneath the mountain. . . ."

The party became a separate entity—far removed, yet surrounding us in sound—as we pushed against each other rhythmically, holding tight, breathing hard.

Moaning.

Gasping.

"Oh, Marcella," I exhaled.

"Oh, baby," she whispered hot. "Rub my button."

Anything, my mind said. But what? "Your button? Where's?"

"Give me yur hand, sweety. Oh, baby." Her hot breath lit my senses on fire as she put my hand beneath her dress and pressed my fingers against the wet and slippery spot between her legs. More and more she rubbed and breathed and gasped. "Don't stop, Ricky. Please. Oh yes. More. Harder. Yes. Do it to me. Here."

I unbuckled my pants. "Yes. Oh, Marcella. Let's."

Suddenly from the kitchen, "Rick? You here, brother?"

"Through the rude wind's wild lament
And the bitter weather."

I startled and let go. Marcella's legs began giving out and she slowly slid to the floor.

"Hey brother. We need some more hors d'oeuvres."

"Mark my footsteps, my good page. . ."

I heard the door handle turn and reached quickly for it.

"Coming," I said in an unsure voice, halfway between a scream and a cough. "Had to get . . ."—cough—"had to get some stuff here."

Marcella was still on the floor, trying to get up. "I'm OK," she whispered. "Go on."

"What's going on, Rick?" Andy asked, as the bright lights of the kitchen made me squint.

"Nothing."

"Brother, you ought to see yourself. Your face is covered with lipstick. Your hair is all messed. Your fly is down. Here's a dish towel. For crying out loud, Rick! What got into you?"

The next thing I knew, Georgey was coming into the kitchen. I scrubbed my face hard and pushed my hair back as best I could.

"Got them cheeseballs, childs?"

"Just bringing them out," Andy said, grabbing the two plates Marcella had been working on. "Ricky was just cleaning up a bit. Here Georgey, you take one and I'll take the other."

"You seen Marcella?" Georgey asked, as they left the kitchen with me behind them.

"She was in the living room, last I saw her," Andy said.

Georgey limped back into the dining room just as the guests were applauding a song. She handed the tray to to Zeke and said, "Here, hold this for me a minute." Then she took

Reginald and Marjorie by the hand and brought them over to a cluster of violinists from the symphony.

"Good evenin'," she said. "This is Reginald and Marjorie Baker. Real good friends of mine. I'm Georgey."

"We all know who Georgey is," one woman said kindly. "Lillian speaks of you all the time."

"Reginald and Marjorie is my next door neighbors."

One of the violinists spoke. "This music, Miss Georgey, is absolutely amazing. Not at all like classical."

"You is so right. I listened to Missus Stoner for years. I got to be able to tell a sonata from a fugue (pardon my French). Then she met Miss Tildalayhu."

"Tildalayhu—that's a peculiar name. Where is she from?"

Marjorie stepped in. "She's from Chicago, up north. Studied with Mahalia Jackson, she did."

"What a gifted singer Mahalia Jackson is."

"You don't mind if I sits, do you?" Georgey asked. "Needs to take a load off." She motioned to Zeke to pass the tray around, but he shook his head "no" and stood like a statue in the middle of the living room. Soon Zeze came over to him with a bottle of beer, trading it for the tray of hors d'oeuvres.

The only people who drank too much that night were Fabien Sevitski and the overweight cellist from the symphony who walked around with a piece of toilet paper hanging out the back of her skirt. Everyone enjoyed themselves and I could both see it in their eyes and feel it in their hearts. They learned about each other in new ways as human beings—both colored and white. The party was an anomaly for 1955.

I saw Marcella as she was leaving with Rozelle—she blew me a kiss—and it was after midnight when we had wiped and put away the last dish.

"Wasn't it wonderful to see who our true friends are?" Mom bubbled.

It sure was," Dad said. "Did you notice how well Zeke got along? I was quite surprised."

"Me too," Andy said. "What did Zeke do for a living?"

"He had a bunch of jobs. Mostly he shined shoes."

"Down at the train station," I added. "He told me how he got beaten up by a couple white guys."

"Where'd he get the money to retire so early? Seems he's been sitting on his porch for years," Andy said.

"I heard he's on disability," Mom said.

"What's disability?" Spike asked.

"It's when you get injured on the job and you can't work anymore. Many employers pay the injured worker until they are of legal retirement age. They have insurance that covers that kind of thing," Dad explained.

"Oh," said Spike, yawning. "Sorry I asked. I'm going to bed."

"Goodnight, sweetheart. Thanks for your help tonight." Mom kissed him and Georgey hugged him good night.

"Prayers?"

"I'll do them in bed." He wandered up the stairs.

"But wait a minute," I said. "Zeke told me that he and his father shined shoes at the railroad station. He didn't work for a big company."

Dad looked at Georgey and shrugged. "You're right, son. He worked there seven days a week until his father died."

"Is this another family secret?" Mom asked.

"I guess you'd call it that."

"You can tell 'em, Doctah. It just don't go no farther than here."

Dad poured the second half of his beer. "Well, let's see. Where to start." He took a sip and leaned back. "When Zeke's father died, he left Zeke a lot of money. Zeke's mother had passed away sometime earlier, and he had no brothers or sisters."

"Left him a lot of money from the shoeshine business?" Mom asked.

"No. During the Depression wealthy men weren't having their shoes shined as often. Times were tough. So, Zeke's father—Patches, they called him—started burglarizing small stores after they closed. Apparently, he had an uncanny knack for picking locks and sliding under half-closed windows. The cleverest thing he did was to not take all the money out of the cash registers—just a little. If there was very little in the drawer, he wouldn't take any at all, because it'd be too obvious. So most businesses didn't miss it until later, and some never missed it at all."

"Zeke's daddy was a crook?" I asked, cringing.

"Zeke's father was a burglar—a very skilled one, at that. I once saw his father's tools. He kept them in an old medicine bag like mine. He also read books about the different values of jewelry." Dad smiled and sipped his beer. "Patches was the best."

Georgey added, "And don't you ever let on you know or ever tell no one. And act surprised if anyone tells you."

"Sure," Andy said, "but if he was stealing . . ."

"Professionally burglarizing," Dad corrected, legitimizing the crime.

"Burglarizing," Andy asserted. "If he was burglarizing small amounts at a time, how did he get enough money to retire?"

Dad spoke again. "Zeke told me his father started his burglar business in 1925. By the mid '30s, he had graduated to the homes of wealthy white people of this town—the Lillys, the Mallorys, even the Moriaritys—breaking into their houses when they went on vacation and stealing jewelry, then fencing it in Louisville or Detroit or Chicago. Much of the jewelry was very expensive. He knew what every piece was worth. As I said, he was a student of the craft—the ultimate pro. He was almost caught only once, and before the police arrived he jumped through a glass window, cutting himself badly, and escaped. He almost died from loss of blood. He told his family he was attacked by a bunch of white men with knives."

"You see," Georgey added, "Zeke never knowed about his daddy until just afore he died in '39 or '40. He was a layin' there in his death bed and told Zeke the whole story. Told him how he did it, how many homes he broke into. Ole Patches had the memry of an elephant, never forgot. Knew the name, the address and what he stole. Had it hidden all round the house 'tween walls and in ceilings."

Dad nodded. "He made Zeke promise on the Bible that he would never be a criminal like his father. Zeke agreed. He must have been completely shocked, because Patches had still gone to the train station every day and shined folks' shoes. Shined their shoes and learned their names."

Georgey added, "and wished them a good trip as they boarded the train on their vacation."

"And broke into their house the next day?" Andy remarked.

"Right," Dad said. "So, Patches told Zeke where the jewelry and the money were hidden, and then he died."

"How much money was there?" Mom asked, her eyes wide.

"Oh, I don't know for sure. Zeke would never say—and I never asked—only that he and Zeze would never want for anything. And they certainly haven't."

"They gives very, very kindly to the church. No one knows 'cept the Reverend."

"And you," Andy said.

"Why you, Georgey?" Mom asked.

"A few years ago Zeke come down with cancer and Zeze and me become real close. The doctah cared for Zeke and the cancer done disappeared—thanks to Zeze and our prayers—but not afore Zeke told the doctah and me and Zeze the whole story."

"You mean Zeze never knew until then?" Mom asked.

"Nope. Colored folks don't nose around when a good thing is happenin'."

"Now," Dad said pointing to us sternly, "this is a Stoner secret. It goes no further than this room. It is not to be repeated." He looked into each of our eyes. "Agreed?"

We agreed, made speechless by the intrigue.

"So, goodnight and see you all in the morning. Georgey will pray that our phone doesn't ring tonight and I won't have to go to the hospital on call."

"Goodness," Georgey scoffed, "after one whole beer tonight. The doctah is getting reckless in his old age."

Mom and Dad headed to their bedroom, Mom kicking off her heels in the hallway.

"Hold on a minute," Georgey said, bowing her head. "Lord Jesus, thank you for this gathering tonight. We is always amazed at how you makes things happen. Keep us wise, great God. And hold the secret of Zeke within our fambly. In the name of your precious Son, Jesus. Amen."

Andy and I took Georgey home.

An issue remained:

"Rick," Andy began, "what's going on between you and Marcella?"

Georgey turned around and looked at me. "Marcella? You mean the colored girl, Marcella?"

"Nothing," I said.

Georgey looked from me to Andy quizzically. "Little Marcella Ames?"

"Just real good friends," I said.

"That's not what Arkie said."

"Oh, Ricky darlin'. You can't start that."

"Thanks a lot, Andy," I said. "I would have thought we could at least keep it in the family."

"We are," he said. "This is Georgey. Remember? We just shared Zeke's secret."

"Oh, my goodness, children. What on earth is goin' on?"

"Just friends? You sure, brother?" Andy asked.

I hesitated. "Kinda sure. I'd like it to be more I think. We've talked about it, about not letting anything get serious. But talking about it makes me want to—you know—see her. She's not like any white girl I know."

"Oh, my goodness sakes alive," Georgey exclaimed, wagging her head slowly. "This ain't no good. Not now. No, no, no. You jes' got over one broken jaw."

"I just want to go out with her. That's all. I don't want to go steady."

"Oh, that's good. She wouldn't look good wearing your Corpse Club pin at Attucks, anyway," Andy smirked.

"Don't be a jerk."

Georgey turned to Andy, "Be nice, child. Be nice."

"OK," Andy said. "If you went out with her, where do you think you would go?"

"I don't know. A movie? Her house? Our house?"

"Let me play this out for you, little brother," he said, looking in the rearview mirror. "Dad drives you on your date. You go into Marcella's neighborhood, pull up in front of her house. You get out and go up to her door. The whole neighborhood is looking out their windows. You meet her very suspicious family and walk back to the car. Dad manages a weak wave to her father. At least one of the neighbors yells at you. 'Go home, white boy.' Dad pulls up in front of the movie theater and you both get out to taunts and threats. A big white guy calls you every name in the book. You try to punch him out and he beats the holy living crap out of you. Welcome to Methodist Hospital with your second busted jaw in six months, and you've set back civil rights in this town by fifty years."

"Such a jerk," I mumbled.

"Andy's right, Ricky darlin'. Everone gets hurt—you, Marcella, her fambly, and ours."

"Didn't you once tell me and Andy about Abraham having sex with a Negro lady named Hagar?"

The car closed in around us as it grew quiet. Then Georgey said, "That was many years ago, honey, in another country. It was OK back then. It most certainly ain't now."

"So, you're telling me we are all for integration as long as it doesn't involve our own family?"

We pulled up to Georgey's house.

No one talked.

Georgey was deep in concentration, pulling on her ear and murmuring "hmm."

Then she spoke as she got out of the car. "I thinks that is what we is sayin'."

"I think that is absolutely what we are saying," Andy added.

We walked her up to the house, she struggling up the five steps to her porch—cane on one side, railing on the other—left leg, left leg, left leg.

As we opened the door we heard a nearby voice in the glow of a cigarette quietly say, "Evenin' Miss Georgella. Whitey brothers. Nice party." It was like someone was hiding in the bushes—a voice to which we were now tied. Georgey never locked her doors—didn't believe in it—and her neighborhood was never broken into. Georgey was home, but our house was also her home. She often said her house was simply another Stoner bedroom, though when you looked out her bedroom window here, you saw a whole new forest of trees and birds and little Negro animals running around.

* * *

Mom held true to her word, and by New Year's Day she had pulled the plug on the American Piano competition. Aunt Weeze wasn't the least disturbed. She knew she was clearly in over her head. Dad said that because of her poor health, she'd never be able to pull off the competition. According to Mom, ridding herself of Aunt Weeze was easier than dumping an old boyfriend. So, Louise Waring once again could become Louise Waring—not half of Waring and Stoner. She'd never have to share the limelight. Her light could now shine.

Mom and Dad listened to her first solo radio broadcast.

MUSIC
(Chopin Etude *7 seconds*)
ANNOUNCER
(*Music down*)

"Good afternoon, ladies and gentlemen, and welcome to an hour of fine classical piano with the music of Louise Waring, one of this country's finest pianists, trained by the great artists of Europe and New York. How fortunate we are to have her play for us and tell us about the music, its meaning, why it was written, and how we can better appreciate it.

"So, without further ado, let me introduce Louise Waring."

"So far so good," Dad said.
"I'll cross my fingers," Mom added.

(*Applause*)
LOUISE WARING

"Good afternoon, everyone. What an absolutely marvelous opportunity to share my music with you. It seems like just yesterday I was getting my start in New York City, beating the streets for auditions, sipping wine in Greenwich Village with famous artists, writers, and musicians. Perhaps my greatest enjoyment was working with 'Lennie' Bernstein. What a treat it is to know such a gifted musician. Lennie always said that I was one of his favorite pianists and looked forward to working with me always. When Lennie wrote 'On the Town,' I was right there by his side. One of his concerns with the music was the song 'New York, New York,' the segue—if I might—and how it would work.

So, let's hear 'New York, New York' and my version of the refrain."

"Oh, my goodness," Mom said, turning up the radio. "She has lost her mind."

"Did she know Leonard Bernstein?" Dad asked.

"She never met him, much less sat next to him while he composed. What in the world is she doing?"

For week number two, Aunt Weeze tried to play some of that hip swinger Elvis Presley's rock 'n' roll music. "Let's listen to 'You Aren't Nothing But a Hound Dog.'" She then briefly recounted the first time she met Elvis.

It was clear by week three that the radio station had applied a hammerlock on her name-dropping and restricted her to factual information only. Meanwhile, at Sid's Jewelers downtown, Aunt Weeze was signing photographs of herself sitting at a piano— "Best of luck, Louise Waring."

A month later, WFBM dropped the show and Aunt Weeze and Sidney Goldstein prepared to move to Santa Fe. "Gobs of music there, Lillian. Sid and I will fit in well. I just feel it."

Fabien Sevitzky was furious with Mom. Mom let everyone know that he had the right to be angry—she had let him down and it might have besmirched his reputation ("besmirched" was Dad's word). She never once blamed anyone but herself. "I am going to spend more time with my family and that's that."

Dad predicted the "Russian Tornado" would blow over.

* * *

333

Mary Clarisa Wright, Shuli's mother, took very sick on New Year's Day. She had no doctor, so Shuli gave Dad's name to the hospital. They ran a series of tests on her, and a week later they determined it was cancer—some kind of stomach or pancreatic cancer. Dad said it didn't make any difference because it had spread everywhere. At the same time, Mary Clarisa's sister Eloise was carrying a deep chest cough that was wearing her out.

Within two weeks and eight months pregnant, Shuli's life changed forever. Her mother was moved to an asylum in Greenfield where she passed away quietly, with Shuli by her side—silent doors swung shut on a silent life. Her Aunt Eloise couldn't help care for an infant and asked Dad if he could find a home for Shuli. Georgey happily welcomed Shuli into her house to be cared for by the neighborhood. "Carin' for a new momma and a baby child is God's message to this old spook. He's watchin' me. Thank you, Lord."

A new chapter in all of our lives began.

Fifty

March approached rapidly, with its shrill sting of winter hiding periodically behind a false warmth that teased us, making us think tomorrow would be summer. Tomorrow, we'd think, convertibles will be convertibles once more and girls will wear sleeveless blouses and walk with sun-tanned legs. Though the spring-flowering trees would begin to produce their swollen buds, a surprise snowstorm brought us back to reality—it always did.

March was the month of the Indiana High School State Basketball Championship—games bigger than any spring snowstorm, more captivating than the 500-mile race, more heart wrenching than a thousand broken jaws, and more fun than a coed skinny dip in the inviting river.

Just like the previous year, Crispus Attucks was favored to take it all, and senior Oscar Robertson was the star. Now, with racial tensions being so high, the town worried about the prospect of a Negro high school winning again, so they ramped up police protection throughout the city. Indianapolis remained controlled. The 1956 Crispus Attucks Tigers also had 6'6 junior Rozelle Thorpe as second string forward. Sophomore Arkansas Johnson just missed making varsity, though he would certainly make the team next year with Oscar Robertson gone. 1957 and '58 would be Arkie's years.

Indianapolis was crazy about high school basketball— good crazy, and bad crazy. The newspapers used the term "Hoop

Crazy," but only if you were from Indianapolis in the '50s could you understand the insanity of March. When the Crispus Attucks Tigers won the state championship in 1955, basketball became our pride and our poison. It was more than just a game. It was excellence achieved by an all-Negro group of young men. Many in the white community were proud of that team and the all-Negro high school. Many others in that same community were angry— angry because their white supremacist beliefs were being debunked. Jealous, spiteful, and close-minded, that insistence festered. During that same time, virtually in the background, Martin Luther King, Jr., was preaching equality, Rosa Parks was peacefully acting out protests against inequality, and Emmett Till's aftermath hung heavily over white communities everywhere.

An all-colored high school winning a state championship in a highly segregated town was threatening in one breath, and prideful in another. Even Mom had memorized the names of all the Attucks' players and could recite them like the Seven Dwarfs—Oscar and Ed, Leon and Bill, and Al Maxey—yet she didn't understand a free throw. "If it's free, why do they have to shoot it? And, if they miss it, it certainly will cost them." The newspapers reported that the Tigers would repeat their efforts again this year without a hitch, and the town's expectations were set at the top of the bar.

* * *

On March 1, three days before the opening game of the championship series, Shuli Wright went into labor. I had heard the phone ring in the middle of the night, heard Dad say, "I'm on

336

my way, Georgey. Keep her calm. Boil some water. Hospital? Sounds like it's too late. We'll do it right there."

A healthy baby girl was delivered by Dad at sunrise that next morning, and Shuli named her Butterfly—Butterfly Wright. Dad called home to let us know. "A Butterfly was born in Indianapolis this morning, thanks to Georgey. All I had to do was cut the cord." We could hear Georgey in the background. "Will you just look at this beautiful child! I could jes poke a straw in that little baby and drink her up. Praise the Lord, sweet Jesus!"

Andy and I drove to school that morning and looked at the kids outside the building. Ranging from ages fourteen to eighteen, not a father or mother in the bunch and few Negroes, their lives seemed so simple and orderly to me—carrying schoolbooks, laughing, running. It was like a phony TV commercial that faked happiness. My family's life seemed richer, deeper, and more real—no actors, no music track. Butterfly Wright, daughter of 16-year-old Baby Shuli, had come into this world kicking and screaming. Her father was nowhere to be found. I instinctively touched my jaw with that memory, wondering if other people's lives were as convoluted as mine.

Butterfly Wright was white with skin as soft and tight as a powdered doll. Her perfectly round black eyes peered out with questions I didn't know the answers to. It could have been God's way of communicating with me—

"Here, Rick. This is what your God looks like. Go ahead. Hold Me. Yes, I'm the one who creates. I am the creator and the created. I'm much more complicated than you will ever know."

Then God spit up fresh, white milk—Her sustenance gleaned from Shuli's breasts and trickling off Her chin into the crevices and folds of Her neck.

"Ricky," Shuli said, "there's a towel on the table. Why don't you hold my baby and wipe off her chin?"

"Me?" I was fifteen and not supposed to be caring for an infant. I still remembered Shuli as Baby Shuli—a kid with flashing cotton panties.. A baby? A mother? How did all this happen?

"Ain't no one else holdin' this child," Shuli said.

I carefully held her in my lap—so scared I'd drop her—and wiped off Butterfly's neck and chin. Georgey's living room smelled heavy of warm, fresh milk, reminding me of a dairy barn in Southern Indiana.

"I was scared, too," Shuli said quietly, sitting beside me. "It wasn't supposed to happen. I was a girl, not a woman."

"Yeah" was all I could get out.

"But right after Miss Georgella and yur daddy delivered that child and set her on my breasts, I wasn't scared no more. Now I'm a momma and I got a child to bring up and care for."

"She's, uh, kinda white, don'tcha think?"

"Most Negro babies are born white, Rickey. She'll darken up real fine, your daddy says. You know your daddy was the one who really named her."

"Dad?"

"We was talking once about my freckles and he told me about a butterfly called Vanessa Cardui, the Painted Lady—light brown with black spots. I asked him if my baby would have freckles. If so, I'd call her Butterfly, 'cause I don't like the name Vanessa—sounds too white. Doctah said I should name her Butterfly anyway—either Butterfly after her momma, or Butterfly after the Painted Lady."

"Neat," I mumbled, always surprised by Dad's reflections and hip-pocket knowledge.

Shuli scooped Butterfly from my lap, smiling. "Miss Georgella, we is gonna need a stake to drive into this zombie's heart. All he can do is sit and say, 'yeah.'"

"I don't know what else to say, Shuli."

"Georgella." We heard Zeke's low, gruff voice from across the street. "Georgella, you got a couple a real big visitors. One's that nigger Arkie, come to visit again. Brought along some good-lookin' womens."

We heard Arkie's voice call out. "Afternoon, Mr. Zeke. This here is Rozelle Thorpe and our friends, Hanna and Marcella." Then he whispered to everyone, "We better go across the street and shake his hand, if you know what's good for you."

"Hell, I know," Zeke began.

"You watch yur mouth, old man," Zeze said.

They walked across the street and up the steps to Zeke's porch, Rozelle lowering his head under the doorway.

"Yeah. I know who Rozelle Thorpe is. You gonna be the backup to Oscar. I reads everthing about my Tigers. Yep."

"Nice to meet you, Mr. Zeke, sir. Arkie tells me a lot about you and Miss Zeze."

"Yur gonna be bigger 'n yur daddy," Zeze said.

"Yes, ma'am. You know my daddy?"

"We went to Attucks together. Zeke here finished 'fore I started," she said, tightening her head rag and adjusting her composure.

Georgey came out onto her porch. "OK Zeke, let the chilluns alone. They didn't come here to see you. They come here to see the Butterfly."

"You go on. Nice talkin' witch ya," Zeke said, picking his ear and nodding.

Georgey held the door for Rozelle, whispering warnings about getting stuck on Zeke's porch. We congregated in Georgey's kitchen like an assorted flock of birds—perching on counters, backs of chairs, and the stove—passing the Butterfly around, oohing and awing, wiping her spills, and teasing each other.

"Hey, Rick. Hope you and Andy are comin' to the game," Arkie said.

"Yeah, a bunch of us are. You dressing?"

"Probably not. Rozelle's dressin'. Looks like he'll get some time."

Rozelle nodded.

Marcella said, "Coach Crowe said he was goin' to use Oscar sparingly, so Rozelle should get a lot of time."

"There's lotta talk about my white friend down here," Arkie said. "Like you was some kind of a monster waitin' for the right time to get even."

"I hope not," I said.

Marcella walked around behind me, secretly put her hand in mine, and squeezed.

"Arkie's just jokin' with you, Rick," she said. "Most folks I talk to think you and yur brother are great."

The rest of the conversation became muffled in my mind as my breath quickened and I squeezed back. I thought about the warmth of her hand and wondered why she did it, while over and over in my mind ran the reasons why I should stay clear of her. At the same time I was also running through the list of possible places where we could meet without anyone knowing. Then she drew small circles in my palm with her fingernail and I felt her breasts rubbing against my back. Arkie noticed. His jaw clinched as he threw a raised eyebrow my way.

"How you gettin' home, Rick?" Rozelle asked.

"Dad's picking me up any minute."

"Rozelle and me got a curfew, so we better get goin'," Arkie said, heading for the door with Rozelle and the girls.

Georgey interjected. "Marcella, darlin', I needs to show you somethin'. Y'all go on ahead, we'll be right along."

I don't know what Georgey said to Marcella behind closed doors, but when she came out of the kitchen a few minutes later, that cute, purple-black, sweet girl looked hang-dog gray, wide-eyed, and petrified.

Fifty-One

March 4, 1956, was the first game of the state tournament season for Crispus Attucks. They would play Evansville Central High School in Indianapolis—a home game—but because Attucks couldn't afford a gymnasium, they scheduled their games in other high school gyms, all integrated. Arkie called at dinnertime.

"Hey, man, I'm playin' tonight. Rozelle, he's sick. Got a temperature of 103. Coach Crowe told me to dress."

Andy drove Baxter, Jim and me to the game. The shouts and cheers rattled the gym's high rafters and bounced from the cinderblock walls to the hard, wooden bleachers. Evansville Central was long on cheers and good-looking cheerleaders, while Attucks went to work early, tearing the game open and building a large lead. By the fourth quarter the second string took the court, and we cheered for Arkie until our voices stung. Midway through the fourth quarter, the Attucks cheerleaders started singing "The Crazy Song." Arkie stole an inbound pass and raced for a layup as the cheer continued. Arkie knew we were there. He looked over his shoulder and grinned as I screamed his name.

It seemed ironic that Arkie played in that first game of the tournament because, as the weeks went on after that, the regular eleven boys were always on the floor. No one got sick, no one was injured, and they didn't lose a game. Game after game Arkie sat behind the team in street clothes with a bus-driver sheen on his butt, yet he was always cheering on his teammates, nosing into the huddles, slapping rear ends.

Fifty-Two

Mom went to choir practice at the Church of the Holy God on Thursday nights. Dad said that one of us should go with her, reasoning that even if she were driving into a poor, white section at night, she shouldn't be alone—even though Dad drove into Frog Island at night by himself, even though Reverend Williams stood outside the church door waiting for her (along with thirty-three other choir members), even though she had a special parking space ten feet from the door, and even though it was possible to get there without having to stop at one light. She was safer in that neighborhood than rich, white Golden Hill—even though rich, white neighborhoods were supposed to be safe (but not for colored people) after dark. Mom simply felt better if one of us drove with her.

One of my major observations about the difference between a white Presbyterian choir and a Negro gospel choir is their enthusiasm. The white choir sits and stands in one place with their hands glued to the hymnal or sheet music. They stand like wooden toy soldiers. They don't put the hymnal down or hold it under their armpits so they can clap their hands. They don't dance in place or rock and sway. They don't shout "Yes!" or "Hallelujah!" Anyone can feel the difference, even the wooden soldiers.

Miss Tildalayhu always asked Mom to warm up the choir and "get 'em disciplined," she said. "We want them to sound like one harmonica, not thirty-three voices."

"I love you all," Mom said to the choir.

Thirty-three faces beamed.

"Georgey says Rozelle's auntie is in the choir. Which one?" Mom asked.

A tall, thin woman raised her hand. "Right here, Miss Lilly. Lulu's my name."

"Isn't Rozelle wonderful?" Mom asked.

"Hallelujah!" several members shouted.

"Takin' our boys to the championship, again."

Mom did a couple of bars of "The Crazy Song" to a chorus of laughter.

"OK. Watch my mouth," Mom said, heavily enunciating. "Do, re, mi, fa, sol, la, ti, do. Let's do it together, listening to the person next to us so that we say it together. Here we go. Do, re, mi, fa, sol, la, ti—now hold ti. Ti. Again. Ti. I want to hear the T . . . Tiiiii. Good. Do, re, mi, fa, sol, la, ti, do. Good. Wonderful! Again. This time we'll run up to Ti and hold it until I lower my hand.

"Do, re, mi, fa, sol, la, tiiiiiiiiiiiiiiiiiiiiiiii, do."

"Wonderful!" Mom exclaimed, finishing with a rhythmic finale, her back hunched and left leg drifting to the side. "Yes!"

I sat on the steps with Arkie, Rozelle, and Reverend Williams. It was a cold, black night and the light over the door burned a yellow halo.

"Smells like snow," Reverend Williams said.

"Yes, sir," Rozelle replied.

We were comfortable with the silence, as if we were alone. The choir started and stopped like hands on a record needle—

beginning a song, stopping, repeating the chorus. Quiet, then music. Quiet, then music.

"Again, from 'Jesus Lord,'" Mom said. Then quiet.

"Yur momma's a wonderful lady," Reverend Williams said.

"Thank you, sir."

"How surprised I was to hear she gave up her radio show."

"And her concerts," I added. "Now she has more time to be with the family. That's real important to her."

"Praise the Lord."

"Reverend Williams, anyone hear from Barrett?" I asked.

"Well, I guess I can tell you." He lit a cigarette—a Camel. "A neighbor says he's in jail up in Chicago."

"What for?" Arkie asked.

"Drugs. The drug scene's big up there. Young boys and girls are exposed to it like we are to cigarettes. Drug dealers give it away to poor folks to get them hooked, so those folks will steal anything to get money. Many poor, young girls are hooked on heroin or cocaine and become prostitutes to support their habit."

"I know some guys at school who sell marijuana," Arkie said.

"At high school?" Reverend Williams asked.

"Sho 'nuf, man," Rozelle said. "Lotta that stuff around. The wild kids smoke it down by the canal. Call it pot."

"Dangerous stuff," Reverend Williams said, shaking his head.

"Hear Dancin' Al can get you some," Arkie said.

"Oh Lord! If that's the case, I don't ever want to see him on this church's grounds. I want you to understand that. You hear me?"

"Yessir," Rozelle mumbled, and Arkie nodded his assent.

"Drugs are the stuff of the devil," Reverend Williams continued. "We must remember our community as it is, as it is now. We got enough temptations. I'm pretty tuned in, I thought. Now Dancin' Al? He's idolized by many young girls. I know drugs can change our community before we even knows it. Lord have mercy."

"He was a regular kind a nigger before he conked his hair," Rozelle said.

Arkie smiled. "The man says his hair is fried, dyed, and laid to the side."

My mind raced to Shuli. What would she have done without Georgey? Without Dad? I couldn't imagine her on the streets. Then my thoughts raced ahead fifteen years to Butterfly and her future. What would her church playground be like?

"We must pray for the Negro community, boys. Pray that Jesus gives us the foresight to see evil comin' and guides us." He looked at each of us with deep concern in his eyes, touched our arms, searched our faces. "I hope you boys don't mind but, at this moment, I am called to pray. Can we bow our heads?

"Blessed Lord Jesus. Here we sit, happy and sad, black and white, poor and rich, scared and brave. We are your children. Lord, guide us. Keep us away from the devil. Steer us like sheep in the field and protect this church's flock. Spread your merciful wings over Arkie and Rozelle and Rick. Make them wise and brave and strong. We also pray for the Negro community as we approach our high school basketball finals—that our victory will help solidify the races, not divide them. Energize young Arkie and Rozelle. And, Lord Jesus, I pray for Alvin Benjamin. We call him Dancin' Al. I pray for a cleansing. Keep him from using his

347

talents for evil purposes. I ask this in Your blessed, blessed name. Amen."

From inside the church Mom said, "Now let's turn out the lights and sing in darkness, listening to each other, feeling not seeing."

The lights clicked off.

Quiet. Then music. Quiet. Then music. The choir as one in the darkness—like an invisible harmonica.

"We can wade into the middle where the healing waters flow.

"It will only take a little to heal a wounded soul."

Rozelle and Reverend Williams stood up and went inside, leaving Arkie and me on the steps counting cricket chirps.

"OK," he started. "Not a lot of time. Before yur momma comes out. The word is out. Marcella Ames is 100 percent off base for you, my friend. Miss Georgella done spoke to the girl and it is over. No more talkin' 'bout it. She promised Hanna she would stay away from you. Got it?"

"That's why I haven't seen her at church or with you and Rozelle?"

"Don't know what happened. Don't wanna know. I hope you understand that messin' with Marcella is dangerous shit. You know that, don't you?"

"Yeah, I know. I really do." My head was nodding self-consciously.

He eyed me. "And?"

"You know what? I kinda wish I was colored, Arkie. It wouldn't be so difficult."

"Sure, you wish you was colored until you go out for dinner or go to the movies or hafta piss or get arrested."

"What happened to all the talk about equality?" I asked.

"You didn't hear that from me. I like my colored high school and my colored girlfriend. You're the only problem I got."

Mom and Andy exited the side door into the parking area.

"Sounded real good, Mrs. Stoner," Arkie said.

"Why thank you, Arkie." She hugged him. "You always know the right things to say."

"Especially to beautiful women," he added.

Fifty-Three

March 27, 1956. Butterfly was 26 days old. Andy, his friend Mark, Jim Moriarity, and I sat high in the bleachers at Butler Fieldhouse in Indianapolis. It was packed—over 12,000 fans gathered to watch the final game of the state tournament—Crispus Attucks High School, all colored, versus Jefferson–Lafayette High School, all white. Coach Crowe at Attucks dressed twelve boys; Arkie was the twelfth. We talked about sitting in the colored section but thought against it—not because of the Negroes; because of the whites. I knew Reverend Williams was there with Reginald and Sonny, maybe Zeke, and the church youth group. I was certain Hanna would be there with Arkie's parents. And Marcella.

Unintentionally, the Attucks team wore white jerseys. The all-white Lafayette team wore black. No one talked about white versus black, though it was on everyone's mind.

By halftime it was obvious that Attucks was going to smother Lafayette. During the last quarter, Coach Crowe put Rozelle and Arkie in the game. The cheerleaders began the chant,

> "Hi-de-hi-de-hi-de-hi;
> Hi-de-hi-de-hi-de-ho
> Skip, bob, beat-um.
> That's the Crazy Song!"

When Arkie hit a 30-foot jumper with a minute left on the clock, Andy, Jim, Mark, and I went wild cheering. At that point there wasn't a racist in the crowd. Black, white, it didn't matter—it was Indianapolis's own hometown team winning the state championship. The final score was 79-57. We worked our way through the crowd onto the courts while the players were cutting the nets. Reporters with flashbulbs and television cameras made it impossible to find Arkie or Rozelle in the forest of glistening black giants. As we were leaving I heard my name called, and I turned around to see Arkie waving me over to meet his mother and father. Marcella and Hanna were there, beaming. Marcella made my mind wander.

That night the Crispus Attucks team ate dinner in a public restaurant in downtown Indianapolis. Linen tablecloths and waiters. It was the first time that Arkie or Rozelle had been inside a public restaurant as patrons, not as busboys.

For the next week our town couldn't stop reliving the celebration. We watched the highlights over and over, especially the clip of Arkie hitting his 30-foot jumper.

"Here comes sophomore Arkansas Johnson. He pulls up. Shoots. Scores! From 30 feet. What a beautiful jumper! Looks like the next Oscar Robertson is out there."

The *Indianapolis Recorder*, an all-Negro newspaper, printed snapshots of the celebration, the nets being cutting down, and interviews with Doug Collins. Families were celebrating. One photograph showed Arkie and Hanna standing next to his mother, who is hugging me. Andy is smiling. I still have that picture.

* * *

After Georgey pulled her aside and put the fear of God in her if she ever got involved with me, Marcella did her best to avoid me. But each time I saw her, my mind took off her clothes piece by piece, imagining every detail of that ebony body. She went out of her way to avoid church functions if I were there, and it stayed that way until Dark Mary Reese of Frog Island introduced her to the ouija board and the mystical powers of certain people's connections to the outer world.

Marcella called me one afternoon out of the blue. She told me that as much as she loved Miss Georgella, she had spoken to Marcella without understanding her connection to—and these are her words—"a deeper, more sensual love than Miss Georgella could possibly understand.

"You see," Marcella continued, "I been talking to a ouija board. These mystical instruments of God listen to your individual questions and physically guide you through a path to honest action."

I'd heard of ouija boards—that they were weird—yet some people swore by them. Still, I had no idea what Marcella was talking about. It sounded like she'd memorized the instruction booklet.

"What path?" I asked.

"OK, Sweetie. I was so tortured after everone said I shouldn't see you again, everone except Dark Mary."

"Who's Dark Mary?"

"Oh, she's wonderful. She lives on Frog Island. A very mystical lady who speaks with God-On-High."

"God-On-High? Is that our God?"

"That's everone's God. Anyway, she said 'Follow your heart' and held my hand and asked the ouija board to reveal my

352

path. And Ricky, oh Ricky, I swear to you the ouija told me that we should go all the way. 'Make love,' the ouija said."

"Are you kidding?" I gulped. "The ouija board told you that?"

"Yes, yes, yes, Ricky. I told the ouija board about our kiss and the shivers that took over my body evertime I thought of it, and I couldn't stop thinking about it. Oh God, Ricky. I was feeling so shameful and bad. I asked the ouija board if my feelings were against God's rules like Miss Georgella said."

"What did the ouija say?"

"Ouija said, NO."

"No?"

"Not 'no we shouldn't do it.' Ouija said 'no, our going all the way was not against God's rules.' It said, 'Be careful, be slow. Make it beautiful.' Can you believe it, Ricky?"

My mouth went dry as I reached for a breath—aroused in anticipation.

"Oh, God, Marcella. I've dreamed of it since that night on the church basketball court," I blurted out.

"Me, too. Can't get you out of my mind."

"Yeah," I drooled on the mouthpiece of the phone and wiped my chin.

"Can we do it, Ricky?"

"Oh yes."

"Tonight?"

"Tonight? Where?"

"Crown Hill Cemetery, across the street from my house. Dark Mary and I found a nice and private place just down the hill from James Witcomb Riley's tomb. A small bunch of trees. If you come from your house up to Riley's tomb, I'll meet you."

"Sure."

"Oh Ricky, it's such a beautiful day. Not a cloud in the sky. I'll bring a blanket."

"How about 6:30?"

"Perfect. You are my man, Rick Stoner. I love you so much."

"Yeah. I love you too. Six thirty."

James Whitcomb Riley's tomb is like a Parthenon and sits on the highest spot in Indianapolis. Dad and Andy and I used to drive to Crown Hill Cemetery and go up its winding road to the top, and from there we could see the Indianapolis skyline.

That night in early May, the redbud trees were bursting with the advent of spring. The sun was low in the sky and sparkling lights from the city shown like fireflies. I could hear music off in the distance—soft doo-wop about love and romance.

As I approached the tomb, I heard Marcella's voice softly calling.

"Over here, sweetie," she waved from beneath a branch of an old sycamore tree.

I came closer and stepped beneath the branches into a secluded alcove, and there Marcella stood, in a sheer satin robe tied loosely in front. I couldn't move—my mouth slowly opened and I felt a rush of desire. Without hesitation she smiled and slowly shook the robe from her shoulders, and in the soft breeze it rippled and floated to the ground—it seemed like forever before it landed. The dappled sunlight traced her body shape—her immense breasts, her stomach, her luscious, black pubic patch. She parted her lips as she breathed, and her deep red lipstick glistened. Everything seemed to move.

My mind was without thought or form, and then she spoke. "Oh honey. Dark Mary came to bless our union. She . . ."

"She?" I asked, shaking my head, blinking my eyes,

returning to reality.

There stood a tall, thin, colored woman, her hair matted and awry, who wore a black robe sprinkled with many small stars. Her face was disfigured by an ugly scar that pulled down the corner of her right eye. She blinked her eyes slowly, unevenly.

I looked at Marcella as she stood there, voluptuously nude, breathing hard. Smiling, she reached for Dark Mary's hand, who grasped it and reached for mine. The trees rustled and there was a strange odor in the air—like something was smoldering. Dark Mary hummed as I looked at her outstretched hand, her long, spiderlike fingers beckoning me. I looked at Marcella as her breasts heaved. I felt my erection pushing against my pants.

And I ran—

Up the side of the hill past Riley's tomb, through the pergola, and down the other side. I thought I heard Marcella's voice calling me and considered turning around—I wanted to go back—but I kept on running—through family plots, around statues, over grave markers. I reached for my wallet, the prophylactic inside. I stopped to catch my breath and looked around—thinking, dreaming about Marcella.Biggest breasts I'd ever seen in any magazine. I scratched my head. My heart slowed down. Something warned me that this wasn't right. Something inside of me, something filled my heart with—I don't know—something.

"Well hell," I thought to myself, heading home, "there'll be a next time."

I wanted to tell Andy. I wanted to tell Arkie. I rehearsed what I would say, but in the end I told no one. I remember what Dad said about secrets, that "some secrets remain secrets—Clark Kent never told anyone he was Superman."

I decided to be Clark Kent.

* * *

A few weeks later—late May—I hitchhiked home after my last class. Georgey wasn't there. I knew she was at her house with Shuli and the Butterfly. We were calling her THE Butterfly, like putting a label on her as being different from other butterflies—more beautiful, more special. Dad started it on her scheduled health checks, when he'd report, "The Butterfly is healthy, as normal and cranky as most butterflies I have cared for. Her mom is tired, also normal and cranky."

When Georgey wasn't there, our house was missing the smell of cookies and the sounds of her shuffling in the kitchen, tinkering about, making this or that. I sat at the kitchen table and read about Attucks and mostly Oscar Robertson, who was still front-page material in the *Indianapolis Star*. There was speculation he'd be chosen "Mr. Basketball" for the state of Indiana at the annual season finale—the All-Star game—where the best players in Indiana played against the best players in Kentucky. He planned to attend the University of Cincinnati, though seventeen other colleges wanted him.

Andy had cut out the scoring summary for last month's championship game and it still sat on the table. Thorpe, nine points and Arkansas Johnson, eleven points—eleven points in one quarter. Arkie would be seventeen this summer, but just starting his junior year. That was common at Attucks and in that era, where colored children often started school late or moved around because of a broken home—dropping out of one school and starting another.

In Indianapolis it could also have been from a lingering sickness on Frog Island, caused in part by untreated water. I hadn't forgotten when the town refused to install an adequate water and sewage system, bypassing Frog Island entirely. That was the year that Squiggy Daniels spent two months in jail for resisting arrest and assault and battery. The town installed sewage pipes to run to its white residents, but the sewage at Frog Island was still the same.

Fifty-Four

I would be sixteen in two months, and not much made sense to me. I would never have a car like Mike's; I had become a reverse Oreo cookie and I suffered from a triple case of Clark Kent's malady of secrets—the fiasco with Arlene in the trailer park, Marcella and our disastrous night, and the truth behind my broken jaw.

The first two—Arlene and Marcella—would make me look stupid. The last—my broken jaw—would have made me look like Superman. I wanted to tell everyone exactly what happened at the Church of the Holy God and to be seen as a wounded warrior. Rumors were rife throughout the Negro community, and many knew the truth. It had leaked among the white community, but only as a rumor—like the Queen of the Congo.

Though the house was silent, I sensed the near soundless creaks and groans—the ones only mice can hear—the growing pains of lumber adjusting to weight, water whispering in the pipes, the furnace kicking in, the refrigerator rumbling to make ice—the sounds that give a home a life.

I heard Andy's old car pull into the driveway. In August it would become mine, because he would be going away to college. I'd have to work this summer to pay Andy, and Dad said he'd make up the difference. All that for a car I really didn't want—a 1933 Ford sedan. It was Andy's image, not Rick Stoner's. I had wanted a '49 red Cadillac convertible with wire wheels and skirts, but that image wasn't me anymore—it was Mike Dunbar's. Though still a beauty on the outside, the car had become angry, opinionated, loud, and self-centered. I wondered what kind of a car Georgey would suggest I own. Probably Andy's. I could hear her say, "God is more interested in your character than your comfort."

"Rick. Are you home?" Andy shouted from the driveway.

"I'm in here."

"Get out here."

I opened the door and saw Andy standing next to his car. Someone had taken a white paintbrush and written "NIGGER LOVER" in large letters on both sides of the car—across both doors. It was a fast job and the paint had run and puddled on the running boards. I stared in disbelief as words fell from my mouth.

"What . . . who . . . how?"

"Who did it?" My first complete sentence.

"Who else?" Andy snapped.

"D'you see him do it?"

"'Course not."

We walked around the car, shaking our heads and touching the paint—still wet.

"We could get lots of turpentine and wipe it off. Probably get most of it," I said.

"Then I'd have a car with white smears on the side."

"Might need to have it painted again."

"The whole car would have to be. You can't just paint the doors. That would look as bad as leaving the white smears. Who's gonna pay for it?"

At that moment Mom and Miss Tildalayhu pulled into the driveway. Two gaping mouths.

"Oh, my goodness," Mom exclaimed, jumping out of her car. "How on earth did that happen?"

Miss Tildalayhu said nothing. She sat meekly—hands in her lap, head down—while just the top of her hat with the yellow hatband hunched over the dash.

"Oh, my goodness," Mom repeated.

"There's a bunch of racists at school," Andy said.

"It's that Dunbar boy, isn't it?"

"Probably, but there's no way to prove it. Mike's not the only racist at Shortridge."

Mom turned around to Miss Tildalayhu, still sitting in the car. "Oh, Tilly, I'm so sorry you had to see this." She turned to Andy.

"You'll have to wash it off."

"Mom, it's enamel. It doesn't wash off. It's like regular car paint."

"Well, we'll buy some black paint and paint over it." She turned once more to Miss Tildalayhu. "Tilly? Are you all right?"

Still sitting in the car, Miss Tildalayhu had begun sobbing. Mom rushed to put her arm around her.

"I'm sorry, Tilly."

"Oh, no," Miss Tildalayhu said. "You should not apologize to me. We should be apologizin' to you. These are things coloreds don't realize, that this happens to white folks who befriend Negroes. Can hatred be more powerful than love?"

"We'll get through this, Tilly. It's just one more step on a long walk."

"We will, Lilly—all with bruised hearts and a deeper faith."

Andy and I sat down on two outdoor chairs alongside the driveway.

"Think about this," Andy said.

"What?"

"We do nothing."

"Why?"

"It's fear, Rick. Racists thrive on fear. Scare the hell out of someone and hide. They expect us to be scared. I'm not. Are you?"

"Not scared, but I'll feel pretty silly driving around in a car that says 'nigger lover' on it. Don't forget, you're the one going away to college."

"Eventually we can have it painted, but first we can use this as a protest. This is the kind of thing Martin Luther King would do. We'll show this town how ugly racism is without fighting them physically."

* * *

I called Arkie that night and told him about the car and what we were thinking of doing. "You lookin' to be shot?" he asked.

Reverend Williams said, "Arkie told me what happened to Andy's car, and what you plan on doing about it. Have you thought this out carefully?"

Georgey encouraged, "I know you boys are doing what you feels you has to, so God bless you both."

Dad sighed. "You better rehearse what you're going to say. This will create quite a stir."

The high school principal asked Andy what he was doing.

361

"I didn't do this, sir. I'm pretty sure it was Mike Dunbar and some of his friends," Andy replied.

"Well, you can't leave it like that."

"Why not?"

"You're going to start a lot of trouble, Andy. You're too nice a kid."

"I think you ought to talk with Dunbar. Ask him if he knows anything about it."

"What are you saying? You won't get rid of the racial slur?"

"I won't. If Mike or the other kids want to, they can. It'll cost more money than I earn to repaint that car."

* * *

After a tumultuous and very visible week, the *Indianapolis Star* called and asked if they could interview Andy and take some pictures. Two days later a picture of Andy and his car in the high school parking lot was published in the *Star* with this story:

LOCAL, WHITE HIGH SCHOOL STUDENT HARRASSED BY WHITE RACIST GROUPS.

Eighteen-year-old Andrew Stoner recently finished his classes at Shortridge High School and walked out to drive his car home. This is what he found in the parking lot. Stoner has an after-school job and says he is saving his money for college. It would cost $103 to have his car repainted. He was asked by *Star* reporter Elton Wilson why that particular slur was painted on his car. Stoner replied, "My family has many colored friends as well as white friends. We are proud and honored to call them friends."

362

He went on to say, "I guess if I were to paint on my car it would say, 'Negro Supporter.'"

Principal Edmond Carson said Stoner is an excellent student-athlete and will attend Kenyon College in the fall. He added, "This is a very courageous stance this young man has taken. He is to be commended. Shortridge High School has a major colored population and we are proud of our integrated school and all of our students."

Andy and I proudly rode around town in his car, mostly to cheers, until the school year was over. There were also people who raised their middle fingers and shouted obscenities. We knew we were in the middle of a cultural whirlpool—hatred, respect, distrust, admiration. Shortridge was strongly divided, and it swirled around us. The colored population was cohesive. Bonded. Hung together. The white population was mostly quiet, not wanting to take sides except for the extremes. Statements like "Just between you and me, I'm 100 percent behind you, but I'm not looking for trouble" were frequent.

May of that year was hot and Mom instituted her cold air storage program: close the windows in the morning and turn on the fans, open the windows just before sunset, turn off the fans. I tried running a fan's air over ice cubes one night.

Andy and I drove Georgey home on one of those hot evenings, parking Andy's car in front of her house. Shuli sat in the swing on her porch with The Butterfly in her arms.

"Well, I guess I know where you boys stand on Negro issues," she said, eyeing the car. "Come on up and sit for a spell."

"I'll fix some cold, cold iced tea," Georgey said.

"Sounds good," Andy said.

We sipped iced tea and watched the sun slide down behind Zeke and Reginald's houses. Soon Zeke came across the street and shook our hands. "You boys is real brave. Doctah King would be proud of you. Zeze and me are honored to be yur friends." His tired eyes were wet with emotion.

A car drove down the street and beeped. Crickets spoke beneath the porch.

"Hear 'em?" Zeke asked.

"Hear who?" Georgey responded, suspiciously.

"Them crickets chirpin' under yur porch here. If you counts the number of them chirps in one minute, then add forty-one, that's the temperature."

"Really?" Andy said.

"That's a new one," Shuli whispered.

"That's what my daddy told me long time ago. I'll show ya. Got my watch on. I'll tell ya when to start and when to stop. Georgella, no blabbin' till it's over. I know that might be tough for ya. And Shuli, you gotta keep that little girl asleep. Here we go. Start."

We sat quietly—Andy counting, Zeke smoking and watching his wristwatch. Another car drove down the street and beeped. We waved. Shuli hummed to herself quietly. Zeke winked as if he knew something no one else knew.

"Stop," he said.

"Seventy-three," Andy said.

"OK. Seventy-three. Got a pencil and some paper, Georgella? We got us some addin' to do."

"That's all right, Mr. Zeke," Andy said. "Seventy-three and forty-one is, let's see, 114."

"There ya go," Zeke said, smiling real big. "It's one hunerd and fourteen degrees outside. Purty danged hot. Uh?"

"Zeke," Georgey sighed, "it's not a hunerd and fourteen degrees. It's not even ninety degrees."

"That's not what the crickets say," Zeke said.

"Zeze," Georgey called. "Zeze. Can you hear me?"

"I hears you, Georgella."

"How hot you think it is?"

"Oh, Lordy. Must be almost ninety."

"Well, it sure as hell feels a hunerd and fourteen to me," Zeke sputtered.

"Me, too," I said. "At least a hundred and fourteen."

"Cigarette?" Zeke asked, smiling and shaking out a Camel.

I laughed. "'Fraid not, sir. Might nigger-lip the butt."

"What you talkin' 'bout?" Georgey asked.

"Oh, nothin'," Zeke said. "Jes' havin' a little fun."

"Well, they don't smoke, Zeke. They're just young boys," Georgey snapped.

"Not as young as you think, Georgella. Two brave men. They should be smokin' by now. Yep. I recommend Camels." He held the pack like in an ad.

"Yur daddy smokes them Pall Mall cigarettes," Georgey said.

"Those are for white folks."

"Zeke!"

"I'm serious as I can be. Ya ever see a nigger with a Pall Mall in his mouth?"

"Can't say I could tell while driving through town," Andy said.

"I sure am glad my little girl ain't hearin' this," Shuli said.

From down the street we heard a moaning sound, but it could have been anything.

"Who's that?" Georgey said.

"What?" Zeke asked.

We listened to the sound, louder than crickets, several houses down. The sound was a person—seemed to be in distress.

Then Sonny called out, several houses south: "Zeke! It's Miss Alice! Better get down here."

"Miss Alice?" Zeke asked. We all peered down the street to Miss Tildalayhu's house. We saw Miss Alice wearing an old nightgown and backing out her front door. She was pulling something very heavy, struggling and moaning.

"Zeke!" Sonny cried.

Then Reginald and Marjorie ran into the street. "Miss Alice!" they called out.

"Ohh," Miss Alice moaned. She was pulling a body out of the house onto the porch.

Andy and I ran from Georgey's porch toward Miss Tildalayhu's house—Reginald, Sonny, and Marjorie ahead of us— racing down the street.

"Miss Alice!" we called.

"Ohh," she moaned again. "My baby!"

We stopped in our tracks. Miss Alice was pulling Miss Tildalayhu—her daughter—out of the house, dragging her down the porch steps, lifeless like caught fish dragged from a boat deck on the dock. Miss Tildalayhu was in her finest floral print dress and hat.

"Oh, my baby," she wailed.

"She ain't breathin'," Sonny said, kneeling next to her.

"Help my baby," Miss Alice pleaded.

Andy knelt down beside Sonny and checked Miss Tildalayhu's pulse on her carotid artery. "Rick, call Dad. Tell him there's no heartbeat. Hurry. I'll try to get her heart going."

"Use Miss Tildalayhu's phone," Marjorie said. "It's right inside the door. Hurry, honey."

"Ohh," Miss Alice wailed.

I raced into Miss Tildalayhu's house and dialed our phone.

"Doctor Stoner," the calm voice on the other end answered.

"Dad! It's Miss Tildalayhu! She's not breathing. There's no heartbeat. She's in her front yard. What should Andy do?"

"I'll call the hospital and get an ambulance there as fast as I can. Tell Andy to try some CPR. I'll be there in five minutes."

I called out to Andy, "Dad says to do CPR. He's on his way—so is the ambulance."

On my way outside, I quickly glanced around Miss Tildalayhu's house. It was spotless—not a dustball anywhere. Shiny framed photographs of nameless people singing in choirs sat on tables in orderly rows—tallest in the back, mouths open, teeth shiny white. You could almost hear them singing "Hallelujah."

Outside, Reginald quietly said, "I think she's dead."

"Oh, heavenly Father," Georgey began, "do what you hasta do to save this woman. It is not her time. Touch her. Save her, great Father."

Zeke slowly shook his head. "Deader 'n a doornail."

Zeze put her arms around Miss Alice and said tenderly, "Come over here, darlin'. Everthing's gonna be jes' fine."

I sat on Miss Tildalayhu's porch steps, watching Andy and her neighbors cluster around her—Georgey praying while Marjorie and Ann Sue knelt, Miss Alice sobbing in Zeze's arms, Shuli holding Butterfly close. Andy was pressing on Miss Tildalayhu's back then pulling her elbows forward, not giving up on CPR. Reginald and Zeke talked in hushed tones while other neighbors were running to the site—the crowd around the crowd continued to grow. Off in the distance I heard a siren and felt relieved.

Dad careened around the corner, stretching the limits of the old Plymouth and screeching to a stop. He and Mom raced through the crowd, Dad carrying his black physician's bag. At Miss Tildalayhu's side, he checked her pulse and quickly pulled a syringe from his bag.

"Nitroglycerin," he whispered to Andy.

Mom carefully removed Miss Tildalayhu's best lavender hat and embraced her. "Oh, Tilly. Please don't die." A police car inched through the crowd, its red lights flashing hot on the surrounding people and houses.

"Lord God, Almighty," Georgey prayed, "help this woman! See us, Lord Jesus! We're here, callin' to you."

The ambulance wheeled around the corner and the crowd parted again. Dad checked Miss Tildalayhu's heartbeat with his stethoscope once more, then took off his jacket and covered her face and upper body.

"No!" Mom screamed, removing the coat from her face. "You can save her, Wayne. Do more! Do something!"

Butterfly awoke and began to cry. Shuli rocked her quietly.

"It's all over," Dad said, chewing on his lip. "She's in God's hands now."

After a moment of stillness, Georgey quietly lifted her voice and began to gently sing "Amazing Grace." The crowd came to life, softly humming and chiming in. Mom held Miss Tildalayhu, her arms wrapped around Dad's coat that covered her.

"T'was Grace that taught
my heart to fear.
And Grace, my fears relieved.
How precious did that Grace appear
the hour I first believed."

Mom's cries of sadness grew as she hugged Miss Tildalayhu tighter.

"Through many dangers, toils and snares
we have already come.
T'was Grace that brought us safe thus far
and Grace will lead us home."

I sat on the porch steps, moved by the music and the drama of a life ending. The red flashing lights spinning across the front porches were like a fireworks' show, while the car headlights shined on where Matilda Lee Hughes lay. Black faces faded in and out of the shadows, while Mom, Dad and Andy glowed in the center.

"When we've been here 10,000 years,
bright shining as the sun.
We've no less days to sing God's praise
than when we've first begun."

Miss Tildalayhu's body was carefully placed in the back of the ambulance, Mom and Georgey touching her until the doors were closed. Then Mom held Georgey, the two women sobbing. Zeze, Shuli and Butterfly, Ann Sue, and Marjorie soon formed a circle of grief around them both. The sky was deep as the stars lay in layers, hushing the neighborhood sounds. A few clouds drifted past—it was time to move on.

This would soon be over.

* * *

The highlight of Miss Tildalayhu's two-hour service at the Church of the Holy God came at the very end. People lined the back of the church and spilled out of its open doors into the street. The scene was truly an artist's palette—bright pastel colors of hats and dresses and sparkling highlights of five-and-dime jewelry mixed in with the somber darkness of men's suits, white socks, and black shoes.

The casket was left open and Miss Tildalayhu looked beautiful, her cheeks powdered and rouged. She was wearing her best lavender hat with its red, silk band, pearl earrings, and a pearl and seashell bracelet. Friends and neighbors shuffled by the open casket—some nodding and smiling with memories, some sobbing to themselves, others leaning over to kiss her then rearranging her hat. The choir sang under Mom's direction, supplemented by loud shouts of "Oh Lord" and "Praise Jesus" from the congregation. Many were on their feet, dancing and singing in the aisles. There were a surprising number of white faces in the congregation—Jim Moriarity with his parents, a cellist from the symphony, the owner of Sandborn's restaurant, and several of Andy's friends.

Then Reverend Williams went over to Mom, who sat with the choir. He took her hand and led her to a seat next to Georgey. Kneeling in front of them, he read from the Bible. "Let not your heart be troubled . . . ." Georgey laid one hand on his head and held Mom's hand with the other. "Miss Tildalayhu has gone to heavenly mansions."

"Heavenly mansions," Georgey moaned.

"Heavenly mansions," Mom quietly mumbled, wiping her nose.

He walked over to the open casket and carefully, lovingly, removed Miss Tildalayhu's hat, brought it over to Georgey and kissed her. Turning around, he faced the open casket.

"Miss Tildalayhu!" he called out in a loud voice. "Matilda! Tilly! There were so many things we should have said to you, but we never did, so many words of love we did not offer while you selflessly gave of your magnificent talents. You jes' got away too fast."

"Too fast, Lord."

"Way too fast."

"Minutes and hours and weeks and months and years. Yes!"

"Hallelujah!"

"Too fast."

"Times of your faithful givin'. Times you gave your talents to the Lord. I never saw a sad face."

"Her smilin' face!"

"Praise the Lord!"

"Hallelujah!"

"I never heard a cry for thanks. It was all done quietly."

"Quietly."

"Joyfully."

"Oh, so beautifully."

"For the glory of our God. So now there's nothin' more to say. Your sweet name and faith will live with us all our lives." He paused with his head down amid whispers of agreement.

371

"Goodnight, Miss Tildalayhu." He grabbed the casket lid, slammed it shut, and said, "Goodnight, my wonderful friend. I know that God is going to give you a good morning." Tears drained his eyes and shined his cheeks.

Mom rose from her pew and conducted the choir in "On That Great Getting-up Morning We Shall Rise." In the back row of the choir, off to the side and out of sight, sat Spike Stoner—extemporaneously bending notes on his harmonica.

Fifty-Five

The official culmination of the basketball season in Indianapolis always took place in June. The state of Indiana put forth its twelve best high school players, and the state of Kentucky did the same. This year they would play against each other at the Butler Fieldhouse in Indianapolis. Oscar Robertson from Crispus Attucks was chosen to be in the starting five, and sports columnists were in agreement that, if Indiana won, Robertson would be voted Mr. Basketball for the state, regardless of his race.

"Hey, you wanna go to the game?" I asked.

"Sure," Jim answered. "Who's driving?"

"Andy."

"Is he driving 'The Nigger Lover'?"

"Yeah, it's part of our protest."

"It's part of your coffin. Count me out." Mark said.

Jim volunteered his parents' station wagon and then Mark agreed to join us. Andy, Jim, and I wore our Shortridge letter sweaters—Andy's for varsity wrestling, Jim's for varsity basketball, and mine for JV tennis. (Mark wondered if he could get a letter for the German Club.)

Before the game began, the announcer introduced the Indiana state champions—Crispus Attucks. They stood center court in their white sweaters with large, black "A's"—the crowd screaming, the team glowing white on black. There was no racial issue that night. It seemed—for that moment anyway—that champions were colorless, like the black gladiators of Rome. Indianapolis's problem was that black champions were not allowed to be permanently real. They existed for the moment and at the white crowd's discretion—like photographs a white man could take down anytime he wanted; like the photograph of the Queen of the Congo, folded and filed away.

The Indiana All-Stars won the game, and Oscar Robertson scored an unprecedented 34 points. We stayed for the ceremonies, moving down to seats four rows from the floor, and white reporters scurried around us like mice in a box of spilled Cheerios. Rozelle and Arkie came over to sit with us for a while. Andy introduced them to Mark and Jim.

"Didn't I meet you before?" Arkie asked Jim. "Hard to remember. You know all you white folks look the same." We all laughed and relaxed, enjoying the victory.

Jim said, "I met you after the state finals. I met Rozelle here in November."

"How's that?" he asked.

"I play for Shortridge. Forward. You guys ate us up. I had one chance. A jumper at the free throw line."

"What happened?" Rozelle asked.

"You blocked it."

"Sorry," Rozelle mumbled.

"Don't be sorry. We got one game with you next year."

"All right, I'll remember. Stand up here so's I can remember you right."

Jim stood up next to Rozelle—at least a 3-inch difference. Rozelle looked down on Jim.

"Rick says you're called Big Jim."

"Big compared to Rick. I got a really big heart. I suppose that's what he means."

Rozelle mussed his hair and laughed. "I'll remember ya. We'll be friends from now on."

Only a trickle of fans remained; it was mostly the media. The players found their girlfriends or families and prepared to leave. Arkie had borrowed his father's car and brought Rozelle, and they left before us. We stopped to buy hot dogs. As we walked out of the fieldhouse, a major commotion met us in the parking lot—screams and shouts, squealing tires. A fight somewhere. We ran to where the activity was and saw Rozelle—nervous, frantic—looking around for someone, someone to help. . Someone!

"Rozelle!" I shouted.

"Man!" Rozelle screamed. "They jumped Arkie!"

"Where is he?" Andy cried.

"They took him."

"Who took him?" I asked.

"I dunno, man. Some white kids."

"Took him?"

"Yeah. Grabbed him, threw a blanket over his head, and stuffed him in a car."

"In a car?"

"Yeah. Bunch a whiteys in a convertible."

"A red one?" I asked.

"Think so. Dark out here."

There were other people there, whites as well. One said, "It was red. I saw it. A Cadillac. Five kids in it."

"Yeah, we saw it, too. All white guys."

"Shit man," Rozelle said. "I was too scared. One guy aimed a rifle at me and I ran. I'm sorry."

"I'll bet a million bucks I know where they're going," I said.

"Me, too," Jim said.

"You know? Come on!" Rozelle prodded. "Where's yur car, man?"

"Over here—let's hurry!"

Andy told several people to go back inside the fieldhouse, call the police, and wait for them.

"Please tell them it was a red Cadillac convertible," I said. "There's only one in town. It belongs to Mike Dunbar."

"Mike Dunbar?"

"That's right."

Jim, Mark, Andy, Rozelle, and I jumped in the car and headed north. The windows were down and the wind raced hectic as we sped along. Mark was curled up in the very back of the station wagon; Andy and Rozelle were in the back seats.

"Where do you think they're taking him?" Andy asked.

"I'm certain it would be the Northside Men's Club," Jim said.

Andy began thinking out loud. "Is this the place where Dad and Mr. Moriarity picked you guys up after Hell Night?"

"That's the one."

"What's a 'Hell Night'?" Rozelle asked.

"It's an initiation night for a club Jim and I belong to. They hold it at this secluded cornfield," I said.

"I thought white people met in fancy restaurants."

"We should have," Jim said.

"What's it look like?" Andy asked.

"It's a cornfield, a few buildings, and a lake."

Andy nodded his head. "I've actually been there. About a year ago. A dirt road that leads to the buildings?"

"A tractor path."

We thought in silence—racing out of town, streetlights whizzing by in cadence.

"Okay guys. I have a plan." Andy said. "Jim, way before we get there, you're gonna need to turn your lights off. We don't want them to know we're coming. Wonder how many there are?"

"One guy with a rifle and uh, four or five others," Rozelle said.

"Rick," Andy said. "If we drop you and Rozelle off before that tractor path, you think you could get around behind them?"

"Yeah, I think so. Have to run across the cornfield. It's about the length of a football field. Then through some trees, as I recall."

"You're right," Jim said. "There's a bunch of trees surrounding the cabins."

"Better take off that white sweater, Rozelle," Mark said from the back. "You'll look like a giant lightning bug."

"Sure," he said, pulling it over his head.

"They're gonna need lights, so we should be able to see them from a distance."

"Dunbar's car lights?"

"Probably. Don't think they'd be stupid enough to build a fire."

"I hope there's only one car," I said. "What'll we do if there's more?"

"We're screwed," Andy replied. "Mark, I'm gonna drop you off at a gas station and you can call the police. Tell them what's happened and where you are. Tell them to meet you at the gas station and you'll show them where to go."

"What if Dunbar and his cronies aren't there?"

"Then Arkie's in big trouble. But I don't think we should wait for the cops. We can change our plan as we go along. So Mark, you tell them to pick you up at the gas station."

"It's right up there, that Phillips 66," Jim said, slowing down. "There's a phone booth. Turn left on that gravel road."

"Jim, let's drive down the road first," Andy said. "See if we can spot them as we drive by. That would make me feel better about this whole plan."

"Don't drive slow," Mark said. "It'll look suspicious. Then circle around back here."

There were no streetlights—only the headlight beams bouncing along the road. We were quiet as the tires crunched the gravel.

Then, "I see somethin'!" Rozelle exclaimed. "I think. Up there. Are those lights?"

We strained our eyes, searching the blackness.

"Yeah, I see them," I said. "Behind the trees. Keep driving, Jim. Don't slow down."

"Definitely car lights. Hurry!" Rozelle said.

"How many car lights?" I asked.

"Couldn't tell," Mark said.

"Me either." Andy.

Three lefts later, we were back at the Phillips gas station.

"OK, Mark. Tell the cops to meet you here. Not at the location. Here. Then you can show them the way."

"Yeah," I said. "It was—what—three miles at the most? On the righthand side. By the time you get there, you'll see Jim's lights and Dunbar's, I hope."

"You need a dime?" I asked.

"I got one. Be careful, you guys. If there's too many, wait for the cops."

"We will, but we're counting on you to back us up."

We dropped off Mark, drove down the road, and stopped. Jim turned off the car lights and we sat—eyes refocusing, moving, searching in the blackness like searching for a thought. Gradually the shroud lifted from our eyes.

"How you doin', Rozelle?" Andy whispered.

"OK, OK. Yeah, I'm fine. A little scared, but fine."

"We all are."

Slowly Jim rolled down the gravel road, hearing the tires crunch like peanuts and crackers. There were no other sounds. Our eyes continued adjusting and clouds drifted past a half-hearted crescent moon, exposing moon-blue cornfields.

"I think I see something," Jim said, stopping.

I got out of the car. "Yeah. Behind that cluster of trees."

"Uh huh."

"There's the lights."

"Let Rozelle and me start from here," I said. "This is as good a place as any."

"OK, OK," Andy said. "You guys get behind Dunbar's car. Let's say it's facing us now. I want you guys behind it. They won't be able to see you 'cause of the lights in their eyes."

"Then what?" I asked.

"We're going to drive up the tractor path with our lights off. We'll turn them on when we get close or if someone spots us. As soon as you see our lights, I want you to race for Dunbar's car, get the keys, and heave 'em. Rozelle, if anyone gets in Rick's way, stomp on 'em. Otherwise, make sure Dunbar doesn't get away."

"Don't he have a rifle?"

"It's a sawed off-shotgun, double-barreled," I said. "He's gonna only get two shots. That's it."

"That's it?" Rozelle sputtered.

"The person with the gun will control this fight," Andy said. "Let's get that gun."

Jim said, "I'd sure like to know how many we're up against. Rick, you and Rozelle do a head count. When we get out of the car, yell out the number. Rozelle says five. Could be more. Could be less. Don't yell till Andy and I are out of the car."

Rozelle and I got out and watched the car silently roll away, heard the crunch of the gravel, saw the sporadic flashes of Jim's brake lights. Then the blackness covered us completely. We took a moment for our eyes to focus.

"Let's go," Rozelle said, heading straight along a foot-high corn row and getting a good headstart.

"Wait for me, Rozelle."

He slowed down. "Sorry."

"I think there's a fence at the end of the field. We'll have to climb over it."

We were both out of breath when we reached the fence and leaned over—our hands on our knees—panting. We could hear voices and clearly see car headlights. One car—I breathed a sigh of relief and then shuddered with fear as I realized what lay ahead of us. "This way. Quietly," I whispered.

Soon we were just 30 feet behind Dunbar's car. We could see the figures clearly—four, not five. They were wearing white hoods with pointed tops, shouting and encouraging each another. Empty beer cans glowed in the headlights. Then a gun fired into the ground. "Ka-plow!"

"Dance, Jim Crowe!" someone screamed and laughed. "Yeah, dance, nigger!"

"Only one more shot left. Let's get closer," I gushed to Rozelle. "Wait for Andy's lights. First, I'll get the keys."

"Sons a bitches," Rozelle mumbled. I could feel the depth of his hatred.

When we were directly behind the Cadillac, I reached out and touched Rozelle, pointing to the boys. Arkie's hands were tied behind his back and another rope in a hangman's noose hung around his neck, connected to a stake in the ground. He stood in the headlights, sweating, bruised, and bleeding. His sweater had been torn from his body and hung loose around his trousers. Someone was holding the sawed-off shotgun—it had to be Dunbar. He had a leather ammo belt filled with shotgun shells buckled around his waist.

In the distance, suddenly Jim's lights came on and his car flew up the tractor path, zigzagging. At that same moment, I crawled over the trunk and into the Cadillac, hoping Dunbar had left the keys. He did. Jerking them out of the ignition, I threw them as far as I could, just as a white hood leaped into the driver's seat to make a getaway. Aiming for his head, I kicked back against the door and leaped out of the car screaming "Four! Just four!"

I saw Dunbar hide his shotgun under a coat on the ground.

To Rozelle I shouted, "Get the gun! It's under Mike's coat, near his left foot. Stand on it!"

Rozelle raced at Mike and straight-armed him in the chest, knocking him back several feet. Then he picked up the shotgun, aiming at Mike. "Your white ass is done, boy," he sneered.

Another white hood raced away across the field, flailing arms and legs.

"Three," I said, "and we got the gun."

"And you two get over here so we can see you," Rozelle said, holding the shotgun and motioning to the other two remaining.

Jim and Andy pulled up facing Mike's car and jumped out. "Just these three?" Andy asked.

"One got away," I said.

Jim untied Arkie's hands and removed the noose from around his neck.

"Give me those ropes," Andy said, taking the hoods off of the two remaining sheets.

"Well, well, Larry, Neil. Why am I not surprised?" He tied their wrists to Jim's bumper. Rozelle pulled the hood from Dunbar's head.

Arkie approached Dunbar, taking the hood and wiping the blood from his face. "This ain't Mississippi, white boy, and I'm no Emmett Till. You is gonna spend some time in jail, but not before I whup yur ass fair and square. Do you know how to fight like a man?"

"I'm not afraid of any nigger," Mike said.

"Good," Arkie said. "I thought you'd be runnin' by now."

Mike took a quick wild swing at Arkie, hoping to catch him off guard. Arkie easily ducked and evaded the swing, pushing Dunbar in the face with an open hand.

"Come on, boy. Let's see yur stuff. Is that it?"

Mike charged him and Arkie stepped sideways, kicking him in the stomach. He got up and Arkie slapped him in the face—once easy, second time hard—a resounding open-handed smack, knocking him backward. Mike swung heavy arms, then Arkie tightly clasped both hands together and swung like a baseball bat, hitting Mike across the face. Blood shot from his nose and mouth and he bounced off Rozelle, knocking the shotgun from Rozelle's grasp.

Mike lay on his side—struggling for consciousness—and grabbed the shotgun.

He swung around on his knees and aimed the gun at Arkie. "You'll pay for this, nigger."

"Well, let's see. You only got one shell left," Rozelle said. "Who's it gonna be for?"

"You honkey twit?" Arkie said, walking toward Mike, taunting him. "Go ahead. Shoot me, you loser. I don't think you've got the guts."

"Hey!" I cried. "That's enough Arkie."

"Enough my ass. You weren't kicked and beaten by four perverted white guys." He slapped Mike across the face, knocking him to the ground. Mike's eyes turned to ice and his jaw hardened.

"You're making this so easy for me, nigger. It's now called self-defense in a white court."

I watched Mike look down at the shotgun and cock it. It seemed to happen in slow motion. I inhaled suddenly and my eyes bugged as Rozelle froze. It was happening! Dunbar was going to kill Arkie! This was no longer a good idea. So, without thinking, I leaped toward the gun.

"No. NO. NOOO!" I screamed, reaching for the barrel. "NOOOOO!" And I landed on Mike.

A concussive explosion reverberated within my chest, jerking my body and shaking the ground. My ears rang—ringgggggggggggg—and my heart throbbed and pounded—dum, dum-dum, dum. My saliva gelled and my skin quit feeling. Deep voices spoke and faded out as blindness overcame me. I remember thinking that I was hit and needed help. Andy screamed my name from a faraway distance—loud but not loud—

"RICK, RICK, R-ICK, R-I-CK."

Someone pulled me off of Mike, limp and covered with blood.

"He's dead," they said.

I was dead.

"Ain't breathin'."

"Oh, shit man." That was Arkie. "Why'd you do that?"

"Mike, too. His head is gone."

Something made me inhale deeply. Then I vomited.

"Dead people don't puke," Andy said.

Arkie, wiping my blood-soaked face with a sheet, slapped me awake.

Then we stared in disbelief

    —at Mike

        —his missing face

            —festoons of drooling gray matter

                —yellow, black, red blood and matted hair.

The gun had blown his head off. The gun barrel had pushed under his chin and exploded when I jumped on him.

My clothes were covered in his violent death and my body sagged from the weight of what just happened. I had killed another person. Could I take it back? Where is Kings X when you really need it? What could I do? Dropping to my knees, I vomited again—choking as images and thoughts raced in through my head. Headlights, sheets like tepees, a hangman's nooses, thick blood. I shook my head and looked over at Mike's headless body. It seemed to twitch.

"Holy shit!" someone yelled. I think it was Rozelle.

Andy dropped down and put his arm around me. "It's ok brother. It's over. There's nothing we can do about it. The cops should be here soon."

We sat stunned, all of us—even Dunbar's two friends securely tied to Jim's bumper—motionless, saying nothing. I stared at my hands and began to sob. Soon we heard sirens and saw flashing red lights come bouncing up the tractor path—then questions and more questions. The squad car radio hissed as ambulances were called. One of the cops called Dad. I heard him say, "Doctor Stoner, this is . . . ." and the rest is blurry—like pages torn from a book where you'll never know what happened. Other squad cars arrived and an ambulance bumped and screamed up the dirt path. More questions. I was washed off and stuffed into the back seat of one of the police cars, listening to the conversation about what happened.

"Yeah. It sure was racial, chief. White sheets all around the site. Hoods, too. Bill Dunbar's boy. Yessir, a real shame. Two colored boys. Yessir. Six whites. Only the one dead, the Dunbar boy. Three Ku Klux Klan sheets. In plain sight. Yessir. Two of the white boys are the Stoner kids who had their car defaced. Yessir. "Nigger Lover," it said. Yessir. Related to the fieldhouse call we got earlier. Yessir. To the hospital. Methodist Hospital. His dad will meet us there. Yessir."

I would be sixteen in two weeks.

I had killed a fellow human.

Fifty-Six

It wouldn't go away—nor should it. Yet, it hung too heavy. No, it would never go away. How do you forget a killing? The act of it happening—doing it, watching it in your mind over and over, a body not responding, hearing the blast of the end of life? A part of my history now, I was the kid who killed Mike Dunbar. Shot him to death.

It was more than an accident—it was an accidental murder. Some suggested maybe I did it on purpose; that maybe I was filled with such anger that the difference between "accident" and "on purpose" was meaningless. A thin scrim of thought separated right from wrong. Maybe I did kill him—murdered him. My anger at what he stood for prompted my recklessness. Maybe I did it on purpose.

Rounds of questions—over and over, the same questions. Then the newspaper reporters and photographs—a photo of Arkie taking the 30-foot jump shot against Jefferson-Lafayette and Rozelle in the distance, class photos of me, Andy, and Jim. To the press, this was as good as the Emmett Till story. It took the lid off the racial jar in Indianapolis. Many whites tried to blame Arkie and said I was covering for him. But everyone who witnessed that night had the same story—even Larry and Neil, the two remaining friends of Dunbar.

"We weren't gonna hurt him. We were just havin' a little fun with a nigger, then Mike pulled out his shotgun and it got scary."

386

Rozelle and Arkie were in custody, and the only reason that I could think of was because they were Negroes. But eventually everyone agreed they were not the ones that pulled the trigger. Dad reminded the police that Larry and Neil were more culpable than Rozelle and Arkie.

"Harassing anyone is a crime, especially with a loaded gun," Dad told the police chief. He wanted the "colored boys" released immediately.

The chief nodded and told his lieutenant, "We'll have to let those niggers loose."

We signed things—official-looking documents. Dad called Uncle Gordon and carefully read everything to him. Jim and Mark's parents were there with a lawyer. It was as if signatures made the death go away.

I'm sure the Dunbars were devastated. Mike was their only child. I wanted to tell them how sorry I was, but Dad said I should leave them alone. Maybe later. I pictured them clearly in my mind, sitting quietly in their house, crying, then not crying. Their remorse and anger—the crying, then the thinking, then the anger, then crying some more—their eyes weeping, chests hurting, hearts aching—until there is nothing left. Nothing but pure, raw hatred. Mr. Dunbar would eventually struggle to his feet, go into his garage, and rub gunoil on his weapons. They would not sit silent. We knew that, but never discussed it.

Andy didn't dare take his car out of the driveway. We put a cover over it. Three days after the case was officially closed, it was stolen and set on fire in front of Arkie's house on Frog Island. The newspaper refused to report it. Things were too hot in our town.

I became a prisoner. Shortridge suggested I take my final exams at home. Mom, Dad, Andy, and I felt it was important not to give into the fear mode. "Not to flaunt our presence, but to maintain our dignity," Dad said.

In spite of the chaos and mixed feelings around town, we decided to attend Andy's graduation from high school.

"He only graduates from high school once," Dad said. "Besides, we cannot—and will not—hide from this tragedy."

Mr. and Mrs. Moriarity, Baxter and his family, and most of Andy's friends and classmates called to say they would be there to support us. Georgey said she was coming and would sit with the family. We dressed up like going to church, and Mom brought binoculars so she could see her boy get his diploma. Three hundred and eighty-seven seniors graduated that year. Friends and family gathered at the football stadium and sat in chairs that ran the length of the field.

No one said anything when we walked down the center aisle to our seats, Georgey limping heavily. A noticeable hush settled in around us. When Andy received his diploma, there was such a round of applause that they delayed the ceremony. Mom and Georgey wept and Dad struggled to hold back his emotions. I was swallowing hard and Spike was brimming with pride.

On a bleacher far at the other end of the field, a lone figure sat. It was Mr. Dunbar. I borrowed Mom's binoculars and focused on him. He wore an old sweatshirt and had his arms folded, his feet on the bleacher seats in front of him. His hair was uncombed and hung around his face—I could see his pain in his red, swollen eyes. Leaning forward, he put his head down, wrapped his arms around his knees, and sobbed. Then he ducked out. I couldn't tell anyone. It hurt too much, knowing I had caused his grief.

When we returned home from the ceremony, Rozelle's car was parked in the driveway. Arkie, Rozelle, Shuli, and The

Butterfly were inside. Shuli had baked cookies and the house smelled like it once did when Georgey was there. It made us remember her input. Made us smile. Made Georgey's cheeks wet.

"I is so hungry my stomach's takin' in washin' and ironin'," she said.

We sat outside on the rotted lawn chairs with busted webbing. Arkie handed Andy a wrapped graduation gift. The card said, "To Andy, whose greatness shines like the cross of Jesus. The friends and neighbors of Frog Island." Inside was a white, satin autograph book with a light blue tassel. Andy opened it and found page after page after page of best wishes from people who lived on Frog Island, including Oscar Robertson. The first page read, "This book is for all the Stoners, but especially for Andy and Rick. May God bless and keep you. Coralee and Robert Johnson." That page was also signed by Zeke and Zeze, Reginald and Marjorie, Sonny and Ann Sue, Reverend Oswald Williams, Georgey, Baby Shuli, and a tiny handprint—The Butterfly.

We tried to make it a time of celebration, but the hurt was too hard.

We saw someone approach while we were sitting there, and turned to see Mr. Dunbar come halfway up the driveway— weaving, sobbing, red-faced, scrunched up in pain like a burl on a tree trunk. Darkened tears had smudged his cheeks as more continued to flow, and his clothes were dirty and wrinkled.

"You killed my son," he slurred. "All of you killed him. You ruined my life. You niggers are the devil. You're all the evilest of evil murderers."

Dad motioned for us to stay still. "Not a word," he whispered.

"God will fry your asses in hell!" Mr. Dunbar screamed. "In hell!" We sat, holding our breath.

Then he stood silently, weaving, and lowered his head. "In hell," he muttered to himself, no longer looking at us. He blew his nose in his hand and wiped it on his pants. Once more, "in hell" and he turned and stumbled down the driveway.

A hush ensued.

"Bussie," Georgey turned to Dad, "go take him home. Tell him how very sorry you and Missus Stoner is about his boy. Pray with him."

Dad got up, wiped his hands on his pants and began to leave.

"Need some help?" Andy asked.

"No, he don't," Georgey replied.

Fifty-Seven

I felt like I was living in a warehouse for explosives—one firecracker would light off, then another, then another. Each day brought another event. Yet somehow it seemed that the big firecrackers were gone. Things were winding down.

I passed my driver's test on my birthday. I had waited sixteen years for that day, and when it came, it meant very little. The insurance company gave Dad $48 for the "Nigger Lover," so he bought a new car and gave his to Andy. I would owe Andy $48 and be able to drive that ugly, faded blue, 1948 Plymouth as soon as Andy left for college.

But the demon didn't go away. He lingered in the deep recesses of my mind, hiding directly behind my eyelids—images of Mike Dunbar, the glow of headlights on his headless, scattered body, the spattered blood and gore, the inconceivability of it all. Images of Mr. and Mrs. Dunbar alone. Their only child. Mike's girlfriend, Patty. I tried not to tally the number of people impacted by my impulsiveness.

Nothing was important any longer. People tiptoed around me, making small talk so the topic of Mike's death wouldn't come up. I called Arkie for some solace, but he was struggling too.

"What are you gonna do, man?" Arkie asked.

"I don't know. I really don't know. Maybe I should take off—go somewhere else where no one knows me—but I don't know where to go. What are you gonna do?"

"Momma and Daddy have an idea. Don't want you to tell no one 'cept yur family. Can't go beyond them."

"Sure."

"I'm thinkin' about joining the Marines."

"Come on, Arkie. You gotta be 18."

"You just gotta look like yur 18 and swear yur 18."

"You serious?"

"Yeah. I think I am. Man, this ain't goin' away. Eventually someone's gonna pop me—that Mr. Dunbar guy, the KKK. So, I figure I'll join up, get out of here, get my high school diploma and come back in five years. Then I'll be just Arkansas Johnson, not the nigger who might have killed a white boy. If I wanna go to college, I'll get money from the military. That's more than I can get if I stay."

We were silent, listening to our breathing. The real tragedy for Arkie was that he would be giving up the one thing he loved the most—basketball. He had often talked about playing college ball a lot, then the Globetrotters. That gun blast blew his dreams away.

"You think I could get in?" I finally said.

"Rick, you look like yur 14. You'd never pass for 18."

"You're no damn help."

"I can't tell you what to do. You have to figure it out yourself."

"I guess you're right. Promise you let me know what you're gonna do."

"Promise."

That night I talked to Mom, Dad, and Georgey about Arkie.

"Can he really lie about his age and get in the Marines?" I asked.

"Oh, yes," Dad said. "The military is desperate for recruits. He looks at least 18."

"Think I could do that?"

Georgey was listening to the conversation from the kitchen. "Y'all jes' hold on now. No talkin' till I gets there." She came in and sat down. "Do Coralee and Robert know what Arkie's plannin'?" she asked.

"Yeah. You think he can get in?"

"Leon got in when he was just 17. Grew hisself a moustache."

"Well, I'm proud of Arkie," Mom said. "That's a big decision for him. He's giving up a lot."

"Yeah."

"I don't think it's going to be easy around here for Arkie if he stays," Dad said, "or you, son."

"What do you mean? I can't get in the Army. What will I do?"

"Your mother and I have been talking about that." He looked at Mom. "Would you consider going away to a private boarding school?"

"Not a military school, I hope."

"No. We found a school in Massachusetts in a town called Worcester. Mom's parents have some connections there."

"Hush now," Georgey said. "I doesn't want to hear that kind a talk. Ricky's bigger than this thing. It'll blow over. I jes' knows it will."

"No, it won't, Georgey," Mom said, reaching for Georgey's hand. "That I'm certain of. Retaliation is part of hatred. Arkie and Ricky are vulnerable."

"Oh, Lord have mercy!"

That night Dad took Georgey home by himself, then made his usual rounds at the hospital. When he returned, he quietly let himself in. He looked ten years older, haggard, shoulders drooping.

"Not a good day," he said from the refrigerator, pouring half a beer. "Not a good day at all."

What else could happen? I wondered.

Mom poured herself the other half. "You mind?"

"Not a bit." He shook his head slowly. We sat around the breakfast table in a soundless vacuum. Dad put his forehead down and said, "Caroline Dunbar killed herself this afternoon."

Our eyes closed in unison. "Oh my God," we whispered.

"She was dead on arrival when I got there. She asphyxiated herself in Mike's car in the garage, the motor running."

I had an instant flash in my mind of Mrs. Dunbar in her fluffy, pink sweater, heavy eyelashes, and black-smeared eyeliner, tears flowing down her cheeks and murmuring her son's name over and over.

"I can't blame her," Andy said, faintly.

"Me neither," Dad replied, his head still resting on the table.

Fifty-Eight

On Saturday, Arkie showed up at our house. He was scheduled to board a bus for Parris Island Marine Base in South Carolina in two days, and we still had one more thing to do before he and I left town. We changed into prison inmate clothes—vertical black stripes on white. A neighbor of Arkie's had two pairs. I bought two gallons of whitewash paint, a large bucket, and two long-handled brushes.

Though it didn't make much sense with so many other important things to be done, we kept coming back to Mary Lou and her name and number in the graffiti-filled tunnel. We would be part of her pain until she was released from her own hell and we got her off that wall. It wouldn't take long to whitewash over it and any other names and numbers, to wash away some of the hurt. We urgently felt a sense of retribution for something Mary Lou didn't do. If we had met her and put a face to the hurt, it would have diminished the pain and we might have forgotten it. We had to act anonymously, and we had to act now.

It was Arkie's idea to appear as inmates on a prison detail, in case any of the Silver Gun Patrol showed up. "They won't mess with a couple a convicts," Arkie said.

We walked through the woods on our property, heading to the canal banks.

"I have to feel good about something," I said.

"Whaddaya mean?"

"Look at all the trouble I've caused."

395

"Stop it, man. Will you please stop it! That kinda talk is really stupid. Yur focusin' on being pathetic and doin' a real good job." He tripped over a tree branch.

"Watch where you're going."

"Focus on bein' a good Christian man who saved his friend's life by leapin' on a loaded gun. Focus on bein' a friend to the Negro community and to the white community. Ain't no one else—'cept maybe yur daddy—who understands that."

We continued walking.

"Arkie, I killed a man!" I screamed. "That's all I . . ."

"You saved a man!" Arkie screamed louder. "You saved my wretched life."

I didn't say anything. At the canal, I pointed to the bridge. "Let's go over there."

"You gotta move on with yur life, man," Arkie said, as we crossed to the other side of the canal.

"There's a path over here down to the tunnel," I said, cutting through the shrubbery then sliding down an incline.

We stood at the entrance and looked up at the arched ceiling, the darkness in the tunnel, the brightness of the opening at the other side. It somehow seemed smaller, less threatening.

"Three years ago," Arkie said.

"Really. Doesn't seem that long."

"We was in the eighth grade."

"Hmm. Guess you're right."

"I'm always right."

We stood, just looking. Finally I opened the two gallons of paint.

"D'you hear me?" he said.

"Yeah. You're always right."

"Right. Especially 'bout you gettin' over this thing, movin' on, thinkin' upbeat, positive. You gotta do that. We both do."

Inside the tunnel, our eyes adjusted to the darkness. We remembered exactly where Mary Lou was.

"Wabash six times seven is forty-two," I said.

"Let's set Mary Lou free."

We painted over the faded message—*Mary Lou wants you. For a great piece call Wabash 6742.*—each brush stroke rinsing her clean. Then we moved on to the other names and numbers, slopping paint around with our long-handle brushes.

"What kind of peoples you s'pose write this kind a crap?"

"Guys who never were successful with women?"

"Short little fat guys with zits who play cops and robbers."

"Watch out. Andy had the worse case of zits I've ever seen."

"Yeah. Straight A's, city wrestling champ, goin' to college. That's not who wrote this kinda stuff." He put his brush down. "Man, I'm done. How 'bout you?"

"Real done. Mary Lou is free—reborn."

I picked up my bucket and threw the remaining contents against the tunnel walls. Arkie did the same. We watched the white paint slowly run down the cement, creating a cleaner place to bury so much hatred.

"Reborn—so is Rick Stoner," Arkie said, wiping his hands on the wall and smearing two smudges on my cheeks.

I did the same to Arkie. "So too, Arkansas Johnson. Reborn."

A cool breeze blew through the tunnel, and I sensed the increased light as we walked out. What a picture we must have made as we walked up the busy street to my house—two teenagers in black and white prisoner garb with white streaks on their faces, carrying old paint pails and long-handle brushes.

Fifty-Nine

The following night I drove Georgey home and walked her into her house. We didn't talk much on the ride. "You is such a careful driver, darlin'. I always feel safe with you, safer than with yur daddy."

"Evenin' Rick," Zeke said quietly from across the street.

"Evening, Zeke."

"Mind steppin' over here fur a minute?"

"Sure," I said, crossing to his porch to meet him.

Zeke was standing with his hands in his pockets. The glow from his television shined a backlight on him in blues and greens, and he squinted with wet eyes.

"Well, I know you is leavin' and you've had the livin' shit kicked out of ya lately." He paused, looking around. "But I'd say yur special, Rick."

He put one arm on my shoulder and I looked deep into his sorrow-filled eyes.

"Zeze and me could never have children, until you come along. You is the apple of my eye and Zeze and me loves ya." He wept. "Loves ya with every ounce of everthing we got."

He pulled something shiny from his pocket and handed it to me. "Keep this with ya always."

He quickly turned and went inside. In my hand was a new Zippo lighter and under the streetlight I read the inscription:

To Whitey

Don't nigger-lip your butt.

With great love and respect

Zeke

I knew he was watching, so I lit a cigarette—a Camel—and walked into Georgey's house.

"Where's Shuli?"

"Next door sittin' for Ann Sue's grandson."

"Hi, Ricky," Shuli called from Ann Sue's porch.

"Hi Shuli. The Butterfly still up?"

"Sleepin' like a rock," she said. "Come on over and keep me company for a spell."

"Go on, darlin'," Georgey said. "Not a word about Arkie. He's gonna have to tell her hisself."

She turned to me and wrapped her arms around my waist. "Oh, Jesus. Jesus, Jesus. How I have prayed to you these last ten months, askin' you what you was doin'. How you could put so much bad stuff on my good fambly? And you finally told me, Jesus. You is buildin' character. These chilluns—all of 'em—are bein' groomed for greatness. We is part of a much bigger, greater thing that's happenin'. Hold my boys, Jesus, especially this one. Amen to ya."

Shuli and I sat in silence on the porch, listening to the air breathe, a trashcan rattle in the alley, Zeke coughing. A police car drove down the street and I stiffened. Shuli and I said nothing. I felt her warm hand reach out and hold my wrist.

"I know yur a wreck. I feel it in my heart," she whispered.

It had been a long and confusing day for me and I felt on the verge of tears, teetering on anger, looking for a place to hide. I felt tired and began shaking my head. She rubbed my back.

"Let's get a Coca-Cola inside."

"Maybe I better get home," I said, as my eyes welled with tears and I covered them with my hands. "Oh, no."

"Now I'm serious, Ricky. You needs someone to talk to. Me. You been there for me. Now I'm here for you. Tell me what's goin' on. See how I can help."

I followed her inside, then changed my mind. "I gotta go."

"No. You can't go. Yur heart is broke."

She handed me a Coke and instinctively I looked at the bottom—Greencastle, Indiana. It was frosty cold and I put it on my forehead and leaned back on the doorway.

"Indianapolis," she said, holding her bottle up.

"Greencastle."

"I don't know why I'm here. I don't know why I'm anywhere. I just don't know a damn thing," I sighed, closing my eyes and letting disturbing thoughts fly by like nightmares. I inhaled and my breath became stuck in overdrive—a small inhale, a gasp, a large inhale—then tears and babbling. I reached out to take hold of Shuli and told her how confused I felt, how unsure about my future. Nothing I had done was right—not even the afternoon when I was with the girl from the trailer park whose name I couldn't remember. I told her about Mary Lou. It felt important to talk about her. Mary Lou was the only real atonement I'd made in my life. More than anything, I couldn't bear the sadness and remorse for killing Mike. The fact that it was accidental didn't make me feel better—it continued to drag me down. I couldn't shake images of his mother's suicide and of Mr. Dunbar, left with no hope, no life, only anger. Where would I go next? For me, there was no light at the end of my tunnel. We stood in the kitchen doorway and Shuli held me tightly while I rambled and cried.

"Oh, Ricky, Ricky. When you hurt, I hurt."

I leaned heavily on her shoulders and sobbed. "I'm trying to be strong."

"You are strong. Yur the strongest man I know. And I know you'll work through this."

I was an empty glass with no more water to spill.

Shuli began to cry. "Oh, Ricky. Please don't give up. Please stay strong. You and Arkie are the strength of my life. Please." She hugged me tighter, sobbing. "Ricky, darlin', you are the single most special person in my life." Holding me and crying.

"You and Butterfly," she added.

"And Arkie," I added.

Big wet smile. "And Georgey, yeah." She laughed. "Especially Georgey."

We chuckled quietly, like two motor scooters idly humming.

"White cotton panties," I whispered suddenly.

"White cotton what?"

"Panties. You were wearing white cotton panties."

"What are you talkin' about?"

"That first time I met you five or six years ago, you kept spinning your dress. I could see your white cotton panties."

She began laughing. "Ricky Stoner! Aren't you silly."

"You were."

"And you remember a little 11-year-old girl's underwear?"

"I do."

"I'm sure that's why I spun my dress."

We smiled as the memory ran through our minds—smiled long enough to etch it in our hearts.

I wiped my eyes hard as I pushed the tears away, and the sounds and smells of the neighborhood returned—voices like doo-wop music in the background, the flutter of birds nearby, a car downshifting, cigarette smoke and a cough, the wonderful smell of perspiration and cooking, the streetlight in front of the house flickering as a cricket chirped the temperature nearby. Reality had returned, and there was nothing else to say. When I left Shuli Wright that night, for a short time, my head felt surprisingly clear.

Several hours later someone painted "nigger lovers" on our mailbox, and the following day I received a death threat in the mail. Every other phrase had the f-word.

Georgey said, "God's callin' from somewhere far away, darlin'. Time to follow Him."

Sixty

Arkie and I sat in Dad's ugly Plymouth in front of Arkie's house. It was dark. The streetlights on Frog Island were far apart or burned out.

"I never had a friend like you, Rick," Arkie said. "Momma and daddy always warned me about white folks—'slave owners,' they called 'em. Cold, ruthless."

"You mean I let you down?"

"Now I'm tryin' to be serious, just for a minute."

"Sorry."

"I just need to tell you what a special friend you are. Like no other friend I ever had. And all this mess will go away some day. I know you're a wreck. So am I. But some day it'll all be over. Momma says we'll be bigger men because of it all. So, you gotta promise me you'll stay in touch while I'm in the Marines. Write to me. Practice swearin' in yur letters."

We smiled at each other weakly and looked away in silence. A dog barked in the distance. A man swore at his wife. She screamed "No!" and swore back. A toilet flushed. "Where'd you put my goddamned cigarettes?" we faintly heard from afar.

Arkie continued, "When I get married, you'll be my best man. And my first boy'll be called Rick." He paused, wet-eyed, and shook his head. "Damn, I'm gonna miss you." Then quickly he shook my hand, got out of the car, and ran up the steps to his house. I left Frog Island finding it hard to see through my tears— soul spent, wasted, weary. I had a mental picture of Arkie inside

403

his house—arms and forehead against the front door door—
crying as hard as I was at the stop sign exiting Frog Island.

Epilogue

I finished high school at a private boarding school in Massachusetts—a long way from Indianapolis in many ways. When I graduated, I went to Indiana University and spent my entire business career as a copywriter in advertising.

Andy graduated from Kenyon College in three years, went to medical school, and interned in orthopedics. In 1970, he operated on Georgey's leg, straightening it so she could walk without her cane. Even though the operation was successful, she never gave up using it. "It's like Moses' staff. It tells who I is." Georgey's greatest concern about the operation, she told Andy, was that "someone's gonna see my doo-whinkus." He had to promise that no one would look.

Arkie joined the Marines and in 1960 he was sent to Viet Nam. He was gunned down on a night raid, when communist guerillas struck at Bien Hoa. He is buried in Arlington National Cemetery, where we leave tears and basketballs whenever we visit.

Spike continued to study the violin and went on to attend the Julliard School. He taught at the School for the Performing Arts in New York until his recent retirement.

Rozelle graduated with honors from the University of Kentucky, where he was a starter for the Wildcats. He received his master's degree in education, coached at Hampton University in Virginia, and has nine children. The oldest is a son named Arkansas Thorpe.

Rumor has it that Marcella ran off with a circus act in 1957. Somehow Dark Mary was involved, but no one really knew for sure. Marcella never contacted her parents, though they searched for her for many years. I never heard from her again and she remains a missing page.

When I graduated from Indiana University, I married Shuli Wright. The Butterfly was six years old at the time. Shuli and I have a son named Arkansas Stoner—nine inches shorter than Arkansas Thorpe. Our Arkie has freckles. We loved and lived in New York City, where I worked until my retirement, and we stayed close to Spike and his family, who lived across town. The Butterfly graduated from Spike's school as a voice major and then majored in music at Indiana University.

Mom died in 1990 on August 28—her birthday. She was 82 and still giving local concerts and teaching. She still arose at 5 a.m. to practice, but on that morning she made it to the kitchen to fix Dad's runny eggs, toast, and strawberry preserves. She had a massive heart attack while sitting at the piano and was found with her head resting on the keys. If Dad wasn't hungry—we all agreed—Mom would still be sitting there today. Mom's funeral was held at the Church of the Holy God, the Reverend Williams presiding. Spike produced the two-hour service and the music—gospel and classical—was spectacular. Not a dry eye remained, especially after Butterfly sang "O God of Mine." And, yes, my dad wept uncontrollably with a smile on his face. Our greatest sadness was that Georgey wasn't there—in person.

Dad died three months later, for no apparent reason. We're pretty certain he just didn't want to live without Mom. Before he died—in a weak moment after several bottles of Blatz Beer—he told me that he and his brother Gordon had bought Georgey her house after the war. They gave it to her for the glory of God. Never told her. Never told anyone. It was handled by a colored lawyer in town—Squiggy Daniel's grandfather. It was a gift without strings—no tears, no thank yous, no strutting—and one of the Stoner boys' greatest secrets. I think she knew. Georgey understood how to accept God's special gifts. Quietly.

Georgey died in 1976 with her family by her side—all of us, including her son Leon. Her small bedroom hardly held us. She was propped up in her bed, wearing an old pink terrycloth bathrobe with coffee stains and cigarette burns.

"Look at God's miraculous ways," she said, holding Mom's hand. "Jes' look at my amazin' fambly. Deeper, stronger, and fuller 'cause a what we been through together. God builds from confusion. Most families don't have God's special kind a confusion. Just smooth, simple lives. They ain't God's chosen children. We is. Black, white, tan, and freckled. My, oh my, what we been through together and lived to laugh about it and to thank our Lord for His special interest in our lives."

Here is her final prayer:

"Oh, Jesus, my Savior. What a wonderful God You have been to this poor ole spook. Please keep my peoples holy. Cover them with Yur wonderful love and wisdom. And keep Yur lovin' arms around them when I am gone. You promise, don't Ya?

OK then, Sweet Jesus. OK.

Amen to ya."